Nothing But Blue Sky

Nothing But Blue Sky

KATHLEEN MacMAHON

SANDYCOVE

an imprint of

PENGUIN BOOKS

SANDYCOVE

UK | USA | Canada | Ireland | Australia
India | New Zealand | South Africa

Sandycove is part of the Penguin Random House group of companies
whose addresses can be found at global.penguinrandomhouse.com.

First published 2020
001

Copyright © Kathleen MacMahon, 2020

The moral right of the author has been asserted

Set in 12.55/14.94 pt Garamond MT Std
Typeset by Jouve (UK), Milton Keynes
Printed and bound in Great Britain by Clays Ltd, Elcograf S.p.A.

A CIP catalogue record for this book is available from the British Library

ISBN: 978–1–844–88475–9

www.greenpenguin.co.uk

MIX
Paper from
responsible sources
FSC® C018179

Penguin Random House is committed to a
sustainable future for our business, our readers
and our planet. This book is made from Forest
Stewardship Council® certified paper.

For Lucy and Clara

I

I went back to Aiguaclara this summer. Primarily, because I had failed to go back the previous year and had come to see that failure as a breach of faith. It was, at the very least, a breach of the tradition that Mary Rose and I had first established on our honeymoon. Throughout our marriage we returned to Aiguaclara for two weeks every summer. Most often it was the same two weeks at the start of July, although one year we had to delay going by a week to facilitate a family wedding. Another year we had to fly home early for a funeral. But there was never a year we did not go, until last year. That was the first time the chain was broken, and I was anxious to repair it by going back.

The other reason I wanted to go back was that it was in Aiguaclara that Mary Rose and I were at our happiest. We had laid claim to it as our place, jealously keeping it a secret from everyone else. Whenever people asked us where we were going on our holidays, we would vaguely mention the Costa Brava. If pressed, we might mention the name of a neighbouring town along the coast, but Aiguaclara was the word that could not be spoken. So precious was it to us that we could not bear the thought of sharing it.

Year after year we landed there, blinking like newborn rabbits after another interminable Irish winter. Pasty and stiff after completing another lap of our lives. Aiguaclara was our pit stop; it was the place where we mended ourselves, marinating gently in a brew of salt water and sunshine. In Aiguaclara, we paused to take stock of our lives, coming to terms with the passing of another year and making plans for the one to come. Aiguaclara was where we held our AGM; it was the place where all of our most illuminating conversations took place, unplanned, over an extra bottle of wine on a random weeknight. Mary Rose and I never had a tree with our initials carved into the bark. There was no bridge with a padlock bolted to the railings as a testament to our love. What we had was Aiguaclara, and it seemed to me that the pain of being there without her could hardly be greater than the pain of being anywhere else without her. At least in Aiguaclara there might be some memory of our lives together that I had until then forgotten. That was the hope I had, in going back.

When you return to a place year upon year there is always the fear that something will have changed. Mary Rose and I first went to Aiguaclara twenty years ago, and every time we went back it was with dread in our hearts that we would find something altered, that the idyll we had found for ourselves would no longer be idyllic. Maybe a new multistorey hotel had been built on the seafront, or a noisy disco opened in the centre of the village. In Ireland, one of those things would no doubt have happened, with planning permission secured in exchange for a brown envelope, but the Spanish seemed determined to keep things just the way they always had been, which to us was an eternally pleasant surprise.

We would fly into Girona, picking up the hire car and pointing it out the road towards the coast, through fields of ladylike sunflowers and farmhouses of dark gold stone. In the distance, sandcastle towns rose out of the low hills. Trees like standing feathers lined the roads. Sun pouring down over everything, casting stencils of shade. The road cut through a dozen dreary villages that seemed to have no industry at all but the roadside sale of ceramic urns and pots.

'How can a whole region survive on the sale of ceramic pots?' I said, the first time we rolled through the town of La Bisbal d'Empordá. Its arched colonnades were more fitting to a place ten times its size. Every second shop seemed to sell ceramic pots.

'I don't know,' Mary Rose said lightly, her voice rising with the question, as if she too would like an answer. That was back at our beginnings, when she was amused by everything I had to say. Her sympathy was worn down in time, and the patterns in her voice flattened, as I insisted on revisiting the same topics over and over again. I find it hard to let things go.

'Who *buys* all these pots?' I would ask, as we drove through La Bisbal on our route to the coast.

'I mean, how many ceramic pots does one town need?'

She would sigh and shift her bare limbs around on the hot seat of the car, her voice trailing off as she answered me with forced patience.

'That I do not know.'

In time it became a joke between us.

'Ah,' I might say, as we spotted the welcome sign on the edge of town. 'La Bisbal. Home of the ceramic pot.'

Mary Rose would set about winding the window down to drown my voice out. The rushing wind lashed her hair across her face as she shouted over it.

'I'm on my holidays! I do not know and do not care who buys those pots or what they do with them. Do you hear that? I DON'T BLOODY CARE!'

In time, a new motorway was built, carrying the coast-bound traffic southwards out of the airport instead of north. The new route went nowhere near La Bisbal d'Empordá, and the mystery of the ceramic pots was never solved. Mary Rose and I learned to identify new landmarks on the route south: a cement factory that provided me with the reassurance of

3

some local industry, a fertilizer plant that gave off a homely stink of manure, a desolate-looking water park. In my treacherous heart I invariably experienced an air pocket of relief that we did not have any children who would beg to be taken to that godforsaken water park. Mary Rose was no doubt thinking the exact opposite. How she would have loved to have had a reason to spend a day there.

'Look, there's the turn,' she would say, pointing out a sign for Platjes.

From there it's only a few short kilometres to the coast. The landmarks accumulate as the holiday countdown begins. A familiar supermarket is followed quickly by a garden centre full of nothing but cactus plants. A kart-racing track. A billboard with a crocodile on it. Our conversation always slowed as we struck out across the last stretch of countryside towards our destination. We peered hungrily at the outlying fields of corn. The final few farmhouses. The last crossroads. Then we were among the pine trees, on a road that plunged in hairpin twists down the mountainside to the sea. All winter long, Mary Rose and I longed for that first glimpse of Aiguaclara through the trees. A necklace of white stone buildings, like square beads strung along the shore. A slash of sandy beach. A shock of batik sea. The spectacle of summer, same as it ever was, and another year somehow or other miraculously weathered.

This year I took the same route from Dublin to Girona. I hired a car at the airport and made for the coast. Through fields and farmhouses that were all bathed in the same burnished gold. Past the fertilizer plant and the water park. Past the garden centre and the kart-racing track. I took the turn-off for Aiguaclara, but this time there was none of the usual fear in my heart of finding something altered. This time I was aware that it was me who had suffered a change, and I wondered how I would find a formula of words to explain it. All the way down the hill, as I threw the hire car around the twists and turns of the road, I was practising in my head the answer I would give to the question I knew I would inevitably be asked when I got there. No matter how many times I say it, it still sounds stubbornly implausible.

2

In returning to Aiguaclara, I was going against the advice of all the friends and family who last summer successfully persuaded me not to go. Last summer, the world and his wife were of a mind that I should not go back, and I found myself adrift on their certainties, because I myself had none.

'I thought it might be good to go.'

'Are you serious?' they all asked me. 'Go back on your *own*?'

What surprised me was that it seemed to everyone to matter so much.

'Why not,' I said. At the time, I was having difficulty weighing any one course of action against another. Like trying to decide what to order when you're not hungry. The salad or the burger. I had no appetite for anything.

'I always go to Aiguaclara,' I said. 'I've been going there every summer for nearly twenty years. I don't see why I wouldn't go back this year.'

'I. Don't. Think. That's. A. Good. Idea,' said my friend Deborah.

She might have been telling me there was a rattlesnake asleep at my feet and I should step, very carefully, away from it. Deborah's voice can come out as a bit of a squeak, especially when she's emotionally invested in what she's saying. When she's called upon to make a speech – which she hates to do – she has a tendency to go skittering off the register. This gives the impression that she's not very competent, an impression that is entirely misleading. Deborah could run the world, if she wanted to, and I should know. As her friend of more than thirty-five years' standing, I have watched her turn from teenage rebel – all black eyeliner and a one-sided ponytail – to the corporate powerhouse she is now. Mother of three teenage boys and a senior partner in a solicitors' firm, Deborah is the most competent person I know, and if there's a bottom to the vast pool of her wisdom I haven't found it yet, which is why I allowed her to persuade me to go with her and Michael on a group holiday to the south of France last year, instead of going back to Aiguaclara. It was a mistake of comical proportions.

Poor Deborah, she took such care to get that holiday right. From the painstakingly chosen location – on a quiet back road between Nice and Antibes – to the carefully curated guest list, Deborah had left nothing to chance. I can only imagine the amount of thought she must have put into assigning me the garden room with the generous couch bed. The box room under the stairs would have been deemed too pointedly single. The big room with the pink curtains too feminine. The double room with the en suite too big and lonely. She would have arrived at the garden room as the least worst option.

There were eight people in our party. 'Safety in numbers,' I imagined Michael saying to Deborah, as they were planning it. Among the other guests were a couple we all knew from our college days, called Tom and Angela. Deborah's childhood friend Cara was there too, along with her partner, Duncan. Deborah had made sure to invite Michael's brother along as well, so that I wouldn't be the only single person. (It was the brother who got the box room.)

We arrived at the house in the late afternoon. Hot and sticky from the journey in the hire car from the airport, we adjourned to our rooms to shower and change. The plan was to meet on the terrace for drinks at five.

I was the first to appear, followed seconds later by Michael. He emerged in his cargo shorts and a crumpled linen shirt, making a fist of his hand to bear the weight of a rattling pitcher of his famous triple-strength Tanqueray and tonic. The other hand trailed a clutch of empty tumblers. I watched him stop for a moment to survey the view. Beyond the bougainvillea that adorned the balustrade was a wide blue bay, dotted with yachts. To the right was the Cap d'Antibes, and to the left was Cap Ferrat. Between the two, an endless succession of planes traversed the empty sky, like plough horses working a large, flat field. By the look on his face, Michael might have been a farmer staring out at a cloud of locusts.

That was the moment for one of us to say something, but we didn't. Neither he nor I made any reference to the planes, and after that nobody would.

'So, here we are,' he said, as he sloshed the gin into our tumblers and collapsed into a chair beside me.

'To your health,' I said, raising my glass to him, but he was already drinking from his.

'God, I miss smoking.' He rested his drink on his bare, hairy knee. The sunlight fell down over him, and he closed his eyes to savour it. For several long seconds I was able to study him, unobserved, and I saw that he was getting old. The dark curls he had so hated as a young man were now tinged with white, as if he'd been painting a ceiling. He had a spray of fine lines around his eyes, and the flesh of his face had begun to hang loose from his bones. My childhood friend had gone and turned into a middle-aged man without my even noticing. It made me wonder what else I hadn't noticed in the year gone by. I felt as if I'd been away on some arduous expedition – somewhere very far and very, very remote, like the Antarctic – and had only just returned.

'Jesus,' I said. 'I think I'd forgotten what the heat is like. I feel like I've just spent the winter in a walk-in freezer.'

'Yeah,' said Michael, opening one eye and training it on me. 'You do look a bit like a frozen turkey.'

'Thanks,' I said, wondering, with little more than a bystander's interest, what would become of me if I were to defrost. Would the blood start flowing in my veins again? It was hard to imagine such a thing.

Deborah was the next to emerge from the house. Her short hair was fluffy after her shower and her dress still bore the creases of her suitcase. Her arms were stick thin and winter pale. She sat down at the table with her back to the house and propped her bare feet up on an empty chair. As she looked out over the bay I saw the bones of her face harden, and there came over her a look of such great weariness that I felt sorry for her. She had tried so hard to think it all through, and now there was this. Something she had failed to anticipate. The presence of all those planes.

At any one time there might have been four of them in the sky. While one made the climb out of the city and flew south towards Corsica, another would already have banked hard to pass back over our heads in the direction of northern Europe. A third might have been coming in to land, cutting through the sky like a knife as it slid down into the city, while yet another made the plodding journey across the bay. Alone among my companions, I studied the planes with interest, trying to guess the trajectory of their journeys. The others pretended they hadn't noticed them. It was a pretence they would be forced to maintain for the entire holiday.

'Fucked if I know where my sunglasses are,' said Michael's brother, Philip, who had appeared, briefly surveyed the view and promptly turned his back to the bay. Leaning his weight against the balustrade, he shielded his eyes with his hand. 'I'm blind as a bat without them.'

I noticed how Philip's voice was becoming more textured with time, taking on a new layer of character with every part he played. Much to all of our bemusement, Philip had become a successful actor, famous in Ireland, if nowhere else, for a terrifying turn as a Dublin drug dealer in a long-running TV show.

'Sláinte,' he said, raising his glass to us as another plane streamed across the sky.

'Look behind ya,' I was tempted to say, thinking of the Gaiety panto.

My mother's sister, Marguerite, always took my brother and me to the Gaiety panto at Christmas time. It was a tradition she kept up long after we had outgrown it, but nobody had the heart to tell her to stop, for fear of hurting her feelings. I remember the acute physical embarrassment I felt at being forced to endure it. I was painfully ashamed for the actors. For my fellow audience members, I had nothing but disdain. They leapt about in their seats and roared themselves hoarse with their 'look behind ya's, while I maintained a rigid silence. That's what I felt like that whole week in Nice. I felt like I was back at the Gaiety panto, a lone envoy from a humourless country, forced to watch as the rest of the world engaged in a facile game of charades.

'Well,' said Deborah, letting her breath out with a long sigh. 'Here we are at last.'

She was tired, I realized. She was tired out, and it was my fault that she was tired. So monstrously absorbed was I in my own titanic grief that I had not until that moment seen how the wake of it had washed over other people's lives, and none more so than Michael's and Deborah's. From that very first day when they appeared, wordlessly, at my door before dawn, they could not have done more for me. They set up camp in my kitchen, fielding phone calls for me and driving reporters away from my door and, finally, pouring me full of whiskey. It was midnight by the time they left. In the weeks that followed, they cooked and cared for me and somehow helped to fill the days that came at me relentlessly and without mercy, each one dark and gaping like the open mouth of a tunnel. Week after week they walked alongside me, and in all that time it did not occur to me how tired they must have been. They were desperately tired and in need of a rest, and now they could not have one because they had brought me along with them on their holiday. For their sake, if for nothing else, I wished I hadn't come. Ahead of us lay seven unimaginably long days. Not since I was twelve and hopelessly homesick on a school trip to Brittany had time taken on such menace. In my head I started a countdown towards the moment when it would be over and I could crawl back under my rock.

'Hey-ho,' said Duncan, appearing on the terrace. He was wearing a tropical shirt that was too small for him. It gaped between the buttons, revealing his pale chest with its red chest hairs. The baggy jeans he wore were so long in the leg that they scraped along the floor at his heels. On his wrist he had one of those copper bands that are supposed to ward off arthritis.

I am always a bit queasy in the presence of Duncan. It's the beard, I suppose. The dope smoking. The shockingly stained teeth. I don't entirely approve of Duncan, even though he's always nice to me, as he is to everyone. I can't seem to get past the vague physical revulsion I have for him. It may come down to the fact that I once slept with Cara, a very long time ago. It happened after a session in Deborah's house one weekend when her parents were away. We were young, and drunk, and I was pathetically inexperienced and painfully awkward, and presumably for one or all of those reasons it was not a success. We hugged each other afterwards and agreed to put it behind us, and for a long time I didn't give it any thought, but there now exists in my mind the horrifying possibility that Cara may have mentioned it to Duncan. I hope she hasn't, but there it is. The possibility that she has.

The other reason I feel queasy in Duncan's presence is because of something he once said to me, something I would like to be able to erase from my mind but can't. It was shortly after he started going out with Cara, and I hardly knew him, when I bumped into him on the street. He was carrying a twelve-pack of toilet paper under his left arm. 'I'd love to stay and chat,' he said, 'but I'm dying for a dump and we've no bog roll in the house, so I just nipped out to get some.'

I am still shocked that Duncan said that to me. Every time I see him, it's the first thing that comes into my head.

'You're such a prude,' Mary Rose used to say. She had a nurse's equanimity in the face of all bodily functions, whereas I was the prisoner of a congenital shyness relating to anything vaguely biological. Nobody ever discussed such things in my house, and it took me many years to consider it normal for people to speak openly to each other – with humour even – about defecation or masturbation or, worst of all, menstruation.

'It's only *human*,' Mary Rose would say.

'Yes,' I would reply, 'that's precisely the problem.'

In so many things, we were the opposite of one another. Together, we might have made one nicely balanced human being.

'Ah,' said Duncan, noisily dragging a sunlounger out of the shade of the awning and into the last of the day's sunshine. 'This is the life.'

Cara came along and settled herself between his legs. She had taken to wearing her black hair in a razor-sharp bob, like Uma Thurman in *Pulp Fiction*. Her fringe hung down over her eyes and I wondered if it obscured her vision. If it did, she didn't seem to mind, but then Cara didn't seem to mind anything any more. Her voice had assumed a whispery quality, as if she was trying not to disturb a sleeping baby, even though it was a long time since Cara's children were babies. Her kids were both adults by then, and Duncan was already a grandfather. They were enjoying a second youth, now that they were footloose and fancy-free. That was Mary Rose's theory, anyway, rolled out to me one night after a party. Mary Rose loved nothing more than to conduct a post-mortem on a party, dissecting the guests' lives at length as she brushed her teeth and scattered her shoes and clothes and underwear about the bedroom, while I collapsed on the bed with relief that the evening was over. I have never entirely understood why people find parties enjoyable.

'Delicious,' said Cara, sipping at her gin and tonic, while another plane flew out over our heads. Looking up, I saw an aeroplane-shaped stencil, cast against the cloudless sky. It looked to me like a shark swimming through a clear blue sea, and I found it very beautiful but did not say so. Plagued by a terrible sense of detachment, I did not say anything, even though I could so easily have found a formula of words to put them all out of their misery.

'Wow,' said Angela, making her entrance. She was wearing a dress of silk so luxuriously thin that it billowed behind her like smoke from a cigarette as she glided towards the edge of the terrace. Mary Rose would have been able to tell me, under her breath, how much the dress had cost.

'Mary Rose would have loved this,' said Angela, lightly, as she surveyed the view.

'Yes, I think we can safely say that Mary Rose would have approved,' said Deborah.

A decision had clearly been made by them all not to ignore the topic of Mary Rose. They were at pains to mention her, dropping her name into conversations with an air of what they must have hoped would sound like normality. Amusing quotes were attributed to her, some of which did not sound to me entirely accurate, but it would have been churlish of me to question them. Particularly curious were the pointed references that were made to her presence at the most inconsequential of events. For example, on that first evening of the holiday, Philip was talking about a disastrous one-man show he had once performed at a café theatre in Dublin, when he broke off from the story.

'If I remember rightly, Mary Rose came to see it,' he said, and there was a revelatory tone to his voice, as if he was recalling something of enormous significance. He might have been telling us that someone famous had been there. Deborah jumped in to agree with him, too vociferously, as if it mattered a damn whether Mary Rose was there or not. There wasn't any point that I could see in adding this minute footnote to her biography.

'You're right,' said Deborah. 'Mary Rose was definitely there. I remember we tried to sneak out halfway through but she left her coat behind, so we had to go back for it.'

It was exhausting to me, and touching at the same time, how my friends took such care to gather up every morsel of her life. They collated these shards of her history with all the white-glove care of archaeologists gathering up the fragments of some precious artefact. It reminded me of an incident when I was a kid and my brother knocked a vase off the hall table at home. The vase was a big, ugly thing, but it had been handed down through my mother's family and it was precious to her. My brother and I had been horsing around in the dark hallway of that terminally miserable house when he knocked against it. The vase fell and broke into a hundred pieces on the diamond-patterned tiles, and while my brother and I froze in anticipation of our inevitable punishment, my mother got down on her hands and knees and started picking up all the pieces, which she placed carefully into a sling she had made of her skirt.

My father stood in the kitchen doorway watching her with contempt. 'What does it matter, woman?' he said. 'The vase is fucked. You might as well get a brush and sweep it out the bloody door.' At the time all I noticed was the rough way he spoke to her, but now I can see that he had a point. There was no sense whatsoever in trying to put that vase back together again.

'The finest local rosé,' announced Michael, ripping the foil from a long, slim bottle and twisting a wine opener into the cork in the violent manner of a man wringing a chicken's neck. 'A disgusting thing under most circumstances, but for some reason it tastes almost palatable here.'

The wine was so cold that it clouded our glasses as he poured.

'Cheers,' said everyone again.

I remember that for supper that night we ate lamb tagine that had been purchased by Deborah at the local *traiteur* and heated by her in the ancient cooker in the kitchen of the rented house. The cooker was exactly the same shade of pale green enamel as the cooker my grandmother used to have in her house in Harold's Cross, and it had the same perilous smell of gas hovering around it. On that cooker my nana would make us sausages that my mother always forced my brother and me to eat, even though they were burnt on the outside and pink in the middle, with bits of gristle in them that you could not chew. You had to swallow them down with a gulp of the MiWadi orange that Nana would serve us in plastic beakers that for some reason smelled of school. 'It's *my* Wadi,' we would say to each other in an endless loop. 'No, it's *my* Wadi . . .' The MiWadi became more and more dilute as Nana aged until, in time, it was no more than homeopathic, but we drank it anyway, because nobody ever turned down anything in my family, on the basis that it was rude to say no. To say yes was too eager. What we were taught to say was 'I don't mind', a habit it took me years to overcome.

'Pass your plates, folks,' said Deborah, standing to serve out helpings of the tagine from the chipped china soup tureen she had found in the kitchen dresser. There was couscous too, and celeriac remoulade. As I held my plate out to be served, I couldn't help but smile. It was far from couscous that I was reared. My father would never countenance any staple other than the potato on our table.

'Delicious,' said Cara.

'Yes, top notch,' said Tom. 'Well done, guys.'

Big Tom, who Michael had acquired in my absence on his first day of college in UCD. I was embarked by then on a course in journalism at the College of Commerce in Rathmines, and by the time I met Tom it was too late for me to veto him. I only ever tolerated him because he had the use of a car. For four years he was our unofficial driver, which gave us a reach we would not otherwise have had as undergraduates. We went to parties in the mountains with wild Protestant girls. There were weekends in the west of Ireland. Forays down to Sherriff Street to buy drugs in the flats. When we left college, we found we no longer had much use for Tom, and we tried to shake him off, but it proved impossible to do so. 'Tom's a goon,' Michael said to me once. 'But he's our goon, and there's no getting rid of him now.'

'Can I propose a toast?' said Tom, clearing his throat in a theatrical manner.

'Hang on,' said Michael, reaching for a bottle. 'Let me top everyone up first.'

'To old friends,' said Tom, in his big barrister's voice. 'To French plonk and, most of all, to holidays.'

'To holidays,' repeated Duncan, and everyone took care to clink their glasses, holding them up for a moment of ceremony before they drank from them, the way a priest holds the chalice up in front of him as an altar boy rings a bell. I had the feeling that what they were toasting was not just holidays but life itself. So much of what was said that week was code for something else.

'The thing about this wine,' Duncan was saying, 'is that it tastes better and better the more you drink of it.'

'It's a U-bend,' said Michael. 'The trick is to look out for the turn.'

Their voices flapped around me, and I had the sense of being out at sea in a small boat. The evening flowed under us, silent and still. But there were dangers lurking beneath the surface, and I knew that they were all taking extreme care to avoid them. As the darkness fell down around us, we sat on into the hot summer evening, getting gently mashed on that cheap rosé, while the mosquitoes feasted on our tender flesh and the blinking lights of the planes wrote their sombre message across the inky sky.

I don't think I have ever in my life felt so abjectly alone as I did that week in Nice among my oldest friends. I had known most of them for nearly forty years. Michael and I were in school together from the time we were twelve. Deborah, I grew up across the road from in Terenure. Cara Heffernan was always in and out of Deborah's house because she was

Deborah's best friend, and Angela I knew from childhood because her mother and mine were cousins. Michael's brother, Philip, was every bit as familiar to me as my own brother. Even Duncan had become part of the furniture, in the time that he'd been seeing Cara. We had all known each other for so long that our friendship had a patina to it, and yet that week in France, I was a stranger among them.

I should say that group holidays are not my thing at the best of times. I can barely go on holiday with *myself*, and the thought of sharing a rented house for seven days with a group of other people is appalling to me. It's an indication of my fragile state of mind that I ever agreed to it. Every moment of every day presented another opportunity to regret it – from the very first morning, when I got up early in the hope of an hour's solitude on the terrace, only to find Duncan cutting his toenails with a pair of clippers on the copy of the *New York Times* that I had bought at the airport and had not yet finished reading. The bathroom I shared with Philip was always full of the steam of his shower and the smells of his ablutions by the time I got to it, and that first day there was a single pubic hair already embedded in the bar of soap.

Breakfast was a tortuous affair, with everyone falling over each other to drive to the local patisserie to get the croissants. ('No, honestly, I'm happy to go . . .' 'Ah, let me go . . .') There ensued another miserable hour of negotiations after breakfast before we could settle on a plan for the day that everyone was happy with. We had two hire cars and three named drivers, which resulted in a hundred different permutations being explored every time we needed to go anywhere. 'I need to stop at the pharmacy,' Cara might say, at which point Angela would say she would go into town with Cara because she wanted to look for a bikini. 'Duncan can drive us,' Cara would say, but then someone would point out that Duncan had already committed to going with Michael to the local vineyard to stock up on some more plonk for dinner. It was all I could do not to climb out the window and start walking for home.

In fairness, they treated me with great kindness. They took every care not to upset me. But I had the sense that they were all a bit afraid of me. There were murmurs in the kitchen late at night. One evening I heard a burst of nervous, almost hysterical, laughter coming from Cara, and then I heard Deborah telling her to shush. Another time I turned at the dinner table to see that Michael had raised a finger to his lips to deter Tom from embarking on a story about an undertaker he once knew. Undertakers were out of bounds. So, too, funerals, and all manners of death. These were all marked out clearly as no-go areas, the way white flags are placed around a minefield, to denote the places it is not safe to step. Also to be avoided were conversations about children – Mary Rose and I had none, and they must have imagined that it was insensitive, or perhaps just boring, to discuss something that I could now never be a part of. In their extreme sensitivity to my feelings they also steered each other away from any mention of weddings, air travel and indeed the entire Arab world. It was while she was on her way to the wedding of a friend's daughter in Egypt that Mary Rose met her death.

There played out over the next week in Nice a farcical situation whereby the others conspired on a daily basis to find a place for us to spend the day where we would not be troubled by the constant presence in the sky of planes. One day we went to Monaco. Another day we drove inland to see the Matisse chapel at Vence. On the third day we decamped to La Garoupe beach on the Cap d'Antibes, but it was worse there, if anything. From the beach we seemed to have a line of sight not just of every plane coming in and out of Nice but of every plane flying southwards over France. I sat on the sand and watched them, and because I knew all the others were thinking of Mary Rose, I thought of her too. I imagined her sitting at a window seat on one of those planes – among the many unnatural things I now know about her is the fact that she was in seat 15A – so I could picture her looking down on the beaches below, and I thought of how very strange it was that we were all sitting on one of those beaches, looking up into the sky and imagining her there.

The next day was muggy, with a heavy suspense in the air that slowed our routine down. It was midday by the time we were all up and about, and nobody had any appetite for another day at the beach, so we stayed around the house, bumping off each other as we came and went from the kitchen to get a drink, or something to eat. By afternoon the cabin fever was rising to a dangerous pitch.

'I thought I might go for a wander around the Old Town,' said Deborah, and I opted to go with her, purely to pre-empt the emergence of another, less attractive, plan. Michael offered to drive us, and I insisted on Deborah taking the front seat, while I crept into the back. Pinned behind a particularly aggressive seat belt, I felt like a kid again. Deborah and Michael could have been my parents, their voices only half heard as we drove around for what seemed like a long time looking for a parking space. I stared out the window, wallowing in my helplessness.

'Look, there's the Negresco,' said Deborah, playing mother. 'And that's the casino . . .'

I pressed my nose against the glass and gazed up at the grand old buildings of the Promenade des Anglais. They were a consolation to me, in their magnificent indifference. They made my suffering seem somehow small and transient.

'It reminds me of the city in one of those Babar the Elephant stories,' said Deborah, and I could see what she meant. With its palm trees and carousels and its striped beach umbrellas, it was a city straight out of a children's storybook.

'Splendid,' I said, meaning it literally.

As we inched along the train of traffic on the promenade, I studied the faces of the people we passed. The faces of the old people, in particular, had something to say to me. These people had survived a war. Their parents had survived – or died in – a war. And yet here they were, walking along the Promenade des Anglais in the sunshine in search of an evening drink. The thought of it made me feel, not better – I never felt better – but somehow different. The pain was still there, the pain was always there, but I had a soothing feeling on top of it, like when you apply a cooling gel to sunburn.

'Now that is skill,' said Michael.

He had managed to shoehorn the hire car into a minuscule parking space by the Opera House. We spilled out and made for the flower market, following the directions on Michael's phone. Deborah wanted to buy some cheese. Michael was looking for spices. As we trailed along the stalls, she paused to look at a display of peaches. He stopped to sample some olives, and I saw the opportunity to do something I had not done since I was a kid. Without saying a word to either of them, I slipped away.

An old habit of mine: for a period of time from when I was about five until I was seven, my mother had to write my address on a piece of paper and pin it to my jacket whenever we left the house, so I could be returned home if I was found wandering. I don't remember ever being lost, but I must have been, because I came home in a squad car once. She was furious with me, but she never said that the reason she was angry was that she loved me and feared that something had happened to me. There was only her anger. At seven, I made my First Confession, and the one sin I could think to confess to the priest was my disobedience to my mother in wandering off. I can't remember what the penance was, but having confessed to it and repented, I never did it again. Not until I found myself in the market in Nice with Michael and Deborah.

Gone for a wander, I said to Deborah in a text, once I was safely clear of the market. Ring me when you're ready to go.

I roamed the streets of the Old Town in search of a decent café. I didn't want to sit in one of those tourist cafés. I wanted a proper café, where women sit stroking their little lapdogs and men do nothing but smoke. I took to the back streets, through the smells of garlic and leather, past the racks of retro postcards and the rails of surprisingly unfashionable clothing, stalked by the ever-present feeling of being without Mary Rose. An awful, anxious feeling, like the kind you have when you've lost some essential thing. A phone, or a wallet, that you cannot live without. The torture is in the belief that it might yet be found, if only you knew where to look.

Eventually, I found a suitable café on a corner, and sat down and ordered myself a Campari. Mary Rose and I once went through a phase of drinking Campari with orange juice and I had a sudden notion to taste it, in the hope that it would bring me back, even for one second, to a time when she was with me. At home, I kept her half-empty bottle of perfume on the bedside table for the same reason, and before I went to sleep I would spray a little of it on to her pillow. I would sometimes even phone her voicemail just to hear her voice, until one day – in a fit of ice-cold efficiency – I closed down her account. I continued to send her the occasional message whenever something happened that would be of interest to her. For example, I sent her a message when Cara's daughter decided to do nursing, because I knew it would please her. I texted her when George Michael died, because – despite the forlorn figure he cut in his later years – he remained for her the golden boy of her teenage dreams. Sometimes I just texted her to say goodnight.

In time the row of texts I had sent her ran down the right-hand side of the screen of my phone, with nothing but blank space on the left-hand side. I had to scroll a long way up to find the last text I got from Mary Rose.

Boarding now, she had written. Love you!!!

Mary Rose was a great woman for saying I love you. A great woman for an exclamation mark, too. In some instances, every single sentence she wrote bore an exclamation mark. Her every sign-off was marked by a slew of XXX's.

The flowers arrived!!! Pink roses, my absolute favourite! Thank you my love!!! XXXX MR

There could have been no clearer illustration of the disparity in our personalities than a comparison of the two columns of our texts to each other. Her texts ran long and were often peppered with emoticons. Mine were short and resolutely emoticon-free. What amazes me now is how this disparity managed to survive, and even flourish, throughout our marriage. In all the years we were together, Mary Rose was never infected by my bottomless capacity for negativity. Nor did her cheerful positivity ever rub off on me.

We did cross-pollinate on occasion. For example, Mary Rose was a dedicated tea drinker when we met. She had an aversion to coffee because some coffee liqueurs had made her sick as a child. There are few things I enjoy as much as a good cup of coffee, especially on holiday, and I wanted very much for Mary Rose to appreciate this. It was on holiday one year in Aiguaclara, worn down by the ubiquity of dreary

English teabags, that she finally agreed to try a cortado. It became one of our great shared pleasures and a rare entry on my side of the balance sheet of our marriage. Mary Rose had brought so many things to my life – off the top of my head I can list the capacity to love and be loved and a cash deposit for a house – while on my side of the balance sheet there was only coffee and the pink roses I took to sending her every year on her birthday. Oh, and dancing. Thanks to a charismatic nun who taught us for a term in sixth class, I was able to dance.

That was a rabbit I pulled out of the hat the first time we were at a wedding together. Once the bride and groom had the first dance out of the way, I took Mary Rose by the waist and swung her out on to the dance floor. I whirled and spun her; I played her out like a yoyo and wound her back in again. She had on a strapless dress, with a full skirt that fell out in a fan every time I tipped her backwards. After the dance was finished, I bent down and kissed her hand. She bit her lip and shook her head in disbelief.

'I can't believe you,' she said, narrowing her eyes at me.

'Just one of my many hidden talents,' I told her, which I fear now was false advertising. I had no more rabbits in the hat, only hang-ups and prejudices, as Mary Rose would soon discover, but I'm not sure it was my intention to mislead her. It may have been, in those early days of our romance, that I had fooled myself into thinking that there might be more to me than even I knew. I was in love with the reflection of myself that I saw in her endlessly startled eyes.

'Le Campari,' said the waiter, and I looked up to see him standing before me with a tray. He set the Campari glass down on the table, snagged the cap off a bottle of orange juice and set that down too, along with an empty ashtray. I stared at the ashtray, thinking how long it had been since I was a person who smoked. It seemed to me that I had become a different person entirely to that young man who had once smoked with blissful impunity. Just like I was a different person now to the happy husband who was once married to Mary Rose. Some new, half-living creature had climbed out of the husk of that husband, someone I hardly even recognized as myself. I took a sip of the Campari, and for a moment it worked some magic in connecting me back to all the previous versions of me.

I found myself watching a man coming along the street. The man was in his late forties, or early fifties perhaps. Tall and thin, with dark hair and a smart suit, he looked a lot like me. As I watched him, he stopped in front of a building across the street. He took a set of keys out of the pocket of his jacket and turned to open the huge fortress door. The door swung open, and I had a glimpse of an ox-blood hallway. Black-and-white tiles. A carved wooden newel post. The man stepped inside, and the door swung closed behind him. There was a brief hesitation before the latch clicked shut.

I was possessed by a tremendous desire to be that man. To turn the key in the lock of that door and slip into his life. I imagined how I would ignore the lift, taking the smooth stone steps two at a time and hitting the light switches on the way up. As a student I once spent a summer living in a *chambre de bonne* in the Bastille, and it took me three months to perfect the art of hitting all the light switches and none of the doorbells on my way up the dark stairwell. It was a source of great pride to me that I had made myself native to that building in the Bastille – with its stone steps that cupped in the middle from centuries of footfall – and I longed to disappear into another building just like it. To vanish without trace into another life. The desire was so strong that I had to close my eyes to make it go away.

Stopping for a drink at the café opposite the Palais de Justice, went the text that came in from Deborah with a ping.

I paid my bill and headed instead for the promenade, finding a free blue chair in a row laid out to face the sea. The water had been emptied of all colour, so that it was almost white, like the sky. On the beach, dogs bounded through the shallows, while groups of young people sat in circles on the stones. A pungent smell of hashish filled the air, fighting with the lavish perfume trails left behind by the women walking the promenade. To the west, a pool of pink light began to spill over the hills behind the city, and above all of this were the planes, endlessly coming in to land.

Their flight path took them on a straight course for the city, so that it seemed for a second or two that they were intent on dive-bombing us, but then they banked and swept along the arc of the bay, coming down into the airport. I concentrated on trying to identify their livery. British Airways was easy. So was easyJet, and some of the Gulf airlines had very helpfully printed the name of their country in block capitals on the undercarriage. That reminded me of Africa, the way the planes had big black letters printed on their underbellies.

I spent a summer in Africa once, as a young freelance, and it retains in my memory a clarity that most other things in my life have lost. I can hardly remember a single episode from my schooldays, for example, and even college is by and large a blur. The twenty-five years I worked as a broadcast journalist seem in retrospect more like one very long and busy day than what must, in fact, have been thousands of them. So much of my past is a fog to me, but I only have to think about Africa and I'm back there, not as a middle-aged man reminiscing, but as a 24-year-old innocent embarked on the adventure of his life.

There was, in particular, an early morning on the border

between Kenya and Sudan. I was standing in the open air outside my hut when I heard the roar of jet engines from the airstrip nearby. A cargo plane was leaving to drop forty-kilo bags of rice and beans out of the sky over southern Sudan. It flew a hundred foot over my head, and on its underbelly I saw printed, in huge black letters, the abbreviation 'UN'. I remember being incredibly impressed by the sight of it, and I ran back into my hut to grab my camera, but I was too late. By the time I came back out, it was no more than a speck in the sky, heading north. I lowered the camera, annoyed that I had missed the photo opportunity.

A picture tells a thousand words; everyone knows that, even the mother I saw later that day at a feeding centre in southern Sudan. There must have been a hundred mothers, with their hundred babies, huddled in an unnatural silence under the shade of a dirty tarpaulin. I circled them with my camera, noticing one baby among them who was the smallest, the sickest, the closest to death. The baby's mother saw me training my camera on him and turned him towards me so I could get a better shot. It was all she could do for him.

It was the picture of that baby, in his Stars and Stripes T-shirt, that accompanied the article I later had published in the *Irish Times*. I never knew what happened to him, never thought to enquire after him – I had not even asked his name. I barely gave him a thought in the years that followed, until the memory of him darted out of a crevice in my mind, nearly thirty years later. Sitting in a blue chair on the Promenade des Anglais, the thought of him caused my heart to crack in my chest. I had a shuddering in my lungs, and I found myself retching, as the grief rose up like vomit in my throat. I closed my eyes and clamped my lips shut, but the tears still leaked out of me. My head fell forward, my shoulders collapsed. I had no power in me to hold my body together. It might almost have been a fit of laughter it was so violent, and I was aware of the public spectacle I must have made, sitting on a blue chair on the Promenade des Anglais sobbing my heart out, but I couldn't stop. I was suddenly and belatedly heartbroken, not just by my own sorrow but by all the other countless sorrows in the world, and I wondered how I had for so long failed to acknowledge them.

'There you are,' said Deborah.

I whipped my head around to see her standing behind my chair. The tears in my eyes caused her to wobble in front of me. She put her two hands on my shoulders and gave them a squeeze.

'We were trying to ring you.'

I put a finger in the corner of one eye and rubbed it, the way you do if you have something trapped there.

'Sorry,' I said. 'My phone must have been on silent.'

'Are you good to go?'

'Sure,' I said, but I looked back out to sea once more. Another plane had appeared out of the white sky in front of us. I watched, transfixed, as it flew straight towards us. It turned, tracing the line of the bay, and then floated down to earth, light as a feather. There was nothing in the world I wanted to do so much as to wait for the next one and see it safely down. I would have liked to sit there all evening, watching those planes coming safely down to earth, but instead I stood and followed my friend to the car.

There were to be fireworks in Nice for Bastille Day. We saw the posters going up about the town. The Jazz Festival was taking place that weekend, and Duncan wanted to go to a concert by some young American singer. He went into town to make enquiries, but the gig was sold out. He consoled himself by rigging up a portable speaker to his smartphone and playing her album to us on the terrace.

'That woman has the voice of a wanton goddess,' he said, rolling a joint with his left hand while his right hand lay like a happy cat on Cara's thigh. I wondered how he had managed to get hold of the dope.

'We saw her when she played the Olympia,' said Cara. 'She was ay-may-zing.'

Mary Rose was right: they were like teenagers, the pair of them. They liked to talk about gigs they'd been to in small venues around Dublin. Often, they would mention open-mic nights in city pubs, and during the summer months they headed off to music festivals around the country, sleeping on an inflatable mattress in the back of Duncan's battered old station wagon. I was unreasonably irritated by all of this, probably because, in another life, I might have enjoyed doing that kind of thing myself. Mary Rose and I seldom went to concerts, and when we did it was the safety of the familiar that we sought out. She liked Paul Simon and Sting. I was more of a Steely Dan man, myself.

Our plan that night was to go and see the fireworks on the Promenade des Anglais, but several circumstances intervened. The first was that Michael chose that evening to produce a bottle of Pernod after dinner, with the result that nobody was capable of driving. The second circumstance was the rain: for the first time since we arrived there had been clouds that day, and by evening the air was cool and dank. Angela, in particular, was not keen on getting caught in the rain.

'We could just watch the fireworks from right here,' suggested Tom, always quick to placate his wife. The way Tom danced around Angela, you could be forgiven for thinking she was a minor European royal. If she had a terminal illness, maybe that would have been some justification for the way Tom rushed into the house to get a rug to wrap around her shoulders. I have in the past seen Tom load up a breakfast tray with coffee and toast and a single nectarine and carry it up to Angela, *in the bath*. 'He's not so much her husband as her guide dog,' Mary Rose once said. Angela Foley, princess of Templeogue Gardens, had made a working animal out of our Tom.

'Why don't I get rugs for *all of us*,' said Deborah pointedly, going into the house and stripping the couches of their coverings. As the first drops of rain began to fall, sporadic and harmless, Michael wound out the overhead awning so that the terrace was covered. Philip and I dragged the chairs and sunloungers into a row along the balustrade, and we each of us made a nest for ourselves with the rugs Deborah handed out. We looked like patients in a Swiss sanatorium.

The fireworks were underwhelming, as they always are unless you are close enough to them to smell the gunpowder, but they provided a welcome diversion from the monotony that had by then descended on our evenings. They had an innocence about them that made me feel sentimental about France, and all that is good in the world. For a short time there, wrapped up in a scratchy rug that smelled faintly of spilled milk, with my free hand holding for dear life on to my glass of Pernod, and the rain sounding a gentle drum roll on the awning, I was almost at peace.

The fireworks had ended, and we were at work clearing away the glasses and empty bottles when we noticed the phones. There was the sound of a ringtone coming from somewhere. At first nobody was sure whose phone it was, but after some searching underneath cushions and rugs it was established that it was Deborah's. By that time Cara's phone was chirping with a flurry of texts. The music on Duncan's kept dropping out as it registered incoming messages. On the dark table in the corner of the terrace, Michael's screen strobed silently with a muted call.

'Something has happened in Nice,' said Cara, checking her texts. Her speech was all speeded up. No whisper to it now.

'No, we're fine,' Deborah was telling whoever it was that had phoned her. She turned her back to us and walked down towards the far end of the terrace.

'We're all grand,' I heard her say. 'We're here in the house. We didn't even know anything about it until you called.'

'Some kind of an attack in Nice,' Duncan was saying, pawing at his screen. 'There's a number of people dead.'

'Fuck it,' said Philip.

'Jesus,' said Michael. 'What else are they saying?'

Already, I knew how it would roll out. After the first urgent notification on the wires, there would be an eerie lull of a minute or two, before the first eyewitness accounts began to break through on social media. Then the unconfirmed sources. The rumours. The false alarms. The local media would have the first hard facts, but it would be an hour at least before there was anything official from the police.

'Looks like a truck drove into the crowd at the fireworks,' said Tom.

'My God,' said Angela. 'We could have been there.' She had swung her legs over the side of her sunlounger. Her hands were cupped over her mouth, her eyes round and staring. 'Did you text the kids?' she asked Tom, moving her hands down to cross them over her heart, as if she had been disturbed while sunbathing topless and didn't want anyone to see her breasts.

'Hang on. I'll do that now.'

Deborah had come off her call and was standing with her phone in her hand, itching for something else to do.

'I'll check Facebook,' she said. 'They've probably put a safety check in place.'

'Good thinking,' said Duncan, gazing at Deborah with dumb admiration, as if he would never in a million years have thought of such a thing.

'Okay,' she said, looking up from her phone. 'I've listed us all as safe and well.'

I remember thinking that she was being a bit melodramatic. We were several miles outside Nice, on a candlelit terrace that floated over the dark hillside like a raft in the middle of the sea. All around us lay nothing but the damp, fragrant night. It was absurd to think of us being in any kind of danger. But of course people would worry. It occurred to me, belatedly, that I should contact Mary Rose's sisters. Mary Rose's sisters would be bound to worry.

'They're saying at least thirty dead now,' said Tom.

'Oh Jesus, no.' Cara was shaking her head. 'Please, no.' She was rolling through her Twitter feed with her middle finger. 'People are posting photos of the bodies. For fuck's sake.'

Inside the house, Michael was trying to turn the TV on. I saw him jabbing at it with the remote control, but I did not go to help him. Instead, I carried on through to the bedroom, where I retrieved my phone from the bottom of my suitcase, turning it on only for long enough to text Jean Anne and Kitty. I had that sense of melodrama again as I typed out the words. It seemed to me absurdly self-important to be registering my own survival, which was clearly of no consequence in the grand scheme of things. It seemed almost unseemly, as if I had greedily chosen to live by grabbing at a long straw and leaving others with no choice but to pull the short ones. I had no feeling of relief, only a bitter sense of the irony of my survival. I would not have cared if I had died.

Safe and well, was what I wrote in the text that I sent to my sisters-in-law.

I hesitated for a moment, considering whether I should forward the text on to my brother, but then I thought, fuck him. I powered the phone off and tossed it back into my suitcase. I passed through the living room, where Michael and Philip were sitting on the edge of the couch with their eyes trained on a French news channel. I plunged back into the darkness of the terrace, seeking refuge on a sunlounger. I had a hum in my ears, which I recognized as the sound of my own isolation. I could find no role for myself in this drama.

'Are you okay?' asked Deborah, coming to sit lightly on the edge of the sunlounger, her hand resting on my arm.

'Why wouldn't I be?'

In the silence that followed I knew that she was finding it hard to understand me. Hard to like me, even. But she persisted in trying.

'I was thinking this might hit you harder than the rest of us.'

'I don't see why.'

'No,' she said, removing her hand and standing up. 'Well, that's good. So long as you're okay.'

I felt badly for Deborah that I had failed to react in the way she expected me to. I was sorry that I had made her dislike me. But the truth was that I could see no connection between what had happened on the Promenade des Anglais that night and what had happened to Mary Rose. In my mind there was no connection between what had happened to Mary Rose and any other thing. To seek out a pattern to these things seemed to me naïve and somehow primitive. It was irritating to me, so I brushed it off.

I have made the same mistake before. Not by virtue of grief but through professional arrogance, I have resisted jumping to what I considered to be amateur conclusions. When Mary Rose poked her head out the kitchen window of a rental house in Kerry to tell me that a plane had crashed into the World Trade Center in New York, for example, I barely looked up from my book.

She was tidying away the lunch and I was sitting in a deck-chair outside the window in an unexpected pool of sunshine.

'It just happened a few minutes ago,' she said.

'Oh, really?'

I assumed that she was attributing unnecessary import-ance to a one-line report at the end of the radio bulletin. It must have been a light plane, I thought. One of those single-engine jobs, flying out of Teterboro or LaGuardia. That kind of thing had happened before.

'The tower is on fire.'

I envisaged a small plume of smoke. Lines of office work-ers filing out of the building. There would be a statement from the Aviation Administration. It would barely warrant a full package on the six o'clock news, and by the nine o'clock news it would be cut back to a reader voice-over.

'Oh?' I said again, so as not to be rude.

'Seemingly, there was a big bang.'

The word 'seemingly' was one that she liked to use. But 'seemingly' could mean anything. It could mean that some-thing only seemed to be the case. It could mean that it was not necessarily true, a concept I had noticed creeping into news broadcasts in recent years. Even the BBC had softened their guidelines. 'It is being reported that . . .' was something you heard more and more, much to my annoyance. I was trained back in the days when you did not report something until you had established it for a fact.

'Hmm,' I said, hoping that would be enough to discour-age her. I would have preferred not to be fed snippets of the news while I was on my holiday, but I never had the heart to tell her this, for fear of hurting her feelings. Eager as a child who brings in wild flowers from the ditch for her teacher, Mary Rose loved to bring me news stories.

'I wonder could it be deliberate?' she said, sticking her head out the window again.

'Oh, I doubt it,' I said, keen to reassure her. 'Probably just an accident.'

When she relayed the news to me that a second plane had struck the South Tower, I joined her at the radio in the kitchen. I had a strange hum in my ears, like static in an empty radio studio. The sense that everything I thought I knew about the world now counted for nothing. I did not realize it then, but we had just entered the age of the implausible. Soon to become the age of the absurd and, again, I did not see that one coming. Not until I was on duty in the newsroom one Christmas Day and saw that a man had been arrested for trying to board a flight out of Amsterdam with explosives in his underpants. I saw it as a flash coming in on the wires, but I almost neglected to carry the story on the grounds that it was too silly, which it was.

I was still on compassionate leave when Trump was elected, and it became clear to me very quickly that it would not be possible to go back. The world had become a Marvel comic book. It had become a James Bond movie, and there was no place in it for a straight man like me. I felt like Jimmy Stewart in *The Man Who Knew Too Much*. 'Well, look here now,' a voice in my mind kept saying, ready to apply logic to the situation. But there was no logic any more. There was no trajectory that you could make out. The news cycle had become a cartoon train, careening off the tracks and headed for the terrifying unknown, and I had somehow stepped off it. I found myself alone in a strangely silent landscape.

'Oh God,' said Cara. 'There's something going on in a restaurant too. They've taken hostages.'

'Looks like the driver's been shot dead,' said Tom. 'Looks like the police have managed to shoot him.'

Their voices sounded very far away. I rested my head back on the slightly damp cushion of the sunlounger and closed my eyes. Shutting out everything else, I zoned in on the sound of a man's voice, coming from the TV inside.

'Plusieurs dizaines de morts . . .'

He was speaking very quickly, and there were only bits of what he said that I understood.

'Un camion blanc . . . pendant le feu d'artifice . . . quatorze juillet.'

Other things I could hear quite distinctly but not translate. They were just sounds to me.

'. . . a foncé dans la foule . . . les tirs des forces de l'ordre.'

Then I heard him say that up to fifty people were between life and death, and I was struck by the phrase because it seemed to me like an accurate description of the state I was in. I was neither dead nor alive but doomed to wander a desolate space between the two. There was me, and separated from me by a thick pane of glass was the world, where all kinds of things happened that I could see and hear but not feel. They were things I cared nothing about. I was in such pain.

I once had a kidney stone, and that was the same order of pain. Pain that blocked out everything around it. You had to grab on to it and ride it out, the way a surfer rides a wave. There were moments when it was almost pleasurable in its stunning, all-encompassing intensity. You had to respect the way it obliterated everything else, made every other person fall away, every other thing irrelevant. That was how I felt that night in Nice. I was ice cold and unreachable by virtue of my own unspeakable suffering. When at last I made it to bed that night, I rolled over on to my side and curled up into a ball. Pulling my knees into my chest, I was overcome by relief that I no longer had to remain upright. No longer had to pretend to care about anything but myself. What I wanted, more than anything, was to be home, with nothing to attend to but my own misery. I promised myself, then and there, never to holiday with anyone again.

So, when January of this year came around, and Deborah gamely suggested that we all spend a week together this summer, I was ready for her. She was thinking Tuscany, she told me, and I pictured her searching the Internet for a villa at the furthest possible remove from any international airport. Good and brave friend that she is, Deborah could not disguise her relief when I told her I was determined to go back to Aiguaclara and, this time, she did not try to dissuade me.

3

It was Mary Rose who discovered Aiguaclara.

In a bed and breakfast in Barcelona, on a sweltering July evening that fell three days into our honeymoon, she lay belly down on the unmade bed and drew a circle with her biro in the guidebook.

'A picturesque village with a small sandy beach, Aiguaclara enjoys crystal-clear waters that reflect the green of the surrounding pine trees,' she read, in her class-prefect voice, only lifting her head to look at me when she had finished.

'Don't move,' I said, enjoying the picturesque view I had, as I emerged from the bathroom, of the twin dimples at the base of her back. I pretended to swat away an imaginary mosquito before coming to kneel over her to claim my dues as her champion. I buried my face in the sticky skin at the back of her neck, but she persisted in reading me snippets from the guidebook, so I grabbed it and launched it across the room. It hit the wall and slid to the floor, as Mary Rose flipped herself over on to her back to challenge me with her guileless blue eyes. With her fair hair streaked like seaweed across her face, she was a mermaid trapped in my nets. I could hardly believe she was mine to keep.

That guidebook still sits on the top shelf of our bookcase, beside the dog-eared copy of *South East Asia on a Shoestring* that was among Mary Rose's possessions when she moved in with me. There's an ancient *Let's Go Europe* that I inherited from an American I once met on a train. *The Rough Guide to*

Venice and the Veneto and the *Time Out Guide to Lisbon* are treasured relics of our first holidays together. With advancing age and prosperity, we accumulated a row of Fodor's city guides. *Alastair Sawday's Special Places to Stay: Morocco* is the last guidebook we bought together. Now that the Internet does our guiding for us, I have no more use for them. They are hopelessly out of date, but I keep them anyway, as artefacts of a more innocent time.

The *Eyewitness Travel Guide* to Spain had a fold-out map of the region, which we used to guide us to Aiguaclara. How quaint it seems now, to use a map! We had to take a few loops of the roundabout in the local town before we found the right turn. Then the heady plunge down the hill, not knowing what to expect at the bottom. The joy of finding the place to be every bit as idyllic as the guidebook had promised. More so, even, in the failing light. The sea was like mirrored glass, the beach a small crescent of golden sand. The buildings along the seafront were all painted white, with cheery awnings and corrugated terracotta roof tiles. With the lights coming on along the promenade, and people already gathering in the restaurants for dinner, it seemed to us as perfect a place as we could have found.

'Not too shabby,' I said, as we parked the car under a huge white oleander bush.

'It's gorgeous,' said Mary Rose, gushing with the enthusiasm I felt but could not express.

That first day in Aiguaclara we marvelled at the colour of the water. The pleasure of the sun on our faces. The warm air on our skin. Over and over again, we commented on these things, while all around us everyone else seemed to be unmoved by them. I remember being struck then – as I have been every time since – of how Europeans assume the pleasures of summer as a birthright. In Spain they speak of *las vacaciones*, by which they mean morning after morning breaking to a clear blue sky, and a long lazy day on the beach, followed by a feast of fish and white wine in a restaurant on the seafront. Back when we first went to Aiguaclara, Mary Rose and I were too Irish by far to take such pleasures for granted.

'Can you believe we're here?' we would ask each other. Standing on the balcony, looking out over that mesmerizing sea, we felt like desert explorers happening upon an oasis that might yet turn out to be a mirage. Swimming at night in the inky sea, under a sky falling down with stars – the buildings along the shoreline lit up like the string of tiny paper houses Mary Rose once bought for our Christmas tree – we said it again.

'I can't believe this is real.'

Summer to us was freezing your arse off on a windswept beach, with a trip to the ice-cream shop if you were lucky. Of course, they never had the ice-cream you wanted. You'd stare at the HB poster, agonizing over your choice, but no matter which one you picked they were always bound to be out of it. One of the things I've noticed about Spain is how they always have the ice-cream you want. I like to watch the children lining up at the freezer in Aiguaclara, on tippy-toes in their togs, pointing to their selection on the ice-cream poster in the full expectation that it will be produced. I try to imagine what it must be like for them, to grow up without a constant undertow of disappointment.

'What a perfect place for children,' said Mary Rose, that first evening we were in Aiguaclara. We sat having our aperitif on the terrace of the hotel, watching little girls in summer dresses set up makeshift shops on the hot stones of the promenade to sell painted rocks to the tourists. The boys played football on the beach and scaled the lifeguards' chair, their shouts and laughter like invisible fireworks in the gently falling night.

'We'll have to come back here every year,' said Mary Rose. 'When we have children.'

That first year we were staying in the old three-star hotel on the promenade. We had signed up to a half-board deal that tied us in to a buffet breakfast and a set dinner in the company of a group of Dutch pensioners. I remember that we were rendered hopelessly institutionalized within days. In subsequent years we drifted up the hill, renting different apartments year upon year, apartments which varied only marginally in the horror of their decor and the discomfort of their beds. One place had two rickety wooden cots we pushed together, making a danger sport of our love-making as we tried to avoid falling into the crevice between them. Another had quasi-pornographic pictures of the owner's children hanging on the walls. And the pillows – oh God, the pillows. I invariably had a crick in my neck by the third day.

'Maybe next year we should splash out on a *slightly* fancier apartment,' said Mary Rose. That was the year we rented an apartment on the seafront, where the wiring was so antiquated that a fuse popped every time you boiled the kettle or turned on the toaster. The apartment was dark and insufferably hot, with just one small window opening from the bedroom on to an internal yard. We were woken before dawn every morning by a ferocious tumbling sound on the wooden staircase as the woman who lived upstairs let her dogs out to run on the beach.

'This apartment,' said Mary Rose, 'is a torture chamber. 'When we're not being electrocuted, we're being subjected to sleep deprivation. I insist on an upgrade next year.'

It must have been around that time that we started using the Internet, because I remember a winter spent browsing pictures of apartments on the home computer at our little house in Ringsend, the two of us huddled in the office space under the stairs. The Internet connection was so slow we spent most of our time looking at an egg timer and listening to crackle on the line.

'This one looks nice,' Mary Rose would say, bringing up a picture of a minimalist living room, with monochrome couches and stainless-steel kitchen appliances, and not a floral-patterned curtain or a tapestry cushion in sight.

'I'm not paying a grand a week for a holiday apartment!'

'I don't see what difference it makes,' said Mary Rose.

'How can you say that? You're talking about four hundred quid in the difference!'

She shrugged. 'In the grand scheme of things, I don't see how it makes any difference.'

It seemed to me then that what separated her from me was not so much a problem of perspective but a cognitive one. I thought there was something wrong with Mary Rose's brain if she couldn't understand the difference between paying six hundred a week for an apartment and paying a thousand. Between paying a tenner for a bottle of wine and twenty quid. Between buying a jumper at full price and waiting for the sales.

'You do know this will be half price the day after tomorrow?' I said one Christmas morning, when I opened the wrapping on a sky-blue cashmere jumper she had bought me.

By the look on her face, I might as well have been telling her there was no Santa Claus.

'But I wanted to give it to you for Christmas.'

'Well, it's your money,' I said, only grudgingly ceding the point because it was Christmas.

In my defence, I should say that I had been reared in a home where we were restricted to using one sheet of toilet paper at a time. My mother turned the collars of my father's shirts, picking them apart and sewing them back inside out, so he'd get a few more years' wear out of them. Any letters that arrived at our house without a postmark were salvaged and the stamps steamed off, so they could be used again. All of which explains why I could not in a million years countenance paying a thousand euro a week for a holiday apartment, when the alternative was to pay six hundred. I insisted on skimping, with predictable consequences.

There was the year we rented a place that was infested by flying ants. Another time, we opened the door of a spare bedroom to find a bat hanging from the ceiling. Always hungry for an opportunity to make a hero of myself in my wife's eyes, I draped a bed sheet over my head and approached the bat with my arms outstretched like a Halloween ghost.

'Don't hurt it!' said Mary Rose, from somewhere behind me.

Through the sheet, I could only barely see the dark blotch the bat made on the wall, but I managed somehow to trap it. As I transported it out to the balcony, I could feel its matchstick bones fluttering with fear inside the bundle I had made of the sheet. It reminded me of making an Airfix plane when I was a kid. The way you had to handle it like hot toast, keeping your hands light and loose, so as not to break it. I held the bundle out over the balcony railing and, with a magician's flourish, I released the bat. He dropped like a stone, and for a moment I was afraid he was going to splatter on the terrace below us, but he recovered just in time, rising up to miraculously clear the pine trees and fly out into the blue sky. What was most miraculous of all was the way Mary Rose looked at me when I came back into the apartment. Nobody had ever looked at me that way, until I met Mary Rose.

'You were amazing!' she said, and her eyes were wide with wonder as she pinned herself against my chest. The kiss she gave me was long and solemn, and it made me feel like a man I had never imagined myself to be. All my life I had fashioned myself as an anti-hero, but Mary Rose made me feel like I was wearing an invisible cape. That was the effect she had on me, and I miss it now that it's gone.

We rented 'the bat cave' for several years in a row, until at last we happened upon a good deal on a tiny house further up the hill. The house belonged to a noisy Yorkshire woman called Jo, who we met one evening down on the seafront. Jo was sitting at a table outside one of the restaurants on the promenade with a group of other migratory English, and we sat down at the table next to them to have our sundowner. It was one of the rhythms of the place that the locals huddled late into the evening on the shaded beach, while the northern Europeans took to the promenade and got pissed in the last of the day's sunshine.

'So, where are *you* from?' asked Jo, leaning towards us. She had blonde hair piled on top of her head in a messy, Brigitte Bardot style and she was wearing nothing but a swimsuit and a sarong, even though she looked to me like she hadn't been near the water in years. Her busty chest had been scorched so many times that you could see the layers where she had peeled and burned and peeled and burned. It reminded me of the walls of our house when we steamed the wallpaper off, revealing layers and layers of previous paint jobs.

'We're from Dublin,' said Mary Rose, looking slightly peeved to be approached in so familiar a manner. There was no snobbery in her, but she had been brought up to observe a certain etiquette in her dealings with people, and she didn't like it to be overlooked.

'Oh, Dublin,' said Jo, knowingly. 'My first husband was from Dublin.'

She laughed a phlegmy, smoker's laugh and reached for the pack of cigarettes on the table, lighting one up in a rush, as if it was an inhaler. She took a quick puff on it and exhaled, slapping herself on the chest in relief.

'Here,' she said, turning to her companions. 'Guess where they're from?'

She supplied the answer without waiting for them to guess.

'I love Dublin,' she told us. 'I always go to Bewley's for me coffee, and Beshoff's for me fish and chips. You can't beat Beshoff's for the fish and chips.'

She leaned over and took a hold of the half-empty jug of sangria that sat fermenting in the heat of the sun. She wore a lot of rings, no doubt the result of a lot of husbands, and they clanged off the glass handle of the jug.

'Here,' she said, 'have some sangria.'

I would have preferred to drink dishwater, but I wasn't quick enough to stop her from slopping some into my glass. Seeing that I had been so easily defeated, Mary Rose meekly submitted too.

'Cheers,' we both said, raising our glasses to Jo and her companions.

'Cheers, ducks,' said Jo.

By the time we had taken our second sip, Jo had offered to show us her house up the hill, with a view to renting it to us at some point in the future. She had plenty of friends she could stay with, she told us, and she'd prefer to rent her house to people she knew, rather than take her chances with strangers on the Internet. That she considered us people she knew, after only just meeting us, was a testament to her freakishly friendly nature, but we were to discover that she was generous too, and kind. She always left a bottle of wine for us on the kitchen counter, and she never raised the rent on us, and when Mary Rose died, I had a very lovely letter from her. I had dropped her an email to let her know we wouldn't be renting her house that summer, and briefly explaining why. She replied, clearly in shock, but she followed the email up with a letter. It was written in purple ink on notepaper adorned with a small garland of pink flowers in each corner, and she enclosed a poem she had photocopied for me from a book she had at home. The poem was a little hackneyed for my liking, but I was very touched by the thought of Jo going to the trouble of photocopying it for me.

Jo's house was only a few hundred metres up the hill, and it had the feel of a lighthouse about it, with just three rooms, one on top of the other, and a spiral staircase connecting them all. Mary Rose and I loved that little house, but I did not phone Jo to reserve it for this year. Afraid of lifting the dust covers on the places of the past, I avoided renting any of the apartments we had stayed in before. In any case I needed an extra bedroom, so I went on the Internet instead and hired for myself, at vast expense, a gleaming modern apartment overlooking the promenade. Mary Rose would have been amazed to hear me say that the cost of it did not seem to me to matter a damn.

That was one of the many unexpected outcomes of her death: it turned my world upside down. Not in a figurative sense, as I had always taken that expression to mean. It *literally* turned my world upside down, so that every position I had ever taken on anything was flipped around, every opinion reversed, every certainty upended. Suddenly, I understood exactly what Mary Rose meant when she said it didn't make a difference what we paid for our holiday apartment. In the unrecognizably altered landscape I found myself in after her death – like the view outside your window after a snowfall, with light and dark reversed – it made absolutely no difference to me what I paid for anything.

The apartment had barely any furniture in it. There were only two white couches in the living room and a glass coffee table. No lace antimacassars, no dried flowers, no china dogs. Mary Rose and I used to have a competition to identify the most hideous thing in our apartment, but this place had no contenders. On the walls were none of the chocolate-box landscapes we had come to expect from holiday rentals. None of the framed needlepoint that decorated the walls of Jo's place, only tastefully framed vintage tourist posters. The vast double bed was blessedly free of the multitude of satin cushions that Jo favoured, cushions we would normally have to bundle into a wardrobe as soon as we arrived. There was not a thing in this impeccable space to trigger any memories, but even so the sight of the welcome pack the agency had left for me on the kitchen counter was enough to cause me a pinprick of pain. The first time we came to Aiguaclara, I remember Mary Rose complaining that the welcome pack was unacceptably stingy, consisting as it did of one box of matches, one miniature bar of soap, two dishwasher tablets and a single J-cloth. Year after year, she said the same thing, and every year I agreed with her. Every year, I suggested that she complain and every year we decided it didn't matter and instead took ourselves off for a stiff drink on the seafront, followed by a trip to Aiguaclara's solitary and criminally overpriced shop to stock up on more soap and dishwasher tablets and J-cloths, among other things.

No doubt every couple has these dialogues that repeat themselves over and over again, and word for word, down through the years. I found them as maddening as the decades of the rosary, but at the same time somehow reassuring. The sense that we were forming our own rings on a tree trunk.

'I wish someone would explain to me why they have so many pharmacies in Spain,' I would say, knowing even as I did so that I had said this to Mary Rose every time we had ever been there. 'There seems to be a pharmacy on every second corner,' I would say, and she would sigh and shrug. I always took this to mean that she didn't care why there are so many pharmacies in Spain, and I never did succeed in getting an answer out of her, but it still baffles me to this day. I wish someone would explain to me why there are so many pharmacies in Spain.

'Did you ever notice how many amputees there are here?' asked Mary Rose once.

It was market day in the local town, and we were browsing the stalls of fake designer handbags and granny knickers. As soon as she said it, I started to see amputees everywhere. Every tenth person seemed to be missing an arm or a leg.

'I wonder is it something to do with the fact that they're all wearing summer clothes?' I suggested. 'Maybe there are just as many amputees in Ireland, only we don't notice them because they're all wearing long sleeves and trousers.'

Mary Rose wasn't convinced. 'Or something to do with all the motorbikes?' she speculated.

We never did solve the mystery. Nor did we ever figure out why there are so many children who wear glasses in Spain. A better health system, maybe? A genetic weakness, passed down through the generations? Part of the fascination of travel was the questions that remained unanswered year upon year.

Our routine on the day of our arrival was always the same. We would open up the apartment and dump our bags inside and, without even stopping to take a shower, we would beat it down the hill for a drink on the seafront. The venue for that first ceremonial drink was always and invariably Can Alicia. For reasons we didn't quite understand, Alicia's was the centre of Aiguaclara's little universe. It was the place people flocked to, ignoring the restaurants and bars on either side, and Mary Rose and I saw no reason to go against this tide. The first drink of the holiday was always on the house, compliments of Alicia, who welcomed us back as old friends with much kissing and laying on of hands.

'*Cuándo han llegado?*' When did we arrive?

Just today.

And how long would we be staying?

'*Dos semanas.*'

'*Qué bien.*'

Mary Rose had studied Spanish for three years in secondary school, before she was forced to trade it in for Chemistry, so she had the ability to conduct a rudimentary conversation and even to translate the odd thing for me. She would always start by asking after Alicia's husband and children, and Alicia would reciprocate by asking after our families and we would reply that everyone was '*bien, todo bien*'.

We might make an attempt to describe our joy at finally seeing some sun.

'*Mucho frío en Irlanda,*' I might say, throwing in an improvised shiver, and Alicia would fill us in on the recent weather in Aiguaclara. There might have been heavy rain in June, and lots of wind. Or perhaps there was no rain, just lots of wind. We were never entirely sure we were hearing her right, but we made up for our confusion by nodding vigorously and babbling back at her in pidgin Spanish.

I might make an attempt to ask her about the economy in Spain, or to give her some news about the economy at home.

'*Muy nervioso*,' I would say, and she would listen to me with great seriousness.

With her hands on her wide-slung hips, and her eyes scouring mine for meaning, she might agree.

'*En todo el mundo*,' she might say. '*Es una época muy nerviosa*.'

A moment of silence might follow, as we came to terms with the fact that the things we wanted to discuss with each other were beyond our powers of language to express.

'*Bueno*,' Alicia might say, taking leave of us to attend to a neighbouring table.

Alicia had a husband called Francesc, who spent his days slumped in a wicker chair in the dark interior of the restaurant, while she bustled from table to table. Francesc had some kind of health problem, the exact nature of which we never did manage to understand. '*Muy difícil*,' she told us. '*Mucho sufrimiento*.' It was our habit to always go inside to say hello to Francesc when we arrived, even though he was barely verbal and would only grunt at us and nod and wave his hands about. Then there came a year when we arrived in Aiguaclara to find the wicker chair gone, and no sign of Francesc, and we did not need words to understand that he had died.

'*Nos queríamos mucho*,' said Alicia, when we sympathized with her. She fluttered her plump hands against her breast. The impression was of the beating wings of a trapped bird.

'We loved each other a lot,' said Mary Rose, by way of translation.

'*Mucho*,' Alicia repeated, and this time she held her hands still against her heart.

'I'm so sorry,' I said.

'*Lo siento mucho*,' said Mary Rose, and by her crumpled face it was clear to me that she did feel it deeply. Mary Rose was the most empathetic person I ever knew. She felt other people's suffering as if it was her own. An exhausting quality, for a nurse. Sometimes, when she came off shift, she would be unable to speak, emptied out of the reserves of emotional energy she poured into the babies in her care. Often in the night I would wake to find the bed beside me empty and, through the open door, I would see her perched on the stairs, with her phone pressed to her ear, her voice a whisper as she spoke to the nurses on the night shift about the condition of some baby she had been nursing during the day. She could not have cared more about those babies if they'd been her own.

'Doesn't it bother you?' she asked me once. 'The things you see.'

'Of course,' I said, thinking of the Reuters footage I had watched that very day, of a man being dragged alive behind a jeep along some dust road in Iraq. In the same feed there were camera rushes of dead livestock floating on flood waters in Bangladesh, and the aftermath of a bus crash in Italy in which a number of children had been killed. Sometimes when I came home after a long day working with such pictures, I would sit in my car outside our house for a moment, looking through the front window to the lamplit living room and beyond it to the cheery yellow kitchen, where Mary Rose might be standing at the cooker, or setting the table for supper. A vase of supermarket tulips on the gingham-covered table, and a bottle of wine uncorked and ready to drink. At moments like those I was acutely aware of my blessings, compared to all the people whose unfortunate lives I was paid to observe on a daily basis, but I never lost a moment's sleep over them, unlike Mary Rose, who often lay awake at night worrying about this or that baby. Proof, if proof were needed, that Mary Rose was a better person than me, but then Mary Rose was a better person than most people, so perhaps I shouldn't be too hard on myself.

'Poor Francesc,' she said, once Alicia had left us alone with our drinks. 'I wonder what happened to him.'

'Who knows,' I said. 'He was pretty old. I reckon his number was up.'

'Yes, but that's the downside to a happy marriage,' said Mary Rose. 'One person has to go before the other. I find that so sad.'

She was no doubt thinking of her mother and father, or perhaps even of us, but all I could think of was my own parents, who would not have that problem. My parents had always made each other miserable, so for one of them to go first would surely be a happy release for the other. Little did I know that my mother's unhappiness would by then be so ingrained in her that she would not be capable of rising out of it. When my father did finally die, she would spend the rest of her days pining for the many opportunities he had given her to practise it. I came to understand that unhappiness is a habit, just as Mary Rose had taught me the habit of happiness. Before I met her, it never even occurred to me to pursue it.

4

Mary Rose and I liked to start our day in Aiguaclara with some people-watching. We would station ourselves each morning under the tamarisk trees on the hotel's terrace, which occupied the near end of the promenade and enjoyed the morning sun. From that vantage point we had a view of all the comings and goings of the place, and within days we came to recognize their patterns. The newsagent at the end of the promenade was the target at that time of the morning for a parade of slow-moving old men who made the ritual journey to buy their paper, returning with a copy of *La Vanguardia* clutched tightly under one arm, like a freshly caught rabbit that might yet escape. Some of them bought the Castilian version, others the Catalan edition, but they all wore the same uniform of pastel polo shirts, pressed shorts and canvas espadrilles.

We observed how Alicia's son, Carlitos, would arrive on a scooter every morning to open up the restaurant. In later years Carlitos would acquire a Segway, but back when we first stayed in Aiguaclara he used one of those children's scooters to get to work. He had tattoos on both arms and the perpetually dazed expression of a dope smoker. Unfairly, we made the assumption that he was a party boy, and we waited for him to sleep it out one morning, but he never did. He always had the restaurant open and the tables and chairs set out on the promenade by ten.

There was a young bald man who came down to the beach every morning at the same time for his swim. He would roll out a cotton towel on the sand and weigh it down carefully at opposite corners with his shoes. He would remove his clothes to reveal a microscopic pair of swimming trunks. Swapping his sunglasses for goggles, he would swim two laps of the bay in a beautiful, languorous front crawl before coming back to sit on his towel and smoke a cigarillo as he dried off. We decided that he was a research scientist, heading in for a long day in the lab. We named him Enrique.

I can generally guess people's names quite accurately, especially if I know their occupation. Every cameraman I've ever worked with has been called Colm, for example. Television production people are invariably called Mary. Taxi drivers tend to be called Maurice, or more commonly now Emmanuel or Samuel. Bartenders are always either Arthur or Martin. Doris and Jim were the names Mary Rose and I gave to the elderly English couple who took a small rubber rib out on the water every morning. He looked like Sean Connery. She looked like his mother, which just went to show you how unfair life was to women, according to Mary Rose.

'You'll probably get better and better looking as you get older,' she said to me, mournfully. 'I'm afraid it's all downhill for me.'

She was twenty-seven then, and golden and pink all over, and I could not imagine her ever being old, but Mary Rose seemed to see our future selves everywhere she looked.

'That's you,' she said, pointing to a decrepit old man who was hobbling down towards the sea. His legs were as bandy as a newborn baby's, his flesh as loose as an oversized suit. His muscles and ligaments were visible through his skin, giving him the grisly appearance of an anatomy model. He was supported on either side by a young and lovely female lifeguard. The lifeguards waded into the water with him, taking great care not to let go of him until he was afloat and knocking out a surprisingly buoyant breaststroke.

'That's what you have to look forward to,' said Mary Rose. 'Even in their dotage, men still have beautiful young women fawning all over them.'

She sighed long and deep.

'It's depressing how far feminism still has to go.'

I remember being surprised by that, because Mary Rose had never struck me as a feminist, which just goes to show how little I knew her at the start. I had taken her for a traditionalist, which she was in a way, but I had failed to consider that her insistence on the importance of family, and roast dinners, and Midnight Mass on Christmas Eve, could co-exist with a righteous indignation at the many injustices women faced on a daily basis. It was something I discovered about her only as time went on.

'Over six thousand Irish women travelled to England for an abortion last year,' she said to me, about five years into our marriage, as the country prepared to face into yet another referendum on the subject. The debate over abortion had been so divisive, on so many occasions in the past, that I dreaded the thought of it rearing its ugly head again.

'The Irish state is failing in its duty to provide adequate healthcare to these women,' said Mary Rose. 'It's as simple as that.'

Despite her position as an employee of a Roman Catholic hospital, she was planning to attend an abortion rights march that was taking place in Dublin that weekend.

'You should come with me,' she said. 'This isn't just a women's issue. This affects everybody.'

'I'm afraid I can't. I'm not allowed to attend any marches or protests.'

As a reporter for a public service broadcaster, I had an

obligation to remain impartial on any matter of controversy, which provided me with a most convenient screen behind which to hide my lifelong habit of ambivalence.

'It's in my contract,' I told her, feigning frustration, when the truth was that I was only too glad of the excuse not to align myself with any cause, no matter how deserving. Walking down Grafton Street, I would raise a hand with polite authority to fend off petitioners on behalf of the people of Palestine or Burma. On my daily walk to work, I would catch the eye of the lone Falun Gong protester as she held a tree pose outside the Chinese embassy, but I never stopped to speak to her, on the basis that this could be misconstrued. I even waved off charity muggers – all those animal-shelter people with their high-vis bibs and their direct-debit mandates primed and ready to go – they didn't stand a chance with me, so impenetrable was I in my cowardly cloak of impartiality. Needless to say, Mary Rose signed up to everything. When she died, I discovered that she had eleven direct-debit mandates going out of her account on a monthly basis – ELEVEN – funding everything from the local chapter of the Vincent de Paul to a project to combat river blindness in Africa. Mary Rose was the ultimate soft touch.

'I'm not allowed to affiliate myself with any charities,' I told her. 'Not allowed to wear any badges or emblems.'

'Makes sense, I suppose,' she said, taking what I said at face value.

With her schoolgirl conscience and her fearless clarity of thought, Mary Rose could not have imagined the grey splodge of doubt that lay at the centre of my soul. I was in no rush to reveal it to her. I figured she would find me out soon enough.

*

'So, what about these people?' she said to me, on one of those first mornings that we lingered over breakfast in the sunshine on the terrace of the Hotel Aiguaclara.

She was referring to an elegant couple, in their sixties perhaps, who were staying in a tall, slender house that opened directly on to the promenade. They seemed at home in the place, greeting the locals with multiple kisses and a short exchange of conversation. We knew they were French because we heard him say to her, with some irritation, '*J'arrive, j'arrive.*'

'Anatole and Brigitte,' I said, without hesitation. 'He's a film director. She was a model, but she gave up work when she married him. They live in a lovely old apartment with parquet floors on the edge of the Marais. They prefer to holiday here, rather than in Antibes, because they can't stand their compatriots.'

'They're fans of Dalí,' said Mary Rose, running with my narrative. 'Anatole wanted to make a movie about him, in the sixties, so they drove down to visit him in Cadaqués but he made a pass at Brigitte, so they came on down here.'

We had just been on a day trip to Dalí's house in Cadaqués, so it was fresh in her mind.

'That was when Franco was in power,' I said. 'They bought the house here on the spur of the moment, using Brigitte's engagement ring as a down payment.'

'Brigitte was pregnant at the time, and when their daughter was born, they called her Claire, after Aiguaclara.'

The daughter was about my age, we guessed, with honey-coloured hair that she wore pinned up in wings at her temples. She had a burly husband we called Jean-Luc, and a small baby who she seemed always to be kissing. '*Mon bebé,*' we heard her say, over and over again, as she leaned in to kiss him repeatedly on the nose.

As well as the daughter, Brigitte and Anatole had two adult sons, both of whom looked like a younger version of Anatole, only slimmer around the waist and without the beard. The older son had an extremely thin wife and three small boys. We called him Olivier and her Valerie, but we didn't bother giving the boys names. The other son was perhaps no more than twenty-five, and he had a very beautiful black girlfriend who was constantly wrapped around him like an ivy creeper. We decided his name was Renaud and hers Ines.

The French people had a traditional Mallorcan fishing boat that they kept moored out in the bay, and most days they would embark on a laborious expedition to transport all the family, and their beach bags, from the tiny pier at the end of the promenade on to the pilot's dinghy and from there out to the boat. We watched as the grandmother and the daughter fussed over the baby, while the men passed the bags into the boat in the manner of villagers passing buckets of water along to quench a fire.

'That will be us, some day,' said Mary Rose, looking at them with undisguised longing. 'Someday we'll be coming here with our children and our grandchildren. I can see us celebrating our fiftieth wedding anniversary here. We'll hire a big house on the front and invite them all to come. If they're still talking to us!'

'Inshallah,' I said, as a shiver of superstition ran through me.

She was so certain of the future and what it would hold for us. I had only a vague anxiety that I did not share her certainties. The only thing I was ever certain about was Mary Rose.

When Mary Rose died, I found a sleeve of old photographs in the drawer of her bedside table. I was surprised to find them, because Mary Rose was hopeless at holding on to things, an anomaly I found it hard at first to square with the rest of her personality. She was such a careful person, in the sense that she always remembered people's birthdays. Not just her family but also her friends – she even remembered the birthday of an old nun who had been kind to her at school, making sure to always send her a card. She scrupulously checked the use-by dates on the food in our fridge, throwing out anything that went even a day beyond its expiry. She recycled meticulously and was assiduous about cleaning the toilet but, to my surprise, she was shockingly careless with her own belongings.

Her clothes were always strewn about our bedroom floor. Jeans in lifeless puddles where she had stepped out of them, T-shirts abandoned inside out with a bra still attached to them. Knickers curled up on themselves like decomposing orange peels. My socks – which she liked to steal instead of ever buying any of her own – separated from their partners and tossed behind the door. When we went to replace our bed, we found dozens of lone socks coated in dust behind the old one.

In the nearly nineteen years that we were married, Mary Rose lost her wedding ring three times. Her engagement ring she lost twice. She said it was because she was always taking her rings off and putting them on again at the hospital – her hands smelled of the Hibiscrub she had to lather on them twenty times a day – but the truth was that she lost everything she had of value. The earrings her parents had given her for her twenty-first were particularly precious to her, but she lost one of them in the sea in Aiguaclara and insisted on throwing the other one after it, because what was the point in keeping one earring as a reminder of what had been lost? She lost sunglasses and handbags and scarves and, most of all, gloves. She lost bankcards and driving licences and, on at least one occasion that I know of, her passport. She lost her phone on a regular basis, and all her photos and contact details with it. She even lost the triple string of pink pearls I had given her as a thirtieth-birthday present, so it was a great surprise to me to find, when eventually I mustered the courage to go through her bedside drawer, an old Kodak sleeve of photos from our honeymoon. How they survived her, I do not know.

The photos were mostly of me. The fancy new camera was a wedding present from her sisters; I remember her buying a roll of film for it at the souvenir shop on the seafront. The first picture she took was of me brandishing the palm of my hand to block the shot.

'At least wait until I've a bit of a suntan before you start taking photographs,' I said.

I was painfully conscious of how white I was. Everybody else on the beach seemed native to the place, by virtue of being nut brown, but I was clearly an impostor. A crasher at a fancy-dress party, where everybody else had the theme in advance.

'Would it kill you to smile?' Mary Rose asked, looking at me through the viewfinder.

'I look like a villain when I smile.'

'You look like a villain when you don't.'

'Maybe I look like one no matter what I do.'

In the photograph she took, I don't resemble a villain so much as I do my father. I'm sitting on my towel on the beach, wearing my panama hat and a pair of swimming trunks, with my arms draped over my knees to hold the international edition of the *Guardian* wide open. My father used to read a newspaper on the beach in Rosslare with the same dogged obstinacy. I remember him struggling to rein in the pages, the way a yachtsman struggles with a sail in a storm-force wind, while my mother looked on nervously, waiting for him to lose his cool. He never would give up on it. Never could see the funny side. I often think of how different all our lives might have been, if only my father had been able to laugh at himself.

'So, what's our plan for the day?' I asked Mary Rose, wondering how long I would be expected to sit on the beach. I was hoping we would only stay there long enough to dry off after our swim. I was itching to get moving.

'No plan,' she said. 'We're on our holidays.'

She was laying her towel out with great care on the sand, securing the corners with her sandals and her handbag. The fourth corner she weighed down with her suncream, which she was in the habit of reapplying about five times an hour. I was struck by how unapologetically she assumed her patch of beach, as if she had as much of a right to it as anyone else. She was at home in the world, whereas I could not shake off the prickly sense that I didn't belong. That the searchlights would come on at any moment, and everyone would stop what they were doing and turn to me as if to say, 'What are you doing here?'

That was the appeal of my job. Working for a national institution, with its instantly recognizable abbreviation and its corporate logo – we even had branded umbrellas – I was the member of a club. Armed with my NUJ card, I could make of myself someone authoritative at a border crossing or a news conference. I was not alone but working within a code of behaviour, scripting to a house style. I loved the sense of belonging I had every time I signed off on a report. Maybe that's why I found myself thinking about work when I was on the beach. It was a form of self-soothing.

The place seemed to me a human hive, teeming with all

manner of barely clothed humanity, but I distracted myself by imagining some disaster occurring. A plane could fall out of the sky over our heads. A forest fire could break out on the hillside behind us. A shark attack could take place in front of my eyes, requiring me to spring into action.

'You know you're supposed to relax on a beach,' said Mary Rose, settling down on her back and closing her eyes.

'Hmm,' I said, continuing my survey of our surroundings. There was a cruise ship on the horizon, and I was imagining how it might start to sink while I sat there watching. I began running through a breathless eyewitness report in my head.

'Janey, it's hot,' said Mary Rose, her voice slurred as if she was drunk.

She had flipped over on to her belly, with her chin resting on a prop she'd made of her arm, a paperback novel splayed out in front of her on the sand. She was wearing a turquoise string bikini, tied in little bows on either hip and behind her neck and back.

'Here, untie my bikini top, will you?' she said. 'I don't want to get tan marks.'

I was actually quite a fan of tan marks, because of the way they highlighted the naughty bits, but I didn't argue with her. I untied her bikini top and let the strings fall to either side, planting a kiss on her shoulder where the sea salt had crusted in tiny flakes.

'Mmmm,' she said, burrowing into the sand with childlike pleasure.

I went back to calculating how long the battery on my phone would last if I had to file a live report. How I would need to scramble a camera crew from Barcelona and find a feed point somewhere. I would be in great demand from other networks as the guy with the most important quality a journalist can possess, a knack for being in the right place at the right time. It was a quality that had so far eluded me, but I lived in hope that my luck could change at any moment.

'Okay,' said Mary Rose. 'I'm too hot. I'm going for another swim.'

As she flipped herself over again, I caught a flash of her bare right breast – white and round as a perfectly formed meringue – before she reached behind her to retie her bikini top.

'Come on, are you coming?'

For the want of anything better to do, I joined her. I was a bit nervous of swimming in the sea because of the thought of all the fish in it, but of course I wasn't going to tell Mary Rose that. Instead I imitated one of those beach dives I'd seen the Spanish men do, wading into the shallows and throwing myself nonchalantly head first into the waves, as if I'd been doing it all my life.

'God, the water's amazing,' she said, breaking the surface like a porpoise, all wet and glistening and fully in her element.

'Amazing,' I repeated, even though to me the sea was hostile terrain, full of things that might sting you or bite you. I was even less at home there than I was on the land.

'The water's so clear,' she said, diving down for a look.

'I'll take your word for it,' I said.

After lunch, Mary Rose bought herself a mask and snorkel, and suggested we take it in turns using it.

'Ah, you're all right,' I said. 'You work away. I'm quite happy here.'

I had seen *Jaws* and had no intention of putting my head under the sea for any prolonged period. I would only go in for long enough to cool down. For actual swimming, I felt safer in a pool.

'There are so many fish out there,' she said, when she came back out. She had the mask pushed back on her head, with the snorkel hanging loose by her ear, and she was raining drops of water down on me as she reached for her towel. In her gasping enthusiasm I saw the little kid she must once have been. The kind of kid I always wanted to be. Golden and suntanned and unafraid.

'If you go over by the rocks you can see sea urchins. I even saw a squid!'

'Thank you,' I said. 'That confirms my very worst fears.'

What's amazing to me now is how she put up with me. How she loved me, despite my best efforts to be unlovable. How she persisted in photographing me in the face of all my protests. The pictures she took on that holiday are mostly of me sitting at various restaurant tables. There's one of me sitting under the feathery pink canopy of the tamarisk trees at the Hotel Aiguaclara. There's me sitting at an indoor table in Alicia's, with a landscape of the bay painted in cheery colours on the tiled wall behind me. A third picture shows me in the local town, sitting over a cup of coffee in the square.

I look exactly the same in every shot, because I have just the one face I show to the world. A mask of assumed indifference, eyebrows ever so slightly furrowed as if to say, 'What is it you want from me?' Unlike Mary Rose, whose face was always in motion, registering a hundred different expressions depending on the moment, so that no two shots of her were ever the same. And yet of all the pictures from our honeymoon – and there are at least thirty of them – only one has her in it. She must have handed someone the camera and asked them to take a picture of us both. She's sitting beside me on the low parapet at the viewpoint on top of the hill. It's evening time in the picture, and the sky is dusky blue. Bursts of yellow light, like small explosions, dot the landscape behind us. Mary Rose has her eyes closed, with one hand raised to paw away a strand of hair that has blown over her face. I wish I had a better honeymoon shot of her, but that's the only one in existence, and I have nobody but myself to blame.

Of the many things I find hard to understand about my life now that she's gone, one of them is why I allowed Mary Rose to take multiple photographs of me, instead of taking the camera out of her hands and turning it on her, my beautiful young wife.

On the first day of my first holiday without her in Aiguaclara, I left my bag in the apartment and headed out again in search of the ritual first drink at Alicia's. My summer shoes were strangely light on my feet, the ground beneath me unfamiliar in its warmth. I felt as weightless as an astronaut. Every step I took, I was rehearsing in my head how I would answer the question Alicia was bound to ask me when I got there. A question that came, as I knew it would, as soon as I stepped into the aisle between the tables on the terrace.

It was barely six o'clock, but already a foreign family were sitting down to dinner. A louche-looking Spanish couple were loitering over the detritus of a long lunch, while a waiter cleared a third table by gathering up the paper tablecloth and with it the crumbs and napkins and prawn shells that littered it, so that only the linen cloth underneath was left, as good as new.

Alicia came out and greeted me with the usual kiss. She stood back and looked around her in confusion. Then she cocked her head to one side and narrowed her eyes as she looked into mine.

'*Pero dónde está Mary Rose?*' she asked. 'Where is Mary Rose?'

5

What happened to Mary Rose still makes no sense to me. Somewhere along the way I had made certain assumptions about what the future held for her. Based on her story so far, I had assumed she would always be happy. I had assumed she would never dream of leaving me. I had assumed, at the very least, that she wouldn't die.

Mary Rose was a reader, and she introduced me to novels. Until I met her, I was strictly a non-fiction man. 'I've no interest in reading something someone else just made up,' I explained to her. 'I don't see the point.'

'That's ridiculous,' she said, rolling her eyes. 'I swear to God, David. For an intelligent person, you can be an awful eejit.'

I had just started a seven-hundred-page history of Stalin's Russia, which I had acquired on a Saturday-morning foray into Waterstones while Mary Rose was having her hair done. The act of plucking it off the table in the bookshop and carrying it up to the till made me feel like the person I had always wanted to be. But it was a hardback and so heavy that I could only hold it up for short periods at a time and, while for the first few pages I was gripped – perhaps more by the image of myself as an avid history buff than by the history itself – it began after that to feel a lot like homework. I persisted with it, one paragraph at a time, rather than give Mary Rose the satisfaction of seeing me abandon it. I was still only a third of the way through it that Christmas when she presented me with a small stack of beautifully lean paperback novels.

'In case you hadn't noticed, I'm a *bloke*,' I told her, as I unwrapped them. 'I like to read history, and the occasional biography, but I do not read fiction, because I'm male.'

'Ah, you're not as male as you think you are,' she said, with a smile.

She was curled up on the couch in a rose velvet robe, just the knob of her knee peeping out from where the robe parted. Her hair was, as always, unbrushed, and last night's make-up had left little specks of black dust, like a sprinkling of soot, under her eyes. Mary Rose was lazy about removing her make-up, one of the slovenly habits that I came to love about her even more than her accomplishments. She was delightfully imperfect.

'What *exactly* do you mean by that?'

'Well, I wouldn't describe you as a *bloke*. Your brother, now, he's a bloke. Tom's definitely a bloke. Even Michael is a bit of a bloke, but you . . .' Her mouth twitched as she tried not to laugh, mischief bubbling away in her eyes. She had the most expressive eyes I ever saw. They were bottomless wells of sorrow, or laughter, or empathy, or concern, depending on the day.

'Come on, out with it,' I said.

'Don't be upset, now, it's one of the things I love about you.'

She reached out to lay the palm of her hand on my cheek. I grabbed hold of her wrist and pulled her towards me.

'What? My inner female?'

She was laughing openly now.

'Don't take it the wrong way. All I mean is that you're not afraid to like girly things. You wear scarves. You eat quiche. You're fussy about the kind of pen you use.'

I thought of Michael's brother, Philip, who once told me I would be categorized as an otter if I were a gay man. Michael would be a wolf, he explained, and Terry a bear. Was that what Mary Rose meant, that I was an otter, not a wolf or a bear?

'All I'm saying,' said Mary Rose, 'is that you've a healthy streak of the female in you.'

I pretended to be affronted, as a form of foreplay, but the truth was that I understood what she meant. My brother would *absolutely* have understood what she meant. Terry had long ago taken to calling me Bunty because of an incident when I was ten and brought home a stack of old annuals I'd picked up in the charity shop in Rathmines for 10p each. Among them were several editions of the *Bunty*, which Terry caught me reading. I saw no reason not to read them, until Terry tormented me for it, just as my father tormented my mother about the historical romances she brought home from the library every week. In my house, the books you chose to read were a stick to beat you with.

The books Mary Rose gave me that year were *A Farewell to Arms*, *Jane Eyre* and *The Great Gatsby*. (I had read *The Great Gatsby* for my Leaving Cert, but I didn't tell her that.) She later induced me to try Steinbeck and Dickens. She introduced me to Evelyn Waugh and Graham Greene, both of whom became great favourites of mine. She even forced *Little Women* on me, on the basis that it was the book she loved most in all the world. But the story of what happened to Mary Rose does not flow like the plots of any of the novels she made me read. There is no narrative thread woven through it from the start, no foreshadowing of major events to come, no delicately balanced formula of cause and effect. When I look around me, the stories of everyone else's lives appear to conform to some kind of logic, but what happened to Mary Rose simply does not add up.

It seems obvious to me, for example, that the poison that ran in my father's veins would in time result in a cancer that would eat him from the inside out. My poor mother was always going to die of a series of strokes so torturously inconclusive that her family would begin to long for the big one. My brother was bound to develop a heart condition, determined as he was to become the size of two men, rather than one. The fact that his wife had an affair with his best friend is no surprise to anyone, least of all myself, because she made a crude pass at me once. Similarly, it seems clear to me that Mary Rose's older sister, Jean Anne, would end up obsessively competing in marathons to escape the crashing boredom of her marriage, and that her younger sister, Kitty, would someday confess to them all over Sunday dinner that she had once had an abortion. In all these stories, I can see the lines that start in the past and run through the present and into the future. They are straight lines, all of them, and as true as railway tracks. It's only in the case of Mary Rose that I can find no trajectory.

What happened to her is not something that happens to a Mary Rose. A Mary Rose is destined to have a large family, and work without complaint until retirement at the job she loves, steering newborn babies through their travails the way a ship's captain steers his crew through a storm. A Mary Rose wears a hat to her daughter's wedding and brings up the gifts and is called upon to dance with the groom. A Mary Rose lives to see varicose veins appear on the backs of her slim, girlish legs as her upper arms thicken, and she is forced to throw out all the clothes she has no hope of ever fitting into again. In the years that follow, she is comforted by the suntan that begins to last from year to year, as the skin of her chest cures in the sun like a leather handbag and her hands accumulate age spots where once she had freckles. A Mary Rose lives to become a very old lady, surrounded by children and grandchildren and perhaps even a handful of great-grandchildren, and a party is held for her ninetieth birthday because she is so precious to them all.

An Elaine might die of a romantic malady. I imagine an Elaine drowning in a river or locking herself away in a convent. A Rebecca could be murdered, by her own husband most likely, and their wedding photograph would be published in all the papers and everyone would say that he had the look of a murderer even then. A Hillary could almost be president, but not quite. A Christine might be jailed for fraud, or espionage, but a Mary Rose is destined to live a long and uneventful life. At least, that's how it seems to me. I can find nothing in her past – not a single thing – that could in any way have prepared me for what the future had in store for her.

She was twenty-six when I met her. A long-waisted creature with unkempt hair the colour of damp hay, she was wearing blue jeans and Converse All Stars with a crisp white shirt: her standard uniform, I would later discover. Her idea of dressing up was to wear a silk blouse with her jeans instead of a cotton one. Personally, I have always found jeans uncomfortable, but I wear them anyway because what else am I going to wear, cords? Everybody wore jeans back then, with varied success, but Mary Rose wore them the way they were supposed to be worn.

She was a few years younger than me, but we found ourselves part of the same group one night in a pub. She would afterwards insist it was Kehoe's where this auspicious meeting took place, but I think it was Mulligan's. In any case, I remember the moment I first set eyes on her. She was struggling to carry three pints of Guinness back from the bar when I offered to give her a hand. The pint I took from her had been badly poured, and the head of it had slopped over the side of the glass like a rogue wave.

'Forgive me if I lick,' I said, kissing her Guinness froth from my fingers.

I was already a reporter on the TV desk by then, and I enjoyed a modicum of low-level, provincial fame – a fame I was ambivalent about: on the one hand I was gratified to have people recognize my existence, but this sense of pride in myself also made me slightly nauseous, because I had been reared to pass through the world unnoticed. Most often what happened was that people only half recognized me. They knew they knew me from somewhere, but they couldn't put their finger on it, so they would embark on an excruciating round of guessing. Is it the rugby club? Do you've kids in such and such a school? Sooner or later I would have to put an end to it. 'I'm on the telly,' I would say as casually as possible – but I had not yet found a way of doing this without coming across as smug or arrogant, or maybe even both.

'I'm David Dowling,' I told Mary Rose, hoping to circumvent this charade, but I could see that she already knew who I was and was shy of me because of it. Her emotions were so close to the surface that they shone through her skin. Any time she was happy or excited or sad or worried, pink patches would appear high up on her cheekbones and her eyes would shimmer with pure blue honesty.

'I know who you are,' she said, incapable of subterfuge even to spare herself embarrassment. It would not have occurred to her.

She was ordinary-looking, or so I thought at the start, but I was to be proven wrong. Her beauty was a secret, revealed only to those who studied her for long enough. Her friends, her family and, of course, me. The other thing that wasn't immediately apparent about Mary Rose was how smart she was. She wore her intelligence so lightly that I didn't fully appreciate it at first. My preoccupation at the time was to impress her with mine.

'I've seen you on the news,' she said.

'Yeah, I've been up the North a lot.'

I'd been covering the talks. Day after day of talks, going long into the night. I stood with the other hacks outside Stormont Castle and smoked, waiting for someone to come out and tell us something – anything – that we could file as copy and thereby justify our expenses, which we needed to throw a fire blanket over the bar tab in the Europa Hotel. All we really did up there in those days was smoke and drink, shuttling ourselves safely by taxi from the Europa to Stormont and back again at all hours of the day and night. The Europa was famously the most bombed hotel in the world, but the dangers were largely past by the time I got there. Not that I gave Mary Rose that impression. On the contrary.

'It can get pretty hairy up there,' I said.

Her eyes widened as she listened.

'In the Protestant areas, especially, they're not too wild about the likes of us.' I leaned in, shouting into her ear to be heard over the noise of the bar.

She tucked her hair back as she listened to me, revealing a small diamond-and-gold stud in her earlobe. There were tiny blonde hairs, like very fine fur, along the line of her jaw.

'I was down in the Harland and Wolff shipyard the other day with a guy from CNN. We were trying to track down some of the UVF lads, to interview them, but things got a bit out of hand. We had to scarper pretty fast. Luckily we'd left the taxi running.'

God, what an arsehole I was.

'It's some place,' I said, gliding along on my own fake bravado. 'Indian territory, for sure.'

'Yes,' said Mary Rose, nodding. 'I worked in the Royal Victoria for a while.'

I could hardly hear her over the noise in the bar. It was like a human bonfire in there, the heat of a hundred bodies thrown together, the crackle of their laughter rising up out of the crush, like branches breaking. The smoke from all their cigarettes had formed a crust on the ceiling.

'You worked where?' I roared.

'The Royal Victoria. In Belfast.'

'Oh, so you're a doctor.'

She turned towards me, shouting into my ear, 'I'm a nurse.'

Now it was my turn to shout into her ear. 'But you worked in Belfast?'

'I was only there for six months.'

'What was it like?' I asked, struggling to regain my advantage.

'It was good. I made some great friends up there. Belfast people are the best.'

I made some noises to indicate that I agreed with her even though, like most reporters, I only ever got to talk to taxi drivers and bar staff.

'But you must have seen some pretty rough stuff, working in the hospital.'

She leaned her head to one side, silent for a moment as she thought about her answer.

'They used to ring the ambulance first,' she said, turning her shimmering blue gaze on me. 'When they carried out a punishment shooting, the IRA would sometimes ring the ambulance first, before they'd even shot the guy. Can you believe that?'

It seemed to me then as accurate a description of the horrors of the Troubles as you could ever find, and I found myself looking at her in a new light. She was no longer just a girl in a bar, she was someone far more formidable than that. Before I left the pub that night, I had asked her out.

'So, was it love at first sight?' Deborah asked me, once she'd managed to worm it out of me that I had a girlfriend. Up until then there had been no one serious – 'Why take on someone else's problems as well as your own?' I would say, whenever Deborah pressed me on my bachelor status – but with Mary Rose it was clear from the start that this was the real thing.

'No,' I said. 'It was wounded pride. I'd behaved like a prick, and I didn't want that to be her lasting impression of me. I had to prove to her I wasn't the person I was pretending to be.'

I believe murderers are sometimes motivated by a similar desire to erase a negative impression. I could have killed Mary Rose, but instead I chose to take her out to dinner.

'What I can't understand is why you agreed,' I said to her, many years later. 'I was such an arsehole. You should never have agreed to go out with me.'

'It was your shoes,' she told me. 'Normally I wouldn't trust a good-looking guy, but when I saw your shoes, I knew I was safe.'

'What about my shoes?' I asked, puffed up with pleasure, even then, that she had described me as good-looking. It has always been a surprise to me that women find me attractive. That anyone would want to sleep with me is one of life's miracles. To be loved by a woman like Mary Rose, I can still hardly believe it.

'Come on,' I asked, prodding her. 'What about my shoes?'

'They were kind of remedial. They had these rubber soles. Not the kind of thing at all that I'd expect from a big-shot TV reporter. If it hadn't been for the shoes, I never would have agreed to go out with you.'

I knew for certain then, if I hadn't known all along, why Mary Rose was the woman for me. She saw through my

74

disguise – through the Thomas Pink shirts and the brass Zippo lighter and the Montblanc fountain pen I insisted on using as props to sustain the fictional character I had created for myself. Mary Rose saw right through all that, to the poor, cowed creature I was inside, and she liked me anyway. How could I not love her?

When I was a kid, my mother always brought my brother and me in on the bus to Clery's department store on O'Connell Street to buy our school shoes. My mother was a country girl, and as such O'Connell Street was where she was comfortable shopping – she would have been a fish out of water among the grandes dames of Dublin on Grafton Street – and she never learned to drive, so the bus was her mode of transport. She had a maternal uncle who worked in Clery's, and once we'd fixed on a pair of shoes, after much prodding of our toes to make sure there was room for us to grow, she would always drop Uncle Leo's name and ask for a discount.

I can't explain the mortification this caused in me. I wanted the floor to open up and swallow me whole. I wanted never, ever to go anywhere with my mother again, but of course I had to follow her back down the sweeping carpeted staircase, waiting in abject misery at the cosmetics counter while she stopped to try on lipsticks. I had to go outside with her and submit to being talked to by her at the bus stop, and sit beside her all the way home, burning up with a treacherous shame. I don't remember Terry being there, but I suppose he must have been. Maybe he sat somewhere else, leaving me to keep faith with our mother alone.

Trips to the barber were similarly excruciating. 'Make sure I get my money's worth,' my mother would say. 'I don't want to be back here with them next week.' The barber never brushed our hair clippings away properly, so there was the purgatory of walking home afterwards with the whole world knowing you'd just been shorn, by the shards of hair on your neck and your poor exposed pink ears.

The embarrassment I felt as a child was a physical thing. I remember being embarrassed to be seen with my parents at Mass on Sunday. I remember the barely disguised dislike in the way my father's customers greeted him in the churchyard afterwards, and the pity in their eyes as they spoke to my mother. All of that was highly embarrassing to me. Worse still was the butcher's shop my father owned, with animal carcasses hanging in the window and our surname written there on the sign for everyone to see. I was embarrassed by our car – Japanese, when all the cool people had French cars. I was embarrassed by the tartan Thermos flask my mother would produce whenever we went to the beach, with its plastic lid that for some reason smelled of raisins. We had these flowery old towels that were gathered and elasticated at the top like curtains, so you could make your own little beach hut for changing out of your swimming togs. My togs were hand-me-downs from my mother's cousin in Clontarf, and by the time they got to me they were wafer thin and flabby with age. I wore a pair of those togs to the school swimming gala in Rathmines pool, and they came right off me when I dived in.

'Not *right* off,' said Mary Rose, the first time I told her that story.

'Right off,' I said.

Her hands flew to her face, her eyes widening with horror.

'I had to turn around, stark naked, and fish around for them in the water.'

Her eyes started to stream with laughter.

'It was deeply traumatizing,' I said, barely twitching a smile. The shame, even twenty years later, was so acute I found it hard to laugh about it. 'It's not that easy,' I said, 'to put on a pair of togs, in the deep end of the pool, with the whole school watching.'

Mary Rose was heaving by now. A little snort came out of her, as she struggled to breathe. 'Stop,' she said. 'I'm going to wet my pants.'

'I'm glad you find it amusing.'

She seemed to find all my sad stories amusing, but then I would tell her a funny story, like the one I told her years later when my father was dying of cancer, and her face would go all sad.

'How was your dad today?' she asked me, on that occasion, as soon as I came in the door. I remember her sitting cross-legged on the couch, painting her nails a barely perceptible shade of pink.

'Bit worse,' I said.

He was in the hospice by then, his organs succumbing one by one to the disease that had started in his bowel. 'Hardly surprising after all that meat,' I heard my brother's wife say, and I wondered were the rest of us headed the same way. There wasn't a day of my childhood that we didn't eat red meat, mainly pork and lamb chops. The better cuts were kept for paying customers.

'He's stopped eating,' I told Mary Rose.

'Well, that's natural,' she said, pausing in her nail painting to look up at me. 'There comes a point when your body starts to shut itself down. It won't be long now.'

The nurses had been saying that for weeks. It's a matter of days, they kept saying, so between us we operated a vigil. It wasn't so bad when there were two of us in the room, but I dreaded being left alone with him. Sometimes he would open his fishy eyes and lie there staring at me, and I would stare back with no clue what to say. A time-stopping, terrifying silence, like the moment when a teacher asks you a question and you can't think of the answer. The silence would only break when I was safely in the car and on the way home, and I would find myself sailing through red lights and crashing stop signs as my brain flooded with all the things I should have said to him. The hot, raw flow of my anger was shocking to me, but it had come too late for me to pour it out on him. That was the worst of it, the way I had to go back in there every day and look at him lying there, so thin that his body made barely a ridge in the neatly made bedsheets. He was unequal to the anger that was in me.

'There was one funny moment,' I told her.

'Oh?' she said, putting a final stroke of polish on her thumb before looking up.

'So, I was sitting there reading my paper, and I realized he was trying to say something to me.'

She folded her fingers into the palm of her hand and blew on her wet nails as if she was playing a little tune on a mouth organ.

'I figured he wanted water, so I poured him some from the jug. I had to sit on the edge of the bed to give it to him, and it was weird because I don't think I'd ever been so close to him before. He was sucking the water from the straw, and afterwards he leaned his head back on the pillow, and he gave this big sigh, like it was the most delicious thing he'd ever tasted.'

It was pathetic how happy I was to have been of service to him, but I did not say this to Mary Rose. I couldn't say it, because it was puzzling to me, and slightly terrifying, that I still wanted his approval. A moment of grace, after all that had gone between us. That's what I was hoping for.

'So, then he starts trying to say something, whispering, like it's the last bit of energy he has . . .'

Mary Rose had paused in her nail painting – one hand done, one still to go – to hear me out.

'"David," he says.' I was imitating my father's deathbed voice, bubbles of anticipation rising in me already, at the thought of how I would make Mary Rose laugh. 'Then he pauses, like he wants to say something really important, but he can't get the words out . . . "David," he goes . . . And I say, "Yes, Dad, what is it?" "David," he says, and I lean in closer, so that I can hear what he's saying . . .'

I paused in the telling of it, for comic timing.

'"David," he says. "You're sitting on my arm."'

Mary Rose's face fell. She clamped her lips together and gave me an upside-down smile.

The room wobbled on me.

'That's a funny story!' I said, with the desperation of someone flailing to stop himself losing his balance on a slippery floor.

She just sighed and leaned her head to one side, her eyes watering.

'Oh, David,' she said, with a scrunched-up expression of pity on her face, like the face you make when you see a child drop an ice-cream. 'I'm so sorry.'

I had only been seeing Mary Rose for a week or two when she invited me to come and meet her family. 'My mum wants you to come for Sunday dinner,' she said, and I succumbed to the invitation as a form of penance that would have to be endured. I figured we would eat the dinner and be out of there in a matter of an hour or so. It had occurred to me that we might even catch a film afterwards, or go for a pint, but as it happened we were there all evening. I had never been at a family meal like it. Nobody seemed in any hurry for it to be over.

It was Mary Rose's younger sister, Kitty, who opened the door for us, barefoot, with wet hair and a towel over her shoulders. She was just out of the shower, she said, before turning and bounding up the stairs. We were halfway through taking our coats off and hanging them on the hall stand when the older sister, Jean Anne, arrived, with her husband, Billy, and their baby. They were laden down with baby paraphernalia, and the bags they carried required a lot of rearranging, so our introductions were somewhat fractured.

'Come on through,' I heard someone calling from further down the hall.

I followed Mary Rose into a warm kitchen, where a long pine table was set for dinner. Her mother was at the Aga, shifting some pots around on the hot plates.

'Mum,' said Mary Rose, 'this is David.'

'David!' her mother said, coming towards me with open arms. 'You're welcome, darling.'

I wasn't to know it then, but she called everyone darling.

'Mrs Murphy,' I said. 'Thanks for having me.'

'Oh, I only go by Moya,' she said, carrying the flowers I'd brought her over to the sink. The flowers were cheap carnations, bought in the petrol station because it was a Sunday and everywhere else was closed, but she handled them as if they were long-stemmed roses. 'I'm thirty years married, but whenever someone calls me Mrs Murphy, I still think they're mistaking me for my mother-in-law.'

She pulled the flowers out of their wrapping and plunged them into a vase.

'They're gorgeous,' she said, lying with consummate grace. 'What a treat, thank you.'

'What's for dinner?' asked Kitty. Her wet hair was tied up now in a knot on top of her head. The towel was gone from her shoulders, but her feet were still bare. She wandered over to the Aga and lifted the lid on one of the pots. 'If there aren't any roast potatoes, I think I might cry.'

I was struck by her expectation of home comforts you can count on, her cheek in demanding they be supplied.

'Hi, Mum,' said Jean Anne, coming into the kitchen with the baby in her arms.

The baby had red blotches on his cheeks, like the blusher the ugly sisters wear in the panto. His hair was damp and plastered to his head, his eyes bright and feverish.

'Are we teething?' asked Mary Rose's mother, coming to kiss him on his sticky forehead. 'You poor little bugger.'

I was surprised she would use that kind of language. I'd heard it from my father of course, but not from my mother. She would never have dared to speak like that.

'Here,' said Mary Rose. 'Give me a go of him.'

Her sister passed her the baby and she buried her face in the hippo flesh at the back of his neck.

'He smells divine.'

'Omigod,' said Jean Anne, leaning in to look at the baby's head. 'What's happened to him?'

Even I could see that a red welt had appeared on the baby's forehead.

'Look,' said Mary Rose, 'it's just Mum's lipstick.' She licked her finger and rubbed the lipstick stain off his head.

'You see, that's where it's handy to have a nurse around,' said Jean Anne's husband. 'Saves us going to accident and emergency with a lipstick stain. We'd look like right eejits.'

He was struggling in his efforts to attach a seat for the baby to the kitchen table.

'Here,' said Jean Anne, throwing her eyes up to heaven. 'Let me do it.'

'What are you all doing in here?' asked Mary Rose's dad,

appearing in the kitchen doorway with a bottle of wine in his hand. A tall man, floppy as a scarecrow, he seemed always to be holding down laughter at some joke or other. 'I've lit a fire in the living room. I've been sitting in there for the past ten minutes, but nobody seems inclined to come and join me.'

They all ignored him.

'You must be David,' he said, transferring the bottle of wine, with some awkwardness, to his left hand so that he could shake mine with his right.

'Willie,' I said, 'nice to meet you.'

'There's a beautiful fire lit in the living room, David, but my wife seems to be determined to hold court in the kitchen.'

'He never learns,' said Kitty, rolling her eyes at me. 'He always lights a fire in the living room, and everyone always ends up in the kitchen.'

I smiled, fighting off the sense I had of some extreme strangeness. There was something very weird to me about this house, but I had trouble pinpointing exactly what it was. It was only when we were sitting down around the table that it occurred to me. These people seemed to actually like each other. They seemed to take genuine pleasure in each other's company. It was a house full of affection, and I had never been in such a house before. I had never even imagined there could be such a thing.

'So, tell me, David, does the journalism run in the family?'

He was going around the table, in the manner of a waiter, pouring out the wine. He made a bad job of it, pouring too fast, so the wine gushed and splashed, but nobody seemed to notice.

'No, I'm the first journalist we've produced. My father's a butcher.' I did not add, as my mother would have done, that he was a *pork* butcher, even though by that point my father had expanded into beef and lamb. A pork butcher was nevertheless a cut above a regular butcher, in my mother's mind, so she always made sure to mention it.

'Like myself,' said Willie, with a chuckle. He was an orthopaedic surgeon, I knew. A man of no apparent ego, he was nonetheless something of a media darling because of his irrepressible volubility. He was happy to be interviewed at the drop of a hat about the health service, but not only that. He could also be asked about politics or books or pretty much anything. He was a programme editor's dream.

'What part of the country are your own people from, David?' asked Moya. She was a Galway woman herself, and she had married into Mayo. She liked to seek out a county connection.

'Jesus, Mum,' said Mary Rose. 'This is turning into Twenty Questions.'

'Oh, don't worry,' I said, 'I don't mind.' And the truth was, I didn't. Their interest was so guileless, so free of all the sharp edges that I was used to encountering around my own parents' table, that I was quite happy to answer their questions.

'You see? He doesn't mind.'

'My mother's from Portarlington,' I said, betraying her yet again by neglecting to mention that she was of Huguenot stock. My mother took great pride in her Huguenot heritage and always hankered after the name she had lost when she married my father. She went from being Bernardine Mazel to plain old Bernie Dowling. Nowadays a woman would hang on to her own name, of course, and maybe even pass it down to her children as a double-barrel, but that would have been unthinkable at the time my mother married my father. She was stuck with his name, as she was with him, for the rest of her days. 'And my father's a Dubliner born and bred.'

The shop in Terenure went back three generations, I told them, and they seemed surprised by that. They took it for granted that everybody came from the country, as they did. To be a genuine Dubliner was a curiosity to them.

'My great-grandfather started the shop in the twenties.'

'That's amazing,' said Moya, and I agreed with her, even though I was not in the least bit amazed.

'My people were digging spuds out of the earth with their bare hands in the twenties,' said Willie, happily helping himself to another slice of roast beef. 'Pass the horseradish there, Kitty. And I'll have another roast potato if someone will spike one for me.'

He passed his fork along the table and Jean Anne stuck it into a roast potato and passed it back.

'David,' said Moya. 'Do me a favour and reach behind you and grab that jug of water on the counter.'

I hopped up to do her bidding.

'Jesus, Moya,' said Willie. 'You're not to be putting our guest to work, for God's sake.'

'Ah, he's hardly a guest,' said Moya. 'Are you, darling?'

And I said no, of course not, touched beyond measure that I had been incorporated with so little ceremony into their happy home.

6

Hard work was the rock my home was founded upon. My brother and I were reared to place great value on parsimony and respectability, and we learned from our parents to practise a jaundiced helplessness in the face of all forms of authority. Reticence was the medium through which we moved, and disappointment hung thick in the air we breathed. There was no accounting at all for happiness in this scheme of things.

When I was growing up, my mother rose and dressed before six every morning, putting in an hour of chores before any of us even came down for breakfast. My father left the house shortly after eight, taking sandwiches with him because he wouldn't countenance closing the shop to come home for lunch. Hot lunches, to him, were the luxury of those who did desk work for a living. My father was made of tougher stuff than that, on his feet for ten hours a day. He would pull the shop's shutters closed on the stroke of six, cleaning down the counters and stowing everything in the fridge, before taking off his apron and bundling it into a bag for my mother to launder. The shop was only three minutes' walk from home, so he was always back by twenty to seven, going straight up the stairs to wash and change before sitting down at the table in expectation of his dinner at seven sharp. Every night after dinner he would sit with his armchair pulled up to the TV, while my mother stood in the kitchen, ironing. She ironed every piece of clothing we ever wore. Every sock, every vest, every pair of underpants. She ironed the towels and the tea towels, and the cloth napkins that she persisted in using even when everyone else started using paper napkins. It was as if, by endlessly ironing, she could somehow smooth all the kinks out of her life and make of it something perfect. It seems to me now that she ironed her life away, instead of making something better of it.

My mother was an educated woman. She had gone as far as the Leaving Cert and even had hopes of becoming a teacher, but her mother died and it fell to her to keep house until her sister, Marguerite, reached adulthood. My father, on the other hand, left school at fifteen to go and work in the shop, and yet he never missed an opportunity to let my mother know that his was the superior intelligence. He lectured her on home economics and world affairs. He sneered at the books she read. He laughed at her most innocent mistakes. I remember one day when we were out in the car, and we had to pull over to make way for an oncoming ambulance, and my mother wondered out loud why it had AMBULANCE spelled backwards on the front bonnet.

'You're not going to tell me you don't know that?' my father asked her. From the back seat, I could see his eyes in the rear-view mirror, glinting with malice.

'I've never noticed it before now,' she said, and I could hear from her voice that she was trying to hold her own.

'Boys?' he said, hoping we'd supply the answer, but neither of us could, or would, so he told her himself. Often in the years that followed, he would come back to it, slapping his hand on his thigh and shaking his head as he laughed for longer than was kind, laughing not with her but at her. She bore his scorn with sad, unsurprised eyes, the way a battered dog bears a beating.

My mother was a social person, but he was relentlessly unkind about her friends. She liked to make herself pretty, but he grilled her over any pathetic little bit of money she might have spent on herself. He even criticized the meals she cooked for us, day in day out, complaining that the apple sauce she served with the pork chops was lumpy, or the roast potatoes undercooked. I remember him once making a list of all the complaints he had about her cooking and handing it to her in the kitchen as he left for work.

'Wasn't he ever nice to her?' asked Mary Rose, when I told her this. 'Was he never kind to her? Did he never pay her a compliment?'

'Not that I remember,' I said, 'but I don't know what happened behind closed doors. They stayed together, that's all I know. I don't think either of them would ever have dreamed of leaving.'

'Do you think they loved each other?'

'God, no. They couldn't stand the sight of each other.'

'But that's really sad,' said Mary Rose.

And I said, 'Yes, I suppose it is.'

Shortly after I met Mary Rose, my aunt Marguerite was knocked down by a car on Middle Abbey Street. She broke her pelvis and had nobody at home to mind her. My mother wanted to invite her to stay, but my father wouldn't have it, so she had to go into a convalescent home while she recovered. She spent her days there doing jigsaw puzzles, but to make the puzzles more challenging she would throw away the box, building the picture piece by piece with nothing to guide her. That was what the early days of my relationship with Mary Rose were like. I had no template for happiness – there was nothing in my experience that offered a picture of what a loving relationship might look like – but, in the same way that a jigsaw comes together piece by piece, an image began to form in my mind of how our future together might appear.

*

We had barely known each other three months when I asked Mary Rose to marry me. I had planned a trip to Venice for Valentine's Day, which fell on a Friday that year, so we flew out on the Thursday. I had a swanky restaurant booked for the Friday night, and a ring on loan from a jeweller friend, and I planned to do the whole thing with some ceremony, instead of which I ended up blurting it out in the local trattoria over a bottle of cheap Montepulciano. It seemed to me at that moment that it wasn't the words that mattered, or the setting. All that mattered was that we move ahead with what, in my mind, had already become a foregone conclusion. I was certain that Mary Rose and I would spend the rest of our lives together, and I was sure she knew it too, so the proposal was really just a formality. I gave no thought to the nuts and bolts of what would follow. All I knew was that I wanted Mary Rose to be my wife, but when I woke up the next morning I found her sitting up in the hotel bed, writing a guest list for a wedding. The list ran, on its first draft, to a hundred and sixty people.

'Hang on a minute,' I said, 'I was thinking small wedding. Maybe just you and me. I was not thinking a big church wedding.'

An image flashed through my mind of my father in a hired morning suit and my mother in a hat with artificial fruit on it. It was a horror show, to my mind, and I knew at once that I couldn't do it.

'You aren't having doubts, are you?' asked Mary Rose, her face a mask of hurt.

I had the stale taste of Montepulciano in my mouth, along with the rank fug of the cigar I had smoked, at the waiter's behest, to celebrate our engagement. We had ordered champagne as well, on top of the two bottles of wine we had already consumed with our meal. These morsels of evidence revealed themselves, like the windows of an Advent calendar opening one by one inside my brain. I remembered getting lost on our way back to the hotel. We kept looping back to the same deserted square. I had to pee into a canal.

'No, of course not,' I said. 'I'm just hungover.'

I flipped over and buried my face in the pillow, remembering only then how I had woken in the night to the sound of music. Not sure if I was awake or dreaming, I had made my way over to the window, where a barge was approaching in the darkness. From the barge came the sound of Bob Marley's voice, singing 'Redemption Song'. The music grew louder as the barge approached, and I stood and watched it slide under the bridge below my window as Mary Rose slept in the bed behind me with my ring on her finger. I had never been a fan of Bob Marley, or of reggae music in general, but I heard it then as if for the first time and was struck by the beauty of it. As sublime a moment as I had ever experienced, it seemed to me as I climbed back into bed, burying my face into her hair that smelled of my cigarettes, that I had received some kind of supernatural blessing. Now the cold morning light was streaming in through the window, picking up the brocade pattern on the curtains and wallpaper, and my wife-to-be was drawing up an elaborate wedding plan on a piece of hotel writing paper.

'Wait,' I said, 'I have to brush my teeth.'

In the bathroom, I leaned my weight on the sink and stared into the mirror, wondering what I had let myself in for. Simpleton that I was, it had not occurred to me that Mary Rose would want all the bells and whistles. I don't know what I was thinking when I asked her to marry me, but the idea of a big church wedding had not been part of my proposal.

*

'I don't believe in God, for starters, do you?'

My mother had frogmarched us to Mass every week as children, more to present the illusion of a united family than out of any genuine religious conviction. It had never really occurred to me that there were people who actually believed in God.

'I do,' said Mary Rose, unashamedly.

We were sitting in the dark breakfast room of the hotel, eating stale cake from the miserable buffet that was laid out for us on a long table. There were some yoghurts too, and a jug of heavily diluted orange juice. A flask of that dismal coffee that Italian hotels for some reason always serve at breakfast.

'Do Italians really *drink* this coffee at breakfast?' I asked. 'Or is it just for the tourists?'

Every time we went to Italy I found myself asking the same question, but I never did get an answer. It became for me one of the many unresolved mysteries in life. I still find it impossible to believe that any self-respecting Italian would willingly drink that woeful coffee.

'Why don't you have tea?' suggested Mary Rose, ever practical, but of course I didn't want tea. I wanted coffee.

'Are you telling me that you believe in God the Father, Creator of heaven and earth?' I asked her, rather nastily. The bad breakfast, and the hangover, had conspired to make me grumpy. 'You believe he sent his only son down to earth to atone for our sins? You believe that Jesus died on the Cross and rose again on the third day? That he ascended into heaven and is seated at the right hand of the Father and will come again on the last day?'

I had been fed all this crap in school and had no patience for it, but my voice that day sounded a hollow note in my ears. My argument seemed hopelessly adolescent, like a gauche attempt to make the case for atheism in a school debating competition. I may even have made that exact case, in a debate against Our Lady's Grove, sometime in the early eighties. My rhetoric had not evolved much since then.

'The next thing, you're going to tell me you believe in the Virgin Birth.'

'Whatever about that, I believe in the Holy Spirit,' said Mary Rose, with great dignity. She spoke with such economy of expression that I did not give her words much weight. I was young at the time and accustomed to measuring an argument by the number of words someone used and not their import.

'I'm sorry, but I can't see myself standing at an altar while some druid waves incense over us and lectures us on conjugal living.' Moral scruples aside, I had a horror of rounding up my few friends and lining them up on one side of a church along with my family. The idea of throwing them all together was enough to make me break out in a cold sweat. I preferred to keep my relationships strictly compartmentalized, like airline meals. 'It's a bit of a circus anyway, isn't it, the whole wedding thing?'

I persuaded her to settle for the registry office and lunch afterwards for a handful of close family and friends in a private room at the Shelbourne Hotel. There were to be no flowers and no wedding car. No professional photographer. No tiered fruit cake. Mary Rose couldn't very well wear a veil, she reasoned, without an aisle to walk down, so instead she wore a diamond clip in her hair. Instead of a bouquet, she carried a spray of roses from her mother's garden. When we stepped out of the registry office on to the grimy footpath of Grand Canal Street, Kitty threw some confetti over us and we walked hand in hand, with our guests trailing after us, through Merrion Square to the Shelbourne. It was clear to me at the time that sanity had prevailed, but now that she's gone I very much regret that Mary Rose did not get the wedding she wanted.

'We live life forwards, we learn it backwards,' said Deborah when I told her that, and it struck me at once as the truest and saddest thing.

In the weeks after Mary Rose died, I couldn't go out the door without being bombarded by the sympathy of strangers. People I hardly knew – people Mary Rose hardly knew – came up to me in the street, or in the supermarket, to offer their condolences. It was the closest I have ever come to understanding what it must be like to be a proper celebrity, rather than the very minor public figure I was before she died. First comes the flash of recognition as people clock you, then a wave of shyness comes over them as they wonder should they approach, followed by a triumph of courage, or bullishness, when they do.

'David,' gasped a colleague I bumped into as I was buying petrol one day. He grabbed my hand in a rush to intimacy and then dropped it again and beetled off without another word. Worse was the guy I met stepping out of the shower in the gym, who threw his bare arm over my shoulder and didn't know what to do next. His flesh on my flesh, his underarm hair hanging between us, as he stammered out his sympathies; I had to unwind myself from him. There were women who wrapped their arms around me in the supermarket in the mistaken belief that they could bring me comfort. Others wept openly as they sympathized with me, which I considered highly inappropriate. I was reminded of a kid in my class in primary school – Johnny Brophy was his name – who always blew out the candles at other people's birthday parties. It turned out the world was full of Johnny Brophys.

There were people who offered me their own tales of

bereavement. People spoke of parents they had 'lost', and brothers and sisters who had 'passed away', and on one occasion a husband who 'went'. (I was tempted to ask where.) I remember bitterly resenting the suggestion that there was any commonality in our experiences. I objected to the implication that what I was going through was at any level normal. I felt like roaring with rage at the suggestion that any other person had ever suffered like I was suffering. My grief was totalitarian; it was self-absorbed in the extreme, and monstrously exclusive.

Worst of all were the people who tried to best me with their tragedies. Like a cat offering the gift of a dead rat, friends and acquaintances offered me stories of suicides and childhood cancers, and in one case a death by lightning strike, as if I might find solace in the knowledge that there were other ends as awful as, or perhaps even more awful than, the end Mary Rose had suffered. I would not listen to those stories. I could not listen to them. I was full up already of grief.

'Sorry for your trouble,' people said to me, a hundred times a day. Or 'Sorry for your loss.' Some of them just said they were sorry. I suppose they meant that they regretted what had happened. That they wished it hadn't happened to me. That they wished it hadn't happened to Mary Rose. Even so, I was confounded by the language they used, with its implication that they were in some way responsible for her death. The words people used were often curiously inaccurate, I noticed. I took everything they said literally.

'We'll take care of your bins for you,' said my neighbours very kindly. 'You shouldn't be worrying about things like that. Not while you're recovering from the death of your wife.' I am not recovering, was what I wanted to say. I am never going to recover.

'It might be good for you to go back to work,' said someone

else. 'It might be good to have a bit of normality.' I remember being puzzled by that, because it seemed to me there would be no such thing as normality for me ever again.

Not since I was in junior school had I paid such attention to the nuts and bolts of language. Certain words took on added significance: words like 'body' and 'wreckage'. The term 'remains' was used, with its heart-crushing accuracy. Verbs became thick with meaning, verbs like 'retrieve' and 'repatriate'. Possessive pronouns jumped out at me by attaching themselves to things that should not by rights have been mentioned in the same sentence as Mary Rose. Her DNA. Her dental records. Her death certificate. It seemed to me an obscenity that these things were now being spoken of as belonging to her.

The funeral Mass – I still can't bring myself to say hers – was held at the vast church near Mary Rose's parents' house in Monkstown. A funeral without a coffin; the priest discreetly placed an easel in the centre aisle instead, and an enlarged photograph of her was produced for display by Jean Anne. What was left of Mary Rose was at that point being held for tests at the Department of Forensic Medicine in Cairo, along with the rest of the victims of the crash. It would be seven months before she was returned to us but, in the meantime, we had decided to go ahead and have a funeral. I think the idea was that it would help us to come to terms with her death but, in some ways, it had the opposite effect. All day long, I had the sense that she wasn't dead at all, only absent, while we held a party in her honour. We played all her favourite tunes. We told funny stories about her, and Willie made a speech, not unlike the speech he had made at our wedding. I couldn't help thinking Mary Rose would be raging with us all that she was missing it.

Because it was a wet day, we lined up at the back of the

church afterwards to receive the mourners, rather than suffering everyone to stand outside in the rain. I was there for over an hour and a half, shaking hands and surrendering myself to tearful hugs, as everybody who had ever known either me or Mary Rose, or any of her family, filed by. The strange thing is that I could have sat down at the end of the day and written a list of every single person who was there that day. I could have described exactly what they were wearing. I could have recorded, word for word, what they said to me. Such was the strange, hyper-alert state of my brain that I had complete recall for the first twenty-four hours, after which a fog descended on me. By the following week I would have struggled to tell you the name of a single person who was there. What I remember now, of that entire day, is very little.

I remember that Kitty forced me to eat a sausage sandwich that morning before we left for the church, and I managed to force it down but have never been able to eat a sausage since. Even the smell of them frying is enough to turn my stomach.

I remember that some woman left a lipstick stain on the collar of my best white shirt and Deborah tried to remove it by spraying Vanish on it when we got to the hotel, where Jean Anne had arranged for soup and sandwiches to be laid on for the mourners. Where Deborah produced the Vanish from I have no idea. All I know is that she seemed fixated on removing that lipstick stain from my collar, as if to do so would solve anything. In the weeks and months that followed I would notice a great desire on the part of women to solve such small and inconsequential things for me. I suppose Deborah's Vanish mania was an early manifestation of that syndrome.

I remember – among all the things I have forgotten – what my old French teacher Mr Tanguy said to me in the hotel after the funeral. Mr Tanguy was a Breton nationalist who had pitched up in Ireland on account of being a Nazi collaborator during the war. He could never go back to France, for fear of being arrested, but he spoke often of his heartache at never setting foot in his homeland again. When we went to Brittany one year on a school trip, a classmate of mine brought Mr Tanguy back a tea towel from St Malo, and Mr Tanguy cried when the boy gave it to him. That incident always made me feel quite tender towards Mr Tanguy, so I was touched to see him at Mary Rose's funeral. I was coming back from the loo when I collided with him in the lobby.

'Your wife must have been a lovely person,' he said to me. 'I've never seen so many people at a funeral. There must have been five hundred people in the church.'

He gripped the sleeve of my jacket with his swollen old hand. He smelled of rolling tobacco and freshly consumed Guinness, with a top note of tuna from the sandwiches that were served.

'I've been counting the number of people who would come to my funeral when I die,' he said, with a comically straight face. 'I'm stuck at seven.'

I had a rush of affection for him and the black humour he brought to bear on his own melancholy.

'Make that eight,' I told him. 'I'll keep an eye out for your death notice.'

I was back in the reception room when I found myself standing with Mary Rose's mother by the French windows. A glass of wine in our hands, we stood side by side facing into the room, which was full of people. The babble of their conversation filled the air. There was the odd burst of laughter. It was extraordinary to me how convivial the gathering appeared. It might have been a book launch.

'Do you know what I've been thinking?' asked Moya, letting her gaze wander the room. I had the sense that she was not so much talking to me as speaking her thoughts out loud.

In her voice I could hear the same detached exhaustion I felt. I had the sense we were watching everything through a pane of glass.

'What?' I asked.

'I've been thinking how everyone has to die sometime. Maybe it doesn't matter so much how it happens. Maybe none of this really matters, in the grand scheme of things.'

I looked at her long and hard.

'That's the only thing anyone has said to me in a very long time that makes any sense,' I told her, my head reeling at the possibility that we had got the scale of it all wrong. That far from being the biggest and most terrible thing that had ever happened to anybody, it was actually the smallest and most ordinary thing that could happen to a person. I felt suddenly – and in truth only very temporarily – exhilarated at the thought that we could choose to shrug our shoulders in the face of death.

How to relate it with as little drama as possible? Any time I tried to rehearse it, it came out sounding absurdly wide of the mark. I felt like a contestant on a TV game show, giving the wrong answer to a question. I could hear a buzzer in my mind, sounding my mistake.

'Where is Mary Rose?' Alicia asked me, for the second time.

'She died,' I said, pointing up at the sky. 'She died in a plane crash.'

I was expecting her eyes to flare up as if I had set a match to them. That was the way most people reacted, but Alicia's expression was different. She made a little falling sound, the way a log fire collapses into itself with barely a whisper when there is no longer enough mass to support it.

'*Qué horror,*' she said, shaking her head very slowly.

And I said yes. *Qué horror.*

7

There was a time when plane crashes were a favourite of mine. There's a choreography to a plane-crash story that I once found shamefully satisfying. A series of set pieces, starting with the shot of the arrivals board in the airport, with the word DELAYED appearing alongside the call number of the doomed flight. RETARDÉ. RETRASADO. The pictures soon roll in of the relatives consoling each other in the arrivals hall. Within hours there will be aerial footage of the crash site. An expanse of sea, or a desolate flank of mountain. The pictures might show debris bobbing around on the surface of the waves. Personal belongings scattered across the hillside. A close-up of a child's shoe or a charred passport. You freeze that shot for five seconds and lay your sign-off over it. For some reason, plane crashes come with a licence to indulge in cliché.

I once worked with a video editor who would not cut a plane-crash story. She would pass it off to someone else, for fear of forfeiting a night's sleep or ruining her holidays or never being able to fly again. Personally, I always found abduction stories much more upsetting. Madeleine McCann, Natascha Kampusch, Elisabeth Fritzl: I hated covering those. I did not like to think there were monsters who could do this to other people in real life. Give me a good plane crash any time, I used to say.

It was a bit of a joke in the office. Whenever news broke on the wires of a passenger plane disappearing off the radar, it would be thrown to me to catch. If you trawl through the news archives of the last twenty years, you will find my byline on most of the plane-crash stories. I must have covered a dozen of them, starting with the Concorde crash in Paris. The Europe Correspondent was on leave at the time, but I had my passport and an overnight bag all packed and ready in the boot of my car, so it fell to me to go.

'I'm sending someone from Belfast as well,' said my editor. 'It's a race to see which of you gets there first.'

I landed at Charles de Gaulle an hour before the other guy, driving a stake with my name on it through the story by filing a radio report from the first phone booth I could find.

'Give me a few words for a level,' said the studio sound operator back in Dublin.

'It has emerged that all of the dead were German pensioners,' I said, 'but it's still sad.'

The sound op made a clicking noise with his tongue.

'One of these days you're going to get yourself in trouble, Dowling. You're lucky I wasn't recording.'

Like most of the sound ops I ever met, he had no sense of humour – unlike all of the reporters I ever knew, who had no sense of seriousness. There was nothing the hacks would not joke about. They traded in black humour, like a secret handshake.

'Where's the hospitality tent?' asked the guy from Belfast, when he joined me at Charles de Gaulle.

Straight out of central casting, he was wearing a creased Kermit the Frog raincoat, its pockets bulging with all the miniatures he had cadged from the drinks trolley on the plane. In those days, reporters took only the occasional break from their drinking to file their stories. Journalism was a mere hobby to them, while the drinking was professional. That night in Paris we drank the bar in the airport hotel dry, high on the heady sense of being at the centre of something.

But it was an illusion, of course. For all our misplaced pride, we were always and forever on the periphery. You are not at the centre of something until you are personally affected by it. I know that now.

When I first started going out with Mary Rose, I was still trying to prove myself as a reporter. Determined to somehow make myself indispensable to the workings of the newsroom, and in constant competition with my colleagues for the best markings, I jumped at any story that came my way. I travelled around the country at a moment's notice, staying in soulless hotels on motorway roundabouts. I covered all the bread-and-butter stories: the party conferences and the ploughing championships; fishing tragedies and fatal road accidents. Any time I wasn't working, I was with Mary Rose, with the result that I never saw my family, something that was not a concern to me but struck her as very odd.

'I still haven't met your mum,' she said to me, when we had been seeing each other for a month or so.

I had been to her parents' house for dinner by then, and I had been their guest for Sunday lunch at their yacht club in Dun Laoghaire. Willie had once had a yacht, apparently, but it sank in Hurricane Charlie and he never replaced it. The club membership he retained, without ever hankering after the doomed yacht. The name of the club was carved on a discreet brass plaque outside the door, with a harp and a crown above it, and I wondered, as we waited for the door to be opened, how this place had somehow managed to blithely ignore the central conflict of our history, or perhaps even embrace it. I had the sense of stepping into an expensively carpeted time capsule.

The interior of the club was all navy-blue leather and

pigeon-coloured walls covered with framed portraits of former commodores. The current members all wore blue blazers with brass buttons and called the staff by their first names. The staff called the club members by their surnames and made sure to throw in their titles – *Dr* Moriarty or *Professor* Doyle – even though the staff were all old enough to be Methuselah's mother. Grown offspring of members were the exception, because the staff had known them since they were seven, which was the age that children had to be to enter the dining room. Forever after, the staff saw them as the children they had once been.

'Hello, Mary Rose,' said an ancient woman we met in the corridor. She was bent into a comma shape from years of ferrying plates to and from the kitchen.

'Hi, Betty,' said Mary Rose. 'Hope you're keeping well?'

'Oh, very well, thanks,' said Betty, as she scurried off.

'Hello, Arthur,' said Mary Rose to the barman. 'Good to see you.'

'Hi, Mary Rose.'

We went through to the drawing room, where her family were already gathered around a roaring fire. Willie jumped up to greet us.

'Daithí,' he said. 'You're most welcome.' It was a habit of his to translate people's names into Irish as an indication of his affection.

'May-Ro,' he said, beaming with pleasure as he leaned in to kiss her.

'Hi, Dad. Hi, Mum.' Mary Rose bent over her mother's armchair to kiss the top of her sleek head. Then she went around the circle and wordlessly kissed her brother-in-law and both of her sisters.

'Hi, Ro,' murmured Kitty, holding her cheek up for the kiss.

I was struck by how foreign their habits were to me. In my

family we never kissed one another, and our names had never evolved or morphed into affectionate abbreviations. What was written on our birth certs might as well have been carved in stone.

I sank into an armchair and took the gin and tonic that was offered me, slipping with ease into the patrician atmosphere of the club. It shocked me how much I liked it there.

'Have a look at the menu,' said Moya, handing me a leather folder. The folder was the same deep blue as the chairs, and it too had a harp and a crown embossed in gold on the front. The fare on offer was reassuringly unfashionable. You could have lamb or beef or chicken or salmon, all served with their requisite stuffings and sauces and, of course, potatoes and seasonal vegetables.

'How nice to see the whole clan assembled,' said a tall, very thin man, wearing a red polo neck under the ubiquitous brass-buttoned blazer. He came and stood with a cadaverous hand resting on the back of Mary Rose's wingback chair, leaning into our circle the way you might lean in through a window. 'Tell me, are you people going west for the new year?'

'We might go down a bit earlier,' said Willie. 'We might even go down on Stephen's Day this year.'

'We thought we'd go down on the twenty-seventh, after the racing,' said the man.

They were like a flock of birds, in the unchanging pattern of their migrations. Even the way the women sat, with their necks stretched up to hold their heads to polite attention: they looked like swans. I had the sense that I was hiding behind a bank of reeds, observing them through a pair of binoculars. It was fascinating to me to see Mary Rose in her natural habitat.

'Late one last night?' I heard her say to Kitty.

'More like early,' said Kitty.

They were so close they could speak to each other in shorthand.

'And now for something new,' said Jean Anne, rolling her eyes.

They were alike, the sisters, but of the three of them it was Kitty who was the looker. She had the fairest hair and the bluest eyes. The finest bone structure. Mary Rose was taller than her, with a wider face, while Jean Anne was skinnier, with meaner features. The dress Kitty wore that day was red, whereas Mary Rose and Jean Anne wore navy blue and grey respectively. Mary Rose had her hair pulled back in a demure ponytail, while Kitty wore hers loose over her shoulders. Kitty's lipstick was vampire red, Mary Rose's a pale shell pink. Jean Anne wore no make-up that I could see, and she had her hair cut short to show that she didn't care. She might as well have been wearing a sign around her neck that said, 'I'm the one with the brains.'

'Of the three of them,' Moya told me many years later, 'Jean Anne is the one I worry about most. Jean Anne is the one who finds it hardest to be happy.'

According to Moya, Kitty was always climbing things as a child – walls, trees, even once an electricity pylon – the more dangerous the better, while Jean Anne was hell-bent on achieving ever more stunning academic results. In later years Kitty turned to men for her adventures, and Jean Anne started competing in marathons instead of exams. Mary Rose was the only one who wasn't forever chasing after something.

'Mary Rose is a typical middle child,' said Moya. 'She never gave me a moment's trouble. Even as a baby, she would sit happily by herself for hours on end. She never once cried to be picked up.'

'Mary Rose is nothing if not her own woman,' Willie said, in the speech he made at our wedding. He said the same thing when he delivered the eulogy at her funeral, only using the past tense instead.

'That was true what Willie said about her,' Michael said to me, in the hotel afterwards. 'I never knew anyone who was so much themselves as Mary Rose.'

'Yes,' I said. 'She had no need to be anything else.'

It was something I had seen in her from the start, without ever knowing how to articulate it. She had been born with a gift for happiness, and she had the privilege of growing up in a house that did nothing to dent it. Nothing had ever gone wrong for her, and she had no reason to think it would. If there was a weakness in Mary Rose, it was that expectation of hers that everything would work out just as she hoped. If I had a hidden strength, it was that I had no such expectations.

When I first met Mary Rose, I was still very much a work in progress. I had set about building a persona for myself on the shaky foundations my family had provided for me. By wearing the right clothes – a uniform of striped shirts and Levi jeans and Hugo Boss suits bought once a year in the January sales – and using the right aftershave – Armani – and smoking the right cigarettes – Marlboro Red – and driving the right car – a second-hand VW Golf – I had made of myself the person I had always wanted to be. Someone like Han Solo in *Star Wars*; it was that gruff charm I had in mind. There was a touch of my secondary-school English teacher in there too, a man barely older than us, who wore a tweed jacket and jeans, and hinted at his experience with women whenever we discussed poetry. I was very taken by a diplomat who came in to give us a career talk in school and spoke of 'living out of a suitcase'. That struck me, in 1982, as impossibly glamorous. I also admired my friend Michael's father, who brought home flowers for his wife and opened the car door for his daughters and taught his sons to be gentlemen. The first feminist I ever knew, he insisted on washing the dishes every night as an exercise in the fair division of household labour. Sadly, Michael's mother was a harridan, which made his father's courtesy to her all the more remarkable.

Michael's father was a chemist, with a shop directly across the road from my father's shop, but where my father's was a ghoulish repository of dismembered animals – their poor legs, like the legs of dancing girls, all hanging in a row on butcher's hooks – Michael's father's shop was a museum of polished glass and gleaming mahogany cabinetry, with bottles lined up on the shelves in beautiful symmetry, and a jar of barley-sugar twists on the counter for any child who wanted one. He was a singer and played the lead, year on year, in the Rathmines and Rathgar Musical Society productions. He was outed as a tax defaulter in the 1990s, but that didn't dent my opinion of him, or raise my own father up in my eyes, even though my father had always prided himself on paying all his taxes.

When I picture him now, I can see him standing behind his butcher's block with a cleaver in his hand and his apron all smeared with dried blood, the colour high in his cheeks from the effort of hacking animals to pieces. To this day I find it difficult to eat anything that shares the same name as a body part, haunted by the memory of the things that appeared on our table with no attempt to disguise them. Ribs and shoulders and neck and belly. A leg, with a knuckle still in it. The gleam of white bone at the centre of a rasher. The memory of the offal we were forced to eat – brains, liver, kidneys – still makes me heave when I think of it. It's a wonder I didn't end up a vegetarian, but then the meat I was reared on was only marginally more disgusting than the overcooked vegetables my mother served up with it. The lumpy sauces. I hate to say it, reluctant to take my father's side in anything, but she was a terrible cook.

When I was a child my brother and I were forced to eat all the food on our plates, a habit that was hard-wired into me by the time I met Mary Rose. Whenever we went out for dinner, I would feel compelled to clear her plate as well as my own. 'How can you still be hungry?' she would ask me, incredulous, and I had to explain to her that hunger was irrelevant. I had been drilled by my mother never to let a morsel of food go to waste. 'But if you're not hungry, it's a waste to eat it,' Mary Rose argued, and I wondered, not for the last time, if it was possible that she had been reared by wolves, so free was she of the shame and guilt that most people of my generation wore as a second skin.

'There's children starving in the world,' my mother used to say, whenever we complained about our food. 'There's children dying for want of the food that you'd have me throw in the bin.' During Lent each year the picture of an emaciated child looked out at us from the Trócaire box on the mantelpiece as further reproof. 'It's not that long ago there were people in your own country dying of hunger,' my mother would say. So then we had the weight on our conscience of famines past as well as present, as we tried to force down another mouthful of corned beef and feel lucky to have it, as my mother wanted us to.

I can see clearly now how, in making life decisions, I have generally chosen the path that leads me as far away from my family as is feasible, as quickly as possible. I chose not to go to university, unlike most of my peers, because a university degree would take three or four years, whereas I could get a diploma in journalism in two. The tools of my chosen trade – a pen and a spiral-bound notebook – were as far removed as could be from the bloody knives my father and brother wore strapped around their waists. The beat I would cover as a reporter was a world away from the suburban isolation of my upbringing.

I had grown up on a respectable middle-class street in the nation's capital, only a few miles from Government Buildings and the Four Courts, but for all the contact I had with those institutions, I might as well have been living on Mars. Our neighbours were all junior civil servants and bank workers and shopkeepers, like my father. Until I started working in journalism, I had never met a politician or a judge or a senior businessperson. I had no inside knowledge of the workings of society, so I had to make it my business to learn them. I committed to memory *Nealon's Guide to the Dáil*, and the IPA Directory that detailed who was who, in what civic institution, in Ireland. I read the newspapers every night with a highlighter pen, marking up the names of people I wanted to remember. I built up a contacts book by trawling the phone book, so that in time I became the go-to person in the newsroom for anyone looking for an out-of-hours number. I drew charts of all the parties in the North – the DUPs and the PUPs and the UUPs – with the names of their various associated terrorist groups written in brackets beside them, where appropriate. I read as many foreign papers as I could get my hands on, filching old copies of the *Guardian* and the *International Herald Tribune* from the newsroom library so I could swot up on events in the Balkans and the Middle East. Armed with all this hard-won knowledge I felt not exactly equal to anyone at work but equipped at least to take them on.

In retrospect I can see that I was hardly a natural. I am good on detail: I might notice the colour and make of a car parked outside my house, or a fallen branch on my route to work. 'You'd be a great witness in a murder investigation,'

Mary Rose used to say to me. She would *not* have been a good witness in a murder investigation. When the shopping centre on the dual carriageway was demolished it was months before she even noticed it was gone. But she had what I don't have, an insatiable interest in people, without which, I can see now, I could never have made a great journalist. I was never any more than a good and diligent imitation of one. It was an accomplished enough act to fool most people but not everyone.

'Hey, David,' said the news editor one morning. 'What's your extension there? I've a call for you.'

It was my brother, Terry, ringing me about a minor emergency. My mother had taken a fall and needed some stitches, but it was the Thursday before Easter and neither my father nor Terry could leave the shop. Could I take her to the hospital? Terry wanted to know. I could, I said, even though it seemed to me that my job was surely more important than theirs. As it happened, we chanced on a rare lull at the accident and emergency, so I was back at work by lunchtime.

'Was that your brother who rang earlier?' the news editor asked me later, with a suspicious expression on her face.

'Yes,' I said, suppressing a treacherous desire to disown him. 'There was a bit of a domestic situation.'

But it wasn't the purpose of the call that interested her.

'Funny, you speak with a completely different accent to him,' she said, and from the bemused way she looked at me I knew that she had me for a fraud. I don't remember being ashamed of myself, only furious that Terry had trespassed upon the sterile and carefully fenced-off life I had created for myself. If anything, the incident only strengthened my resolve to steer clear of my family.

'Does your mother not think it's weird that you haven't brought me to meet her yet?' Mary Rose asked me, when we'd been seeing each other for about six weeks.

I didn't like to say that I hadn't even told my mother about her yet. I told my mother as little as possible about anything at all. I deliberately withheld any information that was personal to me, or in any way important, because I could not bear to have it tossed around in the maddening disorder she brought to every conversation. She was like a painter working before the invention of perspective. She could not sift a thing of consequence from a thing of no consequence. Every topic had equal weight.

'It's very sad,' she might say. 'A boy from Larkfield Gardens killed himself last week. Apparently, he'd been let down by a girl.' With the next breath she'd be complaining that buttermilk was no longer available in the local shop. 'I asked them why they don't stock it any more, and they said people can't be bothered making their own bread. It's more expensive now to make your own bread than it is to buy it. That's what they said.'

I was filled with dread at the thought of drawing Mary Rose into one of those maddening conversations that unfolded in excruciating detail over my mother's kitchen table, but I ran out of excuses. It was the week before Christmas when I finally relented, and I had timed the visit so my father wouldn't be there, but Mary Rose did not suspect this. She was disappointed to miss him.

'I feel bad that we're coming while he's at work,' she said, as I parked the car outside the house.

'Well, there's no way out of that, because he's always at work.'

I went around to open the door for her. With her handbag in one hand and the gift she had brought my mother in the other, she struggled to get out of the car.

'Surely he doesn't work on Sundays,' she said, looking up at the dark, forbidding windows of my childhood home.

'No, but on Sundays he's a misery to himself and others because he's not at work.'

I pushed open the stiff, wrought-iron gate.

'What about Christmas?' Her heels click-clacked on the chequerboard tiles of the garden path. 'He must take time off at Christmas.'

Mary Rose had never even met my father, but even so she was prepared to defend him. She had decided he couldn't be as miserable a man as I said he was. I knew he would have no trouble in proving her wrong. This was the guy who told us as children that the ice-cream van only played its tune when it had run out of ice-cream. I had told Mary Rose that story, but she didn't believe me. She thought I was joking.

'Christmas is the only time of year he does take time off,' I told her, as I rang the doorbell. *PING-pong*. It had a cheery little ring to it that was most misleading.

'He closes the shop at four o'clock on the dot every Christmas Eve, no matter how many turkeys and hams are still there, waiting to be collected. When the pubs close, he gets people coming to the house asking him to open up the shop for them, but he never will. He won't even answer the door. "Serves them right for going to the boozer," he always says.'

I could see from her face that Mary Rose did not believe this story either, but she had no time to press the point because my mother was opening the door. Her watery voice seeped out of the darkness of the hallway.

'I wasn't sure whether I heard the bell. I hope you're not there long. You're not there long, are you?'

I could feel the blood draining down into my feet as I tried to reassure her that we had only just arrived. My mother had the capacity to complicate even the simple act of opening the door. It was exhausting to me how much energy was required to conduct even the most basic exchange with her.

'Would you like some tea?' she asked Mary Rose.

'Tea would be lovely, thank you.'

'I could make coffee, if you prefer?'

'Oh no, tea is perfect.'

'It's no trouble. If you'd prefer coffee, all you have to do is say.'

'Mum,' I said, trying not to growl. 'Let's just have tea.'

Mary Rose handed over the gift she'd brought, and my mother sat down to open it, sliding her fingernail carefully under the Sellotape so as not to tear the wrapping paper.

'Oh, lovely. A candle!'

Attuned to her every nuance, I knew that what she really meant was, what possible use could I have for a candle? The gift Mary Rose had so carefully chosen would be regifted, to my aunt Marguerite most likely, and ideally in the same wrapping. I watched in despair as Mary Rose struggled to make conversation with her. She was so eager to like her. To find some grounds on which they could be friends. The conversation sounded to me like the racket an orchestra makes when it's tuning up. There was no harmony to it.

'You'll have some almond cake,' my mother said, taking up a silver cake slice that had clearly been polished for the occasion. Her almond loaf cake was her stock-in-trade, a dry thing with no icing that she made from an old family recipe. As children, my brother and I longed for the shop cakes we saw in the window of the Kylemore bakery as we walked home from school. They were liberally laced with cream and icing sugar and raspberry jam, and you could almost taste them, just by looking at them. My father considered shop cake a shocking extravagance, so my mother persisted in making her almond loaf cake, even though it was so dry you had to wash every bite of it down with a mouthful of tea.

'You might show me where the bathroom is,' Mary Rose said at last, folding her napkin and placing it on the table.

Glad of any respite, I jumped up and led her up the stairs to the landing, but when I pointed out the bathroom door, she showed no interest in going in there. She was looking all around her, like a detective casing out a crime scene. She took in the brass urn of dried flowers that sat on a wooden plant stand in the alcove on the return. The plum-coloured staircarpet that had never in my lifetime been changed, even though it was threadbare in places from years of footfall. The ugly mahogany tallboy on the upstairs landing, with a glazed Chinese pot on top of it. My mother kept old buttons in that pot.

'Which is your bedroom?' Mary Rose whispered.

I led her across the landing to the middle of three doors, opening it out to reveal the room I had slept in for more than twenty years. It had barely changed since. It still had a wooden framed bed with a quilted satin bedspread on it, and a scuffed chest of drawers with two handles missing, and a leather-topped desk with an anglepoise desk lamp. On the mantelpiece was a model Aer Lingus plane that had been my most treasured possession as a child. Mary Rose went over and picked it up, turning it around in her hands.

'I wanted to be a pilot when I was a kid,' I explained, and for reasons I could not have identified I felt very sad.

Mary Rose took my face in her hands and kissed me most solemnly.

'I love that you kept that plane.'

My romance with aviation began with Richard Scarry. I was six when my aunt Marguerite gave me some books of his for Christmas. The books comprised a series of illustrated scenes from an imaginary city, with all the various professions and trades depicted hard at work. There were shopkeepers and policemen and construction workers and street cleaners and a tuba player, all busily going about their work. There were window cleaners and florists and ditch diggers and clergymen and mothers with their children, all represented as cats and dogs and lions and pigs. There were two tiny green bugs who drove around in a TV van with a camera mounted on the roof, but I never paid them much heed. The page that drew my attention was the one that showed the airport.

I can still picture the fat, cheery plane on the tarmac, with a lone passenger climbing the steps. Waiting to welcome him on board was a mouse in a blue uniform. She had the words 'pretty stewardess' printed beside her, and sitting in the cockpit was a bear, or maybe it was a dog, with the caption 'handsome pilot'. Many years later, I bought one of those books for Mary Rose's nephews and was shocked to find that the pilot was no longer handsome, only a plain old pilot. The stewardess was no longer pretty; she had become a flight attendant. The world had moved on, but some wistful part of me was still back there in a childhood where I had dreamed of one day being that handsome pilot.

The model Aer Lingus plane was a gift from Marguerite, who had brought it back for me from a holiday in Spain. Marguerite was single, and relatively wealthy by virtue of her job as a secretary to the editor of the *Irish Independent*, and she could afford to go on holidays that seemed impossibly glamorous to us, in the late seventies and early eighties. We never went further than Wexford in the summer, but Marguerite went to the Costa del Sol or the Algarve, and once even as far as Greece. Not only that, but she had access to free theatre tickets, and press passes to Funderland, because of her job. She had inside information on the sensational murders of the day and would share these with us freely over a slice of the Bewley's chocolate fudge cake she was in the habit of bringing us whenever she visited. Over and over again, Terry and I pestered her to tell us the story of how poor Bridie Gargan was sunbathing in the Phoenix Park when Malcolm MacArthur pulled up in his car and killed her, or how Charles Self was stabbed fourteen times in his own home with a kitchen knife and left for dead. Marguerite was by far the most exciting figure of my youth and the only person I remember ever showing an interest in me as a human being. It was she who suggested I think of journalism, when it became clear I could not be a pilot.

The traditional narrative in these cases is to tragically fail the test when you find out you're colour-blind, but my reason for not becoming a pilot was more prosaic: I was crap at maths. I don't remember being disappointed when this reality took shape for me, no more than I would have been if I'd been told I could not become an astronaut or a movie star. I had not been brought up to imagine for one moment that life would ever deliver on my dreams. I had been brought up to suppress all forms of ambition, as something boastful and shameful. To strive for nothing that would put you ahead of yourself or any member of your family. To somehow earn a living was all that was required of me, and to do it in a way that would not attract any excitement or undue attention was the expectation of everyone, with the honourable exception of my aunt Marguerite.

Terry followed my father into the family butcher's shop as soon as he left school, so there was no place for me there, even if I had wanted it. I took Marguerite's advice and enrolled in a course in journalism in the technical college in Rathmines. Marguerite had me primed to be a court reporter, which to her mind was the most thrilling beat of all. I was determined to be a foreign correspondent, but I spoke of this to no one. My father would have laughed me out of it. My mother would have been appalled. To her, France was the only truly civilized country in the world. To travel anywhere else was to put yourself at the mercy of insects and oily food, and it would have distressed her greatly to think of me making it my business. She wanted nothing more than to see me safely settled down in Dublin 6.

When I first went to Africa as a young freelancer, my poor mother was convinced that I would die of some dread mosquito-borne disease. When I was sent to Banda Aceh to cover the aftermath of the tsunami, she was convinced I would contract cholera. Nowadays any foreign travel requires a risk assessment to be carried out for the insurance company, but my mother was well ahead of them. In time she came to take some pride in my travels, not for any reason of substance, but because she liked it when her friends and neighbours saw me on TV.

'I see that David is in East Timor,' someone might say to her on the street, and she would nod and pretend to know where East Timor was.

'Dolores Keating said she saw you,' she might tell me afterwards. I always had the sense that my presence in these places was not real for her until one of her friends had reported a sighting of me. 'Where was it you were again?'

'East Timor.'

'Oh yes, East Timor. Dolores has an uncle who's a priest there, apparently.'

God forbid that she should pass on a useful contact to me while I was actually there.

'Whereabouts is he, do you know?'

'Oh, I don't know.' Defensive by nature, she would always clam up in the face of any questions. She must have been a criminal in a past life.

'I wonder what order he's with.'

'I don't think he comes home very often. The other uncle, he lives in Harold's Cross. He has an electrical repair shop. They have a daughter has cystic fibrosis. Or is it cerebral palsy? I can't remember which. It's one or the other.'

That kind of useless information was another of my mother's stock-in-trades, along with the dreaded almond loaf cake.

'Where was it you were again?' she asked.

'East Timor.'

'Oh yes, that's it.'

She took out a pencil and wrote it down in her diary, where she could look it up if anyone asked her. She drew a circle around it and read what she had written back to herself.

'East Timor,' she said, committing it to memory. There was something of the schoolgirl in her efforts to learn the geography of my travels. She had never travelled much herself. A month spent visiting a pen pal in France as a teenager was the extent of it. The way she spoke of it afterwards, you would think she'd been there for years.

'I spent some time in France when I was young,' she would say. 'I lived in a place called Angoulins, near La Rochelle. We went to Île de Ré on our holidays.'

I always had the impression that she mentioned as many place names as possible so as to show off her French accent. The beach at Île de Ré was the nicest beach she'd ever been on, she said, and she wondered if it had changed in all the time since she'd been there. She spoke often, and pointedly, of a desire to go back.

'You must think I'm made of money,' my father always said, any time she dropped these hints.

It was Rosslare every year for us, and a guest house half a mile from the strand. In their later years, my father sometimes stretched to a midweek hotel deal for my mother and himself in Kilkenny, using their free travel passes to get there by train, but she never did persuade him to take her back to Île de Ré. By the time he died, leaving just over half a million euro sitting in cash in his savings account, she was too old and too worn down by life to make the journey. She was forced to settle for the second-hand news of my travels, which were less extensive than she imagined. She never could get a handle on the distinction between the stories I covered from my desk in Dublin, laying wire pictures over my voice, and the stories I filmed on location, with a piece to camera in front of a local landmark to prove it.

'I saw you were in North Korea,' she might say, when I called by to visit her of a Sunday morning. Mary Rose had a yoga class on Sundays, so I often used that time to visit my mother.

'Well, I wasn't actually *in* North Korea. I was only reporting on it,' I might say.

Another time I covered the death of Turkmenbashi, despite the fact that I would struggle to find Turkmenistan on a map. I have filed stories on Chad and Mali from the comfort of my desk in the newsroom. Western Sahara, similarly, has been the focus of my armchair journalism. So too Bangladesh and Mongolia and Tibet. I have compiled an analysis of the effects of climate change on the Maldives. I have presented – in front of a screen in studio – many a report on the war in Syria, but I have never been there.

'So, you're back from Iran,' my mother said, knowledgeably, on another occasion.

'I wasn't actually *in* Iran,' I explained. 'I only did a report on it.'

'Oh?' she said, raising her eyebrows testily. She seemed affronted, as if I had engaged in some kind of subterfuge just to trick her. I tried explaining how she could tell if I was in fact in a place by the clue in my sign-off.

'For example, if I say, "David Dowling, RTÉ NEWS, Pyongyang," then I'm *in* Pyongyang. If I just say, "David Dowling, RTÉ News," then I'm not.'

'I see,' she said, but she seemed sceptical. I had aroused her natural suspicion, and she would never again place her trust in me as a correspondent. When I went to do a series of reports from Burma that would later see me shortlisted for (but not winning) a National Media Award, my mother refused to believe that I had been there.

'Dolores Keating said she saw you in Burma. I didn't like to tell her that you weren't actually there.'

I buried my face in my hands and, in some silent part of me, let out a bloodcurdling scream.

'So, how many countries have you actually been to?' my nephew asked me one day.

My brother Terry's child, he was a scrawny little thing, much like I had been, with a forlorn air about him. He had his vest perpetually hanging out from under his shirt. A constant green stream of snot ran from his nose, and nobody seemed bothered to wipe it away, so it crusted and flaked on his upper lip. Snail trails glistened down the left-hand sleeve of his jumper where he'd used it as a tissue.

'I don't know,' I told him. 'I've lost count.'

Which wasn't to say that I didn't ever count them. Embarrassing as it is to admit, I would sometimes tally them up in my head. I have even, on occasion, taken out my old passports and leafed through them to look at the stamps. I'm not sure I entirely believe what my life has turned out to be – how wildly it has exceeded my expectations – until I see the proof of it in the official stamps in my passport.

'Forty maybe?' I told TJ, slightly disingenuously. I was fairly sure it was thirty-six, and that was counting England, Scotland and Wales as separate entities.

'So, what's the weirdest country you've ever been to?'

The child seemed to have a genuine interest in geography. He always wanted to know the most dangerous place I'd ever been, the hottest, the furthest away. It almost made me warm to him.

'Without a doubt, the Vatican is the weirdest place I've ever been. Straight out of *The Wizard of Oz*. They wear these mad costumes.'

His eyes widened. His breath was laboured and noisy, like Darth Vader's.

'What kind of costumes?'

'Pantaloons. And they carry spears.'

'What are pantaloons?'

'Ridiculous-looking trousers. They have yellow stripes on them, like a wasp.'

'That's mad,' he said, rapt.

'So, where in the world would you most like to go?' I asked him.

'Japan,' he said, just like that. 'And Egypt, and Mongolia.' He had the list all ready in his head.

'And Greenland,' he added. 'Or Iceland, but I'd prefer to go to Greenland.'

'Why Greenland?'

'Because I can't imagine what it looks like.'

'That's a good reason to go somewhere,' I said, feeling surprisingly affectionate towards him, and I wondered why I hadn't paid more attention to him before. I had written him off because he was Terry's kid. But I was my father's child, and nothing like him, I hoped. There was surely hope for TJ too, despite his parentage.

He looked at me, unblinking.

'You should think about becoming a pilot,' I told him, passing the dream of my youth on to him like a baton. 'Then you could go everywhere.'

'Yeah,' he said. 'Maybe. My dad wants me to do business.'

Of course he did. Terry probably had TJ all lined up in his mind to take Dowling & Son to another level. He had already added a fish counter to the shop, replacing the little cashier's booth where my mother used to sit taking in the money at Christmas time. He'd started a line in prepared meats – meatballs, and chicken breasts marinated in a variety of slimy sauces, all oven ready in tinfoil containers – for customers with no time to cook. No doubt he was counting on poor TJ taking the enterprise global.

'You should do whatever *you* want to do,' I told TJ, unable to resist the opportunity to wage a small covert war against my brother, through his son. 'When I was a kid, I wanted to be a pilot, but I ended up doing journalism. If you want to travel, then journalism is a pretty cool job.'

I probably saw more of the world working as a journalist than I would ever have done working for an airline, but I still feel a pang of envy any time I see a pilot at work. I remember waiting for a flight one morning by a glass wall in Dublin airport, and I saw the captain lean out and clean the window of his cockpit with a cloth, the way a driver would clean the windscreen of his car. There was something in the homeliness of it that filled me with a visceral envy. He was so very much at home at the controls of that great steel bird.

In all the years I was travelling for work, I never tired of flying. I loved the drunken wobble of the plane as it made its way out on to the runway. I loved the roar of the engines as they prepared for take-off, and the weight of forward momentum that pinned your body back against the seat as the aircraft left the ground. I enjoyed turbulence, reassured by the reminder that we were *travelling*, through clouds and wind and rain, and not just teleporting from one location to another. I even liked airports: I liked the shimmer of aviation fuel hovering over the tarmac and the open plains of the terminal building, like some industrial savannah, with the flight crews from different airlines moving through the landscape in uniform herds and the passengers nothing but carrion. No matter how often I flew, I was never able to shake off the thrill of it, until Mary Rose died.

8

Mary Rose was afraid of flying.

'Do you know the odds of being killed in a plane crash?' I asked her, the first time we ever flew anywhere together. We were sitting at the gate, waiting for a late-night flight to London, and Mary Rose was shaking a tiny yellow pill into the palm of her hand from a brown plastic bottle she had produced from her handbag.

'Don't,' she said. 'Please don't talk about it.'

Her fear was deaf to all reason and utterly incomprehensible to me. I could not understand why anyone would be frightened of something so improbable.

'It's one in eleven million. I looked it up.'

The glass wall of the terminal building had become a huge mirror, casting a lonely reflection of ourselves back at us. We were sitting side by side in a row of plastic bucket seats, my hand resting on the thigh of her jeans, her head on my shoulder. The pill was starting to work its magic on her. Beyond our reflections I could see the plane we were about to board, like a hologram in the night.

'I'm serious,' she said, in a groggy voice. 'I don't want to talk about it. I don't even want to think about it.'

'Come on. You've more chance of being struck by lightning. You've more chance of being eaten by a shark. Or a crocodile.'

'Don't be ridiculous,' she slurred. 'I never go anywhere where there are crocodiles.'

'Put it another way. You've more chance of winning the Lotto.'

'Which is why I buy tickets,' she said, with an indulgent smile.

Mary Rose was the member of a lottery syndicate at the hospital, and she paid her fiver in diligently every week, even though I kept telling her that lottery tickets were nothing but a tax on stupidity.

'But the money goes to good causes,' she told me, blithely. It was impossible to win an argument with Mary Rose.

Mary Rose and her family were in the habit of sending each other safety updates whenever they travelled anywhere. Any time her parents undertook the four-hour car journey from their home in Dublin to their house in the west of Ireland, her mother would text her to let her know they had arrived. Similarly, whenever we travelled anywhere, Mary Rose would turn on her phone as soon as we landed to send her mother an update. Even on a perfectly routine flight, Mary Rose never failed to let her mother know we had reached our destination alive and well.

'Isn't that a safe assumption?' I asked her, when we landed in London.

'What do you mean?'

'Well, I think it's safe to assume that we arrived. There should be no need for a text. It would only be news if we *didn't* arrive, in which case they'd hear about it soon enough. It would be on the radio bulletins within the hour. The airline would have a passenger manifest. The embassy would be in touch with the families in no time.'

'Don't say things like that,' she said, covering her ears. 'You're talking about it like it could actually happen.'

'You're contradicting your own argument!' I said to her, as

we passed through the cattle pen at passport control. 'Either it's not going to happen, in which case there's nothing to worry about, or it's a likely scenario, in which case you shouldn't fly.'

It became a joke between us. Whenever Mary Rose travelled anywhere without me, I would tell her to text me as soon as she arrived to let me know she had arrived.

The text she sent was always the same: Arrived safe and well.

And I would always text her back: Phew!

It was one of my core beliefs, the faith I had in statistics. It seemed to me that even if you did happen to be in New York on 9/11, or in Bali during the 2002 bombings, the chances of being killed or injured were *still* close to zero. Mary Rose and I happened to be in Morocco in 2011 when a bomb destroyed a café on the Jemaa el-Fnaa square, where we had sat drinking mint tea only a day earlier. By the time the bomb went off we were two hundred miles south, sitting by the pool of our hotel in Taroudant. We received a flurry of calls from concerned family and friends, and I remember thinking that it was a bit excitable of them to worry. There must have been thousands of tourists in Marrakech on that day. There was no reason to think we would be among the dead.

'We're fine,' said Mary Rose, when she rang her sister back. 'A bit shook, but we're grand.'

We did not seem shook to me, stretched out on our sun-loungers by a green-tiled pool in a citrus-scented garden, but I said nothing. I was waiting for a call back from the office. I had phoned in as soon as I heard, offering to go back up to Marrakech to cover the story. Already, I was turning the logistics of it over in my mind. How I would have to find a shirt and tie. A freelance cameraman. An EBU feed point.

'When will they decide?' asked Mary Rose.

I looked at my watch.

'By the afternoon conference,' I said. 'They're watching the wires to see what happens.'

In the end it turned out there were only seventeen dead, and no Irish among them, so it didn't warrant sending me up there.

'Well, that was a close call,' said Mary Rose, at dinner that night.

And I said yes, it was close all right, even though part of me was still itching to get up there.

'I can't stop thinking about those poor people,' said Mary Rose. 'I keep thinking it could have been us.'

We were eating at a small table out in the garden, under the fragrant protection of a neatly planted orange grove. The perimeter fence of the hotel threw another cordon around us, and beyond that again we were encircled by the old walls of the city. Outside the city walls was the desert, under the same stars as us. It made me feel infinitely calm and safe.

'I'm pretty sure we were in that same café yesterday,' said Mary Rose, leaning over the table towards me. 'Imagine if it had been a day later.'

Even if we had been there a day later, I was thinking, what were the chances of us being there at the precise moment the bomb went off? We might have been there an hour later or an hour earlier. It seemed to me that the probabilities were overwhelmingly weighted in our favour, but I did not say so. Even at the time, I knew it was entirely normal of Mary Rose to react in the way that she did. I knew my own reaction was highly abnormal, and yet it did seem to me that I was also right. The chances of us being in precisely that café in Jemaa el-Fnaa, at precisely three minutes before noon on that precise day, were still tremendously low. If anything, the fact that we were in Marrakech the day before, the fact that we were for a short hour sitting in that very café, and that we still managed to escape being killed by the bomb, just went to prove my point that it was almost impossible to beat the statistics and become the victim of a terrorist attack.

It all came down to numbers. There are seven thousand hotel rooms in Morocco – I checked – and an occupancy rate of up to sixty per cent, which would suggest, even by my remedial maths, that there would be over four thousand tourists in the city on any one day, most of whom would be bound to visit the Jemaa el-Fnaa at some point to see the snake charmers and take a glass of mint tea. Add to that the million-odd residents of the city, many of whom might also happen to fancy a glass of mint tea in a café on the Jemaa el-Fnaa. As against those many thousands who might be there at the precise moment the bomb goes off, the number seventeen seemed to me at that time very small. Now I know that the only number that counts is one. One person, in one place, at one moment in time. That's all it takes.

Every time there's a plane crash there's a story of someone who should have been on the flight but for some reason wasn't. In a novel or a movie, this might seem like a cliché, but in journalism, it's guaranteed box office. A 'just add water' story – like the child who gets pulled alive out of the rubble ten days after an earthquake, or the painting someone found in the attic that turns out to be an Old Master, it never fails to get people talking. There is always a guy who misses the flight because he went to the wrong terminal, or a woman who was refused boarding because her passport was out of date.

In Mary Rose's case, there were numerous opportunities for her to be that person and I found myself relentlessly rehashing them. Sleepless, at four in the morning, I agonized over the mechanics of the decisions that had led, one by one, to her death. Like a man tapping the walls of an old library for evidence of a hidden passage, I was trying to find a way around it. A way for me, even now, to circumvent it, but every means of escape was blocked by the evidence of my own intransigence. The conclusion I was forced to reach was that it was the unbending nature of my own views that had left no alternative route by which Mary Rose might have avoided the tragedy that lay in her path.

Starting with the wedding invitation. The bride was the daughter of an old friend of hers. Mary Rose and Oonagh had done nursing together, and when Oonagh married an Egyptian house officer and went back to Cairo with him, she and Mary Rose maintained their friendship by letter and then by email. Oonagh and Ayman came back to Ireland regularly on holiday, but in all the years Mary Rose had never taken them up on their many invitations for us to visit them in Cairo. We discussed it once or twice, but I didn't like the idea of staying in their home – I didn't like the idea of staying in *anyone's* home – and Mary Rose knew they would not countenance us staying in a hotel, so we had never made the trip. But when the wedding invitation arrived, Mary Rose decided then and there that she would go, whether I would accompany her or not. As it happened, I decided not.

'You know I hate weddings.'

I had been to too many of them by then, suffering through the intensely physical boredom of the church service, desperate for it to end so I could throw myself at the drinks table in the hotel. I had struggled through one overcooked beef dinner too many, trapped in conversation with the earnest women on either side of me, who always felt the need to justify their decision to give up work to be with their kids. The drunker they got, the less they were capable of applying the brakes to the talk of their children. I had heard too many interminable speeches, tossing my fiver into the pot to bet on the duration of the best man's drunken ramblings, or the father of the bride's pedantic account of his daughter's life. No matter how long people guessed a speech would be, it always felt ten times longer. At least when I was a smoker there was solace to be found in the gathering outside of like-minded souls, but after I gave up the fags there was nothing to live for, except the inevitable search at the end of the night for Mary Rose's handbag, which would eventually be found underneath one of the tables that had been moved aside for the dancing. Only when the bag was found could we leave.

'I'd prefer a good funeral any day,' I told her.

'That's a terrible thing to say.'

Like all good and normal people, Mary Rose considered weddings to be happy events. She found funerals sad.

'Look,' she said, sifting through the pack of embossed documentation that had arrived with the invite. 'The reception's going to be held in an old palace.'

I could have suggested that we go together, a few days early, and make a holiday of it, but of course I didn't.

'Ayman's mother is going to host a barbecue the next day at her house.'

'I would rather eat my own underpants than go to a barbecue at Ayman's mother's house,' I said.

Would You Rather was a game my brother and I had played as children. It was Terry's invention, of course, and it involved him putting all kinds of hideous scenarios to me and forcing me to choose between them. It was a perfect outlet for his sadistic nature.

'Would you rather be eaten by piranhas or strangled by a boa constrictor?' he might ask, hopping from foot to foot with excitement as he waited for my answer. 'Would you rather stick a knife in your eye or have your right arm chopped off with an axe?' 'Would you rather be buried alive with snakes in your coffin or fed to a tank full of sharks?'

I had told Mary Rose all about Would You Rather, so she knew how it worked.

'I would rather sleep in a tarantula's nest than go to a barbecue at Ayman's mother's house,' I told her. I have never been a big fan of the barbecue. Call me weird, but I don't really enjoy eating burnt food in the rain, as you are invariably forced to do at an Irish barbecue. If it was up to me, they'd be banned.

'Okay,' said Mary Rose. 'Relax. You don't have to go. I'm quite happy to go it alone.'

Even then, I could have told her that I'd be lonely without her. I could have pleaded with her not to go, but I didn't. I was in the process of applying for a promotion at the time – the deputy foreign editor's job was up for grabs, and I was busy preparing for the interview – so it suited me for her to go to Egypt. In her absence, I would be able to devote a hundred per cent of my headspace to the job application, and not have to expend any more energy worrying about her.

'You should go,' I said. 'It will do you good to go.'

She had not been herself for some time, and my hope was that the trip might be the tonic she needed to restore her.

'Are you sure it's safe?' her mother asked me, with a touching degree of faith in my expertise.

And I could have said no. If I had said no, I'm not sure it is safe for her to go to Egypt, what with all the unrest in North Africa, maybe her mother might have persuaded her not to travel. But of course I didn't.

'You'd be in more danger driving from Dublin to Belfast,' I said. 'You'd be in more danger on the Circle Line in London. Cairo's very calm these days, and anyway, Mary Rose won't even be staying in a hotel. She'll be staying with Oonagh and Ayman. The chances of anything happening to her there are next to nil.'

It was a Wednesday afternoon when she left. I had been working late the previous night, so I took the day off in lieu. Mindful that Mary Rose would be travelling through the night, we went back to bed for the afternoon, and when I woke up it was to the roar of the power shower in the en suite. I heard the hairdryer starting up in the spare bedroom, and in the intermittent silences that replaced the roar of the hairdryer, I could hear Mary Rose singing 'Islands in the Stream' in her tuneless voice. Every little detail of that day is forever etched on my brain. Every step in the chronology as clear as it is irreversible.

'Sorry,' she said, coming back into our bedroom. 'Did I wake you?'

'I need to get up anyway. I'll drive you to the airport.'

'Are you sure? I can easily Hailo a cab.'

Yes, I think now, Hailo a cab! Maybe the cab won't show up. Maybe it will get the address wrong. Maybe it will break down on the way to the airport or nudge another car in the queue for the toll bridge. Nothing serious, just enough to require everyone to get out and exchange insurance details. Enough to cause a delay of half an hour, and for Mary Rose to miss her flight to Paris, and lose her connection to Cairo. She could be that woman who missed the flight because of a tiny twist of fate.

'Ah no,' I said. 'Forget the cab. I'm happy to drive you.'

Bam, bam, bam, went her suitcase as I dragged it down the stairs for her.

'What have you got in this thing, a body?'

'The joys of long-haul travel,' she said. 'There's no weight restriction, so I brought five pairs of shoes.'

'Have you got your passport?' I said to her, before we left the house. She checked her handbag for the fiftieth time.

If only her passport had not been there. If only she had taken mine by mistake, without bothering to check it. Even then, her travel schedule might have been derailed. There was no traffic on the road to the airport, and we sailed through the toll plaza, over the East-Link bridge and through the port tunnel, arriving at the airport inside of fifteen minutes.

'Don't bother parking,' she said. 'Just pull up to the drop-off area and I can hop out.'

I never even got out of the car to say goodbye to her. We were both so accustomed to travelling that we attached no ceremony to it. She was nervous anyway, as she always was before a flight, so she was keen to get checked in. She leaned over and gave me a quick kiss on the cheek before getting out of the car, pulling her suitcase out of the back seat and slamming the two doors behind her.

'Well,' she said, leaning in through the half-open passenger window, 'I'll talk to you later.'

'Make sure to let me know you've arrived safely,' I said to her, reprising our old joke.

'No doubt the embassy will be in touch with you if I don't,' she said, returning the ball with a drop shot.

I didn't even stay to watch her walk into the airport. Anxious to get back into town before the rush-hour traffic, I pulled away from the kerb as soon as she was gone. Afterwards, I would often find myself wishing I had sat for a moment and watched her walk through the doors of the terminal, but there was no rewinding even the briefest moment of that day's timeline.

I once dropped a glove from a ski lift and I remember having the same feeling then, of wanting to spool time

9

With great delicacy, Alicia steered me towards a table for two just inside the awning of the restaurant. The terrace was too rowdy for the solitary diner – she must have known I would have been lost out there – while the interior of the restaurant was too gloomy for one man eating alone, but the table she chose for me was just right, perched as it was three steps above the terrace and angled at forty-five degrees to the tables below. I took my seat – back to the wall – with the sense that I was sitting at the edge of a stage, a feeling that chimed with my extreme self-consciousness at eating alone. Alicia's son, Carlitos, materialized behind me, lowering a single menu down in front of my field of vision. I took it from him and felt his hand rest for a moment on my shoulder before he moved away.

I opened out the menu and started reading it from top to bottom, even though I knew it off by heart. I could not escape the feeling that I was acting out a part. Often Mary Rose and I had observed such a lone diner as me, speculating on the reasons for his solitude. Maybe his wife ran off with a toy boy, she would suggest. Maybe their holiday was already booked, and he decided not to waste it. Maybe she was struck down with a vomiting bug. Maybe that's why he was dining alone.

I had her voice running in my head, as if she continued to live and breathe.

'Maybe he *chooses* to holiday alone,' I argued with her. 'Maybe that's the way he likes it.'

'Don't be ridiculous,' she said to me. 'Nobody chooses to holiday alone.'

I looked up from the menu to see Carlitos standing before me like a genie, with his notepad poised to take my order.

'*Listo?*' he asked me, and I said, '*Sí. Sí, estoy listo.*'

I ordered the bacalao to start with, followed by the monk-fish, and a bottle of Albariño.

'*Bueno,*' said Carlitos, tucking his notepad into his pocket. He gathered up the elements of the spare place setting with ruthless efficiency, removing the second knife and fork, the second place mat and the second wine glass. With his free hand, he repositioned the small decorative basil pot to cover the empty space they left behind.

'*Gracias,*' I said, grateful to him for sparing me any senti-mentality. My solitude I could bear – I had myself primed to act it out with great dignity – but I could not have borne any fuss.

'*Gracias,*' I said again, when Carlos brought me the Albariño, pouring out a glass for me with a consummate lack of cere-mony. I took my first sip and sat back in my chair, determined to wait without awkwardness for the arrival of my starter – already I was feeling proud of how well I was playing my part – when I saw Jo swooping in off the promenade, her thick arms spread out like the wings of a big bird, her face already contorted into a display of sympathy as she closed in on me. There was nothing I could do but succumb.

Mary Rose and I had a game we liked to play as we sat down to dinner on the first night of our holiday. Once we'd had a sip of Albariño, but before we'd bothered to look at the menu, we would ask ourselves who we would least like to see coming along the promenade towards us.

'Now,' she would say, setting down her wine glass and

indicating the sweep of the promenade, 'you first. Who would you least like to see coming our way now?'

So happy was I in her company that there was nobody in the world I wanted to see coming along the promenade, but I played along with it anyway to amuse her.

'Terry,' I said. My brother was invariably the last person I wanted to see anywhere, especially on my holiday. 'Terry is undoubtedly the person I would least like to see coming along the promenade now, in his sandals and his holiday shirt.'

'Ah, God,' said Mary Rose. 'Poor Terry.'

How she persisted in trying to find something to like in my brother, despite all the evidence that there existed no such thing, was a mystery to me.

'There must be some good thing you can say about him,' she said to me once. 'Come on, think now. He must have one quality you admire.'

'Oh yes,' I said, without hesitating. 'There is something. If I ever needed to dispose of a corpse Terry would be the first person I'd call.'

'Ah, God,' said Mary Rose then, as she did now. 'Poor Terry.'

'Poor Terry nothing,' I said. 'Now what about you? Who would you least like to see coming along the promenade?'

There were so few people Mary Rose disliked that this was always a challenge. I think that was the thrill of the game for her – to indulge in a nastiness that was not in her nature. Mary Rose loved her parents with unquestioning devotion. Her sisters she admired out of all proportion to their merits. She loved her friends and colleagues and embraced any opportunity to socialize with them, so she always struggled to think of anyone she would not welcome running into on her holidays. One year she suggested her gynaecologist. Another year she came up with an old boyfriend who had cheated on her. But most often she failed to identify anyone. Not to worry, I always had plenty of suggestions for her.

'What about Jackie Fahy?'

Jackie was our next-door neighbour in Ringsend. A man of indeterminate age, with the physical appearance of Chewbacca, he spent most of his time standing outside the bookies smoking and liked to grab a kiss from Mary Rose whenever he got the chance. Even Mary Rose struggled to find the Christian charity to willingly succumb to a kiss from smelly Jackie Fahy.

'How about Jo, with her jug of sangria,' I suggested, unkindly, another time.

Mary Rose slapped me down for that, but I was unrepentant.

'I would rather drink hemlock with Vladimir Putin than share a jug of sangria with Jo and her friends,' I said, on that occasion. But I lived to repent my unkindness. Watching her sweep through the terrace of Alicia's, all love and tears, I felt acutely ashamed of myself for ever making her the butt of our jokes. The truth was that I was glad to see Jo.

'Come on, give us a hug,' she said, her arms stretched out to receive me. I allowed her to swallow me up in her sticky embrace. My face buried in the crook of her neck, I breathed in the hot, peachy smell of her. Glad to have her company, glad above all to be delivered from the role of solitary diner, I happily succumbed to her invitation to join her party on the terrace. I brought my bottle of Albariño with me and poured out a glass for each of them before they had the chance to order any sangria.

'David,' said Jo, jabbing her cigarette hand at me. She moved around the table. 'Bill. Maggie. And our Pru.'

'Bill,' I said, acknowledging each of them in turn. 'Maggie. Pru.'

'David here has recently been bereaved,' announced Jo, raising her wine glass up as I held my breath in dread of what was coming next.

'What I suggest,' said Jo, solemnly, 'is that we help him to get rightly pissed.'

'Hear, hear,' said the others, clinking their glasses, and I had the impression that it would not necessarily have taken a bereavement to bring them on board.

'A very wise course of action,' said Bill.

'Only too glad to help,' said Pru.

'You're too kind,' I said. And truly, I meant it. I was very glad of their kind and cheerful company. I allowed the evening to roll out under me, so different from the one I had envisaged for myself. Instead of cutting a solemn and dignified figure of mourning and retiring early to bed alone in my pristine apartment, I found myself getting wilfully drunk in the company of a band of rowdy Brexiteers. It was a relief to dwell on some crisis other than my own.

'Please tell me you didn't vote Leave,' I said to Jo, as it became clear that each of her friends had. Bill was, even a year later, stubbornly unapologetic.

'Best thing we ever did,' he said. 'Get those buggers off our backs.'

He grinned, and I was reminded of a guy who was in school with me, called Freddy Dooley. Freddie Dooley was the stupidest boy in our class by a long shot, but far from being humiliated by his abject academic failures, he seemed to take pride in them. At exam time every year, when we were all lined up in neat rows in the freezing-cold school hall, Freddie's head would roll on his neck as he watched the clock on the wall, waiting for the first half hour to pass. After half an hour, you were free to leave the exam, and Freddie always did, handing in his empty script and bounding out of the hall. He would appear a moment later in the window, making monkey gestures and lighting a cigarette with exaggerated pleasure as he luxuriated in his freedom. The purpose of this maggot act was to suggest that we were all fools to be still inside. There was a touch of Freddy Dooley about the whole Brexit thing, it seemed to me, as I watched Jo's friend Bill grin the same inane grin.

'All the same,' said Maggie. 'I'm putting in for me Irish passport. Don't fancy getting stuck in the non-EU queue at the airport.'

I tried to keep a lid on my irritation.

'Or being stuck with the NHS,' said Jo. 'I always get me health stuff done here. Bloody brilliant, the Spanish health service. Works like clockwork.'

'There's another reason for getting the Irish passport,' said Maggie, who seemed only to be thinking this through now.

'You're assuming that Catalonia remains in Spain,' I said, 'and doesn't follow your example by committing political suicide.'

'Do you reckon that's where they're headed, then?' asked Jo.

'Looks like it,' I said. 'More's the pity.'

'Hang on,' said Bill. 'I'd have thought you'd be all for the Catalans getting their independence, what with you being Irish.'

'I despise all forms of nationalism,' I said, surprising myself with my own vehemence. It had been so long since I had been vehement about anything – maybe even never – but I suddenly felt very, very vehement about this, and drunk enough to voice it. Mary Rose would have been amazed, if she could have heard me.

'I believe nationalism to be the root of all the evil in the world,' I said. I was thinking of the flags that plagued the North. Union Jacks strung from the telegraph poles.

Tricolours painted on the gable walls. How I hated those flags. I hated to see them appear across Catalonia.

'Far better to concentrate on the things that hold us together than the things that divide us,' I added, with uncharacteristic passion.

'Nicely said.' That was from Jo.

'Right,' said Bill, and I had the impression not that I had won that round but that it had been ceded to me in deference to my bereavement. They were all too decent to pick a fight with a man when he was down.

It was a rare bone of contention between Mary Rose and me – the subject of politics. I had a tendency to become a bit didactic about international affairs, in particular. When someone asked my opinion, I found it hard not to editorialize. It was a side effect of my job, and my own desire to embody it.

'What do you make of this business in Tunisia?' someone might ask me, as I think they did once, at a dinner party.

'Well, who knows?' I said, as a broad opening stroke. I was anxious not to seem like a know-it-all, but there was a silence there for me to fill. People were waiting for me to answer.

'The thing about Tunisia is that there's a very young population,' I said, and I could hear myself slipping into character. I was no longer just David, a reluctant dinner-party guest and the less charming half of David and Mary Rose. I was David Dowling, foreign news correspondent with the national broadcaster, and as such a voice of authority and impartiality.

'Thirty per cent of young people are unemployed, which makes for a highly volatile situation,' I told the table, aware that I was parroting a script I had written earlier in the week, which in turn had been lifted from the news wires. Across the table from me, I could see that Mary Rose had one eyebrow raised, a twitch pulling at the side of her mouth. She alone knew I was only playing a part, and it amused her to see me do it, but she was far too loyal to ever blow my cover in public. It was a different story when we were alone together.

'Oh, would you stop facting!' she would say, cutting me off mid-sentence.

To Mary Rose, my reliance on the facts was nothing but a decoy. A means of circling an argument, rather than going straight to the centre of it. Mary Rose liked to find her way there blindfolded, working off intuition. I wonder now what she'd make of this post-fact world we're living in. She chose to live in a pre-fact world – it seemed to me that Mary Rose took a medieval approach to life – and much as it killed me to admit it, her approach often worked as well if not better than mine.

She had great luck with the horses, for example. Every year, on St Stephen's Day, we would go with some of her friends to the races at Leopardstown. I liked to study the form, wandering out to the paddock before each race. Mary Rose invariably stayed in the bar, picking which nag to back by its name alone, or the stripes the jockey was wearing. Every win she had was a personal victory over me and my general approach to life.

At election time, her vote was determined not by party loyalty or family tradition, but by the same gut instinct that drove everything she did.

'Likeability,' she told me. 'That's what decides elections. People vote for the candidates they like.'

'No, *you* vote for the candidate you like,' I told her. 'I think you'll find that most people vote on the basis of tax policy. And local issues, of course. Hospitals, roads . . .'

'Oh, you believe what you want to believe,' she said, which was her way of winning every argument.

To Mary Rose, all politics was personal. There was no coat of hers that didn't have a badge on it, or a ribbon supporting one charity or other. No car she ever owned was without a slew of bumper stickers. I drew the line at the poster she wanted to put in our front window in support of a local campaign to prevent an incinerator being built on the beach near our house. I had come home to find her standing barefoot on the couch, in leggings and an old T-shirt of mine, with one hand flattening the poster against the window while she used the other to remove the piece of Sellotape she had between her teeth.

'Oh no,' I said. 'No way. No poster.'

It was the naïve display of her convictions that appalled me, rather than any ethical consideration, but I didn't say that to her.

'You know I can't be seen to take sides,' I said, even though in truth it was hard to see Human Resources calling me in to discuss a STOP THE INCINERATOR poster in my window.

'You do know it's going to go ahead,' she said. 'If people don't make a stand, they're going to go ahead and build it.'

'Well, it seems to me they have to build one somewhere.'

I found it hard to see what difference it made. Just like I found it hard to see how it made much difference whether we rinsed every empty tuna can before we recycled it, or whether we turned the taps off while we were brushing our teeth. These were arguments we had over and over again, and still I could not take them seriously.

'I can't believe you,' she said. She was shaking her head very slowly. 'Is there nothing you care about? I swear to God, the world could end, and you'd just stand there shrugging your shoulders.'

I knew the worst thing I could do then was smile, but I couldn't help it. I smiled.

She made bear claws of her hands and gave a furious growl, jumping down from the couch and stomping off into the kitchen without another word, and it seemed to me that I had won that argument, as I would win every subsequent one, because I had no intention of budging. There was nothing she would ever be able to say to convince me that one person's actions could amount to more than a grain of sand on a vast beach. To pretend otherwise was nothing short of laughable. That was my firmly held belief, and there was nothing Mary Rose could have said or done to change it, short of dying.

After Mary Rose died, I found I felt differently about just about everything. Once the first few months had passed – once the anaesthetic of shock had worn off and I had slowly and against my own stubborn inclination begun inexorably to heal – I found to my amazement that I cared about things. The shameful ambivalence I had once flown as a flag of convenience had vanished, and in its place was a virulent sense of peril about the state of the world. What Mary Rose had for so long tried to achieve – for years she had been trying to stir up some passion in me for something outside of myself – was accomplished in one brutal moment by her death. Like the recipient of a transplant organ who acquires some of the characteristics of the donor, I had somehow managed to inherit a portion, at least, of Mary Rose's heart.

I found I cared about the closure of rural post offices and the struggles of independent bookshops. I cared about the trolley crisis – it seemed to me a terrible thing that anyone should have to spend the night on a hospital trolley. The plight of homeless people in Dublin was deeply upsetting to me – all winter I watched as flimsy tents appeared like mushrooms along the canals – and I signed up for a direct debit to two housing charities, even though I knew my contribution was no more than a drop in the ocean. Before Mary Rose died, I would have seen the refugee crisis only in the frame of a news story – as a geopolitical event – but afterwards I saw it as a human tragedy. Free of my public-service obligation, I put my name to a petition calling on the government to take more refugees. It seemed clear to me that we could and should take more refugees from Syria, just as I was in no doubt that Brexit was a terrible mistake. That Catalonia would be better off staying a part of Spain. I found myself wanting very, very much for Catalonia to stay part of Spain.

On my first morning as a widower in Aiguaclara, rough around the edges with a rasping hangover – the previous night's Albariño had formed a nasty film on my tongue that no amount of tooth-brushing had succeeded in removing, and I felt like I had a small axe embedded in my head – I walked out on to the balcony to get some air. There was a very tanned man sitting on the neighbouring balcony, wearing nothing but a pair of shorts. He was writing with great concentration in a notebook, and he was smoking a cigarette made of black tobacco. It was the smell of tobacco that had alerted me to his presence. The railing of my balcony ran from my apartment along the front of his, with only a low wall between us, and slung over his section of railing was a beach towel of the Catalan flag. The towel had not moved since I arrived, suggesting it was there for display purposes rather than to dry off in the sun. It found it quite obnoxious, the display of that towel.

From inside the apartment a dog started barking. A small dog, by the sound of it, although I confess I'm no expert. I never had pets growing up. Mary Rose had a series of King Charles spaniels, the last of which had only recently expired when I came on the scene. She would have liked for us to have a dog, only we worked such long hours. I was dead set against it on the basis that dogs leave hairs all over the place and need constant walking and then they die.

'*Rack, rack, rack,*' went the dog in the apartment next door. The sound of it worked as a scouring brush on my poor bruised brain.

'Ay! Kaya . . .' said the man, or something that sounded like that. Leaving his cigarette streaming black smoke from the ashtray, he shuffled inside in his deck shoes.

I leaned on the balcony railing, contemplating the morning swimmers. The towel occupied the corner of my field of vision, irritating me disproportionately.

'*Rack, rack, rack,*' went the dog inside, and the man said 'Kaya' again, his voice coming from deep inside the apartment. I took this to be the name of the wretched dog.

'Kaya, Kaya, Kaya,' said the man. '*Dios!*'

I reached a hand out and touched the towel, which was bone dry, as I had suspected.

'Don't do it,' I heard Mary Rose say, her eyes wide with suspense.

I spun my head to peer into the next-door apartment, but all I could see was the reflection of the sky in the glass balcony doors. Before I had time to think about the consequences of my actions, I nudged the towel another inch or two over the balcony, watching as it slowly lost traction and quickly fell. It lay on the pavement below, as unthreatening as a dead body. I turned and slipped back into my own apartment, triumphant for a moment until I realized I had no audience. Without Mary Rose to be shocked by me, my little coup seemed sadly pointless. I gathered up my keys and wallet to go downstairs in search of coffee, feeling like the better half of me had been cut away, leaving only the small, nasty half behind.

When Mary Rose was alive, my nasty streak was the foil to her decency. In her sweet and generous presence, I felt free to vent my natural cynicism. My scepticism. My many minor hatreds. I have always hated brunch, for example. I hate the theatre, and jazz, and all group sports. I dislike fat people and have, on occasion, refused to hire a fat tradesman. When a fat person starts using the equipment next to me in the gym, I have been known to move. I won't go to a cinema where they serve popcorn, because I am unable to bear the sound of people munching. The sound of someone biting into an apple, or swallowing a mouthful of tea, makes me gag. Mary Rose liked to drink tea in bed in the mornings and while in the early years she would take herself down-stairs to drink her tea if I complained, it later became her practice to tell me to piss off.

'It's perfectly reasonable for me to drink tea in bed,' she told me. 'What's not reasonable is for you to complain about it, so if you don't like it you can get up and go downstairs where you won't have to listen to me.'

That was the first indication that her tolerance for my intolerances was beginning to run thin. In the years that fol-lowed she called me out for using the word 'knacker' in reference to Travellers, and for referring to old people as 'coffin dodgers'. She revised her early leniency in allowing me to skip the church bit at weddings ('That's just rude,' she said) and took to insisting that we answer the door to chil-dren at Hallowe'en, rather than turning out the lights and pretending we weren't home, which was my preference. She became, with my acquiescence, the arbiter of what was acceptable for me to say and what wasn't. What was accept-able for me to feel and think and do.

'Shush now,' she would say, when I embarked on one of my diatribes.

A hardy annual concerned the feral cats who liked to use the trellis in our back garden as a climbing frame. I would stand at the back window, planning creative ways to eliminate them. 'Those cats are vermin,' I would say, partly to get a rise out of Mary Rose. 'I wonder, if I nailed one of them to the back wall, would it act as a warning sign to the others to stay away?'

'Oh, would you shush,' she would say, without even bothering to look up.

Another time I embarked on a rant about cyclists and how they were taking over the roads. If it was up to me, I told her, they'd all be shot. 'Don't be an arsehole,' she said, drawing the distinction once again between the person I might by my behaviour appear to be (i.e. an arsehole) and the person she knew me to be (i.e. not an arsehole).

We were out to dinner with friends of hers the night my mother had her second stroke. It was only a small stroke, as I explained to them. 'She didn't have the decency to go for the big one,' I said, and because Mary Rose laughed, they all did too. With Mary Rose beside me, I was only one half of a double act – good cop, bad cop – and the fact that she was my partner was enough to vouch for my worth as a human being. Her presence by my side, serene and unflappable, seemed to say, 'Don't mind him, he's actually a lamb.' No matter how awful the things I said, Mary Rose seldom took them seriously, and because she didn't, nobody else did either. Now that she's gone, I find that my jokes more often fall flat. Awkward silences follow my quips. I feel constantly misunderstood. In losing Mary Rose, I have lost the only person who ever fully grasped the fact that, behind all the misanthropy, behind the antipathy to any form of conviviality, I am actually quite a nice person.

'Mary Rose was the saving of you,' Deborah said to me, late one New Year's Eve when we were walking home for want of a taxi. I remember she was barefoot and carrying her high heels by their straps, the way a gamekeeper carries a brace of birds. Mary Rose was up ahead of us with Michael, my coat worn over her shoulders like a cloak. A weave to her as she walked. We had all had too much to drink.

'Imagine if you'd married a woman like your mother,' said Deborah. 'That's what most men do, but it would have been disastrous in your case.'

'How so?'

'Let's face it,' said Deborah, bumping her shoulder against mine. 'You're not exactly easy. The last thing you needed was a woman who would be afraid to stand up to you.'

I pretended to be hurt, but of course Deborah was right. Without Mary Rose there to check my worse instincts, I might have become a monster.

There was one awful incident when she almost broke faith with me. It was a Sunday afternoon, and we were walking the sea wall at Dollymount. Ahead of us a man roughly our age was pushing a very old woman in a wheelchair. They reached the end of the wall and stopped for a moment, looking out to sea.

'Must be tempting for him to slip off the brake,' I said, expecting her to tut mildly, as she often did when I said something unkind, before letting it slide. Instead, she stopped walking and turned to face me.

'Jesus,' she said, looking at me in shock, as if she'd only just seen me for the first time. 'That's really horrible, David.'

She stood with her head tilted to one side and her eyes brimming with disappointment. Disgust, even; she was appalled by what I had said. I'm not sure why that particular thing upset her so much. It seemed to me that I had said far worse things in the past. Maybe I'd gone too far, too often, and this was just the final straw.

'Did you really mean that?' she asked, and I knew that our fate hung on my answer. An answer I would have to give truthfully, as if I was in a courtroom with my hand on the Bible. I think it was the worst moment of my life, up to that point. I had the cold, shameful feeling of being pulled up by a favourite teacher. Not just a teacher, this was my wife, and the person I admired most in the world. I could not bear for her to dislike me, and in that moment it seemed as if she might.

'No,' I said. 'It was just one of those things I say. Of course I didn't mean it.'

She stared at me for what felt like an eternity, and I could see that she was trying to decide whether I was telling her the truth or not. Then she nodded, said, 'All right,' and dropped the tension in her shoulders. She threaded her arm through mine again, resting her head for a moment on my shoulder. We walked on in silence, both of us reeling from the disaster we had so narrowly averted.

10

In the absence of Mary Rose, I kept up our habit of people-watching over coffee every morning at the Hotel Aiguaclara. I ordered a café con leche and some magdalenas from the slow-moving waiter who worked the terrace. The coffee was made with long-life milk, which was what gave it its slightly cloying sweetness. Mary Rose and I once tried to replicate the taste at home by buying long-life milk and heating it in the microwave, but it wasn't the same. All year, I longed for the taste of that delicious coffee.

I drank my first one greedily, promising myself a second one that I would drink more slowly, as the usual stream of old men made the journey down to the shop at the end of the promenade to buy a morning newspaper. Alicia's son arrived on his Segway to open up the restaurant. His hair was thinning, and he had laughter lines like rays of sunshine around his eyes, but he still dressed like a teenage dope smoker. Doris and Jim were long gone, of course. I can't remember when exactly it was that we noticed they weren't there any more, but Enrique our research scientist still came down to the beach for his swim every morning and sat on his towel afterwards to smoke his cigarillo. It cheered me to see that he was still allowing himself the cigarillo. I envied him the pleasure of it.

I was busy watching a strawberry vendor wheeling a heavily laden trolley down the promenade when I noticed that the daughter of the French family had slipped into a chair two tables up from me on the hotel terrace. She was wearing a red sundress, with flat gold sandals. A pair of very large gold-rimmed sunglasses obscured the top half of her face. As I watched her, I noticed that she engaged in none of the fidgeting most people undertake when they're sitting alone. She had no newspaper or book as a prop. She didn't take out her phone to check her messages. She just sat and stared out at the sea, while the waiter studiously ignored her.

Claire was the name Mary Rose and I had given her. When we first came to Aiguaclara she had a baby boy, who by the following year had turned into a wiry toddler. Claire was pregnant again by then, and the third year we came she had a chubby baby girl, who she dressed in little puckered cotton dresses and cotton sun bonnets.

'Isn't she adorable?' said Mary Rose, and I mumbled something vaguely affirmative. Mary Rose and I had just celebrated our second wedding anniversary, and while she longed to bring a child into the equation it seemed to me that the two of us were just fine the way we were, an impression that was only strengthened on that holiday by the sight of young men like me pushing squawling babies up and down the hill in their buggies, and extricating screaming toddlers from the wreckage of a restaurant meal, and fetching water from the sea for the hopeless task of filling a moat made of sand. They might have been working on a chain gang, so relentless were their labours, or so it seemed to me.

Claire spent most of that holiday sitting with the baby on the terrace of their house, under the shade of the sun umbrella, while her burly husband chased the little boy up and down the promenade.

'It's like *The Great Escape*,' said Mary Rose as the little boy made another wild break for freedom. He reminded me of myself as a child, and silently I cheered him on.

At the time Claire's baby seemed to us like any other baby. It was the following year before we noticed that she wasn't.

They were sitting near us in the hotel café: the grandmother, the daughter and the little girl.

'Do you see?' I whispered to Mary Rose.

She said yes, she saw.

The little girl was sitting on Claire's lap. She was eating a chocolate croissant, piece by piece, as the grandmother passed it to her. She can't have been more than eighteen months old, but already her facial features clearly bore the signs of her condition.

'Poor little thing,' said Mary Rose.

'Poor Claire,' I said. 'Poor everybody.'

'Yes,' she said. 'But look how she loves her.'

Mary Rose's face had softened, and a smile came over her as she watched them. The yearning in her for a baby was so great by then that, even in Claire's poor imperfect child, she could see nothing but the love she longed to give her own.

'People don't send flowers,' she said, putting her empty coffee cup down with great finality.

'What do you mean?'

'When those babies are born, nobody sends flowers. It's the saddest thing to see the mum sitting up in the hospital bed, and not a bouquet in sight. It's still a baby, after all. It's still a new little life, coming into the world. Who are we to say there's something wrong with them? Maybe they're just the way they're supposed to be.'

After she died, a colleague of hers told me that Mary Rose sometimes went out and bought flowers herself, for the mothers of those babies. God, she was a good person.

Mary Rose always wanted children. That was something she told me as soon as we got engaged. It was so obvious to her that she saw no need for us to discuss it, and I saw no way to introduce my doubts. Her plan was to get started straight away. By the time we married, Mary Rose's older sister, Jean Anne, already had one child and a second on the way. Kitty was two years younger than Mary Rose, but she was five months pregnant with her first. Mary Rose felt it would be nice for the three of them to have their babies at the same time. She thought it would be nice for the children to have cousins the same age, so she was in a rush to get pregnant as soon as possible. She came off the pill a month before our wedding, figuring that even if she did happen to get pregnant immediately, she could still get away with a few glasses of champagne at the reception. She was taking a chance on having morning sickness on our honeymoon, but neither Jean Anne nor Kitty had suffered from it, so there was no reason to think that Mary Rose would either.

Mary Rose loved babies, so when it came to choosing her specialty, she had opted for neonatal nursing without a moment's doubt. She had trained at the National Maternity Hospital in Holles Street, and apart from a brief stint working for the Royal Victoria in Belfast, she never left Holles Street. To Mary Rose, it was more than just a place of work; it was family. She loved the short walk to work every morning from the little house we bought together in Ringsend, along Pearse Street and up on to Hogan Place, taking a left for the hospital at the shabby corner shop where they sold helium balloons and lurid blue and pink teddy bears to the hospital visitors.

She brought me in there one day, leading me up three flights of narrow marble stairs to the Special Care Baby Unit on the top floor. The building had the feel of an antique submarine, a feeling only heightened by the oilskin-yellow colour of the sharps bins and the sea-green gloss-painted walls. The juxtaposition of high-tech machinery with Victorian infrastructure made you feel like you were in a science-fiction movie. That was where Mary Rose spent the majority of her time, bending over sick babies in their open incubators the way the submarine's captain might pore over his charts. The babies looked more like newborn birds to me than human beings, with their wizened faces and their clawing hands and their eerily transparent skin. They lay cooking under ultraviolet lamps, tangled wires hooking them up to flickering monitors, while their mothers sat wan and silent beside them in stiff chairs. Outside the small, high windows you could see the tops of the trees in Merrion Square.

'Look,' Mary Rose said, stopping in the corridor outside to show me a dense collage of photographs that covered one long wall. There were photographs of twin girls in their First Holy Communion dresses; snapshots of elfin boys, scrubbed and uniformed for the first day of school; the occasional adult child, wearing a deb's dress or a mortarboard.

'Those are our graduates,' she told me proudly.

It was hard for me to believe that the birdlike creatures I had just been shown would ever grow into people like these.

'Extraordinary,' I said, scanning the happy faces in the photographs.

'This is what we do,' said Mary Rose, holding her badge up to bleep us out of the door.

We had been married for only a few months by then, and Mary Rose was still buoyant in the belief that she would soon have a baby of her own. There was no reason for her not to believe it. She was twenty-eight years old and as healthy as the proverbial butcher's dog. But a year went by, and then another, and still there was no sign of a baby, not even the whisper of one.

'Murphy's Law,' she said to me one morning, coming out of the bathroom with another one of those little white wands in her hand. No matter how many times she waved those things, they refused to make her wish come true. 'The hospital's full of young ones who don't want a baby. And then there's the likes of me who'd give anything to be pregnant.'

She tossed the wand into the bin and sat down heavily on the bed, her legs dangling off the edge of it like a child's. I sat down beside her and put my arm around her.

'It'll happen,' I said, without stopping to think whether I believed it or not. I was late for work and didn't have time to get into it.

She turned her face to me.

'Do you think so?' she asked, hanging on my answer as if it was gospel.

'Absolutely,' I said, with as much certainty as I could muster.

But I was beginning to be afraid for her that it wouldn't.

I started to see pregnant women everywhere. In summer, in particular, there was no getting away from them. On the beach in Aiguaclara it seemed to me that every second woman was pregnant. They sat cross-legged in their bikinis, rubbing oil into their bellies. They stood in the shallows, massaging their aching backs with the palms of their hands. In the evenings they billowed along the promenade, flying their voluminous maternity dresses as proudly as spinnakers in the breeze. I was acutely aware of them, because I knew that the sight of them caused Mary Rose pain. She wanted so badly to be pregnant.

She started making charts. She plotted the window of fertility in the middle of her cycle and timed our love-making around it. She started testing the temperature of her cervix and taking homeopathic treatments to aid conception. She submitted herself to a day procedure whereby they injected some dye into her fallopian tubes and watched to see if it came out the other end. I did my bit by squirting some sperm for testing into a paper cup in the bathroom in the doctor's surgery. This was not something I had ever envisaged doing when I married Mary Rose, but I went along with it because she asked me to. At the time I didn't see it as having very much to do with me. Like the choice of curtain fabric for the spare room, or a present for her mother's birthday, it wasn't really something I had an opinion about.

None of the tests showed up any obvious problem, so we signed on for a course of IVF. Again, I had to ejaculate into a paper cup, but this time I was offered the assistance of a dirty magazine, something I declined on the basis that I had images of my own that I preferred to call on. It was a weirdly incongruous experience, like eating an ice-cream on a winter's day just because they're giving them away for free, but I did what I had to do, for Mary Rose.

Keeping the thing a secret from everyone but Mary Rose's sisters and her mother, we succeeded in creating six embryos, which were implanted one by one into Mary Rose's womb over the course of the next eighteen months. Not a one of the embryos took. We embarked on another round of IVF the following year, but this time there were only three embryos resulting. A decision was taken to implant two of them together, to maximize the chance of success. 'The animals went in two by two,' I said, and she slapped me but she was laughing. 'How would you feel about twins?' she asked. But it was not to be. We went back to the clinic for what we had decided would be the final roll of the dice. I sat with Mary Rose and held her hand while a doctor carefully planted the last precious embryo inside her, and then we went home and waited. Ten days later, she emerged from the bathroom very early in the morning with yet another negative pregnancy test.

'I think I knew it, in my heart,' she said, but the tears that rolled down her face suggested otherwise. She cried a river of tears that morning, soaking my chest with them until I could have wrung my T-shirt out.

'I knew I wasn't pregnant,' she said. 'I could feel it in my bones.'

I comforted her as best I could, letting the heartache flow out of her in a hot stream of tears. I cooked her a breakfast of softly poached eggs and tea, and afterwards I ran her a bath with some rose oil in it and sat by her as she cried more tears that ran down her cheeks and into the bathwater. Later, we went for a walk in the Phoenix Park, creeping up on the deer who had gathered under the trees. We stood hand in hand and watched them, trying to soak up some of their grace. Afterwards we stopped off at a pub by the wall of the park, sitting by the fire with our drinks as we let the day settle around what had happened.

'I know this isn't just about me,' she said, generous as always. 'I know this is awful for you too. You're affected by this, just as much as me.'

'Don't worry about me,' I told her. 'I'll be all right.'

My words had a wooden quality that I hoped she could not hear.

'If it wasn't for me, you could have had children. If you'd married someone else.'

'Stop that, now.'

But she persisted, her blue eyes shining with that incurable integrity of hers. It made me feel terrible, to see what a fine person she was, even at her darkest hour. Mary Rose could have been burned at the stake and still maintain her integrity to the end.

'You could always marry someone else, I wouldn't mind. I wouldn't want to stand in the way of you having children.'

'Don't be ridiculous. You know I don't want to be married to anyone else.'

But there was more to it than that. Something I could not bring myself to tell Mary Rose. I did not share her desire to have a child. Like her desire for a church wedding, it was something I had not anticipated when I asked her to marry me. I was thinking only of her, and my desire to attach myself to her for life. And while I did, to my subsequent regret, manage to veto the church wedding, I would not have stood in the way of her having children. I went along with it because she wanted it, and I was sorry for her when it did not come to pass, but I could not rid myself of the ugly slick of relief that lay like the aftermath of an oil spill in my groundwater. A secret I kept from her, out of shame. I never wanted to be a father.

I had watched as the men I knew were reduced one by one to packhorses when their babies were born. I had seen them carting those padded baby bags about the place, and performing fetch for their wives, while all adult conversation disappeared into the vortex that came with every newborn. Any hopes I had of our relationships in time returning to normal were indefinitely suspended. At dinner parties, I listened to my friends talk at length about their five-year-old's prowess on the rugby field, or the twelve-year-old's flair for creative writing. All the lapsed Catholics I knew started going to Mass again, so their children could make their First Holy Communion. All the atheists converted to the Church of Ireland in order to secure a place in the local school.

'It's not so much about religion,' they all said. 'It's the sense of community.'

Mary Rose always bought a picture Bible as a gift for our friends' children on their Communion or Confirmation Day, tucking a fifty-euro note into the holy card she invariably made me countersign. At Christmas time, she always had carefully wrapped gifts under the tree for each of her nieces and nephews and her countless godchildren. I felt aggrieved for her that so many of them had been foisted on her, but she never complained, and never once did she forget a birthday. I was unencumbered by godchildren myself. Every time my brother, Terry, and his wife had another child, Mary Rose wondered would I be chosen, but each time, much to my relief, that honour went elsewhere.

'You'd think your own brother would want to have you as godfather to one of his kids,' said Mary Rose, many times over the years. The lovelessness of my family was something she struggled to get her head around. An eternal optimist, she was convinced the affection was there somewhere, if only she could sniff it out.

'You mind more than I do,' I said to her, on many occasions. 'And anyway, you have enough godchildren for the both of us.'

What I did not say to her was that I was not very fond of children and felt no need to have one attached to me, by some artificial bond of sentiment and sorcery, for the rest of my life.

That summer on the beach in Aiguaclara, I watched as men my age played interminable games of beach tennis with their four-year-olds. *Tac, tac, tac.* Each rally lasted no more than three shots. 'Nice try,' the father would say, as he scrambled to retrieve the ball from the waves. *Tac, tac, tac.* 'Good return!' I lay there thinking I would rather have my toenails pulled out with pliers than play beach tennis with a small child. I figured I didn't have it in me to be a parent. I was not a nice enough person.

I looked up, exasperated, as yet another small boy thundered by my beach towel, sending a spray of wet sand scuttering across the pages of my book. From under a nearby sun umbrella, I saw a baby give me a murderous stare. 'Mum, between my legs hurts,' I heard an English child say. The mother told the child not to pee in the sea or she would get a rash there. Later that day, or maybe it was another day, a small Dutch boy did a turd in his swimming trunks and waddled back up the beach to his father, who was forced to remove it by hand. I rolled over and buried my face in the sand, grateful that I had been spared such indignities. It seemed to me that I had inadvertently pulled off a very lucky escape.

'I wonder should we think about adoption,' she said, one year.

We were on the beach. She was spraying suncream on her toes – I have never in all my life seen anyone take such care applying suncream – and I was drying off after a swim. We were discussing some book we'd both been reading, something by Ian McEwan as I remember, when a jet-skier appeared in the bay. I watched him with narrowed eyes, entertaining violent thoughts for a moment about what I would do if I had a sniper's rifle, and I was about to voice those thoughts to Mary Rose when I checked myself. I was afraid of boring her with the endless repetition of my grievances, grievances that had begun to sound to my ears more and more like my father's. I was starting to bore *myself* with them, which may have been the first step in my mellowing, something I was just congratulating myself on when I realized Mary Rose was talking about adoption.

'What did you say?'

'I wonder should we think about adoption.'

The way she said it, I knew she'd been thinking about it already. She'd probably been thinking of nothing else the whole holiday, and I wondered why she was only bringing it up now. She didn't look at me when she said it. Instead she kept on rubbing the suncream into her toes, rubbing and rubbing long after it was necessary, until I knew she was avoiding looking at me.

'Aren't we a bit old for adoption?' I asked.

She turned and blinked at me, waiting to see what I'd say next. I had my father's voice in my head. 'Children are like farts,' he often said. 'You can just about stand your own.' I could hear those words, but I didn't voice them. I was finally learning to self-censor.

'I'm not a good enough person to raise someone else's child,' I said, falling back on my worst self as a scapegoat.

'Right,' said Mary Rose, putting the suncream back in her bag and rolling over on to her belly. She made a cradle of her arms and laid her head down in it, with her face turned away from me.

'Well, hang on, this is the first I've heard of it,' I said, leaning in to talk to the back of her head. Her hair was flattened a bit where she'd been lying on it, and I could see her scalp where it parted. There was something pathetically melancholy about it. It made me feel awful.

'We can talk it through, if you want,' I said.

But already I was lining up all the arguments against it. Our age was the least of it. There was the notorious difficulty of the adoption process. There would be mountains of paperwork. Numerous infractions of our privacy. Delays and disappointments, followed in the end by a trip to an orphanage in China, or Russia, to take possession of a child who might have any number of problems. We'd be tossing our lives on to a roulette wheel, that was how I felt about adoption, but if it was what Mary Rose wanted I would, of course, go along with it.

'Let's talk about it over dinner.'

She didn't move.

'No,' she said. 'Forget about it.' It was the same voice she sometimes used to tell me to forget about putting the bins out because she'd done it already. 'You don't want to, so let's just forget about it.'

Of course, I should have insisted we talk about it. I should have brought it up again, later that night maybe, over dinner at Alicia's. Out of laziness I think, or maybe it was complacency – out of some fatalistic sense of drift that prevented me from grabbing on to a branch when the waterfall was just up ahead – I didn't. I look back now and wonder why I didn't take that moment and shake it until the truth fell out, but instead I fell back on the hope that Mary Rose would move on, that she would exorcize from her mind the ghosts of the children we could not have, when the fact was that she saw them everywhere.

Mary Rose's parents had a holiday house in the west of Ireland, and it was a tradition for the family to holiday there every August.

'The west,' they called it, using a code word to denote not the entire scraggly west coast of Ireland, but the five square miles around a picturesque fishing village in Connemara where most of the people they knew also had holiday houses. 'We've a place there,' they would say, adding no more specifics. It all seemed to me deliberately obtuse – clandestine even, as if they were going into hiding out there – but in time I came to understand that they were simply speaking a language their own people fully understood. Their people were all country people, most of them from humble backgrounds, who through college education and hard work had made good in Dublin. They all had holiday houses in the west.

Mary Rose's parents bought the place shortly after they

married. They got it 'for a song', as they told me. At that time, it was no more than a derelict cottage with a few out-buildings, at the end of a narrow country lane, but it had the sea just below it and a barely used pier beyond the garden gate. At first, they pitched a tent within its walls and camped there, renovating it bit by bit, as and when they had the money. The original two-bedroomed cottage was restored in the traditional style, with whitewashed walls and a flagstone floor. There was an old open hearth and three tiny, deep windows offering only a prisoner's glimpse of the stone walls and fuchsia bushes beyond. In the seventies, a new kitchen and sunroom were added, all seventies pine, like a sauna, with a mezzanine providing a loft room above the kitchen. An outbuilding was converted into an extra en-suite bed-room in the eighties, and a glass atrium was added in the new millennium to connect them all together. The result was a hideous, homely mess, but Mary Rose and her sisters loved that house the way they had once loved their smelly old dogs. They were blind to its imperfections.

The tradition was for the family to go west for the August bank holiday weekend. They came and went at other times of the year, of course, and the parents generally spent much of the summer there, but the August weekend was the only time when they were all invariably there together. The first time Mary Rose invited me on this annual pilgrimage we took a lift with Kitty in her rust bucket Renault Clio. Kitty was a demon driver, and she had an eye on the clock the whole time, determined to beat her own Dublin-to-Galway land-speed record. We were just past Kinnegad when she spotted her father's Mercedes on the road. Kitty let out three long beeps as she overtook him.

Mary Rose's father always drove a second-hand Mercedes saloon which he would run into the ground before finally and reluctantly giving up on it. His cars always had nicknames and were talked about as if they were members of the family.

'Do you remember Camilla?' Jean Anne might say, reminiscing about a family car long ago consigned to the great scrapyard in the sky. 'She was a great old girl. She had the most beautiful walnut dashboard, and brown leather seats.'

'Betsy was my favourite,' Mary Rose said. 'Betsy was pale blue, and she had a sunroof, so we could all stand up and stick our heads out.'

If my father had heard them, he would have pronounced them all stark raving mad. My father was dispassionate about his cars, as he was about everything he did. He always drove a Japanese model, trading it in for a new one every five years because he said this was the best way of avoiding decreasing returns to scale. Japanese cars were considered more reliable, which was a thing then, because cars were always breaking down. Cars don't seem to break down any more, but there's no style to them either. During my childhood you had to choose between style and reliability, and my father always chose reliability. In almost every respect imaginable, he and Mary Rose's dad were as different as two men could be, and I found myself comparing my father unfavourably to Willie Murphy at nearly every turn.

'You're too kind,' said Willie, beaming with pleasure as I presented him with the bottle of wine I had brought with me as a token of my appreciation for their unstintingly generous hospitality. He swivelled the bottle to study the label. He seemed to take inordinate pleasure in every little thing anyone did for him.

'You shouldn't have,' he said, 'but since you did, I will have to insist you help me drink it.'

The bedrooms in the house in the west were allocated on the basis of need, with the en suite given over to anyone with a baby, which meant that Jean Anne and her husband had it that year. There were two small double bedrooms in the original cottage, one of which was occupied by Mary Rose's parents. Kitty was six months pregnant, so she was installed in the other, on the basis that she would need to be near the bathroom. Mary Rose and I were relegated to the futon in the loft. The following year, Kitty and Jean Anne both had newborns, so there was a fight between them over the en suite. Again, we ended up on the futon in the loft.

Mary Rose hated sleeping in the loft. There was no privacy there, for one thing, because the balcony was open on to the kitchen below. Any sound you made up in the loft could be clearly heard by anyone who happened to have wandered into the kitchen below, which was quite inhibiting for our love-making. Similarly, any sound that was made in the kitchen carried up to the loft, with the result that Mary Rose and I were woken every time anyone boiled a kettle or rattled some plates around in the press.

'I feel like a teenager, sleeping up here. It's like I'm still a kid, and the rest of them are all adults.'

In becoming a mother, Kitty had somehow leapfrogged over Mary Rose and become a more senior person in the family pecking order. Mary Rose had been relegated to the bottom of the heap and nothing would deliver her from it but a baby. Sometimes it seemed to me that Mary Rose longed to have a baby *primarily* so that we would be delivered from the penance of always sleeping in the loft.

'I'm not sure I want to go to the west this year,' she said to me, when we were about five years married. 'I'm not sure I can bear the thought of sleeping on the futon in that bloody loft again.'

Jean Anne had three boys by then, and Kitty had her daughter, so between them they occupied all the bedrooms.

'We could always stay in a B and B in town,' I suggested.

'Oh, I don't know,' said Mary Rose. 'I'm worried my parents would be offended.'

Mary Rose would have died rather than offend anyone, and while I would not have wanted to hurt anyone's feelings, it seemed to me that her family were all a little slow to pick up on the sensitivities of our situation. Not least of them, Jean Anne. I had always had my doubts about Jean Anne because, basically, what kind of a person would choose to become a dentist, but that summer I came to the point of disliking her when I saw how greedily she hunted down compliments for her most recent baby. She was forever doting on him and beseeching everyone else to do the same.

'Isn't he the cutest thing you ever saw?' she said, fluffing up the baby's hair while she was nursing him. 'I love the shape of his head. It's so perfect.'

I felt like slapping her.

'He's amazing,' said Mary Rose, meaning every word of it. As she rested her gaze on her nephew, her eyes glistened with tears that Jean Anne seemed determined not to notice.

'Look at his little toes,' she went on, cupping the baby's bare foot in her hand. 'I can't believe how small they are.'

I saw then how cruelty is like a weed, finding its way into even the most perfect garden. In my own family it ran wild, but even Mary Rose's family was not immune to it. In some ways it was more shocking to find it there, insinuating itself in among all that love.

'He's a beauty,' said Mary Rose, leaning over to stroke the pink sole of the baby's tiny foot with the pad of her little finger. 'He's a beautiful little boy.'

No matter how much pain it caused Mary Rose, she never could bring herself to excuse us from that August week in the west. As Jean Anne's children turned from chubby little boys into stringy teenagers, and Kitty's daughter grew into an even greater terror than Kitty had ever been — as they leapt off the pier and roamed the rock pools in search of crabs — Mary Rose sat stalwart with her sisters on a plaid picnic rug on the beach below the house, scanning the clouds for an ever-elusive patch of blue sky.

There's a diving board mounted to a rocky outcrop at the southern end of the beach in Aiguaclara, and from morning to night the youngsters queue up there for the chance to jump off the board into the sea. The diving board has been there ever since the first time Mary Rose and I went to Aiguaclara – and probably for many years before that – but when I went back this summer, I was shocked to see it had been cordoned off.

I was sitting on the terrace of the Hotel Aiguaclara, savouring the miraculously unchanged taste of the café con leche, when I noticed that a cat's cradle of police tape had been used to isolate the diving board and prevent access to it. My heart sank as I contemplated the possibility that it was to be removed. All across Ireland diving boards had been removed from the old swimming places because the local authorities didn't want to be held responsible for any accidents that might arise. It seemed to me this was most likely the reason the diving board in Aiguaclara had been cordoned off, and I was disproportionately upset at the thought of it. I took it as another step towards the obliteration of all that was good and decent in the world, and it occurred to me all of a sudden that I should not let it go without a fight, so as soon as I had finished my coffee I went over to investigate.

There were two men in worker's overalls and high-vis jackets on the rock by the time I got there. One of them had a large bag of tools with him.

'*Hola*,' I said to them, raising one hand in greeting.

'*Hola*,' they said, without questioning my presence. The one with the tool bag laid it on the ground and bent down to unzip it. The other one took a pack of cigarettes out of his jacket pocket and went to light one.

'*Es finito?*' I asked them, jabbing my finger at the diving board.

They both stopped what they were doing to stare at me.

'*Le plongeoir*,' I said, happening upon the word for it in French, if not in Spanish. '*Es finito?*'

I was clearly not making myself understood. Frustrated by my inability to find the words I needed, I resorted to sign language, drawing my finger across my throat to indicate the demise of the diving board.

'*Tranquilo, hombre*,' said one of the men, clearly alarmed by the violence of the gesture.

It began to dawn on me that, even if I did succeed in securing confirmation that the diving board was to be removed, I would not have the power to express how I felt about it, and what I believed it signified for humanity. Exasperated by my own abject inability to communicate, I waved myself out of the conversation, retreating back over the rock and on to the steps, where I sat and watched the men work. It soon became clear to me that they were not removing the diving board at all, only replacing the screws that bolted it to the rock, and I felt like a fool for jumping the gun. By lunchtime the kids were lining up again to leap off the board into the glimmering green sea.

Mary Rose loved to watch the divers. She liked to sit on the beach below and watch each one approach the end of the slick, wet board. There was a lovely suspense to it, as the diver stood in the loneliness of the moment, arms by his sides, the queue shifting impatiently behind him. You were wondering what grand plan was in the diver's mind: was it to be a twist or a somersault, or would it just be a cannonball or, most disappointingly of all, a pencil dive? A slim, brown slip of a girl might do a cartwheel. A small boy might stand for too long, in an agony of indecision, only to retreat back along the board to the safety of the rock. There was no surprise when a fat kid got to the top of the queue and, inevitably, belly-flopped. Mary Rose winced with empathy while I laughed, and she chastised me for laughing.

'You're so mean,' she said, giving me a sharp little slap, which only made me laugh all the more.

I did not remind her that, as the runt of the litter, I was once the butt of my family's jokes, which I felt gave me the right to laugh at other unfortunates. Mary Rose had never in her life been teased and could not countenance it.

The last time she and I were in Aiguaclara together, we were sitting on the southern end of the beach one evening when we saw the French family gather around the diving board. The sunbathers had thinned out as the shade stretched across the sand, but the last of the day's sunshine made a jade-green pool in the sea beneath the diving board. There might have been a spotlight shining on the place where the divers entered the water.

'Look,' said Mary Rose, sitting up on her towel and hugging her knees into her chest. 'Isn't that Olivier?'

Olivier was the name we had given the older son of the French family. A wide-shouldered man, there was something of Robert Mitchum in the crooked lines of his face, the eyes that seemed to be perpetually smiling, the hair that flopped down over his forehead.

'He looks like a boxer,' said Mary Rose, watching as he took his place at the end of the diving board. He turned half a circle and took a step backwards, so that his heels hung off the edge. Then he made a wide arc with his hands and threw himself into a backflip, coming down head first into the water. There was an outbreak of cheering from his family, who were bunched together in the queue. Perched above them on the rock, I saw Claire. She was sitting with her daughter hugged in close to her as they too watched the diving.

The next one to come to the top of the board was Olivier's brother. He was slightly less stocky, but he had the same boxer's face, all distorted, like a Francis Bacon painting. He stood for a moment, still as a statue, at the edge. Then he raised his arms above his head and fell, in a perfect swan dive, into the sea. He made hardly a splash as he disappeared under the surface. His family gave a cheer, and there was a burst of applause from the little audience on the rock above the diving board.

'Here comes one of Olivier's sons,' Mary Rose whispered to me. I looked across at her and saw that her eyes were lit up with delight.

'He's the image of his dad.'

The young man walked out to the edge and peered down at the drop to the sea. Then he walked back to the base of the diving board, measuring out his steps. He turned and ran the length of it, throwing one hand down with a thump on to the board at the end and cartwheeling off. There was an illusion of stillness, like a flash-frame, as he held the shape of a wheel in the air. Then he was falling, with his arms pinned by his sides and his toes pointed up like a dancer's. Only his back was slightly curved as he went into the water.

'*Bravo*,' Claire called out. '*Magnifique!*'

'*Bravo*,' repeated her daughter, clapping excitedly.

'How old would you say she is?' asked Mary Rose, without taking her eyes off them.

'Who?'

'The girl.'

'I don't know, about sixteen, I suppose. You'd wonder what will become of her.'

'Oh, she'll be fine,' said Mary Rose, with great certainty. 'She won't ever have to suffer like the rest of us do. She'll be protected from all the sorrows of life.'

I was shocked to hear her say that. I think it was the first bitter thing I ever heard her say, and I made a mental note to pursue it with her further, at some time in the future. There was no time to do it right then, because another of the French grandsons was making his way down to the end of the diving board, and Mary Rose had trained all her attention on him. I saw that it was Claire's son. He looked back at the others to make sure they were all watching him, and there was an outbreak of taunting as they urged him on. Claire called out some word of encouragement to him from where she was sitting on the rock. He glanced back at her and gave her a thumbs-up. Then he threw himself into a somersault, pulling his knees in tight to his chest and allowing himself to roll as he fell. He just about had time to straighten up before he entered the water.

There was a roar of approval from the family, and more applause from Claire and the girl, and I realized that Mary Rose was clapping along too. She gave one or two little claps before she became self-conscious and held her hands to her lips in a semblance of prayer. Her eyes were brimming over with emotion, and I could see that she was trying hard not to cry. It was everything that Mary Rose ever wanted for her life, that scene that had just played itself out on the diving board, and I felt very sad for her that she could only watch it from afar.

That's my lasting image of Mary Rose in Aiguaclara. I

wish it wasn't such a lonely one, but for some reason that's the image that has remained strongest in my mind.

'I wonder if our marriage will survive, without children,' she said to me once.

It might have been that year, or maybe it was another year. It's hard to separate one out from the other. What I do remember is that we were in the local town shopping for groceries at the street market. Our arms were weighed down by plastic bags greedily bulging with fruit. Every year in Aiguaclara we feasted on those luscious flat peaches they call paraguayos. To me – reared on a diet of nothing more exotic than apples and oranges – they tasted like the product of some heavenly garden, rather than the fruit of any earthly tree. We ate tomatoes by the kilo, drizzling them with nothing but salt and olive oil. They were so good they needed nothing else.

We bought salted almonds and small green olives that were ladled straight out of the barrel, and cheese-and-ham empanadas made fresh that day by a man with a harelip. After we'd concluded our purchases, we always sat down at one of the tables in the middle of the square for yet another café con leche. The coffee was always served with the same small brown biscuit, individually wrapped in plastic and placed on the saucer with a single cube of sugar. The old men always gathered in the late morning to play dominos and drink coffee in the bar on the corner of the square. It was deeply reassuring to me how things there always seemed to stay the same.

'I love the way the old guys gather in that bar,' I said, for perhaps the hundredth time. Every time I came to the square, I thought about how much I loved it that the old men gathered to pass the time together in that bar, and I voiced the thought to Mary Rose without worrying that I was boring her, because that's what we did. We spoke our thoughts out loud to each other.

'I wonder if our marriage will survive, without children,' she said, out of the blue.

'Where did that come from?' I asked, stunned.

'Children are the glue that keeps people together,' she said. 'It's hard to see how we'll have anything to say to each other, without kids and grandchildren to talk about.'

I was so surprised I didn't know what to say. It was so unlike Mary Rose to be negative about anything. For as long as I had known her, she had been an endless source of positivity. A purveyor of hope and optimism. An inexhaustible dispenser of kindness. Among all our friends, it was accepted that Mary Rose was the hearthstone. She was the fire around which we all gathered to warm our hands. It was inconceivable to me that she would ever be anything other than that.

'We know lots of people whose marriages haven't survived, even with the existence of children.'

I cited Cara, whose marriage had ended when an intern accused her husband of sexual harassment. It turned out that Damian was a serial offender. He had been exposing himself to women in the lift at work for years.

'That's different,' said Mary Rose. 'Cara's husband was a sex pest. She had no choice but to leave him.'

'Okay, I'll give you that. But what about Terry and Liz?'

My brother and his wife were at the time embarked on a trial separation.

'Terry and Liz aren't going to split up,' said Mary Rose, with a snort of derision. 'In their case it's money that's the glue. Once Terry works out how expensive it is to get divorced, he'll be all over Liz again in a flash.'

'Well, how about Kitty?'

Kitty was by then on the rebound from her long and turbulent non-marriage to a colleague in the film industry. She had dyed her hair red and signed up for Tinder.

'Kitty is just Kitty,' said Mary Rose, with her maddening brand of logic.

'So, where does that leave love?' I asked her. 'Surely love is the glue that will keep us together?'

She gave me a pitying look when I said that. 'What if that's not enough?'

In all the years I'd known Mary Rose, she had never once expressed a doubt about us – about me – and it shocked me to hear her do so. The notion that our marriage would not survive had never once occurred to me, and I did not take it seriously even then. I believed that all would be well once she had come to terms with her childlessness.

Her life had for so long been dominated by the desire to become a mother – *our lives* had been dominated by *her* desire to become a mother – and I wanted very much for us to be free of it. I wanted us to enjoy the lovely life we had together – it seemed to me that the life we had built for ourselves was as near perfect as could be – and I wanted Mary Rose to see that too. I had no doubt that in time she would come around to my way of thinking, that our childlessness could, under the right lens, be seen as a good thing. It was a view that only grew in me as the years went by. As our friends sat sober on Saturday nights in their cars outside city-centre discos, waiting for their teenagers to emerge blind drunk and barely clothed, as their disposable incomes were poured into orthodontics and private education and exorbitant insurance premiums for learner drivers who inevitably went on to crash their cars, it seemed to me that Mary Rose and I had a charmed life.

*

'We've so much going for us,' I said to her, over dinner one night at the Japanese restaurant up at the lighthouse.

Mary Rose was wearing a pale pink silk dress. Pink was her colour and roses her scent, from the oil she poured into her bath to the Jo Malone fragrance I took to buying her for her birthday. A jeans girl most of the time, I was always struck by how ladylike she looked when she wore a dress.

'You look like Lauren Bacall,' I whispered across the table to her, as the waiter approached with the wine.

A Verdejo, we had agreed upon, as we agreed on every-thing that mattered, or so it seemed to me. We studied the menus, settling on a shared starter of prawn gyoza. She ordered the sea bass, as I knew she would. I went for the teriyaki chicken. After the waiter had gathered up our menus, he took a lighter from his pocket and lit the candle on our table. The night slowly turned blue. As we sat sipping the crisp green wine in the warm summer air, I was overcome by a sense of how lucky we were. Assuming she would feel the same way, I said it to her, and was shocked to see tears shin-ing in her eyes.

'We both have our dream jobs,' I said, as if she needed convincing.

'I know,' she said, nodding very fast and opening her eyes very wide. 'I know, I know, I know.'

'We have no money worries.'

For Mary Rose that would have been a given – she had none of the squirrelly horror of running out of resources that had been bred into me – but again, she nodded.

'We have a beautiful home and lots of friends.'

She stared at me, and I had the sense that she was listening very hard to what it was that I was saying to her.

'We are surrounded by your lovely family, and we are finally rid of mine.'

Mary Rose didn't like it when I said mean things about my family, but she laughed at that, just a little. My mother had been dead for over a year by then, and her house had been cleared out and sold. Its contents we had carted off, lock, stock and barrel, to an auction house in Rathmines.

'Don't you want to keep anything?' I had asked Terry, as we walked through the house, taking a measure of the job ahead of us.

'Nah,' he said. 'Liz hates brown furniture.'

Their house was all cream-leather couches and pale oak, of the kind that's used to make the cheaper models of coffins. In choosing my mother's, we had stumped up for the mahogany.

'Do you want anything?' Terry asked me.

We were standing in the front room of the house. The good room, my mother always called it. It had a dastardly uncomfortable chaise longue in it, and two wingback chairs upholstered in moss-green velvet with piping on the arms that was threadbare and frayed. There was an upright piano that nobody ever played and a couple of small, round tables for guests to place drinks on, only I hardly ever remember us having any guests. The only time that room was used was on Christmas Day, when we would light the fire that threw out smoke but no heat, and sit awkwardly around it with my father, while my mother ran in and out of the kitchen checking on the turkey, her glass of sherry untouched on the side table, as my father became more and more exasperated with her.

'For God's sake, Bernie, would you ever sit yourself down. The one day in the year when I get to relax with my family and you're up and down like a fiddler's elbow.'

I remember her, with her morning Mass make-up thawing in patches on her face, as she perched on the edge of the

176

chair, her knees falling to the side in helpless submission. A tea towel still in one hand, while with the other hand she held the stem of her sherry glass between her fingers like a cigarette, her face struggling to maintain composure as she itched to get up and baste the turkey and stir the bread sauce and turn the roast potatoes. At the time I had no sympathy for her, infected by my father's irritation at her inability to sit still, but I feel sorry for her now, and her isolation as a lone woman in that household of men.

'Do *you* want anything?' Terry asked me again, as we stood at the centre of the stage that had set the scene for our lives in that house. I looked around the room one last time, with the feeling that it was not an item of furniture I was looking to salvage but something of substance from my childhood that I could carry forward with me into my future.

'No,' I said, turning to look Terry in the eye. 'I don't want anything.'

At the bottom of my mother's wardrobe we found a box of keepsakes that I never knew she had. Terry, of course, knew about it and had long ago rummaged through its contents, but it was new to me, and very touching. In the box she had a little story she had written as a child on four middle pages torn from a copybook. The story was littered with misspellings, but the narrative style was fresh and original. What stood out most was the comment written in the margin. *Definitely shows promise*, was what the teacher had written, in red pen, and my mother had kept it all the years, so precious was it to her. I was very touched by the knowledge that she had once nurtured ambitions of creating something, and I wondered if my own aptitude for English could be traced back to her. I always thought I was an aberration, but it may have been that my mother had a talent that was never realized. If so, it was something she never spoke of, like so many other things in her life. My mother spoke only of things that were of no consequence.

In her box of keepsakes, she had the menu from her wedding breakfast, a dried-out rose from her wedding bouquet, and a paper coaster from the hotel in Tramore where they stayed on their honeymoon. She had the hospital tags from when my brother and I were born, and a bone teething ring someone had given me as a christening gift. On her bedside table we found a desk diary for the last year of her life, filled mainly with shopping lists and household accounts. Opening the diary at a random page, I saw *milk, lightbulbs, bleach* written in the space allocated to a Thursday in May. In the space for the Friday, she had noted: *Gas Bill, 7s.5o.* Her whole life was a list of things to do. I flicked to the back of her diary and found the log she took to keeping in her final years, of my visits to her. Every time I came to see her, she would consult the log and remind me how long it had been since I last darkened her door.

'Twice since Christmas,' she might say, when I tried to defend myself against the accusation that I had no time for her.

'You're so busy,' she would say, 'flying here and there.'

My job, which had once been such a source of pride to her, had become nothing but a stick to beat me with. Her unhappiness, which for so long had been channelled into resenting my father, was unleashed on all of us once he was gone. When I got a call out of the blue one night from my brother to say that she had suffered another, this time fatal, stroke, my primary feeling was one of relief. Her existence had become such a burden to her, and to us, that I was glad it was over.

'We have all the freedom in the world,' I said to Mary Rose, that blue, blue night over dinner at the lighthouse above Aiguaclara. 'We can do whatever we want.'

She nodded, but her eyes were glazed as she stared into mine, and I had the sense that she wasn't hearing me. I did not know it then, but we had reached a fork in the road, one that would carry her one way and me another. If I had listened to her then – if I had talked to her – I might have seen that she could not come with me on the path I had marked out for us. So caught up was I in my own concerns that I didn't even notice we had diverged.

12

The apartment I rented this summer in Aiguaclara had a balcony that sat right over the promenade, and from the balcony I had a dress-circle view of the beach. In the early evenings, after I had showered and changed, I would take a cold beer and some salted nuts out there and sit and watch the day slowly turn to night. The sinking sun fell on the row of houses that wrapped around the far end of the promenade, setting their red awnings on fire. The yellow rocks baked in the last of the day's heat. The sea, which was blue in the morning, became a deep emerald green. The light moved off the beach, driving the sunbathers up the hill, laden down with their beach chairs and their parasols and their inflatable boats. Small children scrambled to climb the lifeguards' chair, now that the lifeguards were gone for the day. At the near end of the beach, a queue still formed for the diving board and one more chance to leap into the sea.

Directly below me were the half-dozen restaurants that lined the seafront. From my vantage point, I could watch over them the way I once watched over the orchestra pit at the panto. As a child, I always found it much more entertaining to study the members of the orchestra than the show itself. One guy's job was to clash the cymbals together at crucial moments, like when the genie appeared in *Aladdin*, or when the clock struck midnight in *Cinderella*. I was fascinated by the idea that this was somebody's *job*.

Every weekend evening in Aiguaclara, some musicians would appear down the seafront. In recent years, it was a ragbag trio of sweet-looking, scruffy young men who made their way along the promenade, stopping to play a few tunes outside each of the restaurants and gathering donations afterwards from the restaurant's customers. There was a very tall double-bass player, and a long-haired trombonist and a wiry little banjo player, and they all sang along with their instruments in raucous harmony. Their repertoire was limited: they played 'When the Saints' and 'Pay Me My Money Down' and 'When You're Smiling', over and over again. Any time I hear any of those songs, no matter where I am, I think of summer in Aiguaclara.

Mary Rose and I were in the habit of having our aperitif at the restaurant we called the New Place, which occupies the bend in the promenade and enjoys the biggest slice of evening sun. It became a mark of our long association with Aiguaclara that we persisted in calling it the New Place long after it was new; it must have appeared the second or third year we were there, making us a proud part of Aiguaclara's pre-history. We only ever had our aperitifs at the New Place; for dinner we would always take ourselves on down to Alicia's, and only when Alicia's was full up would we settle for a table at one of the less popular places in between. It was a source of endless fascination to me why Alicia's place always had a queue forming down the promenade, while the other restaurants were all empty. The menus were practically identical, and any variation in the quality of the food was negligible. The only difference was that everyone seemed to know that Alicia's was the place to go.

'Look,' I would say to Mary Rose, as we drank our aperitifs on the terrace of the New Place. 'Alicia's is already full up and there are only two people in Fernando's.'

Fernando would be standing at the door of his restaurant, his hands clasped behind his back, nodding and smiling to everyone as they walked on by to Alicia's.

'Oh, I can't bear it,' Mary Rose would say. 'It's too sad. Maybe if we eat there tonight it will encourage more people to come. I'm not sure I can walk past him.'

Mary Rose was so soft. So quick to offer herself up to help. She had none of my pathological detachment.

'Not our problem,' was what I always said. I preferred to eat in Alicia's, even though the truth was that the chips weren't as good there as they were in Fernando's. The paella was better at the New Place, but they were still all somehow missing something that you got at Alicia's. That's why everyone went there.

'*Hola*,' Fernando would say, lifting a hand to us as we walked by. '*Buenas tardes.*'

'*Buenas tardes*,' I would reply, without the slightest hint of guilt. I knew poor Mary Rose would be suffering until we were happily settled on the terrace at Alicia's with our menus in our hands.

'We'll go to Fernando's another night,' I'd say, to make her feel better. But we never did go to Fernando's, unless there was no table free at Alicia's.

The French family were loyal patrons of Alicia's. They had the house right next door, so they never even had to worry about securing a table. They would set up their own cutlery and glasses and bread and wine on the long wooden dining table of their own terrace, and then the waiter from Alicia's would come and take their order. In all the years that Mary Rose and I observed them, this ritual never changed.

From my balcony, I watched them gather. The grandmother appeared first, with a large vase of flowers held carefully in both hands. It was a measure of how very much at home they were in Aiguaclara that they bought flowers. It would never have occurred to me to buy flowers while on holiday.

The grandfather came out next, carrying a bottle of wine, which he set down on the table. He shouted something to someone inside, but I couldn't hear what it was that he said. It was a silent movie I was watching, to the joyous soundtrack of the vagabond band, who were now stationed right below my balcony.

'*When you're smiling, when you're smiling, the whole world smiles with you . . .*'

The two adult sons of the French family appeared and sat down at the table with the grandparents. The older one was losing his hair, I noticed. Looking down on him from above, I had a clear view of the bare patch of skin at the whorl of his scalp. His father, miraculously, still had a full head of hair even though, by my reckoning, he can't have been much shy of eighty. The two sons and the grandmother sat at the table smoking away with impunity, while the grandfather talked. Every year, I was amazed to see how many of them still smoked.

There was some commotion as the grandchildren were summoned up from the beach. The three eldest grandsons, who were small children when Mary Rose and I first came to Aiguaclara, were by now all in their twenties. The eldest of them had a girlfriend with him this year, a timid little blonde thing who stuck so close to him as to be almost an appendage. The four of them trailed up off the beach and disappeared inside the house, presumably to get dressed for dinner.

There was a fourth grandson, half black, who I knew was the child of the younger son. He was, of course, half white too – it has always struck me as strange that the white bit goes unmentioned – and I put his age at about twelve. The beautiful long-necked black girl who had mothered this child – the girl Mary Rose and I had christened Ines – had disappeared from the line-up many years ago, but the child was always there with his father. Dripping wet and wearing nothing but a pair of swimming trunks and a beach towel tied about his neck as a cape, he scrambled up the steps on to the promenade and threw himself down at the table. His grandmother jumped up and ushered him inside the house, wrapping his towel around him as she went.

Claire came out carrying a large glass salad bowl, which she set down on the table. The older grandchildren reappeared one by one, dressed in jeans and freshly ironed shirts, their hair all damp from the shower. The little girlfriend was wearing a pretty blue dress, with a light shawl draped elegantly over her slim brown shoulders. I knew Mary Rose would say, 'How French can you be?'

At last the grandmother came out with the boy in tow and they all pulled their chairs closer to the table in readiness for dinner. There was much pouring of wine, and passing around of bread and salad, and the waiter was called over from Alicia's to take their order. The band had by then moved off to the other end of the promenade, so I was able to hear the hum of their conversation rising along with their cigarette smoke from the table, but I couldn't pick out any one thing that was said. I was just about to tear myself away from my observation post to go down in search of dinner when I noticed something that struck me as strange. Neither of Claire's children was there.

I had a very clear image in my mind of the girl, in particular. She had sand-coloured hair, cut in a very short bob. She wore it tucked behind her ears, with a clip to secure it. The haircut left her neck exposed and vulnerable and, from the back, she had the look of a newborn baby in the way her head sat low on her shoulders. Her hairstyle went unchanged from year to year as she grew from a tiny girl of three, four, five, to an adolescent of fourteen, fifteen, sixteen. Her body shape changed, and she grew in height, but there was a silence about her that was always the same. It anchored the family around her.

Whether they were setting out for a day in their boat or gathering for dinner on the terrace of their house, the girl was a stillness at the centre of them. We watched as an uncle took her hand to help her step down off the pier and into the pilot's inflatable dinghy. With infinite patience, a cousin unwrapped her ice-cream for her. Another applied suncream to her shoulders. Most touching of all was the way her brother behaved around her. He seemed always to be performing for her benefit – whether he was jumping off the diving board into the sea, or playing football with his cousins on the beach, he always searched his sister out to make sure she was watching. Every goal he scored was for her benefit. Every backflip was a gift to her. He was her own personal champion.

'There's such a fine line between heartbreak and love,' said Mary Rose one day, as we watched him take his sister for a circuit of the bay in a small rubber dinghy. She was sitting upright inside the boat, and he had set himself up as a human outboard motor at the back. She was adult-sized by then, and the weight of her caused the boat to sag in the water, but he kicked with all his might, driving her right around the whole perimeter of the swimming buoys. She rode along with all the composure of a queen.

'Isn't it wonderful to see how much they love her?' Mary Rose said to me another morning, as we watched the grandparents bring the girl down to the beach with them when they went for their morning swim. They would have orchestrated this to give Claire and her husband a lie-in, was Mary Rose's guess.

185

'It must be tiring for them,' I said. 'Somebody has to be with her all the time.'

As usual, I saw nothing but the downside.

The grandparents wore matching bathrobes: his was green, hers red. The girl was already dressed, in a navy-blue dress with a pattern of sailing boats on it. Her tawny hair was brushed and secured, as always, with a clip.

'They take such good care of her,' said Mary Rose, watching as the grandparents settled the girl on the beach to wait for them. Only when the girl was safely seated on the sand did they slip off their bathrobes and wander down to the water. They entered it gingerly, inching forward until they were up to their waists. Then they let go of the seabed with a little leap of faith. They swam side by side as far as the line of buoys that divided the swimming area from the boats. Then they swam back, their heads turning towards each other every so often in conversation. All the time they were swimming, the girl was scooping sand up in her hands and letting it fall through her fingers. Scooping, and sifting. Scooping and sifting. There was a grace to her absorption that I found very compelling. It made me conscious of the extreme busyness of the world. The absurdity of our endless restlessness. I had a desire to sit, like her, sifting sand through my fingers for the sheer pleasure of it. Not since I was a kid had I done such a thing.

When we were kids, we invariably spent our two-week summer holiday on the strand in Rosslare. The sand there was fine and golden and as intractable as the desert. It always ended up in the ham sandwiches we had for our lunch, and my mother always complained that it somehow managed to make its way into the tea she had poured at the breakfast table that morning into her tartan flask. She would serve the tea in old mugs that she kept in her picnic basket for this express purpose, passing one on to my father, who would have been sitting fully clothed under the shelter of a sand-bank. My father only ever went so far as to remove his jumper and shoes and socks on the beach. I never saw his legs exposed. Never once saw him swim. He took no discernible pleasure in the holiday.

I can picture him, even now, battling to defend his news-paper against the wind. Every so often he might venture off into the sand dunes to complain about the noise coming from some other family's portable radio. The distorted sound of Gary Newman, or The Pretenders, coming from some-where behind us. I seem to remember hearing Chrissie Hynde singing 'Brass in Pocket' as my father went over the top.

'People have no consideration,' he would say, sitting back down with the brief satisfaction of a bout won. He would go back to reading his newspaper, but we could all see that he was only waiting for the radio to start up again, so he could dive back into the dunes for another confrontation. My father lived to do battle with his fellow human beings. As the day wore on, he would find fault with the sandwiches my mother had pre-pared: too much butter, not enough mustard. He would refuse to wear a hat and then complain that evening about being sun-burnt. He would rant about the rubbish that accumulated on the fringes of the beach as the day progressed.

'Aren't people just disgusting?' he would say. 'They really are the filthiest of animals, the way they leave a trail of destruc-tion behind them everywhere they go.' And so on, and so on. I remember the glazed expression my mother would adopt as she was subjected to his constant barrage of outrage. I can only imagine what feelings were churning inside her. I never remember her saying anything to contradict him. Maybe she did, when my brother and I were out of earshot, but if so, I was unaware of it.

There was this game my brother and I liked to play on the beach in Rosslare; it was called Nothing Coming. What you had to do was lie on your belly on the wet sand, with your head facing up the beach and your feet just out of reach of the waterline, and you had to close your eyes and chant, 'Nothing coming, nothing coming, nothing coming.' The idea was to see how many times you could say it before a wave broke over you. The thrill was in the unpredictability of the waves. You knew one was coming but you didn't know when.

Sometimes a small wave would break over you, sending a rush of cold water up between your legs, like a backwards pee, but still you would be able to carry on chanting.

'Nothing coming, nothing coming . . .'

When the big one crashed over you, the shock of it was always brand new. Even though you knew it was coming, even though you had been waiting for it, it still always took you by surprise. A vicious wall of water came tumbling down on you. Salt water in your eyes, your ears, your mouth, so that you couldn't see or hear or breathe. Just when you thought you were sure to die, the wave would release you, leaving you lying exposed on the sand, heart pounding, head reeling. You felt like you had been swallowed up by a sea monster and unexpectedly spat out again. That's how I felt when Mary Rose died.

After Mary Rose died, I found myself waking every morning at ten to five, choking for breath. Not ten past five, not five to five. It was always, for some reason, ten to five.

'It's your lungs,' said Kitty, when I told her. Like people quarantined with the same disease, we were in the habit of comparing our symptoms.

'Why my lungs?' I asked.

'In Chinese medicine, grief resides in the lungs.'

'Yeah, but what's the deal with ten to five? Same time every day. It's very specific.'

'God knows,' said Kitty, lighting up a cigarette. She'd taken up smoking again after Mary Rose died, on the basis that, fuck it, what did it matter? I had considered joining her, but I'd been off them for too long. I had the desire for a fag but not the ability to smoke it. The one time I tried, it made me gag.

The antidepressants the doctor gave me helped with the choking, and they did take the edge off the feeling that I had nothing to live for, but they didn't help with the early rising. Even in Aiguaclara, where I slept the hot, leaden sleep of a patient under anaesthetic, I still woke every morning at ten to five. The thin cotton sheet that covered me only added to the sense that I was in an operating theatre, waking from surgery.

Every morning, I would stagger into the bathroom and stare at myself in the mirror, surprised to find myself still alive. There was always that feeling in the mornings – as if I too had been on the plane with Mary Rose and somehow escaped death. I understood for the first time how correct it was to say that she was 'survived by her husband'. I had seen that expression used in obituaries without ever giving it a thought, but it turned out to be a term of great precision. I had survived Mary Rose only barely. I was struggling to survive her.

Pulling the rug from my bed I would venture out not on to the balcony but on to the tiny terrace at the rear of the apartment. It faced backwards, towards the dark hillside, where my loneliness found a refuge in the sounds of the birds and animals who had the run of the place in the hour before dawn. I liked to close my eyes and train my ears on them, listening to the sound of pigeons clearing their throats in ever receding relays up the hillside. A buzzard, its call like the sound of a small firework being launched. A lone barking dog, barking, barking, barking, until I wondered would it ever stop. I imagined it tethered to a wall in a dark, empty house somewhere, and longed for it to be released. Swallows darted about, like stones flung from one side of the skyscape to the other. As the light began to come up, I watched the arcs they made, and the plunges, trying to figure out if there was a pattern to them. If there was, I never spotted it.

13

There's a hiking trail that runs along the coast through Aigua-clara. The 'Camí de Ronda', it's called. Constructed to keep track of smugglers, it consists of a two-hundred-kilometre stretch of paths and steps that weaves around the cliffs and coves of the Costa Brava, sometimes rising high above the dazzling green sea, other times plunging down to traverse a stony beach. Mary Rose and I had it in mind to walk the entire trail some day, but it was a plan that we postponed year after year, opting instead to spend most of our holiday lazing around on the beach. We would sometimes walk for an hour or two north along the path from Aiguaclara, passing through a pine forest and out on to the coast again at Aiguablava. The furthest we ever got south was the small cove at Cala Perdida, accessible only on foot or by boat, where a woman called Lupita ran a small restaurant in the summertime out of her family's old boathouse. It was part of our holiday ritual to go to Cala Perdida at least once for lunch, and I saw no reason to abandon this ritual just because Mary Rose was not with me.

It's about a mile to Cala Perdida from the beach at Aigua-clara, and the path is so familiar to me that I could walk it with a hood over my head. It starts inauspiciously at the southern end of the beach, where the sand gives way to stone. A flight of rough steps takes you up over the lumpy protrusion of rock where the diving board juts out over the sea. The steps are carpeted with pine needles, and there are generally some pine cones scattered about. I once saw a snake there: an innocuous little sliver of a thing which was insufficient to the flash of fear he struck in me. He swished away as soon as I approached, and it was only after he had disappeared again that I mentioned him to Mary Rose. She squealed and sprang back with comic-book alarm, allowing me to step into the role of gallant knight by ushering her onwards. Forever after, Mary Rose would step gingerly over that portion of the path, remembering a snake she had never even seen. Poor maligned little snake; I think fondly of him every time I pass that spot.

Once the diving board is behind you, the path curves around the far side of the promontory until it runs aground on a flat moonscape of rock, where a small slipway leads down to the sea from a brick boat shed. You have to pick your way across the rock pools to regain the trail, which climbs steeply to run along the edge of a deep ravine. A hundred foot down is the churning, marbled sea. A boy fell here once, many years ago, and we heard his mother's screams as the rescue boat brought them around the headland and transferred him into the ambulance that was waiting at the pier. We never heard what became of the boy, but when we came back the next year a brand-new handrail had been erected along the edge of the ravine. When you looked down you could still hear the tumbling echo of his mother's screams, and the silence of his fall. You could almost imagine it was you.

Beyond the ravine is a flat, forested area that sits high on a bluff above Cala Perdida. The water in the cove below is gemstone green and dappled with rocks as you descend the stone steps all the way down the cliff side to the beach, where six small tables sit under a makeshift awning at the side of the boathouse. The kitchen consists of no more than a camping stove; the staff, of Lupita's daughter and some teenage grandchildren. One year, Mary Rose offered to give Lupita's granddaughter English lessons, and the child – a sweet, slow-moving girl with eyelids that hung heavy over her shy, brown eyes – spent an hour every afternoon at the table in our apartment, making laborious notes in a copybook, her tongue sticking out of the corner of her mouth as she worked. I saw no improvement in her English as the week went on, but Mary Rose ploughed ahead valiantly. By the end of two weeks even Mary Rose had to admit that the problem went deeper than language.

'*Hola*, Lupita,' I said, as I stepped under the shade of the awning.

She came forward, wiping her hands on the frilly, old-fashioned apron she wore. We kissed on both cheeks, and she asked me how I was.

I said I was well.

'*Venga*,' she said, opening her arm out to indicate an empty table.

I sat down.

'*Estás solo?*' she asked me. 'Are you alone?'

Her eyes wandered back up the cliff steps. She was obviously expecting to see Mary Rose following me down.

'*Sí*,' I said, grateful for her tact. '*Estoy solo.*'

'*Muy bien*,' she said, and that was that.

She brought me a beer, without asking if I wanted one, and I was touched by this small intimacy. I ordered the calamari, with fried potatoes and a mixed salad, even though I knew I would struggle to finish it. As I waited for the food to arrive, I tried to assume the air of someone who likes to be alone, but I found it hard to know what to do with my arms and legs. I didn't quite know where to look. If I looked for too long in the direction of the kitchen, Lupita might feel I wanted her to come and talk to me. If I studied the people at the other tables for too long it would seem rude, so I stared out to sea instead, studying the comings and goings of some kayakers with what I hoped was a semblance of genuine interest. I still had not quite got the hang of dining alone.

I was sitting down on the stones digesting my lunch when the French family arrived by boat. I saw them rounding the headland and identified their boat almost immediately by the French tricolour they flew from the mast in addition to the yellow and red Catalan flag. The mast was in the shape of a cross, which gave the boat the look of some primitive mission vessel as it approached. They dropped anchor out beyond the swimming area and prepared to come to shore.

I watched as they stripped down to their swimwear. The boat wobbled alarmingly with their movements, their laughter bouncing off the water.

'*Attention!*' I heard the grandfather say, as he grabbed hold of the mast to steady himself.

One of the grandsons threw himself off the deck of the boat, resurfacing with a flick of his hair that threw an arc of droplets through the air.

'*Vas-y*,' he said, holding his arms up out of the water, like a polo player angling for the ball.

The grandmother passed a plastic bucket over the edge of the boat and he took it. There was a splash as another of the grandsons jumped in. Another plastic bucket was handed down. Then the grandmother climbed backwards down the steps of the boat, letting herself slip gingerly into the water. She was followed, somewhat less elegantly, by the grandfather, still wearing his panama hat. The last into the water was the woman Mary Rose and I called Claire. She had her hair piled on top of her head, and she was wearing her dark glasses as if they were a part of her. She swam slowly, keeping her chin carefully above the water.

Their progress was haphazard. The boys swam an exuberant front crawl, racing each other to the shore. The grandparents bobbed along, nudging their buckets along with them. At one point the grandmother stopped to tread water and wave to someone up on the cliff path. The grandfather rolled on to his back for a while, staring up at the sky. The daughter swam slowly by, paying him no attention. When she reached the shore, she crept out of the water, using her hands to steady herself on the slippery, wet stones. Only when she had arrived at the dry reaches of the beach did she attempt to stand. The old couple emerged together, negotiating the stones with surprising ease. They were wearing rock shoes, and they carried the plastic buckets, which I saw were full of their clothes. They immediately set about unpacking them, retrieving their shirts and dresses and wallets and sunglasses.

'*Tiens*,' the old lady said to the daughter, holding a black dress out to her. She covered herself up in a white linen shift and began to climb the beach towards the restaurant. The old man and the two boys laid claim to a table underneath the awning, but the daughter made no move to follow them. Instead, she sat down on the stones, just a yard or two away from me, with her feet planted apart and her arms folded over her knees. She was wearing a black strapless swimsuit and her fingernails were painted blood red, I noticed.

Directly in front of us a pair of teenage girls were mincing their way across the stones and into the water. A snorkeller was nosing around the caves to the left of the cove and, to the right, a small boy stood with a fishing net on top of a large rock. A young couple lay on the deck of one of the boats, dozing in each other's arms. The French woman was studying the scene the way a woman in a gallery might study a painting. I was sitting beside her, studying the same scene, so it seemed odd to me not to comment on it.

'I never get tired of looking at that water,' I said.

'Yes,' she replied, without taking her eyes off the sea. 'It takes its colour from the trees, I think. That's why it's so green.'

I didn't even bother pretending I had not seen her before.

'You've been coming here a long time.'

She gave no indication that she had ever noticed me.

'My parents bought a place here when I was a kid. We come every year.'

'But you don't have your children with you this time.'

'No,' she said, and she repeated what I had said, very precisely. 'No, I don't have my children with me this time.'

She paused, and I expected her to say something else, but she didn't. The pause went on for too long, long enough for me to know something was wrong. I am finely attuned to these things, from working in television. Often, it's the background noises that tell the story. You can describe the effect of a bomb in Baghdad, for example, by rattling off the casualty numbers. You can show pictures of the stretchers arriving at the hospital, with a close-up of the blood pooling on the tiled floor, but it's the sound of a woman's scream, from somewhere off camera, that tells the horror of it in a way no words or pictures could convey. In the same way a silence in the wrong place is a powerful thing.

'My children were both in the Bataclan . . .'

She left the sentence hanging, as if she was about to add something else, but nothing came. I could have told her I knew all about that hanging clause. You feel you should say something more, but the truth is, there is no more to say. And I knew better than to offer her any words of comfort or condolence. Instead I sat in silence as the shock of the thing she had told me broke over me like a wave. And broke, and broke.

'My wife died in a plane crash,' I told her. Not to add my tragedy to hers. What I wanted her to know was that I belonged to the same terrible club as her. That I knew not to fill the space around her tragedy with words that were of no help to her, only sounds that made no sense. I wanted her to know that I understood.

She nodded, to show me she'd heard, but she showed no surprise at my revelation. Maybe she had lost the capacity to be surprised when her children were killed. She lifted her sunglasses on to the crown of her head as she turned to face me. She had eyes the colour of autumn leaves, somewhere between brown and yellow.

'So you know what it's like, then.'

From the restaurant behind us, there was a burst of laughter. I looked out at the green sea, marbled here and there by dark rocks beneath the surface. I looked up at the steep, green walls of the ravine. At the trees that leaned, for some reason, into the wind, and the perfect blue sky.

'The days are so long,' she said. 'I never imagined a day could be so long. The time seemed to go so quickly, before.'

I said nothing, aware of my breathing shuddering as she spoke. Of my heart swelling in my chest and the blood pooling at my feet. A knot of nausea forming in my stomach as I succumbed again to the physicality of grief. It was like an old illness that never entirely goes away – like malaria or amoebic dysentery – rising up in you again any time you're run down. I felt sick just listening to her.

'I spend the whole day waiting for six o'clock, when I can have my first drink. I drink a bottle of wine with the dinner and then I go to bed and take a pill so I can sleep. The next morning, I wake up, and I have to do the same thing all over again.'

I had the sense that she was saying all this to me because

she could. Because I knew it already and would not be shocked. She was saying things to me that she could not say to anyone else.

'I'm nearly fifty-two years old,' she told me. 'It's possible that I have another thirty years to live. Maybe even forty.' She raised her eyebrows, widened her eyes. 'I don't know how I'm going to do it.'

'*Cou-cou!*' I heard her family call down to her. '*À table.*'

She shouted something back to them and rose to her feet. 'Excuse me,' she said. 'I must go and eat lunch.'

She pulled her dress over her head and drew her sunglasses down over her eyes. Then she flipped her hand to me in a little wave and set off up the beach. After she was gone, the thing that stayed in my mind was not anything she had said to me, but those blood-red fingernails. Her two children were dead, and she had no more reason to go on living, but here she was, in her black swimsuit, on a beach in Catalonia, and she had somehow mustered the energy to paint her nails red. I was struck by this evidence of her courage.

When I got back to the apartment that evening, I looked it up on the Internet. Feeling shabby for doing it, I googled 'Down syndrome' and 'Bataclan', and straight away a slew of articles appeared. GIRL WITH DOWN SYNDROME AMONG VICTIMS OF HORROR ATTACK, went one headline. VICTIM OF BATACLAN MASSACRE HAD SPECIAL NEEDS, said another. The girl was called Élodie, and her brother's name was Tristan. He was a big music fan and had bought his sister the concert tickets as a birthday gift. Élodie was found dead at the scene, but Tristan died later in hospital. He was nineteen years old. She was just about to turn seventeen.

There were many more articles, but I couldn't bear to read any further. It seemed ghoulish to do so, and the last thing I wanted to be was a ghoul. I shut down the browser on my phone and powered it off, but there was no shutting down the image of Claire's daughter, lying dead on the floor of the Bataclan theatre, and her brother nearby, dying. Not since Mary Rose had been killed had I been so upset by anything. I was aware that it was a measure of my progress that I was capable of feeling sorrow for something outside of myself, and I was almost proud of myself for it. For so long I had been incapable of empathy, but the loss of the French woman's children occupied a space in the centre of my mind all evening, the way a very tall person occupies your view when they sit in front of you at the cinema. It took me a long time to get to sleep that night.

14

In the weeks and months after Mary Rose died, I dreamed of her almost every night. At first, I dreamed that she was trying to get into the house, but her keys wouldn't work. She was trying to open her car, but the zapper was useless. She wanted to pay for something, but her credit card had been declined.

'I can't get any money out of the bank machine,' she told me. 'I keep putting my card in, but the machine keeps telling me that my account is no longer valid.'

I was the one who had closed down her accounts, of course. There was a hiatus at first while we waited for the Egyptians to issue a death certificate but, once they produced it, I was able to proceed with the considerable paperwork that is generated by a death. Mary Rose's sisters dealt with her clothes – they came one day armed with a roll of black refuse bags and cleared out her wardrobe. All I asked was that they take her things to the recycling centre and not to a charity shop. I could not bear the thought that I might one day bump into a stranger wearing some item of Mary Rose's clothing.

'Make sure to keep whatever you want,' I told Kitty and Jean Anne, before shutting myself away in the study.

Jean Anne selected the Hermès silk scarf I had bought Mary Rose for her fortieth birthday. Kitty chose a black rabbit-fur jacket she had always coveted. For myself, I kept nothing, only the straw hat Mary Rose always brought with her on holidays. I left the hat on the high shelf in the hallway of our house, where it belonged. I liked to see it there as I came down the stairs in the morning. I could not have borne the sight of Mary Rose's coats in the hallway. I was relieved to see her robes disappear from the hook on the back of the bathroom door. Her underwear drawer was mercifully emptied of everything but a long-exhausted lavender bag, and her shoes were gathered up and discreetly disappeared. Her shoes held a particular poignancy and I could not stand to see them lying around the house, with the imprint of her feet still visible on the insoles. But there was something about the straw hat that subverted the tragic. The sight of it sitting there on the shelf in the hallway always made me smile.

'My wife has died,' I told the person I finally managed to speak to in the bank, after I'd spent an hour negotiating their call answering system. 'I need to close down her accounts.'

'Hold on,' the person said. 'I'll put you through to the deceased person's department.'

I was tempted to make a ghost sound when the call connected, but I didn't.

'Because you're a named driver on your wife's policy,' said the man at the car insurance firm, 'your policy will no longer be valid if your wife doesn't continue on as the policy holder.'

'Sure,' I said. 'But what I'm finding it hard to understand is how my wife can continue to be the policy holder, when she's *dead*. She won't be driving anywhere any time soon.'

I thought of Raymond O'Halpin, who was the chief sub when I started out in radio. One of the first stories I ever wrote up for him was an account of a fatal road accident in Donegal. What I wrote was: 'The dead man was driving between Donegal town and Letterkenny in the early hours of this morning, when he struck an oncoming vehicle.' To my mortification, Raymond pulled me up on it in the middle of the newsroom. 'Since when, Mr Dowling, have you known dead men to be capable of driving automobiles?' It took me weeks to recover from the humiliation – months, years. Every time I thought of it, I wanted to crawl under a rock and cry. What a brittle creature I was, with a shell so thin that any minor transgression could crack it open.

'Were you punished as a child when you did something wrong?' Mary Rose asked me once.

We were washing up together after dinner at her parents' house, and I had let a Waterford crystal glass strike the bottom of the Belfast sink. A wedge of crystal the size of a lemon slice came away from the rim. It was a clean break, I could see, as I fished the broken piece out of the sink, and I tried fitting it back together, as if I could somehow make the glass whole again.

'Don't worry about it,' said Mary Rose, looking over my arm. 'I've tried fixing them before. It doesn't really work.'

Standing there holding the precious broken glass, I was overcome by what I can only describe as panic. I wanted to run away and hide somewhere. I could not bear to own up to what I had done.

'Will you tell your parents that you broke it?' I asked her.

There came over her face an expression of tender consternation.

'It's okay,' she said, raining concern down on me with her molten blue eyes. 'Nobody gets into trouble in this house for breaking something by accident.'

I nodded and placed the broken glass in full view on the kitchen counter, but the feeling of dread did not go away. I had been formed in a house where there was no such thing as an accident, and while I was reluctant to believe that my upbringing had hard-wired me to be defensive and prone to subterfuge, Mary Rose seemed to think it was an open-and-shut case.

'Where's the Nicky Mosse oven dish?' she asked me once, referring to an oval earthenware dish that her mother had given her for Christmas. The dish had a cheerful pattern of red apples on it, and Mary Rose was especially fond of it.

'I don't know,' I said, hoping she would drop the subject, but she started hunting in all the kitchen cupboards for it.

'That's weird. We only used it the other day for the bread-and-butter pudding.'

This I knew, because I had been the one who took it out of the oven to serve up the pudding. The dish was still hot when I immersed it in the sink to soak the crust off, and it cracked in two in the cold water. I hid the pieces in the black wheelie bin outside, taking care to seal them inside a plastic bag and stash the bag under some other rubbish, so there was no chance of Mary Rose finding them.

'Did you put it somewhere else maybe?' she asked me.

I shook my head and pretended to be at a loss as to the whereabouts of the dish.

'Look,' she said, after she'd established that it was in none of the kitchen cupboards. After she'd looked in the fridge, and the oven, and the sideboard in the dining area. 'I don't mind if it's broken. I just want to know where it is, so I can stop searching for it.'

'I don't know why you're asking me,' I said. 'I've no idea where it is.'

From the way she looked at me I think she knew that I was lying, but she didn't pursue it. She just narrowed her eyes and nodded at me, very slowly and sadly. I remember feeling defensive then, because I had the sense that Mary Rose saw a pathology to my behaviour that I could not perceive myself. She believed that I was a product of the family that had produced me, and the house that had for so long sheltered me, while I was still labouring under the illusion that I was a free agent. That there was nothing in the past that was driving the present, when in fact it was the past that was pulling the present by the nose. Every time my father ever put me down. Every time my mother ever lowered her eyes to the table instead of rising to my defence. The past was a river that carried me with it, but I did not see that then, except in tiny glimpses of truth reflected back at me in Mary Rose's clear blue eyes. Looking at my childhood through Mary Rose's eyes, I see now how unpleasant it was, and how it need not have been so.

When my brother and I were children there was a game we sometimes played called Houdini. It involved him tying me to a kitchen chair with the orange nylon rope my mother kept in a kitchen drawer for use as a clothes line. Terry would tie my hands behind my back with the rope and attach it by a series of laborious knots to the bars of the kitchen chair. I had to somehow wriggle out of my bonds, while Terry ran the stopwatch on his digital wristwatch to see how long it would take me to get free. If I managed to free myself within the hour, I won. If I had to beg him to release me, he won.

'You call that a *game*?' said Mary Rose.

'Sure, it was only a bit of harmless fun,' I said, in my father's voice.

Another of the games we played as children was called Splash. It involved me crossing the Dodder weir in my bare feet, while Terry and his friends used long branches to try to knock me into the water. I expected Mary Rose to laugh when I told her this, but she didn't. She didn't even smile.

'You were bullied,' she said. 'Your brother bullied you.'

'Ah no,' I told her, shaking my head. 'Sure, that was just the way of it then.'

Mary Rose had no brothers, so how would she know?

'The boys I knew were always giving each other Chinese burns,' I explained. 'They used to pull the wings off butterflies and put bangers up cat's arses on Hallowe'en. That's just what boys did, when I was a kid.'

'Did *you* ever pull the wings off a butterfly?' she asked me, horrified.

'Well, no,' I said, which was true. I never did pull a wing off a butterfly or put a banger up a cat's arse. Those were all things my brother did, and I was led to believe it was a sign of weakness in me that I didn't join in. I only came to understand later, through Mary Rose's eyes, that I was a better person than my brother, and that this was something I should by rights be proud and not ashamed of, as I had once been. Of course, it seems obvious now, but it wasn't obvious then, not to me at least.

When I was a kid my brother played rugby, whereas I didn't. Rugby terrified me – I was small for my age and afraid of the prospect of boys twice my size bearing down on me with the intention of knocking me to the ground – so I preferred to play soccer, a preference my father and my brother poured scorn on, because soccer at that time was not considered a worthy game. Soccer was 'Peil Luther', the Englishman's football. It was a working-class game, played only in the housing estates of north Dublin, whereas rugby was a middle-class game, played by the likes of us. More nuanced even than that: rugby was a leg-up to a class one rung above us on the social ladder. We lived in a two-storey red-brick house on a narrow, tree-less terraced street, while my brother's rugby-playing friends lived mostly in three-storey houses, on wider streets lined with large trees. Infected by the microcosmic snobberies of the country we lived in, my parents were elevated in their own eyes by my brother's rugby-playing career and spoke of it at every opportunity.

'So, do you play rugby too?' a visiting school friend of my father's once asked me.

One of the rare occasions I remember us ever having a visitor. One of the rare occasions my father ever produced anything like a friend. This man was a priest, home on holiday from his work on the missions in Brazil. He had been invited to eat with us, and my mother had been ironing linens to befit a papal conclave. My father had for once produced a bottle of wine, and we were all assembled around the table in the dining room, which had a stale smell of disuse that even the raft of beeswax candles my mother had lit could not dispel.

'Oh no,' said my father. 'David's not a rugby player. David prefers to read comics and play with toy planes, God help us.'

'Did your mother not stick up for you?' Mary Rose asked me, when I told her this story.

'No,' I said, and it did seem strange to me, when I thought about it. That was how I came to see that my mother had been cowed, just as I was, while we all pretended not to notice. In the same way that we pretended not to notice that my father was a miser and a small-minded bigot, and that my aunt Marguerite was a lesbian and that this was the reason she was eventually discouraged from coming to our house by my father. All those things were there, in plain sight, but I chose not to see them. That was the way of it then.

It was very sad to see the effect Mary Rose's death had on her parents. Living with myself every day, I saw no visible difference in my own appearance. I looked much the same as I always had, and people made a point of telling me I looked well, as if that meant anything, but Willie and Moya looked terrible. Moya had been such a good-looking woman when I met her, small-boned and pretty like Kitty, with bright eyes that touched on everything with the glinting interest of a bird. Despite her delicate build, there was a strength to her that I always found impressive. This was a woman who would think nothing of cooking dinner for twenty people, or washing all the windows in the house, but in the wake of Mary Rose's death her strength abandoned her. She seemed unsurprised by what had happened to Mary Rose, as if she had been waiting for this thing all her life without knowing exactly how or why it would come, and now that it had, there was no point in putting up a fight. She could hang up her boots.

Willie was the opposite. Before, he had been a man of bounding innocence, a man who took delight in all the blessings life had showered upon him without ever for a moment worrying that they would be taken away, but what happened to Mary Rose shattered this innocence. Where once he had been pink and buoyantly upright, he became grey and pathetically stooped. Of course, he was over eighty when Mary Rose died, but whereas before her death he might have passed for seventy, now he looked ninety. It was shocking to see.

'Willie,' I said, when I went to see them on what would have been Mary Rose's birthday, the first since she'd died. It was typical of Mary Rose that she'd always marked her own birthday by sending her mother flowers. 'It's her day as much as mine,' she used to say. 'She's the one who deserves the flowers.' After Mary Rose died, I decided I would carry on the tradition, so I texted Willie that morning to tell him I'd call round.

'David,' he said, putting his hand on my shoulder and drawing me into the hall. There was none of the Daithí from him now. None of the bonhomie. He was in permanently funereal mode.

I went ahead of him into the kitchen, where the Aga was

cold and bare of pots and pans. There were no plants on the windowsill. No happy muddle of postcards and bills on the table. In all the years I'd been going there, the kitchen always smelled of roasting meat or lemon cake or freshly brewed coffee, but now it smelled of nothing but cleaning detergent.

'Here,' I said, holding out the flowers, which I had chosen with great care in the florist's on my way. They were a far cry from the filling-station carnations I had brought for Moya the first time I visited that house, with my veneer of panache that she no doubt saw through. I remember how she gripped my fingers in her hand and squeezed them hard as she kissed me goodbye, and I understood that she was warning me, with what I would soon come to know as her fierce brand of love, to be good to her girl.

'For Moya,' I told Willie, handing the flowers to him.

He nodded and carried them over to the sink, dunking them into a jug of water without taking them out of their wrapping.

'How is she?' I asked him.

'Ah,' he said, trailing off on the word. 'She's upstairs lying down. You'll have to excuse her.'

'And you? How are you, Willie?'

'Oh, I'm well enough.' He looked around the kitchen as if he'd never been there before.

'No news on the BEA investigation,' he said, referring to the French civil aviation bureau with all the fluency of an aviation industry professional. I had seen this before in the parents of a sick child who become as knowledgeable about the child's drugs and vital statistics as the doctors; the relatives of the victim of an unsolved murder who become more effective at media lobbying than any PR person; the subjects of medical misadventure who sit up at night poring over legal documents until they become lay experts in litigation.

In the same way, Willie had, in the ninth decade of his life, developed a specialist knowledge of plane-crash investigations. He had brushed off his schoolboy French to bore through long technical documents. He'd hired a translator to help him negotiate the Arabic.

'Nothing from the Egyptians, of course. They were supposed to publish their report by May, but there's no sign of it.'

'No surprise,' I said.

'No. But there is something I'd like to show you. Come into my study for a minute . . .'

He moved towards the door, then turned back and pointed at me.

'Do you want tea?'

'No, no, I'm grand, thanks.'

We passed back out through the hall and I cast a glance upstairs to where Moya was lying, medicated no doubt, in her bedroom. I had a heavy sense of her being up there, and I wondered could she hear our voices. I felt I was betraying her by indulging Willie's obsession with the progress of the investigation. I knew that she, like me, didn't want to know.

'Now,' said Willie, turning on the light in his study.

I saw there were files piled high on the desk, files on the leather armchair by the window, boxes of files on the floor. It was worse than the last time I'd been there, which was worse than the time before. The only indication of Willie's previous life was the skeleton he had on a stand in the corner of the room – I knew it had been a graduation present from his godfather – and the clay model of a golfer one of Jean Anne's kids had made him one year for Christmas. Everything else was plane-crash stuff.

'Where to find it is the thing,' he was saying, rummaging through a pile of papers on the desk, while I waited.

I studied the bulletin board he had on the wall above his

desk. It was a serial killer's collage of maps and photographs and charts. One graphic showed a map with France in the top left-hand corner and Egypt down in the bottom right. An unbroken line traced the flight path of MS804 all the way as far as Karpathos in Greece, with a tiny little black image of a plane moving only a small distance past the island before the flight path broke into a dotted line, and a dialogue box noted the failure of repeated attempts to make contact with the pilot at 00.27 GMT. Another dialogue box noted that the plane disappeared from radar at 00.30.

'Where did I put the bloody thing?' said Willie, sitting down heavily in the carver chair he had at his desk. He started fumbling through a pile of papers in his lap.

I couldn't take my eyes off the bulletin board. There were pictures of the wreckage: mangled pieces of metal and a battered sneaker laid out in a warehouse, on what looked like green lino. I don't know how Willie could bear to have those photographs on his wall, but I suppose he hardly saw them, so buried was he in the facts. The forensics. The politics of it.

'Okay, here it is,' he said, reaching into the breast pocket of his shirt for his reading glasses. 'Let me see. Yes, that's it.'

He started reading bits out to me. Something about avionics. Something about the 'fall rate'. The field of debris.

'Makes sense, when you think about it,' he said, looking up at me over his glasses.

'Could be something in it, all right,' I said, wishing for his sake that I cared.

'I'm going to Paris again next week,' he told me, as he shuffled back out to the kitchen. 'I want to shake a few trees.'

'Oh, good,' I said. 'Hopefully something will come of that.'

I don't know what he made of my disinterest, but he never commented on it, and I never tried to explain it to him. I had my own way of mourning Mary Rose, as pointless and psychologically dubious as his was, if not more so, but I mentioned it to nobody. We were each of us in our own bubble of grief, like astronauts moving through the same other-worldly terrain, unable to communicate with each other except by hand signal. Each word we spoke seemed to drop into a pool of silence.

Willie filled the kettle from the tap and turned it on. Went to the fridge for the milk, taking care to pour some from the carton into a jug before he set it out on the table. He took the sugar bowl down out of a cupboard. Found a spoon for it in a drawer. Every movement was slow and deliberate, like a child who has only recently been trusted with the tea making.

He walked over to the door.

'Moya,' he called up the stairs. 'David's here if you want to come down for tea.'

He waited there a minute, but when there was no answer he came back into the kitchen and poured the boiling water into the teapot, carrying it over to the table with great care.

'I'm afraid I don't have any biscuits to offer you,' he said, sitting down at last.

'Don't worry, Willie. I don't need any biscuits. I'm happy with the tea.'

'You'll have to forgive her,' he said, rubbing his face with his hands, as if he was trying to rub something away. 'This is a hard day for her.'

'I know it is.'

'She's turned her face to the wall.'

What could I say? We drank our tea, and we talked about this and that without really saying anything much. It was only when he was seeing me out that he locked eyes with me.

'I won't let go of it, David,' he said. 'I won't give up until I know what happened.'

'I know you won't, Willie,' I said, when what I really wanted to tell him was that, for his own sake, for Moya's sake if nothing else, it might be better if he did.

In the year after Mary Rose died, my dreams of her began to thin out. In time I dreamed of her not every night but perhaps only once or twice a week. The nature of the dreams changed too. Whereas at first I had the sense that she was lost and looking for a way home, after a while she seemed to be pursuing another life, in some other place. In one of my recurring dreams she was a violinist in an orchestra – bear in mind that Mary Rose had not a musical note in her head – in another she had signed up with the US Army and was being posted to Afghanistan. On the third night of my holiday in Aiguaclara she appeared to me in a new dream. In this one, she had cut her hair short, and she looked tanned and happy.

'I like where I'm living now,' she told me.

I woke with a feeling of great relief. I had not realized how much I worried about Mary Rose, and how anxious I was about her well-being, as if she was only missing and not in fact gone from this earth. It made me very glad to hear that she was all right.

15

The French woman was sitting at a table on the hotel terrace the next morning when I arrived down for my coffee. I looked around for somewhere to sit, searching out a place at some remove from her, but the only free table was the one next to her, so I had no choice but to sit down at it. I was anxious that she might think I had chosen the table next to her deliberately.

'Hello,' I said, as I pulled a chair back and sat into it.

'Oh, hello.' She put her coffee cup down and turned to face me. She had not seen me until that moment.

'Busy here this morning,' I said, in the hope that this would serve as an illustration of why I had been left with no recourse but to take the table next to hers. Instead it ended up sounding like a lame effort at small talk.

'Oh yes,' she said, graciously. 'Maybe it's because it's the weekend. It's always busy here at the weekends.'

She had excellent but strongly accented English.

'There seem to be more Americans here this year,' I said. And it was true. I had been hearing Americans everywhere. No doubt there had been an article in the *New York Times* describing Aiguaclara as the hidden gem of the Mediterranean. 'When we first came here it was all Dutch,' I added, cringing at the inanity of my own conversation. I was like an instrument that was hopelessly out of tune. I had lost my capacity for idle talk.

'Are you English?' she asked me.

'No, I'm Irish. I'm from Dublin.'

'Oh yes, Dublin,' she said with a lift in her voice, and I was aware of the twinge of guilt I always suffer at being so effortlessly elevated in the eyes of strangers by virtue of my nationality alone. It has never seemed fair to me, the automatic popularity that comes of being Irish, compared to the poor Belgians or the Germans or, God help them, people from Luxembourg.

'You're French?' I said, without waiting for an answer. 'From Paris?'

'I live in Paris, but I'm from Toulouse, originally. My parents still live there.'

So that explained the geography of it. They did not have far to come.

'I never asked your name, by the way. I'm David.'

'Oh yes,' she said, holding out her hand. 'I'm Claire.'

I tried to contain my surprise.

'Claire,' I said, briefly taking her hand in mine. 'It's nice to meet you.'

Her name was Claire!

Of all the amazing things, Mary Rose and I had guessed her name right. I could not get over the coincidence of it. The sheer improbability of it. More than that: it was a personal victory for Mary Rose, who believed in miracles. A defeat for me and my faith in statistics. As soon as Claire had paid her bill and left, I took out my phone to text Mary Rose. I still had her number stored in my phone, with a laughing picture of her attached to the caller ID.

Guess what, I wrote. The French woman in Aiguaclara is called Claire!

I pressed send, imagining her delight at getting the text. I could see her blue eyes widening. She would bite down on her bottom lip and shake her head slowly in amazement. 'I don't believe it,' she would say, when what she really meant was that she did believe it. Mary Rose was a great believer. She believed in everything.

The face of my phone went dark for a moment, then lit up again with an incoming call. It was Mary Rose calling me. Her laughing face, urging me to answer. My heart stalled as I answered.

'Hello?'

There was a short pause, and then I heard a man's voice on the other end.

'Who is this? Why are you sending me messages?'

His accent was not Irish. He sounded like the Romanian builder who did our kitchen extension. I found myself wondering *was* it the Romanian builder who did our kitchen extension, and if so, how on earth did he come to have Mary Rose's phone?

'This is David Dowling,' I said, struggling to get the words out. The rhythm of my heart had been lost. It was pumping too fast now, in an effort to make up for that skipped beat.

'David Dowling?' he said. 'I don't know any David Dowling.'

I could feel the blood rushing to my head. I felt very unwell, as if I might vomit or faint.

'You seem to have my wife's phone,' I said, gulping at the air like a drowning man. I was desperate for some little kindness.

'No,' said the man, immediately defensive. 'This is *my* phone. I buy it from Carphone Warehouse. I have receipt.'

The conversation began to take on a nightmare complexion. I felt the beach in front of me tilt, and the promenade with it, as if it was no more than a slide badly mounted on a projector.

'I'm sorry,' I said. 'I mean that you seem to have my wife's *number*. This is my wife's number.'

'No. This is not your wife's number. This is *my* number.'

My stomach lurched and I could almost imagine it falling out of me and rolling under the table.

'It *was* my wife's number,' I said, desperate now for some morsel of understanding. 'Before she died, this was her number.'

'Please,' he said, indignantly. 'I ask you. Not to use this number again.'

The phone call dropped out and I was left with a frozen image on the screen of Mary Rose laughing. Another second and the screen went black. I felt as if I had stumbled into another ditch of grief. The landscape of my bereavement was like that: it was like walking through a bog in the dark. You never knew when you might be swallowed up by it.

When Mary Rose died, the airline paid for me to see a counsellor.

'So, Mary Rose's parents have this house in the west of Ireland,' I told him.

The counsellor nodded, and he blinked his eyes at me, but he did not speak. He said very little in general, but he was a very active listener. He had all these little tricks to show you that he was listening and not nodding off, for his eighty euro an hour.

'There's a loft room above the kitchen where she and I always slept, and the loft room has this pitch-pine beam running right across it.'

I used my hand to show how the beam ran across the room, at forehead height.

'The first few times I stayed there, I kept walking into that bloody beam.'

The counsellor nodded and inclined his head forward a little, to show me that he was waiting to hear what was coming next.

'That's what I feel like now,' I told him. 'I feel like there's a low hanging wooden beam, right in front of me, and I keep walking slap bang into it. A hundred times a day I walk into that beam, and the pain hits me, right here, between the eyes.'

To illustrate my point, I thumped myself hard on the forehead with the heel of my hand. There was a dull thud but no pain. I had not managed to replicate the shock of it.

'I wonder if I'm ever going to get used to that beam being there. I wonder if I'll ever learn not to walk into it.'

The counsellor leaned back in his chair and crossed his legs.

'What do you think?' he asked me.

He made a point of never offering me any answers. All he did was occasionally throw my own questions back at me.

'I have no idea,' I said. 'I don't know if I even *want* the pain to go away. Sometimes it feels like it's the only thing I still have of Mary Rose.'

In time I could have told him that I never did learn to duck to avoid the pain of losing her. What happened was that I found myself stumbling into it less and less often. Imperceptibly at first: whereas at the start it happened to me a hundred times a day, by the time a month had gone by I was struck by the blow of it perhaps only ninety-five times a day. Another month and it hit me only ninety times in a twenty-four-hour period, and by the time a year had passed, there was sometimes a whole hour when I did not collide with the pain of it. It wasn't that it was any less painful when I did, just that the intervals in between got longer and longer. That's how I came to understand that I was healing.

16

It turned out that Claire's father was not called Anatole, as Mary Rose and I had surmised, but Lionel. He was an architect, not a film director, and he and his wife lived, not in a grand old apartment in Paris, but in a modern house in Toulouse that he himself had designed. His wife was called Beatrice, not Brigitte. The one thing Mary Rose and I had been right about, apart from the bull's eye we had scored with Claire's name, was that they despised the French. That was why they chose to holiday in Catalonia.

All this, I discovered on my first walk with Claire. She had expressed an interest in my ramblings that first morning we spoke on the hotel terrace, and I invited her to come along with me the following day. We agreed to rendezvous over coffee at the hotel, but as soon as this plan was formed I regretted it. All day and throughout that evening, I felt as unsafe as a snail who has ventured out of its shell. What I wanted more than anything was to crawl back in there, but I could see no way of cancelling the plan.

The next morning, I arrived on the hotel terrace to find Claire already seated at a table under the plumed pink branches of a tamarisk tree. She had a cup of coffee in front of her, and she was buttering a large piece of toasted baguette. She smiled when she saw me.

'Good morning,' I said, but I hesitated to sit down. I could not sit at a neighbouring table, as I had done before, but it seemed overly familiar to take a chair at hers without being asked. I was conscious of how little I knew her.

'Aren't you going to take a coffee?' she asked, and I took that as an invitation to sit with her. I signalled my order to the waiter, who for once caught my eye.

'Miracles never cease,' I said, and she laughed.

She was wearing a black vest top and a pair of smartly tailored black shorts, and her hair was raked into a ponytail at the back of her head. The red nail polish had been removed, I noticed.

'I thought we'd walk through the forest as far as Aiguablava.'

I tried to make it sound casual, but the truth was that I had planned our route meticulously. I was nervous at the prospect of spending the morning with a stranger, and I wanted to leave nothing to chance. I had even thought to pack an extra bottle of water for her in my knapsack, not only to ensure that we had enough, but because I dreaded the intimacy of offering her mine.

'We can take the coastal path from Aiguablava as far as Fornells.'

'Oh yes,' she said, 'that works.'

When we had finished our coffee, we struck off up the road that leads out of Aiguaclara, through a conurbation of holiday homes and a row of tennis courts, into the forest. The pavement was too narrow for us to walk side by side, so I stepped out on to the road, taking care not to walk too fast for Claire. She walked a little slower than me, so I had to keep correcting my pace. I wasn't sure whether I should make conversation. I would have preferred not to, but to walk in silence was awkward. You have to know somebody very well to walk with them in silence.

'Are you familiar with this road?' I asked her.

'Oh yes. This is the road we take when we drive to Begur. But I've never walked it before.'

'The turn-off is up here,' I said, indicating the signpost that directed hikers off the road and through the forest. It was signalled by a red-and-white painted flag that was replicated on tree trunks here and there along the trail. I held out my arm to indicate that she should go ahead of me. She looked up into my face briefly, as if to check something, and then she walked on.

'Do you know the names of these trees?' I asked her, for something to say. The pines I knew, but there were other species I could not identify. I have never been good on trees.

She turned, briefly.

'I know the names, but not in English. In French we say *pins*.'

I could have tried to explain that it was not the pine trees I meant but the others. Instead I let the misunderstanding lie. Let her think me an idiot, what did I care.

She stopped at a fork in the path to study the markings on the trees. To the left, a pine trunk was marked with a flag with an X through it. The path to the right was the correct one, I knew, but I hung back, not wanting to be a know-it-all.

'This way?'

She was pointing to the right.

'Yes, I think so.'

A hundred yards down the path, I could see a tree trunk marked with the red-and-white flag.

'Oh yes,' she said, registering it at last.

The sun leaked through the gaps in the leaf canopy as we walked. At one point the path came out from under the trees and ran through a meadow that was dotted with red poppies.

'All we're missing is the Yellow Brick Road,' I said.

'Oh yes,' she said, and smiled.

'I might stop to take some water,' she said, after another minute or two.

'Good idea. It's getting hot.'

I couldn't help but notice how every little thing needed to be negotiated between us. To stop. To drink. To set off again. Mary Rose and I were so entirely in tune with each other that we had long ago dispensed with any need for such communications. Like lifelong dance partners, we hardly needed to speak. We could anticipate each other's every move.

'I don't feel like cooking tonight,' she might say on a rainy Wednesday, and I would tell her I'd already booked us a table at the local pizza place. 'I thought we might go walking this weekend,' I would say, thinking out loud, and she would say that was just what she was thinking – she was thinking we'd go walking in the mountains, and have an early supper afterwards in the Roundwood Inn. 'How about stew this Sunday?' she might suggest, and I would agree that a beef stew was just the thing for Sunday, and would we invite her parents? Day by day, week by week, our lives unfolded with a choreography so long practised that we didn't even have to think about it. It was only in its absence that I became aware of it. If I ever wanted to share my life with another woman, every little detail would have to be ironed out laboriously. I wasn't sure I had the energy for it.

'Should we stop and rest here for a while?' I suggested, when we got beyond the crowded beach at Aiguablava. The path led around the headland to a small inlet with a private slipway and a short stretch of rocky shore where we could sit in peace.

She looked at her watch.

'It's nearly midday,' she said with some surprise, and I felt a sense of accomplishment in the fact that I had, at least, helped her to pass some of the time that weighed so heavily on her. I could do that for her, if nothing else.

*

'So, what was I?' she asked me, as we sat on the rocks and looked out at the teal-coloured sea.

I had confessed to her our voyeuristic interest in her family, explaining how Mary Rose and I had watched them from afar, attributing names and professions to them all.

'Your father was a film director,' I told her. 'Your mother was a model.'

'I will be sure to tell her that,' she said. 'She will be delighted.'

We were alone in the cove, apart from two girls sunbathing topless on a nearby rock. There was something grotesque about their exposed breasts – they reminded me of the chicken fillets laid out on stainless-steel trays in the window of my father's shop. Don't get me wrong, I am a fan of breasts, especially small upright ones, but I've never been able to appreciate them in public. Never understood how men can sit around and feast their eyes on Page 3 girls in plain view of the rest of the world. The whole point of nudity, to me, is that it's experienced in privacy.

'We decided your brothers were amateur boxers, as young men.'

She smiled. Shook her head.

'They were cyclists, actually. My brother Edo broke his nose once, in a fall from his bicycle. Maybe that's why you thought he was a boxer.'

'He became a politician, we decided.'

She laughed at that. 'I can actually imagine him as a politician!'

I did not mention that we also had him for a serial philanderer.

'Actually, Edo works at the university,' she told me. 'He's an economist.'

So it would be students he'd be sleeping with then, I thought.

'What about Christophe?' she asked. Christophe was her younger brother. 'What was Christophe in your movie?'

'Oh, Christophe was a drug dealer.'

She clapped her hands together in a delighted little bout of applause. 'So, Christophe was the black mutton.'

I smiled but did not point out her mistake.

'He likes to smoke marijuana, Christophe. When he was young, he smoked *a lot* of marijuana.'

I knew that just by looking at him.

'He doesn't deal drugs though? This is too disappointing.'

She laughed at that, and I was surprised by how happy it made me to be the cause of her laughter. I felt the glow of a good deed.

'Actually, he's an architect. He works at my father's office.'

She used the same words over and over again, I noticed. It reminded me of those exercises you have to do when you're learning a language. Write ten sentences using the word 'actually'.

'So, what was I?'

She hugged her legs in to her chest, resting her chin on her knees as she waited for my answer.

'You were a food writer. You wrote a cookery column for *Le Monde*.'

'Not bad,' she said. 'I'm an editor, actually. I work at a fashion magazine, in Paris.'

Hence the red nails, I thought.

'I work in the media too,' I told her. 'At least, I did, before Mary Rose died. I'm not sure what I do now.'

Something shifted in me when Mary Rose died. I began to see reporting as a ridiculous job. I couldn't see the point in it.

'Don't you work now?'

'I couldn't go back. Not after what happened. I couldn't find the headspace for it.'

Of all the professional people I encountered in the aftermath of the crash, the reporters alone seemed to me to have no useful purpose. The airline officials who surrounded us in those early days were at least the purveyors of first-hand information. The embassy staff offered practical assistance in handling logistics. The plane-crash investigators might one day establish what had happened, but the reporters who swarmed around me were nothing but an annoyance, and I could not see myself ever rejoining their ranks. For the first time in my life, I wished I had a practical skill. I would have liked to be a doctor or an engineer. I would even have settled for being a plumber or an electrician. I had notions of signing up for a night course in DIY. I wanted very much to be useful, but I didn't quite know how.

'I don't know what I would have done without my work,' said Claire. 'For me, it's the only way to survive the day.'

'I'd like to work again,' I said, learning the truth of what I was saying only as the words were coming out of my mouth. 'I'm not sure what I want to do. I need to think of something new.'

I had blood money coming to me from the airline. Already they had made an interim payment to me of twenty-five thousand dollars, through their insurance company. This, added to the voluntary redundancy package I took from work, and the not inconsiderable sum of money I had inherited from my parents, would keep me covered for the foreseeable future. I was suddenly and unexpectedly rich, largely because of the loss of Mary Rose. A feeling like being washed up on a desert island, bereft and alone but surrounded by bountiful beauty and sunshine.

'It's a strange thing to receive a payment for the life of your wife,' I said to Claire.

I had not yet decided what to do with the money. I could

donate it to a charity in Mary Rose's name. I could share it out among her sisters or her godchildren. Then again, I could keep it. I'm ashamed to say that this was beginning to emerge as the most attractive option.

'After Tristan and Élodie died, I wanted to make an account,' said Claire, breathing a sigh in through her nose and out again.

I did not at first understand what she meant.

'I started counting everything.' She held up a thumb. 'I counted all the money we spent on their baby clothes and all the toys my husband bought for them and everything we spent on their bedrooms. I counted the cost of all the food they ate and all the medicine we had to buy for them.' For each item on her list she opened out another finger. 'The haircuts. The new shoes. The picture books.' She had run out of fingers, but the list went on. 'Private speech therapy for Élodie,' she said. 'A guitar for Tristan. A trip to Bristol, for him to learn English.'

I found myself getting sadder and sadder as I listened to her.

'Skis,' she said. 'Ski boots. Ski helmets. Ski school.'

The topless girls were packing up. They pulled their clothes and shoes out of their beach bags and dressed themselves. They rolled up their towels and stashed their fags away in their bags, casting one last look behind them before they left, to make sure they had forgotten nothing. I heard their voices spiral away from us as they climbed the steps, but Claire's went on.

'All the music lessons. The cinema tickets. The ice-creams. Imagine, I counted up how many ice-creams we bought them every summer.'

I remembered, then, how an airline once lost a suitcase of mine and I had to fill out a form for the insurance company detailing everything that was in the suitcase. It was hard to remember every single thing, and even when I did manage to compile a list it was somehow inadequate to describe what had been lost. In that suitcase was a belt Mary Rose had bought for me in Barcelona on our honeymoon, and a pair of brogues that I had owned for so long they were worn soft in all the right places. There was no point in putting down a replacement value for those things, because I did not want them replaced. I wanted the old ones back. Claire's list was similarly pointless, and yet I understood her desire to quantify her loss. To attach a number to it that would somehow represent the enormity of what had been taken from her. What she wanted was a reckoning.

'Did you ever reach a total?' I asked her.

She shrugged. 'It was a lot of money.' She held her hand up, with her fist tightly clenched as if she was holding some small thing that might at any moment escape.

'It was a lot of money,' she said again. 'And in one moment . . .' She threw open the fingers of her hand, releasing the invisible thing she was holding into the air.

'. . . Pouf, it was gone.'

17

There's a difference between losing a child – or two children in Claire's case – and losing a wife. That's what I discovered on my walks with her. Whereas at first it seemed to me that we had a lot in common – we had both been bereaved, after all, and in the cruellest of circumstances – I soon learned that the terrain we had travelled was different in almost every imaginable way.

'I think it's different for everyone,' she said. 'That's what makes it so difficult.'

It was our second time walking together, and this time we had taken the car south along the coast, parking it at the top of a local hill, which allowed us to take the path down to the sea. The views were spectacular.

'What do you mean?' I asked her.

'When Tristan and Élodie were killed, my husband reacted very differently from me.'

She was walking just ahead of me. She had her arms out on either side of her, balancing herself with the help of an invisible railing as she negotiated the rocky path down the hillside.

'He was very angry. He wanted somebody to blame.'

The orange clay of the path was bone dry and carpeted with pine needles and loose stones. To walk downhill required a certain amount of care, so we were both looking at our feet as we went. Every so often Claire would pause for a second and look back to make sure I was listening.

'All day, he was taking calls from journalists. He was so busy with this, it was like a job for him.'

Many times, I had been the journalist on the other end of that line, so I knew how it worked. In the aftermath of the incident – a bomb, or a shooting, or whatever it might have been – the bereaved person is demented. Loaded with filthy adrenaline and desperate to talk about what happened, they answer the phone at all hours of the day and night. They are unskilled and unguarded, and they invariably say more than they should. They are easy prey, and the journalist picks them off without compunction.

'Every day, he was on the radio.'

Of course he was.

'Then, one day, I came downstairs and there were . . .' She stopped on the path, and I came to a stop beside her. She was wearing her dark glasses, so I couldn't see her eyes, only my own reflection in the lenses. Behind her a single speedboat cut a streak through the hazy blue of the bay. 'There were all these *people* in my living room. They had cameras and lights, and they were moving all the furniture around. *My* furniture, they were picking it up and moving it around.'

I winced, knowing only too well what they were doing. They would have placed an armchair in the corner, away from the window, where they could get the right angle on the lights. A framed photograph of the children would have been moved from a table elsewhere in the room and placed on a shelf or a piece of furniture behind the chair, where it would be clearly in shot.

'I couldn't stand it,' she said, shaking her head as she turned and began to pick her way down the hill again. 'I went to stay with my parents. I'm not sure Hugo even noticed I was gone.'

It occurred to me then that I had at least enjoyed the luxury of owning Mary Rose's death. Mary Rose's parents and her sisters were of course also bereaved, but as the husband I was at the very top of the hierarchy of mourning, in a position I had to share with nobody. Poor Claire had been forced to share it with her husband.

'I think he was really crazy,' she told me. 'Especially when the journalists stopped calling him – then he started to go completely crazy. He couldn't believe they weren't interested in the story any more.'

I had been there too, on the other side. No matter how big the story, there always comes a moment when a new one breaks and the reporters move on. It can happen as suddenly as a gunshot, scaring the crows out of the trees.

'Hugo was so angry. He started calling them on their portable phones.'

I remembered with a lick of guilt all the times when a family member would ring me on my mobile, long after I'd left a story behind me. How I would hear their name and struggle to remember the details of the case, maybe even the name of their loved one. I had become a stranger to them, when once I had pretended to be their friend.

'He even went to one guy's house on a Sunday,' said Claire. 'The guy had to call the police when Hugo wouldn't leave.'

Maybe that was why I didn't give any interviews after Mary Rose died. I knew the life cycle all too well, and I couldn't bear to subject myself to the inevitable humiliation that would ensue. I left all that to Mary Rose's dad.

'He sounds like my wife's father,' I told Claire. 'He's obsessed with finding out what happened.'

'What does her mother do?'

'She does nothing,' I said. 'She's just waiting to die.'

Claire nodded. 'She's old,' she said. 'Hopefully, she won't have to wait for very long.'

That barren grief was something I could well understand; it was the other type I found hard to relate to. The kind Mary Rose's sisters embarked on, harnessing its horsepower and turning it to good causes. When Mary Rose died, Kitty held a singalong *Dirty Dancing* in her honour at an art-house cinema in Dublin. Jean Anne organized a group of friends to run the Dublin Marathon in her name.

'They had T-shirts printed up and everything,' I told Claire. 'They raised enough money to buy an incubator for a hospital in Africa.'

Aren't they amazing, was what everyone said. And I said yes, they are amazing, because it *was* amazing to me, what they had done. I was amazed beyond the point of comprehension as to how they found the energy for it. I could not find the energy for anything other than breathing.

'And you, what did you do?'

'Me?' I had not told anyone this, for fear of worrying them, but I could tell Claire. I could tell her anything, just as she could tell me anything, and neither of us would be shocked or upset or even surprised, because we had both of us lost the capacity for all of those things.

'Sure,' she said with a shrug.

'I drove out to Dublin airport every day. I drove around the back of the airport and parked my car by the side of the road, where I could watch the planes taking off.'

Sometimes I would see other plane spotters there, but I stayed in my car, taking care not to make eye contact with them. I would tilt my seat back, like I was in the front row at the cinema, and peer up out of the windscreen as plane after plane heaved itself into the air over my head. They flew so low that their silver bellies blocked out the sky and the sound of their engines filled the air. In that moment, there was nothing else.

'Sometimes I sat there for hours, just watching the planes.'

'Was it a bomb?' Claire asked, pausing again on the path.

'I don't know. They don't think so, now.'

It seemed extraordinary to me that we were tossing that word between us so casually. There we were, following a winding path down a quiet hillside in Catalonia, with pleasure boats in the bay and sunbathers on the beaches, and we were talking about a bomb, like it was a normal thing. A bomb!

'At first they thought it was,' I told Claire. 'They said they'd found explosives in some of the wreckage. There were traces of it on the bodies, they said. Then we heard that wasn't true. Now they think it was the co-pilot's phone. They think the phone overheated while it was charging and caused a fire in the cockpit.'

'My God,' she said.

'The thing is, I'm not sure I care. It seems a bit weird to me that I don't care, but there it is. I don't care.'

'No,' she said, very firmly. 'I don't think it's weird. It's not weird at all. Why would you care what happened? It makes no difference. It won't bring her back.'

We had reached a curve in the path, where a low wall provided a lookout point, so we stopped for a water break. Sitting on the wall, we were looking down on the winding coastline that lay ahead of us. We could see the beach we were aiming for, with tiny little people dotted about on towels on the sand and swimmers rolling about in the waves and toy pedalos tethered to chains in the shallows.

'What about you?' I asked her.

'Oh yes,' she said, as if she had forgotten where she was in all of this and was only now remembering. 'Me.'

She was looking at the view, but I had the sense that she wasn't seeing it.

'When the ambulance people found Élodie, there was a young man with her,' she told me. 'A complete stranger, imagine! He was sitting on the floor beside her, and he was holding her hand. He waited with her until they took her away.' She turned to me. 'Afterwards, I wanted very much to meet that young man.'

'I can well understand that.'

'I became obsessed with finding him. I didn't care about the investigation or the politics, but I wanted very much to find that man.' She shrugged. 'So you see, we all have our obsessions.'

'Did you find him?'

'Oh yes,' she said, and she turned away from me again, facing out to sea as she spoke. 'I found him eventually. He was from Scotland, actually – from Glasgow in Scotland – but he came to see me in Paris, and I was able to thank him. It was very important for me to know that there was some-body with Élodie that day. It was important for me to know that there was a good person with her, in between all that evil. I had some peace, because of that.'

'I'm glad,' I said. 'I'm glad you found him.'

'Now, come on,' she said, slapping her hands down on the fronts of her thighs. 'Let's get moving or we'll never get there.'

She brushed the dust from the back of her shorts and set off down the path, with me following behind her. We walked fast, and mostly in silence, all the way down to the sea. The sun was directly above us and mercilessly hot, and by the time we reached the beach a swim was the only thing on my mind.

Claire pulled off her T-shirt to reveal the swimsuit she was wearing underneath her clothes. I had my togs in my back-pack, so I had to perform an awkward manoeuvre to change under the cover of a towel. Not since I was in my twenties had I felt so gauche in the presence of a woman. I was raw and exposed, without the protection of my marital status. I felt stripped of a layer of dignity. Thankfully, Claire went ahead of me into the water, leaving me to conclude my contortions in private. By the time I got in, she was already a hundred metres out, swimming a careful, bobbing breaststroke with her head up out of the water and her sunglasses still on. I dived under the surface, registering a shudder of pleasure at the shock of immersing my head in cold water. I had none of the old horror of what was under there, thanks to a course of swimming lessons I had taken in my local pool over the winter, one of the things I had forced myself to do to somehow fill my days now that I was no longer working. 'Not bad for a man,' was the grudging praise the swimming teacher had for me when I swam my first full length, but thanks to her I was now capable of doing a passable front crawl without fear of drowning.

'I forgot to bring some underwear with me,' said Claire, when we were back on the beach.

'Don't worry, we're in no rush. We can wait for your swimsuit to dry before we walk back.'

I laid my towel out for her and sat down beside her on the sand, thinking of nothing but the healing feeling of the heat drying my skin and the hollow rumble of hunger in my belly. I went digging in my rucksack and produced a bread roll I had buttered that morning in the apartment and filled with slices of Manchego cheese.

'Here,' I said, breaking it into two halves and handing the larger one to her. 'You might need something to keep you going.'

'Oh yes,' she said, 'thank you.'

I expected her to nibble at the roll, but she devoured it in no time. It made me happy that she had eaten it so heartily, and I wished I had brought more food with me. All I had left were some flat peaches, which I distributed between us. We ate them in dribbling silence, and I studied the sea in front of us, trying to gauge how far out it was to the marker buoys that separated the swimming area from the boats. There was a man swimming from buoy to buoy in a steady front crawl, and I watched him, trying to guess how far it was between each one. It could be two hundred metres, I figured, which would make a swim of at least a kilometre, if you went right down to the other end of the bay. I was thinking I would like to try it some day when I noticed that Claire was watching a pair of teenage boys who were playing in the waves. She was lying on her back, propped up on her elbows with her hands splayed on the sand, and she was watching the two boys very intently from behind her sunglasses.

The boys were beautiful as only boys of that age can be, their bodies slick as leaping salmons as they reached for the football they were lobbing between them. They were so lean you could count every one of their vertebrae, their shoulder blades as prominent as their hip bones. They were a miracle of skin and bone.

'*Ay, tío!*' I heard one of them shout, as he dived after a wide ball.

The other lad allowed himself to fall backwards, whirling his arms for comic effect as he hit the water with a slap.

From the angle I had on Claire, I could see that there were tears welling up behind her sunglasses and it struck me then that her grieving would be endless. Like the waves that kept breaking every few moments on the sand, it would keep on coming and there would be no end to it, not ever. No matter how long she lived, Claire would always be the mother of those two never-to-be-forgotten children. She would age them, month by month, as if they were alive, and every year that went by she would mourn all the things that had been lost with them. The birthdays. The graduations. A wedding, for Tristan perhaps, if not for Élodie. The possibility of grandchildren. What was lost to Claire was not just the past but the future too, and she would be living with the lack of it forever.

It was the same for Mary Rose's parents. Moya would always have three daughters. Willie would always count himself as the father of three girls. Jean Anne would remain the eldest, and Kitty the youngest, but there would remain between them the vivid presence of that beloved middle sister. For me it was different. I would forever mourn the loss of Mary Rose. I would miss her, forever, but my relationship with her ended on the day she died.

'You and your wife never had children?' Claire asked me.

'No,' I said. 'We never did.'

18

Mary Rose did get pregnant, once. It was the year before she died, January, as I remember. The conflict in eastern Ukraine had escalated and I had hopes that the foreign desk might send me out there. It seems strange to me now that, up until so very recently, I was still trying to build my career. Still trying to chase after some image I had of myself as a veteran foreign correspondent, when what I was, at best, was a conscientious functionary. It seems to me now that I could just as easily have built a career as a moderately successful accountant or solicitor. I was a hard worker, and I was bright enough to assimilate and regurgitate information, but I was never a real hack.

I have worked with reporters who would get out of their beds to investigate a loud noise on the street, in case it had the makings of a story. I've known journalists to unearth scoops while they were in hospital and file the copy from their sickbeds. A colleague of mine once tracked down the Bulgarian gang who had skimmed his credit card, and broke the story on the nine o'clock news. And while I did once entertain the notion that I was one of a kind with them, I left that behind me in the newsroom when I departed, along with a raincoat I forgot to take with me. It's probably still on the coat stand behind my desk, but I can't go back for it. It belongs to another time – I might as well try to go back to fifth-century Japan as go back to a time when I cared so much about work that I was hell-bent on getting myself sent to eastern Ukraine.

It's hard to imagine it now – now that I know that the time I had with Mary Rose was finite and fast running out – but I was so preoccupied with myself that winter that I was not, to my great regret, paying much attention to my wife. I had no reason to think that I should have been paying attention to her, any more than was usual, but if I had been, I might have noticed some small thing. An absence perhaps of the yellow Tampax wrappers that gathered in the wastebasket in our bathroom with cruel regularity every twenty-seven days. A deeper quality to her sleep, like a hibernating bear. She did not at first realize she was pregnant, she later told me. There were none of the symptoms she had been taught to expect – no nausea, no vomiting, no sudden increase in her sense of smell – so she assumed it was the start of the menopause and entered into it with private sorrow. The first indication she had that she was pregnant was when she was at her yoga class one day and started bleeding.

I was editing a package for the lunchtime bulletin when she rang me. The clock on my screen read 12.52, and I still had a section of script to cover with pictures or there would be a black hole in the middle of the package.

'Can I ring you back in five minutes?' I asked her, thinking it was odd that she was ringing me just before the bulletin. Mindful always of other people's lives, Mary Rose never rang me just before a bulletin.

'Okay,' she said. 'I'm in the hospital.'

'I thought you weren't working today.'

'I'm not.'

I didn't have time to ask her to explain. At the edge of my mind was some benign explanation, something that never formed itself into words but that she would no doubt illuminate when I rang her back. Feeling only the slightest touch of unease, I went back to editing my package, which I filed

237

in time to make the lead slot on the bulletin. By the time I got to Holles Street, Mary Rose had lost the child she had not even known she was carrying.

'Mary Rose is fine,' said the Indian nurse who led me along the corridor towards her. 'But she lost the baby.'

The word 'baby', so lovingly enunciated. It was a shock to me to hear it. Until that moment, I had not entirely understood what had happened. All that Mary Rose had said on the phone was that she was bleeding, but I had not understood why.

'We gave her some diazepam to settle her,' said the nurse, in a sweetly soothing voice. 'She's resting now.'

She led me into a ward where Mary Rose was curled on her side in a bed, with a dull expression in her eyes that frightened me more than anything she had told me on the phone. I experienced a moment of cowardice when the nurse very kindly hung back as we approached the bed. It was all I could do not to beg her to stay.

'Thank God you're okay,' I said, leaning in to kiss Mary Rose on the forehead.

Her arm lay outside the covers, a padded white plaster on the back of her hand. I sat down in the chair beside the bed and took her fingers in mine. Her eyes were dry, as if they'd been drained, but I could feel tears welling up in mine.

'Well, you,' I said.

'Well,' she said, and we sat for a long time in silence, staring into each other's eyes.

'I'm glad I was pregnant,' she said at last, in a voice I had only ever heard before in the departure lounge of an airport, the words rendered weightless by the tranquilliser in her bloodstream. 'It's nice to know I was pregnant, even if I didn't know it at the time. I think I'll always be glad that I was once pregnant.'

*

When I first met Mary Rose, she was a person who was capable of anything. Aside from her skills as a nurse, she could cook and sew buttons on shirts and darn socks and make bread. 'There's not much point in feminism if we only end up becoming as useless as men,' was something she said. She could drill holes in a wall and hang a shelf or a painting perfectly straight. She could change the wheel of her car without assistance and check the oil and water and the air pressure of the tyres. She could speak rudimentary Spanish and Italian as well as reasonably fluent French. And she could ski.

When we were growing up, nobody went skiing. Skiing was something Europeans did and, back then, we did not presume to think of ourselves as Europeans. That was before the days of cheap air travel, before the free travel area and the euro and the rising tide of prosperity resulted in planeloads of Irish people jetting off to the Alps and the Dolomites every winter in their Lidl and Aldi ski gear. Most Irish people never even went on sun holidays when I was a child. You were lucky if you made it as far as the Isle of Man. But Mary Rose and her family spent a week every winter in a ski resort in Switzerland because her mother loved to ski.

Never was the disparity in our upbringings so apparent as the first time she and I went on a ski trip together. She had her own boots, of course, while I had to hire a pair from a local shop. When I put them on, they were damp and sweaty inside, like socks someone else had been wearing on a long forced march. I struggled to even stand in my skis and Mary Rose was obliged to tow me to the start of the button lift, where I proceeded to tumble off the button every time I tried to grab hold of it, bringing the whole lift to a shuddering halt and sorely trying the patience of the surly lift attendant. In time, I managed to achieve a certain level of proficiency and I came to enjoy our subsequent ski holidays as much as, if not more than, Mary Rose did, but never in all the years did I manage to attain her level of nonchalant grace. She was a beautiful skier, which was why I was so shocked to see her lose her nerve.

It was February, barely a month after her miscarriage, and we had tagged along with a group of my friends on their annual trip to a resort near Morzine. It was Mary Rose who had insisted we go. Our tradition had always been to go skiing alone, during the school term when the resorts were child-free, despite repeated invitations from Deborah and Michael to join their expedition during the February mid-term.

'I think we should go with them this year,' said Mary Rose. 'It might be fun.'

Fun was not a word I associated with group activities, but perhaps because of the miscarriage I put up no protest.

It was night-time when we arrived, pulling up in our mini-bus outside a picture-postcard Alpine ski hotel. From the antique skis that decorated the wall of the bar to the cheery patchwork quilt on the bed and the smell of cedar rising up through the stairwell from the sauna in the basement, everything was just as it should be. We ate cheese fondue that night, and after dinner we played cards and drank Amaretto in front of the fire in the hotel bar, and I remember thinking how churlish it had been of me not to want to come. I felt very fond of my friends that night, and lucky to have them, and I even began to contemplate a future where Mary Rose and I might holiday with them again.

'Time to hit the hay,' Michael announced, after the third round of Amarettos.

Mary Rose was half asleep already, her head lying heavy as a stone on my shoulder. I had to heave her to her feet and drag her up the stairs.

'I'm too tired to brush my teeth,' she said, peeling her

clothes off and climbing in between the sheets in her bra and knickers. She curled on her side and I fell in behind her, sliding my knees into the backs of hers and threading my arm in the space between her arm and her waist. Her hair smelled of woodsmoke from the fire, and a thought formed in my head, but I fell asleep before I could voice it.

I woke at one point during the night to the lonely boom of an explosion sounding far up the mountain. Through the window, I could see nothing but darkness. I imagined men rising from their beds in the village to drive up the empty ski slopes and plant dynamite in the snow to blow away the risk of avalanche. Boom, went another one. Feeling as safe as a rabbit in its burrow, I closed my eyes and went back to sleep.

'I'm not sure about this,' Mary Rose said to me, as we rode up the mountain in the gondola the next morning. Already the first skiers were coming down the slopes below us. We could see them but not hear them, sealed in as we were in an eerie glass bubble.

'About what?' I asked her.

'About the skiing,' she said, working the space between her eyebrows into two deep vertical lines. 'I feel a bit nervous.'

'Oh, you'll be grand,' I told her. The mantra of my childhood. If I had been poised to enter the lion enclosure in Dublin Zoo, my father would have told me I'd be grand.

'Sure, you could do this in your sleep,' I told her. 'It's like riding a bike. You never lose it.'

It was only when we had been deposited at the top of the second set of lifts that I saw she was genuinely afraid. She stood, awkward on her skis and petrified by the sight of the valley far below. The lift continued to dump little clusters of skiers behind her. She was so unsteady I feared they would topple her over as they passed.

'Don't leave me,' she said, and there was a note of panic in her voice as she held out her hand to me. I reached back and took hold of her, towing her to a place of safety, as she had once towed me. I was struck by the reversal in our roles, but I was not overly alarmed. If anything, I may have been pleased to be the more confident skier at last. All day, I took pride in looking out for her, letting her go ahead of me at the top of each slope and waiting at the bottom until she had safely joined me.

'Is Mary Rose all right?' Deborah said to me that night at dinner.

Cara was there, and Tom and Angela, and all their hulking adult and almost-adult kids. The kids were relegated to the far end of the table, where they were attacking each other with fondue forks. Mary Rose and Michael were sitting across from me, holding a heated debate about *Charlie Hebdo* and Islam. Michael was arguing strenuously for the cartoonist's freedom of expression, but not for the freedom to wear a burka. Mary Rose was taking the opposite view: a woman should be free to wear whatever religious symbols she wants, she was saying, but newspapers and magazines should not be free to offend anyone's religious sensibilities. To Mary Rose, it was all about respect.

'I'm worried about her,' said Deborah.

'Why do you ask that?' I said, turning to her in surprise.

Deborah had not been told about the miscarriage, because Mary Rose had insisted nobody be told. Apart from her colleagues in the hospital, nobody but she and I knew, and that was the way she wanted to keep it. It seemed to me that it comforted her to carry the secret about with her, as if it was the baby itself that she was still carrying, and not the loss of it. So long as she kept it a secret, she had it to herself.

'She just seems . . .' She paused, searching for the right word.

'Seems what?' I asked.

'I don't know. She's not herself. She seems . . .'

I waited for her to find the word she was looking for.

'. . . unmoored,' she said at last.

I looked across the table and saw Mary Rose listening, with her eyebrows raised, to something Michael was saying. Her cheeks were scuffed with pink, and her eyes were bright, and she seemed to me just as she always was.

'Really?'

'Yes,' said Deborah, firmly. 'She's all at sea, the poor doll.'

'Right,' I said, knowing only one thing for sure, and that was that I could trust in Deborah's judgement.

All my life, Deborah has – almost literally – been my portal to an understanding of women. She lived across the road from me when we were growing up, and it was in her house that I found a parallel universe to balance the deficits in mine.

There were four girls in Deborah's family – two older than her and one younger – but there might as well have been fourteen of them for all the sound and fury they whipped up. There was always someone in that house sobbing, or wailing, or screaming with rage or laughter. Someone freaking out because a piece of clothing had been borrowed without permission, or a phone message forgotten. Deborah's sisters seemed always to be washing their hair, wrapping their heads up in bath towels that they twisted into precarious turbans. They spent hours attacking each other's heads with implements that looked more like fire irons to me than beauty paraphernalia. They used strange contraptions to separate out their toes while they painted their nails. They curled their eyelashes with metal clamps and ripped the hair off their legs using scalding pots of hot wax, all with a blithe disregard for my presence among them.

As Deborah's friend – only Deborah, the tomboy, would have had a boy as a best friend – I passed through that house without disturbing so much as a molecule in the air. I might as well have been the Invisible Man, so little attention did they pay me. This gave me the opportunity to observe Deborah's sisters up close on a daily basis, and to get some inkling of what it was to be female. I looked on in fascination as they covered their faces with strange masks and lay cucumber slices over their eyes. I saw how they dried their tights on the rail of the Aga, and conditioned their hair with mayonnaise, and stored their nail polish in the fridge. I watched them zip and unzip each other's dresses, and fasten and unfasten each other's necklaces, and from them I developed a lifelong love of the little rituals of womanhood.

In my house, any show of womanliness was a thing to be ashamed of. I don't remember my mother ever washing her hair, although of course she must have, maybe when we were all out of the house. She had a robe that she kept on a hanger on the back of her bedroom door, but I don't remember ever seeing her wearing it; she was always fully clothed before we were out of bed. While she pegged all our underpants out to dry on the clothes line in the back garden, she dried her own underwear furtively, on the radiator in her bedroom, making sure to put it away in her drawer before my father came home from work. I do remember him once taking her to task after he came across an 'unmentionable' in the bathroom bin, but that was the only evidence I can remember of the monthly cycles she no doubt experienced. She never used the word 'pregnancy', talking only of the time when she was 'expecting' us, and I know that Terry and I had both been bottle-fed. My father disapproved of breastfeeding: I remember him once making a tutting sound with his tongue when we were out for a rare lunch in a hotel and a young woman at the next table began feeding her baby. When my mother was hospitalized for a week – I think she would have been in her late forties – we were told only that it was 'women's trouble'. None of us visited her, and when she came home from the hospital no concession was made to her recuperation; it was business again as usual.

'Let's face it,' said Deborah one night when we were huddled in the back lane behind my house, smoking Silk Cut Purples she'd filched from her mum's handbag, 'your parents are not normal.'

Hers was a different kind of unhappy house, as messy and noisy as mine was silent and sterile. Her parents would later separate – a development my mother would speak of forever afterwards as a tragedy – but when we were teenagers, they spent most of their time shouting at each other. It was as refreshing to me as a thunderstorm, after the tension that hung in the air between my parents.

'It's a wonder anyone could breathe in that house,' Deborah told Mary Rose once. 'The air in there would cut you dead.'

We had been friends since Christmas of third year. Before that we had walked to and from school every day for two years along the same route without ever acknowledging each other's existence. She and one or other of her sisters would trundle along one side of the road, wearing their school uniforms as if they'd been thrown over them, with their long socks pushed down and their skirts rolled up at the waist, while I walked on the other side of the road, alone. We might never have spoken to each other, but for the fire in Mrs Staunton's house.

It was late December, and we were on our way home in the dark. There were Christmas trees in the windows of the houses we passed, the smell of burning coal in the air. A fire brigade passed us at full tilt, siren roaring, and turned into our street. I remember feeling a thrill at the thought that it might be going to my house – that something might actually be about to *happen* to us – and I was disappointed when I saw it stop outside Mrs Staunton's. There was a new smell now, of burning wood, and a horrible sound. It was as if the bones of the house were all being snapped.

Mrs Staunton was standing out in the street in her house-coat. She was one of those old ladies who dressed herself and her front door in similar housecoats; one of those old ladies who was always outside polishing her brasses and calling for her cat. She once paid me a fiver to feed that cat while she was on holiday, and I took a strong dislike to him. He was an annoying cat, and I had no sympathy for him when he was reported missing on the day of the fire. I found myself standing beside Deborah in the small crowd that had gathered on the far side of the street to watch the house being consumed from within, while Mrs Staunton stood at the railings, wailing for her missing cat. I don't know what possessed me, but I started, very, very quietly, to miaow.

I heard Deborah make a little sound, like a squawk. I miaowed again and heard her splutter. All it took was one more miaow and she doubled up on herself, ponytail inverted as she choked on her laughter. She had a most unladylike laugh, like a sudden allergic reaction, all snot and tears. I remember feeling a tremendous surge of power when I first triggered that snorting laugh in Deborah, and it sparked a friendship between us that has changed very little between then and now. Deborah is the only person who is never in the least bit shocked by the things I say. She alone always finds me funny.

It was from Deborah that I learned how to behave around women, and without her I fear what might have become of me. She was the one who told me what to wear the first time I ever went to a disco. When Cliona Lambert invited me to the Muckross Debs, it was Deborah who instructed me on the right chocolates to buy, and the corsage to give her. Years later, after I decided to ask Mary Rose to marry me, it was Deborah who advised me on the choice of ring. So, when she told me, that night in Morzine, that Mary Rose was not well, I did not for a second doubt her, only wondered why I had not noticed it myself.

'Are you all right, Mary Rose?' I asked, when we were in the bathroom brushing our teeth. 'Deborah said you don't seem yourself.'

She hesitated. 'I don't know,' she said, looking back at me through the mirror with vacant eyes. 'I don't know what's happening to me.'

I wrapped my arms around her and hugged her in close. Planting a kiss on her ear, I breathed in the woodsmoke smell of her.

'Come on to bed,' I said. 'We'll talk about it better in the dark.'

'I feel depleted,' she explained, as she lay in my arms. She paused to zoom in on the right words. 'I feel like a battery that's going dead. I feel like I'm ready for the scrapheap.'

'Maybe you should take a break from work,' I suggested. 'Those hours you work are brutal.'

She turned in my arms, facing towards the window and the luminous mountain moon.

'Then I'd only be home all day by myself,' was what she said. 'You can't take a break from yourself. That's what I really want, to take a holiday from myself.'

I pulled her in even tighter to me and kissed her hard skull, through her hair. I listened to her breathing, shallow and sleepless. I looked out the window at the same night sky

247

she was looking at, but she might as well have been a million miles away. I had the sense that it was only the shell of her I had in my arms. She had gone somewhere else, somewhere I couldn't reach her. All I could think to do was wait and hope that she would eventually come back to me.

Since Mary Rose died, I have come to understand the particular pain of regret, something I never had cause to think about before. I have often found myself reading those potted interviews that appear in the Sunday magazines, where celebrities are asked if they have any regrets. Most say they don't believe in them or that they have none. I probably would have said the same thing myself, before Mary Rose died. Now I think it's an absurd thing to say. How could anyone possibly have no regrets?

I regret ever encouraging Mary Rose to go to Egypt. At the time I thought it would be good for her to go. She had been so sad, for so long, that I thought it might do her good to get away. I hoped it might be a turning point for her, that by spending some time with her old friend she might recover something of herself and come back renewed. I'd like to be able to say that was the reason I didn't go with her, but it wasn't. I didn't go, because I didn't want to. I wanted to stay home and concentrate on work, and I very much regret that.

I regret that I did not pay more attention to the difficulties she was having. Even now, I am being disingenuous. I was aware of the difficulties she was having, but I ignored them, and I really, really regret that.

Most of all I regret not telling her more often that I loved her. 'I love you,' was something Mary Rose said at the drop of a hat. She said it in tears and in laughter. Sometimes she said it just as a greeting, like most people say hello or goodbye. It was a sign-off that she and her family used in every conversation. As they saw each other to the door. Before they hung up the phone. Nobody in my family ever told anybody they loved them. It was not something I felt comfortable saying. And yet I did. Love her. I just hope she knew.

'She knew,' said Deborah, when I confided in her. 'Of course she knew. How could she not?'

I had been over this a million times in my head. Through many sleepless nights, I had conducted a forensic review of my record as a husband. Never once did I cheat on Mary Rose, never did I so much as raise my voice to her or ever say anything deliberately unkind. I never forgot her birthday or our anniversary. I never failed to send her roses on Valentine's Day and yet, for all that, there were sins of omission. Blind spots that I had consciously allowed to creep in between us. They troubled me in the months after her death more than anything I could ever have done or said.

I remember there was one night, in particular, when I came home from work late and saw the light on in the bedroom. Instead of going straight in, I sat in the car listening to the radio until I saw the light go out. I pretended to myself that I wanted to hear the end of the discussion that was taking place, but the truth of it was that I wanted to avoid a conversation with Mary Rose. Talking to her at that time was like trying to pick up water, and I was tired of trying to do it and failing.

'I let her down,' I confessed to Deborah.

We were out for drinks in a trendy new cocktail lounge on the quays. Tom's nephew owned the place, and we were there to support him, although whatever money we put behind the bar that night could not have compensated for the loss of cool we must have caused by being there. We must have raised the median age by at least ten years, but we did enjoy the cocktails. Mine was a whiskey sour, and it worked some kind of magic in loosening my tongue.

'I pretended not to notice what was going on with her,' I said, remembering how I went about my life as normal, even though I knew that she was struggling to carry the weight of her troubles. It's a terrible thing to acknowledge, but I remember feeling I had reached the edge of my love for Mary Rose. I found myself standing at the frontier where my life stopped and hers started, with the voice of a sentry in my head saying here and no further. I could not have known it at the time, but Mary Rose had reached that point too, and was preparing to step across it. I only learned that later.

'She'd signed up to go to Lebanon with the Red Cross,' I told Deborah. Even the act of speaking those words caused a crackling in my chest, as if I'd poured hot liquid over ice.

'I know,' said Deborah, without so much as blinking.

I had been just about to tell her how I found out. How I was cleaning the fridge one day when the landline rang. On the other end was a woman with a mid-European accent who asked for Mary Rose. I told her that Mary Rose had died, and she in turn explained that she was ringing about the volunteer register. Oh yes, I said, the volunteer register. It turned out that Mary Rose had signed up for a six-month rotation in a refugee camp in Lebanon. Her name had just come up, and they were ringing to check if she was still available to go. I was about to explain all of this to Deborah, but it was unnecessary now because she already knew.

'So she told you.'

'We discussed it.'

There was something about having a conversation with Deborah that made me feel like I had altitude sickness. Her brain seemed to work at a higher level than mine. It seemed to get more oxygen.

'What the fuck,' I said, staring out the window at the fast-flowing river down below. The water was tinted a sickly green by a spotlight mounted under a nearby bridge. I felt queasy looking at it.

'David,' said Deborah, in a low, insistent voice.

I turned to look at her, and she leaned in towards me, holding her ridiculous fishbowl of a drink in her two hands. 'Listen to me, now. This was about Mary Rose, not about you.'

In that moment I did not believe her.

'Tell me,' I said. 'I can take it.' Although I wasn't sure I could. I took a long slurp of my whiskey sour. 'Was she planning on leaving me?'

I felt sick to the stomach even thinking it, but I'd been turning it over in my head all week and it seemed like the only logical conclusion.

'No!' said Deborah, choking on her drink. 'What gave you that idea?'

'Well, why else would she hatch a secret escape plan?'

'Mary Rose had no more notion of leaving you than you had of leaving her. She just needed some time out. She hadn't mentioned it to you because she wasn't sure it would happen.'

Deborah somehow managed to make it all sound completely normal.

'She wasn't sure you'd understand,' she added.

'Try me,' I said.

Deborah took another long slurp of her cocktail through its short little straw before going on.

'She was finding it hard to see the future. The rest of us all have our lives marked out for us by our kids, but you and Mary Rose didn't have that, and it troubled her. She couldn't see her way forward.'

Mary Rose had tried to say this to me, more than once, and I had made a joke of it. We can buy a camper van, I told her, start smoking dope and going to music festivals like

Duncan and Cara. Mary Rose had laughed when I said that, but I see now that I had failed to adequately listen to what she was trying to say to me.

'She was at a crossroads in her life,' said Deborah. 'A cross-roads, a crisis, call it what you like. She was getting to that age.'

I could feel my brain moving at a snail's pace towards some dawning revelation.

'Are you trying to tell me that Mary Rose was going through the menopause?'

I had seen the grey hairs start to appear at her temples and assumed that she was embracing them with her customary lack of vanity. She made no attempt to cover them up, despite her mother's suggestion that she should, so I concluded that they didn't bother her. She had mentioned that her periods had become less regular, but I took it for granted that she would accept this with her trademark common sense. I had felt the sadness rising up in her like a flood tide at night and, idiot that I was, I had assumed it would in time recede.

'Well, we're all going through the menopause, whether we know it or not,' said Deborah, glancing across the low table to where Cara and Angela were sunk into deep leather arm-chairs, nursing their giant drinks. 'But it's different for women who haven't had children, because there's a mourning process involved.'

'I never got that,' I confessed to Deborah. 'I never really got the children thing.'

With the ice-cold logic of my second whiskey sour it seemed to me that it was as simple as that. I had never under-stood my wife's devastating desire for a child, and, in failing to understand it, I had failed her. It was as simple as that.

'Most men don't,' said Deborah. 'But then, Mary Rose knew that.'

A hush fell on the room, even though it was full of people.

At every table they sat in giddy huddles, while waiters with trays moved among them taking orders, but I might have been sitting alone with Deborah in a forest clearing for all the awareness I had of them. I felt like a character in a fairy tale who comes face to face with an oracle. It seemed to me that Deborah was in possession of some precious truth, one that might deliver me from my suffering and finally set me free.

'Did she tell you that?'

'Of course. We often talked about it.'

Through all the years I had kept it a secret. Through all the years I had felt guilty about it, and worried that Mary Rose would find out. Now Deborah was telling me that she knew all along.

'Mary Rose was a *midwife*,' she said, addressing me as if I was a simpleton. 'She worked in a maternity hospital. She knew that men only fall in love with their children when they set eyes on them. She saw how they stumble into the delivery room like rabbits in the headlights and then come out like they've discovered the secret of the universe. The penny doesn't drop for most men until they're holding that little person in their arms. Mary Rose, of all people, knew that.'

'Right,' I said, wondering how on earth I had managed to get so far through life and still understand it so little.

19

Eight months after Mary Rose died, I received a letter from a woman I had not seen in nearly thirty years, telling me I had a daughter. The letter arrived in a pale blue envelope with a Norwegian stamp on it. My name and address had been handwritten on the front of the envelope, but there was a return address in Oslo on a printed sticker on the back. I assumed it was a letter of sympathy from some acquaintance of Mary Rose. There had been so many of those letters, each and every one of them written with such thought and care that they never failed to move me. The kindness of people was a revelation.

I opened the envelope and slid out a single page of matching blue notepaper, covered in careful upright handwriting. I didn't recognize the handwriting, and I'm ashamed to say that even the name at the bottom meant nothing to me at first. I think it was the surname that threw me – the letter was signed Britta Nygard – a surname I had long ago forgotten if ever I knew it in the first place. It was only when I concentrated on her first name that I remembered who she was. Horrified at the thought that I could ever have not remembered, I turned my attention to the content of her letter.

She had learned of my wife's death by chance, after she entered my name into an Internet search engine in a moment of curiosity, for which she apologized. The article she happened upon was one that appeared in the *Irish Times* the day after Mary Rose's funeral. I remembered the article, which had appeared on the front page, accompanied by a picture of me and Mary Rose's sisters standing outside the church in Monkstown. All of us were dressed in black, and I was holding a large black umbrella over their heads as the rain poured down. I remember clocking the photographer as he framed that picture and knowing, immediately, that it would be on the front page: it had all the elements. In the letter, Britta offered me her sincere condolences on my wife's death, and she went on to say that she believed she owed me an apology. For many years, she had kept something a secret from me. At first, she was convinced that this was the right thing to do, but in time she had become troubled by it. When she read in the newspaper that my wife had died, she decided it was time to tell me that I had a daughter.

'Her name is Elisa,' Britta wrote. 'She is twenty-five years old. She is a nurse working here in the hospital in Oslo. She is a wonderful person.'

In the next paragraph, Britta told me that Elisa was herself the mother of a three-year-old child called Astrid. She apologized again for not telling me sooner. She asked for my forgiveness. 'I have no explanation for you,' she said, 'only that I was once full of certainties and now I have none, just the wish not to waste any more of my time on old mistakes.'

She signed it simply 'Britta'.

Of course I remembered her. I remembered, in great clarity, the airstrip at Lokichoggio. I remembered the jagged hills and the heat-bleached sky and the wobble of aviation fuel in the warm air. Sacks of food stacked like sandbags on the tarmac, and rows of planes waiting patiently on the runway. The planes were drab and dirty and naked of any livery. All they had were the letters on their tail fins. UN. WFP. There was a magnificence to it that I struggled to put into words. At that time, I was desperate to put everything into words.

I had come to Africa on a mission to make a proper journalist of myself. Tired of working the night shift at a Dublin newspaper, I had looked around the world for a patch nobody was covering. The war in Lebanon was the big foreign story of the time, and it was more than adequately serviced by a number of veteran reporters. Iraq was starting to make headlines in a squabble with Kuwait over oil, but I dismissed that as having limited interest for an Irish audience. It seemed to me that Africa was the most fertile ground for me. Nelson Mandela had just been released from prison. The civil war in Ethiopia had come to an end, but there was a famine in southern Sudan that was to my mind under-reported. I decided to take myself there.

I flew into Nairobi and cadged a lift from an Irish aid agency to the border post of Lokichoggio. Loki was at that time a boom town, unnaturally swollen with aid workers and their apparatus. Guest houses had sprung up out of the scrub to provide for the nurses and doctors and logistics people who were flooding in from northern Europe. Some of the guest houses had even dug rudimentary swimming pools for the aid workers. They served whiskey and beer and fried chicken or Nile perch, and every evening the young pilots and nurses gathered to leave their expenses behind the bar. There was all the heady atmosphere of a risk-free war.

The Norwegians were driving the aid effort and Britta was handling logistics for one of those Norwegian agencies. The first time I saw her she was standing under the wing of a cargo plane, counting off boxes of supplies as they were loaded into the cavernous hold. She had dark glasses, worn on her head like a hairband. The clipboard in her hand gave her an air of great competence. I approached her to ask if there was a spare seat for me on the plane.

'You want to hitch a lift to a famine?' she said, in an Abba accent.

'Sure.'

I had to get into southern Sudan, but I had no money to pay for my fare.

'It's raining over there,' she said. 'We can't land today. Maybe tomorrow.'

Her diction had a beautiful precision to it.

'In the meantime, we must wait it out.'

I saw her again that afternoon at the pool in my guest house. The pool was the shape of a kidney bean and strewn with debris and dead insects, but that didn't stop Britta from swimming in it.

'Come on,' she said.

I looked behind me to see if she was talking to someone else, but it seemed that she meant me. There was nothing in my life up until then that could have prepared me for an invitation from a Scandinavian girl to take a dip with her in a swimming pool at a guest house in the African wilderness. Scandinavian girls were the stuff of the Benny Hill programmes that my father watched when I was a child, giving no indication of enjoyment as he sat with his wingback chair pulled up close to the tiny colour TV he had only bought because my mother complained that ours was the only house on the street that didn't have one. I was small for my age then and would not stretch out to full height until I was sixteen. The idea that some Scandinavian girl would one day come on to me was so far beyond my imaginings that even ten years later, six foot one and no longer scrawny, I found it hard to believe.

'Aren't you getting in?'

She was peeling off her T-shirt and trousers to reveal a startlingly white bra and pants. All my life I have had a preference for women in plain white underwear over any manner of satin or lace, and it occurs to me now that this preference can be traced back to Britta, three years older than me and a world more sophisticated, in her white cotton underwear at the pool in Loki.

'I didn't bring my togs,' I said, feeling ridiculous.

I had brought a rucksack with me, meticulously packed with a mosquito net, water-purification tablets, a compass and a penknife. I had malarial tablets too, and chemist-grade quinine, and citronella candles and a torch with spare batteries. I was like William Boot in Evelyn Waugh's *Scoop*; I had everything but the canoe. But I did not have togs.

'You can swim in your underwear,' said Britta. 'That's what we all do.'

My boxer shorts were made of flimsy striped cotton, my skin deathly white from a lifetime of underexposure to the sun, but I had the hopefulness of youth, so I peeled off and jumped in with her, and it was at that moment that I felt my life at last begin. I was twenty-four years old. I was in Africa. I was swimming in my underwear, in a pool in the middle of nowhere, with a worldly Scandinavian woman. The little runt that I once was, and who I once feared I would always be, was at last in my past. I floated on my back, looked up at the overcast sky and gave out a roar of joy.

We must have eaten together that evening at one of the low coffee tables of what the guest house rather euphemistically called its 'restaurant'. We must have taken it in turns to buy each other rounds of barely cooled beer from the rusty refrigerator. We must have smoked one cigarette after another, because everyone in that place smoked from morning until night. The pilots smoked while they flew the planes, allowing the ash to fall down on to the Ordnance Survey maps they used to navigate. The nurses smoked as they tended patients, letting a cigarette dangle from their mouths as they adjusted a drip. The logistics people smoked as they supervised the re-fuelling of the aircraft. That's how I remember it anyway, but it may not be true. It's so long ago.

What I do remember is being with Britta in the tiny hut where I slept. It was early morning, and the light was coming in through the cracks in the woven walls. Our clothes lay intertwined on the single chair at the foot of my bed, our boots upended on the nails that were hammered into the roof beams. Britta had a fear of a spider climbing into her boots while she slept. She feared snakes too and would always make me tuck the bedsheet carefully around our legs before we slept. The walls of the hut didn't meet the floor, so there was nothing to prevent a snake coming in.

The rains in southern Sudan lasted a week. Day after day we sat by the pool and drank beer and played gin rummy. Night after night we repaired to my hut and took our chances with the spiders and the snakes. Each night promised to be our last. There was always the expectation that by the next morning the rains would have stopped, and we would be able to fly out, so we made the most of that one night together, over and over again for a week.

After seven days the rains did finally stop, and she gave me a lift into southern Sudan. From the windows of the plane as we came in to land, we saw people, as tall and thin as their shadows, beginning to converge on us from all directions. Jeeps arrived, splattered with mud, to oversee the distribution of the supplies we had brought. Britta stepped straight into a heated dialogue about transport with a small, bespectacled African. I fell in with a guy from an Irish agency who offered to take me to their feeding centre. He had the engine running on his jeep for fear it would cut out and he would not be able to start it again. There was no opportunity to say a proper goodbye to Britta.

'I'm off,' I said, barely pausing as I walked by her.

She lifted her head and called after me, 'I might see you in Nairobi.'

'Sure,' I said, but I'm not certain if she even heard me.

I raised a hand to her as we drove off. I was high on the sense that life was finally happening to me. It seemed to be happening all by itself, and with so little effort from me that I took it for granted that it would from now on continue to happen with the same beautiful ease. I imagined there was nothing I had to do but ride along.

I did not see her in Nairobi. I did look out for her in the bars where the aid workers all hung out. In the Carnivore restaurant on the Langata Road, where I had dinner with the Irish consul, I expected at any moment to see her appear at the door with a gaggle of other long-limbed Scandinavians. I excused myself from the table and went to the loo, taking the long way back around the edge of the restaurant, in case I had somehow managed to miss her. The place was full of people just like her, but none of them was her.

At the guest house where I was staying, I rose every morning in the expectation that I would find her sitting with one bare, brown foot propped up on the seat of her chair, smoking a cigarette and writing in her journal. I lingered over a second coffee in the breakfast area, working over my notes and expecting at every moment to hear her voice. To look up and find her standing over me. Later, I manufactured an excuse to pass by a hotel where some of the aid workers stayed, stepping into the lobby to ask where I might buy an international newspaper. I heard the lift ping and looked up to see the doors open, but it was an African man in a business suit who emerged, not Britta.

For three days, I roamed Nairobi on my own private safari.

While the tourists piled into jeeps to hit the game parks in the hope of sighting a white rhino, I prowled the city on the lookout for a dark-haired Norwegian woman. In the taxi on the way to the airport, I peered out the window at the silent streams of people walking to work in the dark morning, and even then I was expecting somehow to see her. Right up to the very last minute, when I was sitting in the departure area waiting for my flight out, I was sure I would see her, but I didn't.

I had no idea where she was, and whether I'd missed her by a day or an hour. She might have arrived at the Carnivore minutes after we had paid up and left, scanning the place for me, just as I had looked for her. She might have been in the next lift down in the hotel I visited. She might have approached the same concierge, enquiring after a newspaper or a place to change dollars. She might have arrived at my guest house in a taxi just as mine pulled away. I would never know.

Nowadays, of course, I would have posted a breezy message on her Facebook page: Hey, I'm in Nairobi, where are you at? I would have sent her a text message: Passing through Nairobi this weekend, would love to see you if you're around. But there were no mobiles back then, no social media. Our lives were governed by chance in a way that young people now could not understand, which I think explains why Britta did not track me down to tell me she was pregnant. We were not in the habit of bending fate to our will. We allowed life to take its course, making only the most feeble of efforts to steer ourselves away from danger and towards our desires. The forces that had carried us away from each other were beyond our control. That's how we would have seen it then.

I can hardly remember her now. I have a picture in my mind of her face, but it's only a single frame. I can't make her move or smile or talk. Wait, she's talking to me now, she's saying something very earnest, and I'm laughing. It was the one linguistic error I heard her make in the week I spent with her. She referred to a man who walked with 'a lump'. When I pointed out her mistake, she laughed herself to tears along with me. I remember being very struck by her good nature and liking her very much for it. It was a mark of the confidence she carried about with her, something I saw as peculiarly Nordic. I was Irish and would not have taken it so well if it was me, but she gave me a glimpse of a different way to be, and I'm grateful to her for that.

I feel badly now, when I think of how little thought I gave her afterwards. It seems very strange to me that I allowed myself to forget her so entirely, when the memories were there all along, if only I'd had the inclination to seek them out. I remember the way her tan ended at the top of her thighs, where her shorts started, so that when she took her shorts off, she looked as if she was wearing stockings. I remember the patterns in her voice, and the careful way she went about combining the crisp consonants of her near-perfect English with the long vowels of her native tongue. I remember the stray hairs at the back of her neck that worked their way free of her ponytail as the day went on, and the tiny blue tattoo of a dolphin on her left shoulder blade. She'd had the tattoo done in Amsterdam, she told me, and I wondered briefly whether she could have caught AIDS from the tattooist's needle. I think we may even have discussed safe sex, but neither of us had condoms, and abstinence was not an option, so we quickly abandoned the discussion. It never occurred to me that she would get pregnant. All we thought of in those days was AIDS.

The consequence of all of this was that I now had a daughter, and a granddaughter. In an instant, I had become a father. A grandfather. I had to read Britta's letter three times before I was sure I understood. I had to piece the words together to form sentences. I had to pull back from them and try to see them in their entirety. It was like trying to understand particle physics. It was too big a concept for my brain to take in. I read the letter a fourth time, and only after the fourth reading did I finally come to understand it. For the second time in my life, Britta Nygard had offered me a glimpse of a new way to be.

20

'She's coming here,' I told Claire.

It was our third walk together, and we were taking a rest after heading north along the coastal path out of Palamós towards the beach at Castell. The place where we had stopped was a small cove lined with boathouses that had been converted into charming summer huts. Their wooden doors and window shutters were painted in different primary colours. One of them was geranium red. Another sunshine yellow. A third was sky blue and another bottle green. There were wooden boats moored on the stony beach, a well to draw water, a scattering of trees and, of course, the ubiquitous Catalan flag, flying from one of the boathouses.

Claire and I sat hunched over our knees on the stones as we drew breath.

'She's coming here tomorrow,' I said.

'Who, the Norwegian woman?'

'No, no,' I said. 'My daughter, Elisa.'

Was I imagining it or did she seem relieved?

'She's coming here tomorrow, with my granddaughter.'

The words still sounded strange in my mouth. It did not seem to me that I had earned the right to use them, and yet what other words could I use? There was no other way to describe my relationship to these people who were, essentially, strangers to me. They were also my only living blood relatives, apart from Terry and his boys. Their names were written indelibly on the branch of our family tree that had, unbeknownst to me, taken root in Norway. They had inherited my DNA, with some of my characteristics no doubt, and some of my aberrations, maybe even those of my mother and father too. The thought of it was appalling to me, and yet also somehow thrilling. I still hadn't untangled it in my head.

'How old is the little girl?'

'She's just turned four, I gather.'

I could not pretend to have any of the facts first-hand.

'It's a lovely age.'

'Is it?' I asked, with all the helplessness of someone who is told the many virtues of a city they have never visited. All I could do was nod.

'Oh yes, they're wonderful at that age. They become little people when they're four.'

Once again, I was struck by her courage. There must have been pain for her in every word of this conversation, in every breath of it, and yet she ventured forth.

'I look forward to meeting her,' she said to me, 'your granddaughter.'

As she looked into my eyes, I felt that she was urging me forward too.

'Yes,' I told her. 'You and me both.'

Setting out from Aiguaclara every day with Claire on our walks, I felt as gauche as a courting teenager. We were both of us past fifty, I was a widower and she was recently separated from her husband, and yet there was in our daily excursions the sense of something youthfully clandestine. Perhaps because of the dark and private nature of the things we talked about, I felt on returning as if we had been doing something we shouldn't be doing. A feeling I remember from when, as a teenager, I would find myself kissing some girl in the middle of the afternoon on her parents' couch, only to have to straighten up my school uniform and greet them on their return from work as if nothing had happened.

I was not kissing Claire, of course. I had not even ventured to touch her. Our explorations of each other were purely conversational, but no less intimate for it. With every step we took we probed each other's raw and tender places, tentative and fumbling but venturing further and further each time.

'I could not be with my husband after what happened,' she told me. 'I could not talk with him. Some of the time I could not force myself to look at him.'

We had stopped for a cold beer at a bar on the beach. Incongruous, the situations we found ourselves in. To be talking about such sorrow against the backdrop of a Mediterranean summer. Sailboats on the horizon line. Swimmers in the water. A group of youngsters playing a noisy game of volleyball on the beach.

'We disagreed about the children, you see.'

From the table next to us, there was a burst of laughter. We both turned to see what the joke was, but we were too late. Claire waited for the sound to die down before she continued.

'Hugo's philosophy was so different from mine. My family are . . .' She paused, turning the beer bottle around in her hand as she searched for the right word. 'My family are soft, but Hugo's family, they were so hard. Hugo always wanted me to be hard with the children, especially with Tristan. We had a lot of fights about that.'

She was staring at the beer bottle, as if she was very carefully studying the small print on the label, as she spoke.

'Tristan loved to play music, but Hugo wanted him to play rugby. Hugo was always asking Tristan to go to rugby matches with him. Hugo wanted him to be big and strong, like him, but Tristan was a small boy. He was not the boy his father wished him to be.'

I could have told her that I was all too familiar with that scenario, but I did not want to interrupt her.

'Tristan wanted to study music,' she said. 'But Hugo insisted he go to the university, to study political science.'

She rolled her head on her neck, as if her thoughts needed a swirl.

'I lost that fight,' she said, raising her eyebrows to indicate her helplessness as she looked up at me. 'Hugo could not see it from my point of view.'

I noticed how she pronounced her vowels like an English person. She had learned her English in High Wycombe, in Buckinghamshire, and retained certain quaintly English pronunciation points.

'You see, he was wrong, and I was right. Tristan was unhappy at the university. It was the last year of his life, and he was unhappy.'

She closed her eyes and, with them still closed, she continued to speak.

'I can't forgive Hugo for that.'

She opened her eyes again to look at me, and we sat for some time – maybe as long as a minute – without either of us saying anything.

'Will we walk?' I said to her, after a while.

'Yes,' she said, very decisively, and she stood up. 'Let's walk.'

It was late afternoon by the time we arrived back in Aiguaclara, sticky and sunburnt and ready for a swim.

'Hey-ho,' said Jo, when we ran into her on the way down the hill. She was no doubt bound for Alicia's and a sundowner. Or six.

'Hi, Jo,' I said, overcome by a teenage feeling all over again. 'This is Claire.'

'Hi, Claire,' said Jo, leaning in to kiss her with that mother-hen friendliness she offered everyone she met.

'Join me for a drink?' she asked.

'Another time,' I said. 'We need to swim.'

The 'we' seemed to me to imply too much, and I had to fight the urge to correct it. Claire and I were not a 'we', and I did not want anyone to think we were. I was acutely aware of what people might think as they saw us sitting on the bench by the promenade, unlacing our walking shoes and peeling off our socks. I was embarrassed to think that people observing us might jump to conclusions. If Mary Rose were watching, she would surely jump to a conclusion.

'Okay?' I said, holding out a hand to help Claire step down on to the beach. We deposited our shoes and socks with our bags on the sand. Peeling our clothes off and tossing them on top of our bags, we made our way down to the shore. As we entered the water side by side, dipping our heads underneath and surfacing together, I was reminded of Claire's parents and how Mary Rose and I had often observed them swimming together just like this. Unwilling to fall into such an obvious pattern, I took off in a fast crawl towards the diving board, leaving Claire to bob along by herself towards the marker buoys. I swam two circuits of the swimming area, making sure that she was already out of the water before I emerged.

'So, dinner?' I said, as I gave my hair a quick rub of my towel.

We had idly touched on the possibility of having dinner together that night, in a nearby hilltop town.

'Oh yes,' she said, making a sarong of her towel and tucking the corner of it under her arm, as women have done for time immemorial. It's a ritual I have always loved to watch, just as I love to watch the way women lift their arms to wind their hair into a bun on their heads. The way they smooth their skirts down over their thighs when they sit down. I watched Claire bend to pick up her bag and her walking shoes, all businesslike now as she made her way, barefoot, towards the steps. She paused, looking back over her shoulder briefly.

'Seven?' she said.

And I said, 'Yes, seven bells.'

As it happened, we did not have dinner together that night. I was all ready, freshly showered and dressed in a clean shirt and steadying myself with a drink on the balcony, when I got a text from her.

I'm sorry, the text said, offering no explanation. I can't.

I think it was only then that I understood the depths of her difficulties. We had spoken of them at length, hers and mine, and I knew, for example, that she had been prescribed one kind of pill to help her sleep and another pill to help her through the day. We had compared antidepressants, as teenagers might swap the names of the bands they like. Have you tried Lexapro? I asked. I prefer Sertraline, she said. We were both of us medicated to make the grief bearable, but even so I came to understand that hers was greater than mine, and not diminishing.

Some of the things she told me were unbearable even to listen to. Like the dress she had bought Élodie for her seventeenth birthday. A dress Élodie never got to wear. They laid her out in it instead.

'It was made of light blue silk,' Claire told me, 'with a gold . . . wait, what's the word?' She mimed the action of tying a ribbon about her waist.

'A sash?' I suggested.

'A sash,' she said, pleased that I had found the word she was looking for. 'Élodie loved that dress.' She smiled, as she remembered. 'When she tried it on in the shop, she was so happy that she made a circle. She said she felt like a princess in that dress.'

I had an urge to put my hands over my ears when she told me that. There was a noise to that kind of sorrow, like the noise an orchestra makes when it works towards the crescendo. I have always hated the crescendo; I can never understand why it's there, until afterwards, when the sound of a solitary flute is all the more beautiful for the cacophony that preceded it. That's what grief is like: an unbearable crescendo of noise, followed only very intermittently by moments of respite that are almost as painful in their beauty.

No problem, I wrote, in the text I sent back to Claire. I understand.

Two hours later I got another text from her, and I knew that she had just come back up for air and looked around her and remembered that the world was still turning.

Good luck with your daughter, she said.

21

I had met Elisa just once before. A meeting that was arranged only after we had corresponded tentatively for several weeks. It was Britta I had contacted first, on the email address she had given me, and then I talked to her on the phone. She was the one who urged me to contact Elisa, assuring me that our daughter would be glad to hear from me. I'm not sure I would have known how to negotiate those awkward initial steps without Deborah's help. It was Deborah I went to when I got Britta's letter, landing on her doorstep unannounced on a wet Tuesday morning in January, when she was about to leave for work. Incapable of speech, I handed her the letter and waited for her to read it.

'Oh, my God,' she said, looking at me with shining eyes. 'How wonderful!'

'Really?' I said. I still didn't know what to make of it.

She brought me inside and we sank, both of us still wearing our coats, into the deep velvet couch in her vast open-plan kitchen as she read the letter again. The house was empty and quiet, but there was a fug of burnt toast in the air and a smell of freshly made coffee.

'Don't you see?' she said, lifting her head up from the letter. 'This is a gift. It's life's gift to you, whether you know it or not.'

I had a hum in my ears, like the sound of a basement generator, and a weird, fluttery feeling in my chest that made me wonder if I was having a heart attack. To avoid looking directly at Deborah, I glanced around the room, where

I must have sat a hundred times before, taking in the framed studio portraits on the walls of her and Michael and the children, the baby pictures on the mantelpiece, the photos on the side tables of graduations and debs dances and family holidays.

'I don't know if I can do this,' I said, feeling more lost than I had ever felt in all my life. More lost even than when Mary Rose died. I had no horizon line, nothing to hold on to for balance. I was hoping Deborah would understand.

'Oh, David,' she said. 'David, David, David, my old friend. Forgive me for a moment if I rant.' She took a deep breath, fuelling herself for what was to come. When she spoke, her voice sounded practised, as if this was a speech she'd been waiting to give for a very long time.

'As you know, David, I've got three kids. I love them all dearly, but it has cost me twenty years of my life to rear them. You may remember that I vomited continually the whole time I was pregnant with Ben. I lost three pints of blood having Luke. I suffered a Bell's palsy from the trauma of Hannah's birth. Then there was Ben's asthma, and all the nights I had to sleep on the floor in the hospital. There was Luke's accident with the bike – we had a week in Crumlin when we didn't know if he was going to live or die. Not to count all the nights they were teething. All the nights they woke up with nightmares or fevers. All the days they couldn't go to the crèche and I had to pretend I was the one who was sick, to get a day off work.'

Did I know all of this? I must have been aware of it at the time, surely, but, apart from Luke's bicycle accident, I didn't remember Deborah ever struggling to manage the demands of motherhood. There was one evening when she arrived for dinner at Tom and Angela's only to fall asleep on the couch before we sat down to eat, but that was easily explained by the fact that she had two small babies at the time. I once saw her lose her temper during a children's party at her house, when some of the boys started a food fight with the cupcakes she had baked, but she stabilized as soon as she had a glass of wine in her hand. Deborah was my oldest and dearest – perhaps even my only – friend, but it occurred to me now that there was so much of her life that I didn't know.

'In twenty years,' she said, 'I haven't had a bath without someone disturbing me to ask me if we have any milk, or Sellotape . . .'

It seemed like this was the start of another list, but she got tired of it and changed tack.

'You,' she said, accusingly, 'have lived a life of splendid isolation. You were married to an angel, who heartbreakingly for all of us was taken too soon, and now you find yourself unexpectedly alone in middle age and drowning in self-pity.'

That seemed a bit harsh, but I didn't want to interrupt her, not while she was on a roll.

'Then into your life comes a daughter you never knew you had, and a little granddaughter.'

It seemed absurdly dramatic, the way she said it. It seemed to have no place in the narrative of my life. It was like something that would happen in a movie.

'This is something that can only happen in the life of a man,' said Deborah, opening her eyes wide and shaking her head in exasperation. I was shocked she had said that, and not a little disoriented. Ever since we first became friends, Deborah and I had been on the same side in life, comrades in the trenches of our suburban upbringing. In adulthood, we were allies against a world that didn't always get the joke. She and I were always on the same team, or so I thought, until she threw my gender at me. I felt like my lifelong doubles partner had hopped over the net and started serving

273

ace after ace at me from the other side of the court. All I could do was surrender myself to the barrage.

'You really are unbelievable,' she said. 'You're getting a freebie, you jammy bugger, and you don't even know how lucky you are!'

'It sounds almost comical, when you put it like that,' I ventured.

'It is comical!' she spluttered. 'It's bloody hilarious – it's life's latest hilarious joke, at the expense of women.'

She was laughing, but I was afraid to laugh along with her, not until I knew where this was going.

'I can't help but wonder what Mary Rose would think,' I said.

'Mary Rose would think it was wonderful,' she replied, without skipping a beat. She stood up and started fumbling in her pockets for her car keys. 'Now, listen,' she said. 'I need to get to work, so we'll have to continue this later.'

'Wait,' I said. 'What should I do?'

Deborah did not hesitate to give me an answer, ready as she always was to be the boss of things.

'Write to this Britta Nygard,' she said, speaking very slowly, and with great emphasis on her pronunciation, as if she was speaking to someone who didn't have full command of English. 'Thank her, from the bottom of your heart, for raising your daughter alone all these years, and for having the courage and generosity to share her with you now. Tell her you're eternally grateful.'

'Okay,' I said, getting to my feet. 'That's what I'll do, so.'

Elisa and I arranged to meet in London, both of us wary of a meeting on home ground. I suggested the Royal Academy, because I had been there a few years previously with Mary Rose to see a Hockney exhibition. It seemed to me that the

Royal Academy offered the right combination of a central location and a dignified environment. There was the added benefit of the exhibits, in case we found the meeting awkward and needed a decoy. There's a café in the basement where Mary Rose and I had lunch on that occasion, and it was nice, in so far as I remembered. I had a clear picture of the café in my mind, which was another reason why I chose it as a venue. I needed somewhere that I could visualize for my meeting with Elisa.

I pictured us sitting opposite each other at a small square table, my daughter and I. She had sent me some photographs during our initial email exchange, so I was able to create an image of her in my mind. She was dark-haired, like her mother, and she had a long face, with a broad mouth that projected stubbornness, or so it seemed from the first photograph I saw. In the next photograph she was smiling, so I had to revise my opinion of her. The child she held in her arms was fairer than her, with a solemn little face that was somehow familiar to me.

In the days before I left, I wondered, inconclusively, whether I should bring her a gift. I postponed the decision repeatedly, until the morning of my flight when I found myself wandering in vague desperation around the duty-free area, considering the purchase of a bottle of perfume, or a silk scarf, or some item of Irish pottery, but all of these things seemed pathetically inadequate to the occasion. I drifted towards the gate without making a decision one way or the other, but I was dogged by the feeling that I should be bringing her *something*. On the plane I combed the in-flight shopping magazine, but there was nothing remotely suitable. When I landed in London, there were no shops, only newsagents and snack stalls on my path through the airport to the Tube, so I boarded the train empty-handed. Making my way up above ground again into the bleached landscape of Piccadilly, surrounded on all sides by colourless stone buildings topped with Union Jack flags flying against a colourless sky, I felt hopelessly anxious and unprepared.

London was cold and grey and pregnant everywhere with the advent of Brexit. I had not been there since the vote, and I was surprised by how sad I felt about it. Every little London thing seemed to me to scream of the break-up that was to come, from the hanging baskets outside the pubs to the tiles on the walls of the Tube stations we passed through. I first travelled to London by boat and train the summer I was sixteen, and it seemed to me then the most exciting place in the world. I remember walking up the King's Road as young men not much older than me roared past in open-top cars, and girls like gazelles brought the traffic to a stop. London felt to me like a bigger, cooler brother; now it felt like that brother was abruptly leaving home in a fury of recriminations, with no plans ever to return. I had a mad urge to accost people on the street and tell them not to do it, and I couldn't help but notice how far I had slipped from the role I had once played, of dispassionate reporter. I had become a civilian, and the irrational and sentimental attitude I now took to world affairs was proof of the fact.

I was an hour early for my appointment with my daughter at the Royal Academy, so I wandered on a whim into Fortnum & Mason in the renewed hope of finding her a present. I roamed the racks of biscuits and jams, luxuriating in the shop's plush red carpet under my travel-sore feet. I picked up a tin of chocolate-covered almonds, wondering whether that might make a nice present to bring Elisa, but it was only £8.95, which seemed a bit on the mean side. I contemplated buying her some Turkish Delight, because the wooden box it came in was so nice, but then I decided that Turkish Delight was too risky: what if she hated it? In the end I settled on a perfectly round drum of truffles in the shop's signature turquoise colour. It seemed to me a suitably classy offering, while still falling within the realm of a token, something that carried no emotional weight and incurred no risk of failure. I paid for it with a card and tucked it into my coat pocket. Heading back out on to Piccadilly, I felt slightly more prepared for the meeting than I had done before.

We had arranged to meet in the entrance lobby, in case it was raining, but it was a clear day and I was twenty minutes early, so I decided to while away some time sitting on a bench outside. I had stored Elisa's picture on my phone in case I needed help recognizing her, but as I studied the faces of every young woman who approached the gallery entrance it seemed to me that any one of them could be her. She would be wearing a green coat, she had told me, but there were women in green coats everywhere. Did she mean khaki green, I wondered, or lime green? Did an anorak qualify as a coat? I started to worry that I wouldn't recognize her and took out my phone to refresh her face in my mind. The face in the picture was clearly not the face of any of the women I had seen, so I began to relax again, and wait.

As it happened, I knew her immediately. I knew her not because she *looked* like Britta exactly but because she *was* like her. In the self-possessed way she bore her head on her shoulders, in her elegantly elongated neck and her gliding walk, she might have been the woman I met more than a quarter of a century earlier on the airstrip in Loki.

I stood up and waited as she walked towards me. She had on a green coat, as promised. I had not expected it to be quite so green. She had long, very straight dark hair that fell down over the coat like a curtain. She was wearing black biker boots, and she had a floppy handbag slung across her chest. These were the things I noticed about her first. I raised my hand in recognition, and she raised hers in response, but we were not yet close enough to speak. Her face was very pale, her lips dark red. Her breath made a cloud in the air in front of her as she walked.

'Elisa,' I said, stepping towards her.

'David.'

As soon as I heard her say my name, I was instantly relieved of an anxiety that had been troubling me more than I had realized. I had been worried that she would call me Dad, glossing over the fact that we were strangers to each other and casting me in a role that I had no idea how to play. Even as a schoolboy, I had detested role play – I've enough difficulty making of myself one plausible human being without taking on another – but so long as I was David, I could play along with anything. I placed a light hand on her arm and kissed her, with excessive formality, on both cheeks. Her skin was cold, and she smelled faintly of tobacco. I wondered if she was a smoker, or did she live with one.

'So, how was your trip?' I asked, guiding her towards the steps of the Royal Academy.

'It was fine, thanks. I flew over yesterday.'

She glanced across at me as she negotiated the climb. Just as I was trying to get the measure of her, so too was she, of me.

'I spent the night with a friend, in Croydon.'

It occurred to me that she might have been anxious coming to meet me, maybe that was why she had come a day early. Maybe she needed a night drinking wine with a friend, in preparation for what was to come.

'South London,' I said.

'Yes, it was handy for Gatwick.'

I led her inside, observing her as best I could in snatched glances. She had a strong face, her features connected by

278

straight lines, like the lines that map out a constellation of stars.

'I thought we'd eat in the café,' I said, pointing the way. 'It's a bit less stuffy than the restaurant.'

As I followed her down the stairs to the basement, I was touched to see a wobble in the white line of her scalp where she had parted her hair. It made me feel protective of her, and I remembered with a little shock that she was my daughter. Maybe I was primed by nature to protect her.

'Yes, just two of us,' I told the waiter, holding two fingers up, in the manner of a Boy Scout.

While we waited for the table, I helped her out of her coat. She pulled the scarf she wore from her neck and threaded it through her coat sleeve, so as not to lose it. So, she's a careful person, I thought.

'After you,' I said, motioning for her to follow the waiter to the table.

We sat down and studied the menus. She ordered the quiche, while I ordered the fish pie, and I persuaded her to join me in partaking of a glass of white wine. I knew I was nervous by the strength of my desire for the glass of wine. There was a brief hiatus after we handed back the menus and before the wine arrived, when it was just the two of us, sitting across from each other with nothing for it but to look each other in the eye. That might have been the opportunity for a moment of reckoning, but neither of us availed of it and the moment passed.

The waiter arrived with the wine.

'So, your mother tells me you're a nurse.'

'Yes,' she replied, pausing to take a sip of her wine. I saw that she had pale blue eyes, framed by very dark eyelashes. 'I work at a large hospital in Oslo.'

'My wife was a neonatal nurse,' I told her.

I took it that she knew my wife had died. There was no need to tell her, and yet I wanted to. I had a childish desire for her sympathy.

'I'm specializing in geriatric nursing,' she said.

'Geriatric nursing. That's great.'

So, she was a good person, this daughter of mine. Only a good person would choose to practise geriatric medicine. It wasn't pride I felt in her but wonder at the way all these good women had made a habit of landing in my life. I thought of Deborah, and Britta, and Mary Rose, and now Elisa. I had done nothing to deserve any of them but there they were anyway, like a genetic streak running through my timeline.

'Your mother is a good person,' I said, straying across the barrier between thought and speech.

'Yes,' she said, startled by the non sequitur. She was fingering the stem of her wine glass, perhaps out of nerves. 'Yes, she is. She's a wonderful person.'

I could see Britta in her now, in glimpses that came and went, like a hologram. I could not have picked out what feature it was that reminded me of her, the way women always seem to be able to do. I couldn't have said that it was the eyes that gave it away, or the mouth, or the cheekbones. All I knew was that I could see her mother flickering in and out of her as we spoke. I found it distracting, but also pleasing, to see Britta in her, and I wondered what someone else might see of me in this lovely young woman.

'Would we risk another glass?' I asked her, when the food arrived. We had each of us only a finger of wine left in our glasses and there seemed to me no reason not to have another one, except that perhaps she would think me a lush.

'Why not?' she said, with the faintest trace of a wink, as if to say that she was on my side. I experienced an inordinate flood of relief and knocked back the end of my first glass.

She was not angry with me, as I had feared. She was not upset with me, or with her mother, for depriving her for so long of a father. In fact, none of the things that I had been worrying about came to pass over the course of that perfectly pleasant lunch. There was no sentimental rush to compare the shape of our fingernails, no gushing interest in all the particulars of my ghastly family. It might almost have been a business meeting, so careful were we to respect each other's boundaries. After I had paid the bill, we wandered out of the gallery and said our goodbyes under the winter white sky. It was only when I was back out on Piccadilly that I remembered I had forgotten to give her the drum of Fortnum & Mason chocolates.

It was Deborah and Michael's idea for me to invite Elisa and her daughter to Aiguaclara. I would not have thought of it myself, and even if I had done, I would have ruled it out again straight away, but they were insistent.

'I don't know,' I said, when what I really meant was that I didn't want to.

What I wanted was to go to Aiguaclara alone with my memories of Mary Rose. The last thing I wanted was to have two strangers with me.

'You should invite them,' said Michael, echoing his wife's words. I had the feeling this had been discussed already, in my absence. 'What harm can it do?'

We were sitting on high stools at their kitchen island, with a glass of red wine in our hands, while Michael cooked us steak and chips. Deborah had set out a bowl of salted pistachios, which we were cracking our way through.

'But what if they say yes?' I asked.

I have for many years had a policy of never committing myself to things that I might live to regret, ever since the time I signed up, under duress, to a programme offering mentoring to young journalists and spent the next year trying to extricate myself from it. I knew that, if I invited Elisa to Aiguaclara and she accepted my invitation, I would no doubt spend the intervening months regretting it. Dreading it, even. I tried explaining this to Deborah and Michael, but they were having none of it.

'Has it occurred to you,' he said, roaring at me through a cloud of smoke from the grill, 'that this relationship might be important to her, if not to you? She is your daughter, after all.'

'You need to get to know her,' said Deborah, breaking a stubborn pistachio shell open with the help of her teeth. 'You need to meet the little girl. What better way than to spend a few days on holiday together.'

'That poor girl spent the first twenty-five years of her life without a father,' said Michael, as he speared our steaks with a giant-sized fork and lifted them on to a chopping board. 'And when she finally gets one it turns out to be *you*. The least you could do is spend some time with her.'

It was the closest they could come to saying what Mary Rose would have put more plainly.

'David,' I could hear her saying, 'don't be an arsehole.'

It was her voice I had in my head when I emailed Elisa the next day to issue the invitation. I waited, nervous as a cat, for her reply. Several hours went by, during which time I checked my email every few minutes, not sure whether I wanted her to say yes or no. When at last she did respond – she'd been at work, she explained, and couldn't check her mail – it was with a crisp affirmative. She'd be happy to come. The dates worked well for her. I was surprised by how pleased I was to hear that she was coming.

22

Elisa and Astrid were travelling on a flight from Oslo that was due to land in Barcelona at 10.40 a.m. I figured the drive to the airport wouldn't take me more than three hours, but I wanted to allow for unforeseen circumstances, like a traffic jam on the motorway, or an accident or something. I wanted at all costs to be there in the arrivals hall to greet them, so I left Aiguaclara on the dot of seven.

I drove up the hill, against the train of traffic that was at that time of the morning headed downhill. It was composed mainly of small vans delivering supplies to the restaurants. There were waiters on their motorbikes, heading in to work. The odd German, arriving to catch the early dive boat. I was like a lone sheep going against the direction of the flock.

The local town at that time of the morning was turned in on itself. There were none of the shoppers you usually saw on the streets. No children in the playgrounds as I passed. Instead, through the open doors of bakeries, I saw women laying out bread on shelves. I saw groups of men standing in bars, taking their morning coffee. The town itself was like a stage set, with the light creeping up on the buildings from behind. The Catalan flags hanging from the balconies took on an added significance. Like Chekhov's gun, it seemed to me they had been placed there on purpose, as essential props in a plot that was yet to play out.

I skirted the roundabouts on the edge of town, taking the road south past vast glass-walled speedboat shops, and stores that displayed ready-made swimming pools. There were desolate restaurants surrounded by empty car parks. Garden centres and more garden centres, selling all manner of elaborate statuary more suited to a cemetery than a garden. It was a relief to get on to the autopista, with its overhead signs pointing reassuringly to Barcelona. The word was loaded with significance for me now, as it had never been before. It seemed to signal not just a place on the map but a landmark in my life. As the motorway signs steadily ate away at the kilometres that remained of my journey I had the sense of time running at fast forward.

I arrived at the airport pathetically early. Even by the time I had parked the car and found my way into the terminal building, it was only half past nine. The flight board showed an estimated arrival time of 10.32. The precision of the estimate reassured me that the flight was safely on its way, that its progress was being monitored, moment by moment, by an air traffic controller. I had never thought to worry about these things before.

When Mary Rose died, people assumed that I would automatically become an anxious flyer. On the day her plane disappeared off the radar, the airline offered to fly us to Paris to be with the other families waiting for news at Charles de Gaulle. We could have flown to Cairo to be with the Egyptian relatives, who had by then gathered at the other end. Jean Anne and Kitty both said they couldn't face the thought of flying, and Mary Rose's mother was too distraught to travel, but Willie was of a mind to go. I pictured us cooped up in Gallic silence with dozens of strangers in a softly furnished room in Charles de Gaulle. I imagined us in Cairo, listening to the cries of the Egyptian relatives as the news trickled in. I couldn't decide which was worse, so I persuaded Willie we should remain at home and leave the Irish embassy officials to do the waiting for us.

When Deborah suggested the holiday in Nice, two months later, she broached the topic of air travel with extreme care.

'There's an Aer Lingus flight from Dublin. Ryanair go there too, but I was thinking we might drive down, if you prefer?'

'Seriously?' I said. The only people I knew who took the ferry to France were friends with young families, bound for campsites in Brittany. The idea of it was enough to make me go green at the gills.

'I just thought you might prefer not to fly,' said Deborah, and I felt that disconnect again between the rest of the world and me. I was no more concerned about flying than someone whose relative has been killed in a car crash is afraid to step into a car. I had nothing against planes per se, and it did not occur to me to worry that another one would crash, not until I found myself waiting at Barcelona airport for my daughter and granddaughter to arrive on a flight from Oslo.

I was acutely aware of them sitting on the plane. Of their tremendous vulnerability as human beings made of tender flesh and brittle bones, strapped by flimsy belts into an aluminium cylinder and flying through thin air at ten thousand feet. I remember I once interviewed an air traffic controller, many years ago, and he told me that the aircraft call signs he sees on his computer screens every day are normally just a string of letters and numbers, but that the moment a flight is in jeopardy the numbers become a plane full of people. That's how I felt as I checked the flight board for news of Elisa and Astrid's flight, but I was not thinking of the two hundred or so passengers on the plane. I was thinking only of two.

I sat down to have a coffee while I waited. From where I was sitting, I had a view of the sliding glass doors that opened every few seconds to spill out arriving passengers. There were taxi drivers holding up handwritten signs or iPads with passengers' names on them. A girl waited, holding a bunch of yellow sunflowers. I watched a young man emerge, with a rucksack on his back and his passport still in his hand. He looked around, scanning the arrivals area, and I wondered if the girl with the sunflowers was there for him, but she gave no sign of recognition. Instead, a plump, middle-aged woman rushed up to the young man, coming to stand in front of him with her two hands holding his face as if it was a precious urn. He gripped her about the waist and buried his head in the crook of her neck, and I wondered what might have occurred between them to bring such solemnity to their greeting.

There was a young woman talking on the phone at the table next to me.

'*Te quiero*,' I heard her say. And again, '*Te quiero un montón*.'

The rest of her conversation was incomprehensible to me. All I understood was the word *papi* and the word *mañana*. Then came her sign-off.

'*Te quiero, te quiero, te quiero*,' she said, in a burst of love, like automatic gunfire. Once the call was disconnected, she took a moment to gather herself, then stood up to leave.

Two men replaced her at the table. They both looked to be in their thirties. One of them was black and slender. The other was thicker set and white. The black guy carried a tray that he set down on the table, while the white guy parked their two wheelie bags carefully beside it. When they sat down, they set about unwrapping their sandwiches and taking the lids off their coffee cups, and one of them said something that made the other laugh. The laughing man heaved and shook, his eyes streaming with tears as he laughed. When his laughter was exhausted, he looked in wonder at his companion, who beamed with pleasure at being the cause of such joy.

At one table a mother's eyes hung on the face of her little boy, who was eating a tub of pasta, piece by piece, with his chubby little fingers. At another, a young couple sat linked by both hands as they gazed into each other's eyes. Over by the sliding doors, the girl with the sunflowers squealed when she saw her friend emerge. The friend let go of her bags and stood with her arms stretched wide for a hug. I watched her with an overwhelming sense of déjà vu. I knew I had witnessed this exact scene before, but I couldn't remember when, not for a moment. Then I got it: it was the airport scene from *Love Actually*, a movie Mary Rose had made me watch, under protest, every Christmas. To think that I was now a participant in this saccharine pantomime was an irony that could only have been fully appreciated by Mary Rose. I longed to tell her and watch her throw her head back and laugh.

That was the thought that was in my mind when the doors slid back again to reveal Elisa, casually dressed in blue jeans and a white T-shirt. She was dragging a wheelie suitcase in one hand, and had her little girl trailing her by the other hand. The child wore a small backpack, and in her arms she had a close hold on some kind of stuffed creature. She ducked behind her mother when I came forward to greet them.

I lay a hand on Elisa's shoulder and kissed her.

'It's good to have you here,' I said, taking the handle of her suitcase.

'It's good to be here,' she said, with that conspiratorial smile.

The child I did not attempt to communicate with, because she was so clearly shy of me. I was shy of her too; I didn't know what to say to her. On the drive back to Aiguaclara, as Elisa and I gently advanced our knowledge of each other in a series of cautious reveals, obeying unspoken rules as if we were playing a card game, I stole the odd glance in the rear-view mirror to look at Astrid, who was strapped into the car seat I had hired for her and fast asleep.

The inflatable pink flamingo I bought for Astrid on her first afternoon in Aiguaclara was a major factor in progressing my relationship with her beyond her initial wariness.

She had spotted the inflatables as soon as we got out of the car.

'Mama,' she said, tugging on Elisa's arm and pointing at the array of plastic floating devices hanging from the awning of the souvenir shop on the promenade. There were neon lilos and cheery yellow boats and all manner of inflatable rings and floating chairs. While Elisa was getting herself installed in the apartment, I offered to bring Astrid down to the shop so she could take her pick. She looked to her mother for a translation, which ran so long that I took it to contain some kind of inducement.

All I recognized was the word *bestefar*, which I had been told meant 'grandfather'. I was inordinately touched by the use of it, as if I had been paid a great compliment. I very much wanted to be a *bestefar* to Astrid, but I had no idea what it entailed.

'Will you come with me?' I asked her.

The child looked up at me with terminal seriousness as she gave me her hand.

I'm not sure I had ever held a small child's hand before. I had certainly never before been so *aware* of holding a child's hand. It rested inside mine, still and trusting, as we took the lift down to the ground floor. I chatted to her, even though I knew she couldn't understand what I was saying. I wasn't sure whether I felt the need to reassure her or myself.

'Now,' I said, standing with her underneath the shop's awning. 'What's it to be?'

Without the slightest hesitation, she pointed to the pink flamingo.

'Are you sure, now? You're sure you don't want a boat or a doughnut?'

The inflatable doughnut had pink frosting on it and multi-coloured sprinkles, and it seemed to me the kind of thing a little girl would like.

She shook her head and said something in her own language. The only word I could make out was 'flamingo'. I was interested to discover that it was the same word in Norwegian as it was in English. It seemed to offer the hope of some communication between us. We might build a whole relationship using the word 'flamingo' as a foundation stone.

'You want the flamingo?'

She gave me a grave nod, so I had the shopkeeper unhook the flamingo and hand it over to her. I was impressed by the clarity of her decision-making, and a bit ashamed of my own efforts to derail it. It was intriguing to me that this determined little person was in fact my granddaughter. I could not see the resemblance to me. Elisa, we had established, looked like her maternal grandmother, but the child, according to Deborah and Michael, took after me. They had studied the photographs Elisa had given me, analysing her little face at length and pronouncing her the image of me.

'Can't you see? She has your nose and your eyes. She has the same shape face as you. The same chin. Jesus, David, can you not see it?'

'She's the head off you,' said Michael.

I still could not see it, not in the detail of her features, but the child was, all the same, in some way familiar to me. She reminded me of someone, but who that person might be I could not have said. It was a strange feeling, as if I had met her somewhere before.

'Come on,' I said to her. Let's try out this flamingo of yours.'

To my deep gratification, she spent most of that afternoon riding high on the waves on the back of that pink flamingo, while her mother waded waist-deep in the water alongside her. I kept an eye on them from my spot on the beach. Beside me was all the clutter of their belongings: their towels and their beach bag and their clothes and their two pairs of sandals. I felt a smug pride in this evidence of their attachment to me, and I wondered what a stranger would make of our little group. Might they think that Elisa was my wife and Astrid our child? Anyone observing us would surely conclude from our body language that we were not man and wife, but would they guess that I was Elisa's father? Mary Rose would be bound to guess, if she were the observer. I imagined her, sitting with a coffee on the terrace of the Hotel Aiguaclara, piecing the puzzle of our story together.

'The child is the image of him,' she would say. 'I wonder could he be the grandfather, but then what happened to his wife? And where's the daughter's husband?'

Even Mary Rose, with her great capacity for human interest, would struggle to solve it.

The beach in Aiguaclara takes on a special magic in the late afternoon. There's an alchemy to the light at that time of day, whereby the sea and the rocks and the sinking sun all become one. The heat of the day dissipates like smoke over the hillside, as hour after precious hour falls away. The feeling of sand pouring through an egg timer. The approach of evening can be staved off for only so long.

'I think it's enough for us,' said Elisa, standing up from her towel.

We had spent the last hour reading, while Astrid napped

under a sun umbrella, taking it in turns to swim so the child would not be left alone. I couldn't help but think how amazed Mary Rose would be to see me swim a lap of the buoys with such confidence. How amused she would be to see me happily while away the day on the beach. Maybe it's the onset of middle age, or maybe it's the antidepressants, but I no longer find the close proximity of so many naked people intolerable. I am now perfectly content to spend hour after hour on the beach, observing them in all their strange shapes and forms. As the afternoon wears on, I'm reluctant to pack up and leave – something I see as a measure of the distance I've travelled as a human being – so when Elisa told me it was time for her and Astrid to go up to the apartment, I helped her gather up her stuff, but I didn't go with her. I figured she might like the place to herself for a while.

'I'll be up in an hour or so,' I told her.

'No problem,' she said.

When she was gone, I lay back on the sand with my hat over my face, so that when I opened my eyes I was looking at the sky through a kaleidoscope of straw. There was a pinball feeling in my ears from all the swimming, along with a pouring sensation, like warm oil finding its way through a channel.

Tac, tac, tac went the beach bats. '*Op der op,*' I heard someone say, as a baby cried. The showers hissed, then stopped. Hissed, then stopped. An outboard motor whirred and abruptly dropped out. Then came the sound of someone shouting.

I lifted my hat off my face and sat up to see a woman standing with her feet planted wide apart in the sand, like a volleyball player, as she berated a small boy. The boy was crying inconsolably in the face of her rage, which went on and on. I couldn't understand the language the woman was speaking – it might have been Russian – but by the piece of plastic she was waving around in her hand I deduced that he'd broken something belonging to her.

There was a man sitting under a beach umbrella nearby, with a baby girl in his lap, and he was watching the drama unfold with a sad look on his face. The woman kept shouting, and the little boy kept weeping, and the man under the umbrella kept on watching. Eventually the woman stormed away, and the little boy crept in under the beach umbrella with his father. He sat down with his head bent in defeat, and his father draped an arm around his shaking shoulders.

I watched in horror. In my mind, I was that small boy. The parent who sheltered me was my mother. The storm that raged around us was my father's anger, his hatreds, his contempt. My father was never physically violent, so far as I know. He never so much as raised a hand to me, but then he didn't have to. He had weapon enough in his words.

'You'll make a pansy of that boy,' he used to say, whenever my mother showed me a kindness. 'You'll ruin him. Make a mammy's boy of him.'

Even so, she would sometimes slip a flat bar of Dairy Milk into my school lunch as a surprise. She would buy new socks for me if she was in town and leave them on my bed. When I was studying for exams, she would sometimes carry a mug of tea up to me at my desk, with a finger of her much-maligned almond loaf cake, which in that sugar-deprived era would have been most welcome. It surprised me to remember those furtive little attempts of hers to show me love, and I was overcome by a wave of guilt that I had somehow managed to forget them.

I closed my eyes for a moment to steady myself against the barrage of sorrow that fell down on me, and when I opened them again the disgraced child was out from under the umbrella. He had a lilo under his arm and was clearly asking permission to go down to the water. Permission granted, he ran down the slope of the beach and into the shallows, launching himself on to the lilo and paddling away like a surfer. The angry mother was back, and the father had transferred the baby to her to be fed. I watched the little boy floating out to sea on his lilo. The father was lying back on the sand now, his head supported by his hands, his elbows out either side of him. The mother was cradling the baby in the shade of the umbrella. Peace had been restored, but I knew that none of them would ever fully recover from the dent that had been made in what should have been a happy family day at the beach. Like a scratch in the paintwork of a new car, or a rip in a piece of fabric, a little bit of happiness had been lost, and no amount of mending could restore it to what it had been before.

It occurred to me then, in the manner of a revelation, why I had never wanted children. It was not, as I had for so long convinced myself, that a child would threaten the happiness Mary Rose and I had been so lucky to share. My fear was the very opposite: that I would be a threat to the child's happiness. I was afraid that the misery my own parents had inflicted on me would be passed on, like a poisoned chalice, to any child of mine. Fifty-one years old and still only slowly coming to some understanding of my life, I sat on a beach on the Costa Brava, digesting the terrifying knowledge that we hold in our hands each other's fragile hearts, and can treat them as gently or as roughly as we please.

It was evening before I ran into Claire. I was just finishing a chapter of my book on the beach when I saw the little boat with the French flag pull up to its mooring. Claire's parents were with her, and her brother Christophe, and his son. I lingered for a few minutes, watching them all pile into the pilot's rib. When I saw them disembarking at the pier, I gathered up my towel and suncream and headed up off the beach, stopping to shower the sand off my feet before I climbed the steps on to the promenade. She was standing right there when I straightened up.

'Did they arrive?' she asked me, most solicitously.

'They did. They're up in the apartment. The child is having a nap.'

'Oh, that's good. She must be tired, after the flight.'

'Yes, they had an early start.'

'You must invite them to my parents' celebration,' she said. 'My parents are going to be fifty-five years married tomorrow, and we're having a party to celebrate. We would very much like for the three of you to be our guests.'

In her voice I could hear a note of forced enthusiasm. It was the note you strike when someone surprises you by ringing, unexpectedly, on your door, and you must stir yourself to invite them in.

'We'd be delighted to come,' I told her, surprised to find that I wasn't just saying it for her sake. I actually meant it.

'Count us in,' I said.

23

At the time Mary Rose died, I remember thinking there could be no more happy occasions in my life. I remember saying as much to Deborah that first Christmas.

'It's just part of the ongoing nightmare,' I said to her, when she asked me how I was coping. 'Christmas, New Year, they're all just things to be endured now.'

I had taken to turning off the radio, unable to bear the thickening of emotions brought in by December. Every ad on the radio seemed to have been designed to make me feel bad.

'If you can just get through *this* Christmas,' said Deborah. 'Nothing will ever be as bad again.'

I didn't believe her.

'*Every* Christmas from now on will be like this,' I told her. 'Every birthday. Every anniversary. The same goes for Mary Rose's family. All the weddings, all the christenings, they'll all be sad occasions now, because of what happened to Mary Rose.'

Deborah was listening to me very intently, with her head cocked slightly to the side.

'With respect,' she said, 'I think you're wrong.'

I waited for her to explain.

'I know what you're saying, and of course there will be a moment of sadness, always, that Mary Rose isn't there. But the happy occasions will still be happy occasions, because that's how life works. Happiness trumps sadness, every time. If it didn't, we couldn't survive.'

I did not believe her. Did not want to believe – couldn't

believe – that life would go on. That the cloud cast over us by Mary Rose's death would one day clear and we would all find ourselves, some day in the future, enjoying things again, without her. It was unimaginable to me how that could happen, and yet I found myself, barely fourteen months after her death, accepting an invitation from Claire to a party to celebrate the occasion of her parents' wedding anniversary. Stranger still, I found myself *looking forward* to the party. Given the choice to go or not to go, I would have chosen to go.

'We're all to wear white,' I told Elisa. 'For some reason, they want everyone dressed in white.'

I thought of those photographs you see in *Vanity Fair*. Groups of actors, or captains of industry, all dressed in white. Claire's parents were no doubt going for the same effect. At any other time in my life this dress code would have sent me running for the hills, but so many of my certainties had by then dissolved that I had entered a strangely pliable phase. I identified a crisp white shirt to wear with my blue jeans, which I felt would satisfy the spirit, if not the letter, of the dress code.

'I have a white dress for Astrid, but I'm not sure I have anything white for me,' said Elisa.

She was wearing a Japanese-style robe, her hair wet from the shower, and she was hanging her freshly rinsed swimsuit over the balcony railings to dry. I had noticed that she always rinsed her swimsuit out in fresh water after coming up off the beach, something I had never done, and never known Mary Rose to do. Several times a day, I was struck by little things about her that were foreign to me. She was family, and yet she was not family, because she had been reared apart from me.

It was the same when I first lived with Mary Rose. So many of her habits were strange to me, and mine to her, that it was alarming at times to think how we would manage to meld our lives together. In the first flush of love, we had blithely assumed that we were a perfect fit for each other, but when it came down to the small things it turned out that some of our edges did not quite align. Like two pieces of joinery that had been prefabricated in the workshop, it would take some sanding to smooth them out.

For example, Mary Rose liked to keep the eggs in a bowl on the kitchen counter, whereas I was accustomed to them being stored in the fridge. She bought Barry's Tea; I liked Lyons better. Mary Rose always took her breakfast standing up, a slice of toast in her hand and a mug of tea on the go, as she wandered about the place putting preparations in place for the day. I had been brought up to set the table for breakfast each night before I went to bed and sit down fully dressed the next morning to eat it. She left the immersion on all the time, while I had been reared under pain of death to turn it off as soon as the bathwater was heated. When Mary Rose paired socks, she joined them only by the cuff, whereas I had learned from my mother to pull one sock all the way inside the other.

In the same way I noticed how Elisa draped the dishcloth over the tap in the kitchen sink, rather than folding it on the side. The toothbrushes she and the child used were electric, unlike mine, and they each had a brightly coloured facecloth that they laid out each night to dry on the lip of the bath. Neither Mary Rose nor I ever used a facecloth; she always used oval pads of cotton wool to clean her face at night. Mary Rose and I wore shoes even when we were in the house; I noticed that Elisa and Astrid were in the habit of leaving theirs at the front door.

I have no doubt that all my little habits were as strange to them as theirs were to me, but Elisa gave no indication of it.

It was Astrid who gave it away. She would sit on the white couch with a picture book in her lap, her matchstick legs barely reaching the edge of the seat and her eyes as wide as saucers as she watched me moving about the apartment. She was like the *Mona Lisa*; no matter where I went, her eyes were on me.

'I only have a white T-shirt,' said Elisa, emerging from her bedroom to seek my approval. She looked worried, her square, solemn face all scrunched up.

'I'm sure the T-shirt will do fine.'

She went looking for the iron and proceeded to press the child's white sundress with meticulous care. She ironed her own T-shirt too, and the red linen skirt she had chosen to wear, pressing the folds of its front pleat together with as much attention as she would have done if she were suturing a wound, her head bowed low in concentration as she guided the nose of the iron along the length of the pleat.

She disappeared into her bedroom with the ironed clothes, reappearing a short time later with her hair dry and sleek and shining. She wore no make-up, as far as I could see, but she had a thin gold chain around her neck and gold studs in her ears, and on her feet she wore a pair of Roman sandals. The white dress that Astrid wore was puckered at the chest, with straps that were held together by a little bow at her shoulders. Her white hair was side-parted and held in place behind her ear by a small polka-dot clip.

'Okay?' I said, checking I had my keys and my wallet. 'Are you ready?'

'Let's go,' said Elisa, fetching her handbag from the table.

We rode down together in the small lift, the three of us pressed close together and silent as we waited for the lift doors to open on to the lobby area.

'We have no gift,' said Elisa, with a sudden flash of anxiety.

'Don't worry,' I said, 'it's not expected.'

I had told Elisa no more about Claire's tragedy than the bare essentials, but even then I had seen her face stumble under the weight of it, and I wondered if she saw me as somehow jinxed. First the wife who died in a plane crash, now this friend who had lost both her children in a terrorist attack. Looking at it through Elisa's eyes, it seemed to me relentlessly morbid, and I wondered if she feared being contaminated by these tragedies that seemed to gather around me. If so, she gave no sign of it. I watched her step out onto the promenade, with her little girl's hand in hers, and it seemed to me that she had all of her mother's remarkable self-possession.

Claire's people were already gathering on the terrace of their house as we approached. Moving around the giant candles that had been positioned along the dining table, they looked like moths, all dressed in white.

'David,' said Claire's mother, coming to greet us. Her short white hair was damp and wavy; her lips, a thin dash of coral against her suntanned face. She wore a simple white shift dress, with a collar about her neck of battered silver.

I congratulated her and thanked her for including us in their celebration.

'This is my daughter, Elisa,' I said, my head reeling at the implausibility of it. It would not seem odd to anyone but me that this young woman was my daughter. It would seem to a stranger the most normal thing in the world, but to me it was still distinctly strange.

'Nice to meet you,' said Elisa, in English that could almost be native.

'My granddaughter, Astrid,' I said, watching Beatrice's face soften as her eyes settled on the child.

'How old are you, Astrid?' asked Beatrice, but the child shrank away from her.

'She's four,' Elisa said. 'She's a bit shy.'

'It's normal,' said Beatrice, shrugging it off. Even though she spoke in English, everything she said still sounded French, as if it had been translated only in the narrowest sense, word for word.

'Now, come. Take a glass of champagne with us.'

Claire's father was dispensing champagne flutes. We both took one and flitted among the moths, greeted by each of them with multiple kisses. They accepted us into their circle with hardly a ripple, and I wondered what Claire had told them about us, if anything.

'This is my daughter, Elisa,' I said, over and over again. 'My granddaughter, Astrid.'

The more times I said it, the more convincing it began to sound to me. Like the tables we learned to chant in junior school – five times one is five, five times two is ten – there came a time when you stopped questioning the meaning of it and took it for fact.

'We're so glad you could join us,' said Christophe, sparking his lighter and holding his cigarette to the flame. He made a yawn of his mouth to gobble up the smoke, talking all the time as he exhaled. 'An outsider is a very valuable commodity at a family party. It keeps everyone on their best behaviour.'

'Glad to oblige,' I said, raising my glass to him, although I found it difficult to imagine anyone at this party behaving badly. Except Christophe himself, perhaps. I could easily imagine Christophe causing trouble.

'Claire tells me you're from Dublin,' he said. 'I stayed with a family in Dublin once. They lived in Churchtown.'

I had one ear out for Elisa as I listened to him. 'No, I'm from Norway,' I heard her say to Edo's wife, while Christophe was describing to me in post-traumatic detail the food he was given by the family in Churchtown. He remembered with horror the frozen burgers and the Birds Eye potato waffles that were pulled out of the depths of their vast chest freezer. The Yoplait chocolate yoghurt and the Angel Delight that were served up on a nightly basis in place of dessert. I took pleasure in telling him that those very things were considered delicacies when I was a child. We prized them far above the drab, home-made food my mother insisted on cooking.

I looked around for Claire and spotted her sitting alone with her glass of champagne at the end of the table. I was struck by how out of place she looked sitting down, while everyone else was still standing.

'Excuse me,' I said to Christophe, when he moved towards the table to put out his cigarette. 'I should go and say hello to Claire.'

I bent down to kiss her on both cheeks.

'Are you all right?' I whispered.

'Oh yes,' she said, without hesitation. 'Yes, I'm fine.'

She was a little too emphatic, as if she was trying to convince herself. Even as she spoke, I saw a surge of desperation in her eyes and I knew that she was struggling to rise to the buoyancy of the occasion. I knew all too well that feeling, like an anchor in your heart that threatens to pull you under.

'Come and meet my daughter,' I said, offering her my hand. I helped her up and, even when she was standing, I kept my hand hovering behind her, as if to stop her from falling. We walked over to where Elisa was standing with Edo and his wife.

'Elisa, I'd like you to meet Claire.'

Elisa turned and leaned in to kiss Claire once, twice, on the cheeks. Claire's hand rested for a moment on Elisa's arm and I saw something pass between them. Something intimate and tender, born of what each of them knew about the other. It was amazing to me, how women could so easily establish a friendship.

'Where's your little girl?' Claire asked.

Elisa looked about the place for her, spotting her at last over at the edge of Alicia's terrace, where a small dog was tethered to a table leg while its owners ate. Astrid was down on her hunkers, petting the dog.

'Astrid, *kom hit.*'

Claire placed her hand on Astrid's smooth white head, resting the hand there for a moment as the child stared up at her. It occurred to me that Astrid was not altogether unlike Claire's own daughter had been at that age. She had the same short blonde bob, held in place by a polka-dot clip. No doubt every little thing reminded Claire of Élodie.

'She's beautiful,' Claire told Elisa, and I saw to my relief that the desperation was gone from her eyes.

Someone clapped their hands, two short claps, and I heard Claire's mother shout, *'Allez, à table.'*

I felt the smallest tug on the sleeve of my shirt and understood that Claire wanted me to stick close by her. She slipped into a chair on the near side of the table, facing on to the promenade, and I sat down beside her before anyone else could. Christophe seated Elisa opposite us, with Astrid at the head of the table between Elisa and Claire. Two cushions were produced to raise Astrid up on her chair. Elisa fell straight away into easy conversation with Edo's boys, who were not much younger than her. One of them offered her a cigarette and she accepted it, drawing on it with such delicacy that I guessed she was only an occasional smoker. Astrid reached for a piece of bread from the bread basket and began to eat it, crumb by crumb, like a little bird.

'Would you like some water?' Claire asked her. When the

child nodded, Claire poured a glass a third full and pushed it towards her.

Alicia's son came to stand with his order book at Beatrice's shoulder. If he was surprised to see me with my feet under the French people's table, he gave no sign of it. He moved around the table taking people's orders, then, tucking his order book into his pocket, bounced back into the restaurant on his platform sneakers.

A large bowl of salad was passed along the table, and a plate of cold meats. More wine was poured. A water jug was replenished. I had a curious sensation of things falling into place, like a full house forming in your hand when you're playing poker. I looked out to the darkening bay, where the sea shifted ever so slightly under the boats. The light was gone already off the beach and the sky had turned a deep, velvety blue. The diving board had disappeared into the night, but there were shouts rising off the water from a few late swimmers. Down on the sand, you could make out the darting shadows of children playing hide-and-seek among the kayaks. The lights along the promenade were warm and yellow, the restaurants cheerily crowded with diners as the vagabond band made their way along the seafront.

'*When you're smiling*,' they sang, in raucous harmony. '*When you're smiling, the whole world smiles with you . . .*'

I saw that Christophe was in negotiation with his son over something. The boy was shooting glances at Astrid. His father said something to him and the boy nodded, then pushed his chair back and stood up.

'He wants to know if he can take the little girl down to the beach.'

Elisa translated for Astrid, who considered this carefully, then climbed down off her chair to go with him.

'*Attends*,' said Claire. The child's clip had slipped from her

303

head, hanging on by just a single hair. Claire bent down to fix the clip back in place.

'*Vas-y*,' she said, watching as the boy led Astrid gingerly down the steps and on to the sand.

Looking across the table, I saw Elisa nodding with widened eyes at something one of Edo's boys was saying. The docile girlfriend was animated now, interrupting him to say something that made everyone laugh. Edo's wife turned her head, too late, to hear what the joke was. On her left was Edo, who was refilling his wine glass with fierce concentration. Beatrice sat at the far end of the table, looking slightly stunned, her husband's thick old hand resting on her leathery forearm. I caught her eye and smiled, and she sent a smile back down the table to me. It might have been a radio signal, sent out across a stormy sea. Alpha . . . Lima . . . Lima . . . *All is well.*

'Say cheese,' said Christophe, hovering behind Elisa with a camera. I felt Claire straighten up beside me for the photo. I had been about to drink some wine from my glass, but I put it back down on the table instead, making a play of smiling with my eyes. I have always tried to avoid smiling for photographs, because it makes me feel ridiculous, but on this occasion Christophe did not let me away with it. 'Come on,' he said, 'smile.' Elisa turned from the waist, one arm draped over the back of her chair, to face the camera, and an image flashed through my mind of how we would appear in the photograph, Elisa, Claire and I. Like a tea-set cobbled together from three depleted services – a milk jug from one, a cup and saucer from another, and a sugar bowl from a third – in the image that formed in my mind we were curiously complete.

Claire whispered something in my ear, but I couldn't hear what it was that she said. Her voice seemed to be coming from very far away.

The band had moved along the promenade, their voices fainter now. Christophe turned his camera on us with another flash. Down on the beach, his son was sitting with my granddaughter at the top of the lifeguards' chair, their white clothes flagged against the black night. Elisa was bending her head to light another cigarette from the lighter Edo's son held out to her, her free hand tucking her hair back behind her ear so it wouldn't fall into the flame. Claire's father gave a shout, from the other end of the table, and everyone laughed. From the restaurant, I watched Carlitos emerge with a row of dinner plates balanced up his arm. I saw it all as if I was watching it from above – the rowdy candlelit table, where even now plates of griddled fish were being passed from hand to hand, where Astrid was scrambling to climb up on her chair and Elisa was blowing on her chips to cool them. I saw it as Mary Rose would have seen it, through shining eyes, and I was struck by the sense of how wonderful life is, and how sad, and how strange that it can even be both of these things at the very same time.

Acknowledgements

It has been my great pleasure to work with the wonderful people at Sandycove. Patricia Deevy is a mighty editor and this book is infinitely better for her input. Michael McLoughlin and his team on Nassau Street have been a joy from the start. Caroline Pretty did a great job on the copy-edit, as did Viki Ottewill on the cover. My agent Marianne Gunn O'Connor has been unstinting in her faith in my work. Thanks also to Vicki Satlow for her enthusiasm for this novel. I was blessed to have Patrick Scott as an early reader – his feedback was invaluable. So too the thoughts of Nic Le Duc, Hilary McGouran and Valerie Bistany. I am, as always, grateful to Cormac Kinsella for his many kindnesses to me. Henrietta McKervey is a wonderful comrade in arms. Mary Reynolds is a saint to put up with me. Martin Walsh, Declan Meade and Dan Bolger all offered encouragement when it was most needed. Final thanks to my family, who are unendingly patient and understanding of the demands my work places on both me and them. Thank you, Des, Kev and Meg. Thank you, Lucy and Clara. Thank you, Mark.